ALSO BY P. D. JAMES

Cover Her Face
A Mind to Murder
Unnatural Causes
Shroud for a Nightingale
An Unsuitable Job for a Woman
The Black Tower
Death of an Expert Witness
Innocent Blood
The Skull Beneath the Skin

NON-FICTION

The Maul and the Pear Tree
(WITH T. A. CRITCHLEY)

A
TASTE
FOR
DEATH

A TASTE FOR DEATH

P. D. James

LESTER
&ORPEN
DENNYS
PUBLISHERS

FIRST CANADIAN EDITION

Canadian Cataloguing in Publication Data

James, P. D., 1920–

A taste for death

ISBN 0-88619-142-4 (bound).

I. Title.

PR6060.A56T37   1986   823'.914   c86-093801-8

Manufactured in the U.S.A. for

Lester & Orpen Dennys Limited
78 Sullivan Street
Toronto, Ontario
Canada M5T 1C1

To my daughters,
Clare and Jane,
and in memory of their father,
Connor Bantry White

Author's Note

My apologies are due to the inhabitants of Campden Hill Square for my temerity in erecting a Sir John Soane house to disrupt the symmetry of their terraces and to the Diocese of London for providing, surplus to pastoral requirements, a Sir Arthur Blomfield basilica and its campanile on the banks of the Grand Union Canal. Other places described are recognizably part of London. It is the more important to state, therefore, that all the events described in the novel are fictional and all the characters, living and dead, wholly imaginary.

I am grateful to the Director and staff of the Metropolitan Police Forensic Science Laboratory for their generous help with the scientific details.

Some can gaze and not be sick,
But I could never learn the trick.
There's this to say for blood and breath,
They give a man a taste for death.

—A. E. HOUSMAN

Book One   Death of a Baronet   1

Book Two   Next of Kin   89

Book Three   Helping with Enquiries   171

Book Four   Devices and Desires   231

Book Five   Rhesus Positive   309

Book Six   Mortal Consequences   369

Book Seven   Aftermath   449

BOOK ONE

Death of a Baronet

1
⊠

The bodies were discovered at eight forty-five on the morning of Wednesday 18 September by Miss Emily Wharton, a sixty-five-year-old spinster of the parish of St. Matthew's in Paddington, London, and Darren Wilkes, aged ten, of no particular parish as far as he knew or cared. This unlikely pair of companions had left Miss Wharton's flat in Crowhurst Gardens just before half past eight to walk the half-mile stretch of the Grand Union Canal to St. Matthew's Church. Here Miss Wharton, as was her custom each Wednesday and Friday, would weed out the dead flowers from the vase in front of the statue of the Virgin, scrape the wax and candle stubs from the brass holders, dust the two rows of chairs in the Lady Chapel, which would be adequate for the small congregation expected at that morning's early Mass, and make everything ready for the arrival at nine twenty of Father Barnes.

It was on a similar mission seven months earlier that she had first met Darren. He had been playing alone on the towpath, if anything as purposeless as hurling old beer cans into the canal could be described as playing, and she had paused to say good morning to him. Perhaps he had been surprised to be greeted by an adult who didn't either admonish or cross-examine him. For whatever reason, after his initial expressionless stare, he had attached himself to her, at first dawdling behind, then circling round her, as might a stray dog, and finally trotting at her side. When they had reached St. Matthew's Church he had followed her inside as naturally as if they had set out together that morning.

It was apparent to Miss Wharton, on that first day, that he had never been inside a church before, but neither then nor on any subsequent visit did he evince the least curiosity about its purpose. He had prowled contentedly in and out of the vestry and bell room while she got on with her chores, had watched critically while she had arranged her six daffodils eked out with foliage in the vase at the foot of the Virgin and had viewed with the bland indifference of childhood Miss Wharton's frequent genuflections, obviously taking these sudden bobbings to be one more manifestation of the peculiar antics of adults.

But she had met him on the towpath the next week and the one following. After the third visit he had, without invitation, walked home with her and had shared her tin of tomato soup and her fish fingers. The meal, like a ritual communion, had confirmed the curious, unspoken, mutual dependence which bound them. But by then she had known, with a mixture of gratitude and anxiety, that he had become necessary to her. On their visits to St. Matthew's he always left the church, mysteriously present one moment and the next gone, when the first members of the congregation began to trickle in. After the service, she would find him loitering on the towpath, and he would join her as if they hadn't parted. Miss Wharton had never mentioned his name to Father Barnes or to anyone else at St. Matthew's and, as far as she knew, he had never, in his secretive world of childhood, mentioned hers. She knew as little about him now, his parents, his life, as she had at their first meeting.

But that had been seven months ago, a chill morning in mid-February, when the bushes which screened the canal walk from the neighbouring council estate had been tangled thickets of lifeless thorn; when the branches of the ash trees had been black with buds so tight that it seemed impossible they could ever crack into greenness; and the thin denuded wands of willow, drooping over the canal, had cut delicate feathers on the quickening stream. Now high summer was browning and mellowing into autumn. Miss Wharton, briefly closing her eyes as she trudged through the mush of fallen leaves, thought that she could still scent, above the smell of sluggish water and damp earth, a trace of the heady elderberry flowers of June. It was that smell which on summer mornings most clearly brought back to her the lanes of her Shropshire childhood. She dreaded the onset of winter, and on waking this morning she had thought that she could smell its breath in the air. Although it hadn't rained for a week, the path was slippery with mud, deadening sound. They walked under the leaves in an ominous quietness. Even the tinny clatter of the sparrows was stilled. But to their right the ditch which bordered the canal was still lush with its summer greenness, its grasses thick over the split tyres, discarded mattresses and scraps of clothing rotting in its depths, and the torn and laden boughs of the willow dropped their thin leaves onto a surface which seemed too oily and stagnant to suck them in.

It was eight forty-five and they were nearing the church, passing now into one of the low tunnels that spanned the canal. Darren, who liked best this part of the walk, gave a whoop and rushed into the tunnel, hollering for an echo and running his hands, like pale starfish, along the brick walls. She followed his leaping figure, half-dreading the moment when she would pass through the arch into that claustrophobic, dank, river-smelling darkness and would hear, unnaturally loud, the suck of the canal against the paving stones and the slow drip of water from the low roof. She quickened her pace, and within minutes the half moon of brightness at the end of the tunnel had widened to receive them again into the daylight and he was back, shivering at her side.

She said:

"It's very cold, Darren. Oughtn't you to be wearing your parka?" He hunched his thin shoulders and shook his head. She was amazed at how little he wore and how impervious he was to the cold. Sometimes it seemed to her that he preferred to live in a perpetual shiver. Surely wrapping up well on a chill autumn morning wasn't considered unmanly? And he looked so nice in his parka. She had been relieved when he first appeared in it; it was bright blue striped with red, expensive, obviously new, a reassuring sign that the mother she had never met and of whom he never spoke tried to take good care of him.

Wednesday was her day for replacing the flowers, and this morning she was carrying a small tissue-wrapped bunch of pink roses and one of small white chrysanthemums. The stems were wet and she felt the dampness seeping through her woollen gloves. The flowers were tight-budded, but one was beginning to open and a transitory evocation of summer came to her, bringing with it an old anxiety. Darren often arrived on their church morning with a gift of flowers. These, he had told her, were from Uncle Frank's stall at Brixton. But could that really be true? And then there was the smoked salmon, last Friday's gift, brought to her flat just before suppertime. He told her he had been given it by Uncle Joe, who kept a café up Kilburn way. But the slivers, so moist, so delicious, had been interleaved with greaseproof paper, and the white tray in which they lay had looked so very like the ones she had looked at with hopeless longing in Marks and Spencer, except that someone had torn off the label. He had sat opposite her, watching her while she ate, making an extravagant moue of distaste when she suggested that he share it, but staring at her with a concentrated, almost angry, satisfaction, rather, she thought, as a mother might watch a convalescent child taking her first mouthful. But she had eaten it, and with the delicious taste still lingering on her palate it had seemed ungrateful to cross-question him. But the presents were getting more frequent. If he brought her any more, then they would have to have a little talk.

Suddenly, he gave a yell, raced furiously ahead and leapt up at an overhanging bough. There he swung, thin legs jerking, the white, thick-soled running shoes looking incongruously heavy for the bony legs. He was given to these sudden spurts of activity, running ahead to hide among the bushes and jump out at her, leaping across puddles, rummaging for broken bottles and cans in the ditch and hurling them with a desperate intensity into the water. She would pretend to be frightened when he jumped out, would call out to him to be careful when he crept along an overhanging branch and hung, skimming the water. But on the whole, she rejoiced in his liveliness. It was less worry than the lethargy which so often seemed to overcome him. Now, watching his grinning monkey face as he swung, arm over arm, the frantic twisting of his body, the silver of the delicate ribcage under the pale flesh where the jacket had parted from his jeans, she felt a surge of love so painful that it was like a thrust to the heart. And with the pain came again the old anxiety. As he dropped beside her she said:

"Darren, are you sure your mother doesn't mind your helping me with St. Matthew's?"

"Naw, that's OK, I told ya."

"You come to the flat so often. It's lovely for me, but are you quite sure she doesn't mind?"

"Look, I told ya. It's OK."

"But wouldn't it be better if I came to see her, just to meet her, so that she knows who you're with?"

"She knows. Anyway, she ain't at home. She's off visiting me Uncle Ron at Romford."

Another uncle. How could she possibly keep track of them? But a fresh anxiety surfaced.

"Then who is looking after you, Darren? Who is at home?"

"No one. I'm sleepin' with a neighbour till she comes back. I'm OK."

"And what about school today?"

"I told ya. I don't have to go. It's a holiday, see, it's a holiday! I told ya!"

His voice had become high, almost hysterical. Then, as she didn't speak, he fell in beside her and said more calmly:

"They got Andrex at forty-eight pee a double roll up at Notting Hill. That new supermarket. I could get ya a couple of rolls if you're interested."

He must, she thought, spend a lot of time in supermarkets, shopping for his mother, perhaps, on his way home from school. He was clever at finding bargains, reporting back to her about the special offers, the cheaper lines. She said:

"I'll try to get up there myself, Darren. That's a very good price."

"Yeah, that's what I thought. It's a good price. First time I seen 'em under fifty pee."

For almost the whole of their walk their objective had been in sight: the green copper cupola of the soaring campanile of Arthur Blomfield's extraordinary Romanesque basilica, build in 1870 on the bank of this sluggish urban waterway with as much confidence as if he had erected it on the Venetian Grand Canal. Miss Wharton, on her first visit to St. Matthew's, nine years previously, had decided that it was expedient to admire it since it was her parish church and offered what she described as Catholic privileges. She had then put its architecture firmly out of her mind, together with her yearnings for Norman arches, carved reredos and familiar Early English spires. She supposed that she had now got used to it. But she was still slightly surprised when she found Father Barnes showing round groups of visitors, experts interested in Victorian architecture, who enthused over the baldachin, admired the Pre-Raphaelite paintings on the eight panels of the pulpit or set up their tripods to photograph the apse, and who compared it, in confident, unecclesiastical tones (surely even experts ought to lower their voices in church) with the cathedral of Torcello near Venice or with Blomfield's similar basilica at Jericho in Oxford.

And now, as always, with dramatic suddenness, it loomed before them. They passed through the turnstile in the canal railings and took the gravel path to the porch of the south door, the one to which Miss Wharton had a key. This led to the Little Vestry, where she would hang up her coat, and to the kitchen, where she would wash out the vases and arrange the fresh flowers. As they reached the door she glanced down at the small flower bed which gardeners in the congregation were trying to cultivate with more optimism than success in the unrewarding soil at the side of the path.

"Oh look, Darren, how pretty. The first dahlias. I never thought they'd flower. No, don't pick them. They look so nice there." He had bent down, his hand among the grasses, but as she spoke he straightened up and thrust a grubby fist into his pocket.

"Don't you want 'em for the BVM?"

"We've got your uncle's roses for Our Lady." If only they were his uncle's! I shall have to ask him, she thought. I can't go on like this, offering Our Lady stolen flowers, if they were stolen. But suppose they weren't and I accuse him? I shall destroy everything there is between us. I can't lose him now. And it might put the idea of theft into his head. The half-remembered phrases fell into her mind: corrupting innocence, an occasion of sin. She thought, I shall have to think about it. But not now, not yet.

She rummaged in her handbag for the key on its wooden key ring and tried to fit it into the lock. But she couldn't get it in. Puzzled, but not yet worried, she tried the doorknob and the heavy iron-bound door swung open. It was already unlocked, a key in place on the other side. The passage was quiet, unlit, the oak door to the Little Vestry on the left tightly closed. So Father Barnes must already be here. But how strange that he should arrive before her. And why hadn't he left on the passage light? As her gloved hand found the switch, Darren scampered past her, up to the wrought-iron grille which separated the passage from the nave of the church. He liked to light a candle when they arrived, thrusting thin arms through the grille to reach the candleholder and the coin box. Early in their walk she had handed him the usual tenpenny piece, and now she heard a faint tinkle and watched while he stuck his candle in the socket and reached for the matches in their brass holder.

And it was then, in that moment, that she felt the first twitch of anxiety. Some premonition alerted her subconscious; earlier disquiets and a vague sense of unease came together and focussed into fear. A faint smell, alien yet horribly familiar; the sense of a recent presence; the possible significance of that unlocked outer door; the dark passageway. Suddenly she knew that something was dreadfully wrong. Instinctively she called out:

"Darren!"

He turned and looked at her face. And then, immediately, he was back at her side.

Gently at first, and then with one sharp movement, she opened the door. Her eyes dazzled with light. The long fluorescent tube which disfigured the ceiling was on, its brightness eclipsing the gentle glow from the passageway. And she saw horror itself.

There were two of them, and she knew instantly, and with absolute certainty, that they were dead. The room was a shambles. Their throats had been cut and they lay like butchered animals in a waste of blood. Instinctively she thrust Darren behind her. But she was too late. He, too, had seen. He didn't scream but she felt him tremble and he made a small, pathetic groan, like an angry puppy. She pushed him back into the passage, closed the door, and leaned against it. She was aware of a desperate coldness, of the tumultuous thudding of her heart. It seemed to have swollen in her chest, huge and hot, and its painful drumming shook her frail body as if to burst it apart. And the smell, which at first had been tentative, elusive, no more than an alien tincture on the air, now seemed to seep into the passage with the strong effluvium of death.

She pressed her back against the door, grateful for the support of its solid carved oak. But neither its strength nor her tightly closed eyes could shut out horror. Brightly lit as on a stage, she saw the bodies still, more garish, more brightly lit than when they had first met her horrified eyes. One corpse had slipped from the low single bed to the right of the door and lay staring up at her, the mouth open, the head almost cleft from the body. She saw again the severed vessels, sticking like corrugated pipes through the clotted blood. The second was propped, ungainly as a rag doll, against the far wall. His head had dropped forward and over his chest a great mat of blood had spread like a bib. A brown and blue woollen cap was still on his head but askew. His right eye was hidden, but the left leered at her with a dreadful knowingness. Thus mutilated, it seemed to her everything human had drained away from them with their blood: life, identity, dignity. They no longer looked like men. And the blood was everywhere. It seemed to her that she herself was drowning in blood. Blood drummed in her ears, blood gurgled like vomit in her throat, blood splashed in bright globules against the retinas of her closed eyes. The images of death she was powerless to shut out swam before her in a swirl of blood, dissolved, re-formed, and then dissolved again, but always in blood. And then she heard Darren's voice, felt the tug of his hand on her sleeve.

"We gotta get outer here before the filth arrive. Come on. We ain't seen nothin', nothin'. We ain't been 'ere."

His voice squeaked with fear. He clutched at her arm. Through the thin tweed, his grubby fingers bit, sharp as teeth. Gently she prised them loose. When she spoke, she was surprised at the calmness of her voice.

"That's nonsense, Darren. Of course they won't suspect us. Running away . . . now, that would look suspicious."

She hustled him along the passage.

"I'll stay here. You go for help. We must lock the door. No one must come in. I'll wait here and you fetch Father Barnes. You know the vicarage? It's the corner flat in that block on Harrow Road. He'll know what to do. He'll call the police."

"But you can't stay 'ere on your own. Suppose 'e's still here? In the church, waitin' and watchin'? We gotta keep together. OK?"

The authority in his childish voice disconcerted her.

"But it doesn't seem right, Darren, to leave them. Not both of us. It seems, well, callous, wrong. I ought to stay."

"That's daft. You can't do nothin'. They're dead, stiff. You saw 'em."

He made a swift gesture of drawing a knife across his throat, rolled up his eyes and gagged. The sound was horribly realistic, a gush of blood in the throat. She cried out:

"Oh, don't, Darren, please don't!"

Immediately he was conciliatory, his voice calmer. He put his hand in hers. "Better come along with me to Father Barnes." She looked down at him, piteously, as if she were the child.

"If you think so, Darren."

He had regained his mastery now. The small body almost swaggered. "Yeah, that's what I think. Come along with me." He was excited. She heard it in the raised treble, saw it in the bright eyes. He was no longer shocked and he wasn't really upset. It had been silly to think that she needed to protect him from the horror. That spurt of fear at the thought of the police had passed. Brought up on those bright, flickering images of violence, could he distinguish between them and reality, she wondered. Perhaps it was more merciful that, protected by his innocence, he shouldn't be able to. He put a thin arm around her shoulders, helping her to the door, and she leaned against him, feeling the sharp bones under her arm.

How kind he is, she thought, how sweet, this dear, dear child. She would have to talk to him about the flowers and the salmon. But she needn't think about that now, not now.

They were outside. The air, fresh and cold, smelled to her as sweet as a sea breeze. But when, together, they had pulled shut the heavy door with its iron-decorated bands, she found she couldn't fit the key into the lock. Her fingers were jumping rhythmically, as if in spasm. He took the key from her and, stretching high, thrust it into the lock. And then her legs gently folded and she subsided slowly on the step, ungainly as a marionette. He looked down at her.

"You all right?"

"I'm afraid I can't walk, Darren. I'll be better soon. But I have to stay here. You fetch Father Barnes. But hurry!"

As he still hesitated, she said:

"The murderer, he can't be still inside. The door was unlocked when we arrived. He must have left after he'd—he wouldn't hang about inside waiting to be caught, would he?"

How odd, she thought, that my mind can reason that out while my body seems to have given up.

But it was true. He couldn't still be there, hiding in the church, knife in hand. Not unless they had died very recently. But the blood hadn't looked fresh . . . Or had it? Her bowels suddenly churned. Oh God, she prayed, don't let that happen, not now. I'll never get to the lavatory. I can't make it past that door. She thought of the humiliation, of Father Barnes coming, the police. It was bad enough to be slumped here like a heap of old clothes.

"Hurry," she said. "I'll be all right. But hurry!"

He made off, running very fast. When he had gone, she still lay there, fighting the terrible loosening of her bowels, the need to vomit. She tried to pray but, strangely, the words seemed to have got muddled up. "May the souls of the righteous, in the mercy of Christ, rest in peace." But perhaps they hadn't been the righteous. There ought to be a prayer that would do for all men, all the murdered bodies all over the world. Perhaps there was. She would have to ask Father Barnes. He would be sure to know.

And then came a new and different terror. What had she done with her key? She looked down at the one clutched in her hand. This was weighted with a large wooden tag charred at the end, where Father Barnes had put it down too close to a gas flame. So this was his spare key, the one he kept at the vicarage. It must be the one they had found in the lock and she had handed it to Darren to relock the door. So what had she done with hers? She rummaged frantically in her handbag as if the key were a vital clue, its loss disastrous, seeing in imagination a phalanx of accusing eyes, the police demanding she account for it, Father Barnes's tired and dispirited face. But her scrabbling fingers found it safe between her purse and the bag lining, and she drew it out with a moan of relief. She must have automatically put it away when she found the door already open. But how odd that she couldn't remember! Everything was a blank between their arrival and the moment in which she had thrust open the Little Vestry door.

She was aware of a dark shadow looming beside her. She looked up and saw Father Barnes. Relief flooded her heart. She said:

"You've rung the police, Father?"

"Not yet. I thought it was better to see for myself, in case the boy was playing tricks."

So they must have stepped past her, into the church, into that dreadful room. How odd that, huddled in the corner, she hadn't even noticed. Impatience rose like vomit in her throat. She wanted to cry out, "Well, now you've seen!" She had thought that when he arrived everything would be all right. No, not all right but better, made sense of. Somewhere there were the right words and he would speak them. But looking at him, she knew that he brought no comfort. She looked up at his face, unattractively blotched by the morning chill, at the grubby stubble, at the two brittle hairs at the corners of his mouth, at the trace of blackened blood in the left nostril, as if he had had a nosebleed, at the eyes, still gummy with sleep. How silly to think that he would bring his strength, would somehow make the horror bearable. He didn't even know what to do. It had been the same over the Christmas decorations. Mrs. Noakes had always done the pulpit, ever since Father Collins's time. And then Lilly Moore had suggested that it wasn't fair, that they ought to take turns at the pulpit and the font. He should have made up his mind and stood firm. It was always the same. But what a time to be thinking of Christmas decorations, her mind a tangle of hollyberries and gaudy poinsettias, red as blood. But it hadn't been so very red, more a reddish brown.

Poor Father Barnes, she thought, irritation dissolving into sentimentality. He's a failure like me, both failures. She was aware of Darren shivering beside her. Someone ought to take him home. Oh God, she thought, what will this do to him, to both of us? Father Barnes was still standing beside her, twisting the door key in his ungloved hands. She said gently:

"Father, we have to get the police."

"The police. Of course. Yes, we must call the police. I'll phone from the vicarage."

But still he hesitated. On an impulse she asked:

"Do you know them, Father?"

"Oh yes, yes. The tramp. That's Harry Mack. Poor Harry. He sleeps in the porch sometimes."

He didn't need to tell her that. She knew that Harry liked to doss down in the porch. She had taken her turn at clearing up after him, the crumbs, the paper bags, the discarded bottles, sometimes even worse things. She ought to have recognized Harry, that woollen hat, the jacket. She tried not to dwell on why it was that she hadn't. She asked, with the same gentleness:

"And the other, Father. Did you recognize him?"

He looked down at her. She saw his fear, his bewilderment, and above all, a kind of astonishment at the enormity of the complications that lay ahead. He said slowly, not looking at her:

"The other is Paul Berowne. Sir Paul Berowne. He is—he was—a Minister of the Crown."

2

⊠

As soon as he had left the Commissioner's office and was back in his own room Commander Adam Dalgliesh rang Chief Inspector John Massingham. The receiver was snatched at the first ring and Massingham's disciplined impatience came across as strongly as his voice. Dalgliesh said:

"The Commissioner has had a word with the Home Office. We're to take this one, John. The new squad will officially be in existence on Monday anyway, so we're only jumping the gun by five days. And Paul Berowne may still technically be the Member for Hertfordshire North East. He wrote to the Chancellor of the Exchequer to apply for the Chiltern Hundreds on Saturday, apparently, and no one seems quite sure whether the resignation dates from the day the letter was received or the date the warrant is signed by the Chancellor. Anyway, all that is academic. We take the case."

But Massingham was uninterested in the procedural details for the resignation of a parliamentary seat. He said:

"Division are sure, sir, that the body is Sir Paul Berowne?"

"One of the bodies. Don't forget the tramp. Yes, it's Berowne. There's evidence of identity at the scene, and the parish priest knew him, apparently. It wasn't the first time Berowne had spent the night in St. Matthew's Church vestry."

"An odd place to choose to sleep."

"Or to die. Have you spoken to Inspector Miskin?"

Once they had begun working together they would both be calling her Kate, but now Dalgliesh gave her her rank. Massingham said:

"She's off today, sir, but I managed to get her at her flat. I've asked Robins to collect her gear and she'll meet us at the scene. I've alerted the rest of the team."

"Right, John. Get the Rover, will you. I'll meet you outside. Four minutes."

It crossed his mind that Massingham might not have been too displeased had Kate Miskin already left her flat and been impossible to contact. The new squad had been set up in C1 to investigate serious crimes which, for political or other reasons, needed particularly sensitive handling. It had been so self-evident to Dalgliesh that the squad would need a senior woman detective that he had devoted his energy to choosing the right one rather than to speculating how well she would fit into the team. He had selected the twenty-seven-year-old Kate Miskin on her record and her performance at interview, satisfied that she had the qualities for which he was looking. They were also the ones he most admired in a detective: intelligence, courage, discretion and common sense. What else she might have to contribute remained to be seen. He knew that she and Massingham had worked together before when he had been a newly promoted divisional detective inspector and she a sergeant. It was rumoured that the relationship had at times been stormy. But Massingham had learned to discipline some of his prejudices since then, as he had the notorious Massingham temper. And a fresh, even an iconoclastic, influence, even a little healthy rivalry, could be more effective operationally than the collusive and machismo freemasonry which frequently bound together a team of all male officers.

Dalgliesh began rapidly but methodically to clear his desk, then checked his murder bag. He had told Massingham four minutes, and he would be there. Already he had moved, as if by a conscious act of will, into a world in which time was precisely measured, details obsessively noticed, the senses preternaturally alert to sound, smell, sight, the flick of an eyelid, the timbre of a voice. He had been called from this office to so many bodies, in such different settings, such different states of dissolution, old, young, pathetic, horrifying, having in common only the one fact, that they were violently dead and by another's hand. But this body was different. For the first time in his career, he had known and liked the victim. He told himself that it was pointless to speculate what difference, if any, this would make to the investigation. Already he knew that the difference was there.

The Commissioner had said:

"His throat is cut, possibly by his own hand. But there's a second body, a tramp. This case is likely to be messy in more ways than one."

His reaction to the news had been partly predictable and partly complex and more disturbing. There had been the natural initial shock of disbelief at hearing of the unexpected death of any person even casually known. He would have felt no less if he'd been told that Berowne was dead of a coronary or killed in a car smash. But this had been followed by a sense of personal outrage, an emptiness and then a surge of melancholy, not strong enough to be called grief but keener than mere regret, which had surprised him by its intensity. But it hadn't been strong enough to make him say "I can't take this case. I'm too involved, too committed."

Waiting briefly for the lift, he told himself that he was no more involved than he would be in any other case. Berowne was dead. It was his business to find out how and why. Commitment was to the job, to the living, not to the dead.

He had hardly passed through the swing doors when Massingham drove up the ramp with the Rover. Getting in beside him, Dalgliesh asked:

"Fingerprints and photography, they're on their way?"

"Yes, sir."

"And the lab?"

"They're sending a senior biologist. She'll meet us there."

"Did you manage to get Dr. Kynaston?"

"No, sir, only the housekeeper. He's been in New England visiting his daughter. He always goes there in the fall. He was due back at Heathrow on BA flight 214 arriving at seven twenty-five. It's landed, but he's probably stuck on the Westway by now."

"Keep on trying his home until he arrives."

"Doc Greeley is available, sir. Kynaston will be jet-lagged."

"I want Kynaston, jet-lagged or not."

Massingham said:

"Only the best for this cadaver."

Something in his voice, a tinge of amusement, even contempt, irritated Dalgliesh. He thought, My God, am I getting over-sensitive about this death even before I've seen the body? He fastened his seat belt without speaking and the Rover slid gently into Broadway, the road he had crossed less than a fortnight earlier on his way to see Sir Paul Berowne.

Gazing straight ahead, only half-aware of a world outside the claustrophobic comfort of the car, of Massingham's hands stroking the wheel, the almost soundless changing of the gears, the pattern of traffic lights, he deliberately let his mind slip free of the present and of all conjecture about what lay ahead, and remembered, by an exercise of mental recall, as if something important depended on his getting it right, every moment of that last meeting with the dead man.

3

⊠

It was Thursday 5 September and he was about to leave his office to drive to Bramshill Police College to begin a series of lectures to the Senior Command Course when the call came through from the Private Office. Berowne's private secretary spoke after the manner of his kind. Sir Paul would be grateful if Commander Dalgliesh could spare a few minutes to see him. It would be convenient if he could come at once. Sir Paul would be leaving his office to join a party of his constituents at the House in about an hour.

Dalgliesh liked Berowne, but the summons was inconvenient. He was not expected at Bramshill until after luncheon and had planned to take his time over the journey to north Hampshire, visiting churches at Sherbourne St. John and Winchfield and lunching at a pub near Stratfield Saye before arriving at Bramshill in time for the usual courtesies with the commandant before his two-thirty lecture. It occurred to him that he had reached the age when a man looks forward to his pleasures less keenly than in youth but is disproportionately aggrieved when his plans are upset. There had been the usual time-consuming, wearying and slightly acrimonious preliminaries to the setting up of the new squad in C1, and already his mind was reaching out with relief to the solitary contemplation of alabaster effigies, sixteenth-century glass and the awesome decorations of Winchfield. But it looked as if Paul Berowne wasn't proposing to take much time over their meeting. His plans might still be possible. He left his grip in the office, put on his tweed coat against a blustery autumnal morning and cut through St. James's Park Station to the Department.

As he pushed his way through the swing doors he thought again how much he had preferred the Gothic splendour of the old building in White-hall. It must, he recognized, have been infuriating and inconvenient to work in. It had, after all, been built at a time when the rooms were heated by coal fires tended by an army of minions and when a score of carefully composed handwritten minutes by the Department's legendary eccentrics were adequate to control events which now required three divisions and a couple of under-secretaries. This new building was no doubt excellent of its kind, but if the intention had been to express confident authority tempered by humanity, he wasn't sure that the architect had succeeded. It looked more suitable for a multinational corporation than for a great Department of State. He particularly missed the huge oil portraits which had dignified that impressive Whitehall staircase, intrigued always by the techniques by which artists of varying talents had coped with the challenge of dignifying the ordinary and occasionally unprepossessing features of their sitters by the visual exploitation of magnificent robes and by imposing on their pudgy faces the stern consciousness of imperial power. But at least they had removed the studio photograph of a royal princess which until recently had graced the entrance hall. It had looked more suitable for a West End hairdressing salon.

He was smilingly recognized at the reception desk, but his credentials were still carefully scrutinized and he was required to await the escorting messenger, even though he had attended enough meetings in the building to be reasonably familiar with these particular corridors of power. Few of the elderly male messengers now remained, and for some years the Department had recruited women. They shepherded their charges with a cheerful, maternal competence as if to reassure them that the place might look like a prison but was as gently beneficent as a nursing home and that they were only there for their own good.

He was finally shown into the outer office. The House was still in recess for the summer and the room was unnaturally quiet. One of the typewriters was shrouded and a single clerk was collating papers with none of the urgency which normally powered a Minister's private office. It would have been a different scene a few weeks earlier. He thought, not for the first time, that a system which required Ministers to run their departments, fulfill their parliamentary responsibilities and spend the week-end listening to the grievances of their constituents might have been de-signed to ensure that major decisions were made by men and women tired to the point of exhaustion. It certainly ensured that they were heavily dependent on their permanent officials. Strong Ministers were still their own men; the weaker degenerated into marionettes. Not that this would necessarily worry them. Departmental heads were adept at concealing from their puppets even the gentlest jerk of strings and wire. But Dalgliesh hadn't needed his private source of department gossip to know that there was nothing of this limp subservience about Paul Berowne.

He came forward from behind his desk and held out his hand as if this were a first meeting. His was a face stern, even a little melancholy, in repose, which was transfigured when he smiled. He smiled now. He said:

"I'm sorry to bring you here at short notice. I'm glad we managed to catch you. It isn't particularly important, but I think it may become so."

Dalgliesh could never see him without being reminded of the portrait of his ancestor, Sir Hugo Berowne, in the National Portrait Gallery. Sir Hugo had been undistinguished except for a passionate, if ineffective, allegiance to his king. His only notable recorded act had been to commission Van Dyke to paint his portrait. But it had been enough to ensure him, at least pictorially, a vicarious immortality. The manor house in Hampshire had long since passed from the family, the fortune was diminished; but Sir Hugo's long and melancholy face framed by a collar of exquisite lace still stared with arrogant condescension at the passing crowd, the definitive seventeenth-century Royalist gentleman. The present baronet's likeness to him was almost uncanny. Here was the same long-boned face, the high cheekbones tapering to a pointed chin, the same widely spaced eyes with the droop of the left eyelid, the same long-fingered pale hands, the same steady but slightly ironic gaze.

Dalgliesh saw that his desk top was almost clear. It was a necessary ploy for an overworked man who wanted to stay sane. You dealt with one thing at a time, gave it your whole attention, decided it, then put it aside. At this moment he managed to convey that the one thing requiring attention was comparatively unimportant, a short communication on a sheet of quarto-sized white writing paper. He handed it over. Dalgliesh read:

"The Member for Hertfordshire North East, despite his fascist tendencies, is a notable liberal when it comes to women's rights. But perhaps women should beware; proximity to this elegant baronet can be lethal. His first wife was killed in a car accident; he was driving. Theresa Nolan, who nursed his mother and slept in his house, killed herself after an abortion. It was he who knew where to find the body. The naked body of Diana Travers, his domestic servant, was found drowned at his wife's Thames-side birthday party, a party at which he was expected to be present. Once is a private tragedy, twice is bad luck, three times looks like carelessness."

Dalgliesh said:

"Typed with an electric golf-ball machine. They're not the easiest to identify. And the paper is from a pad of ordinary commercial bond sold in thousands. Not much help there. Have you any idea who could have sent it?"

"None. One gets used to the usual abusive or pornographic letters. They're part of the job."

Dalgliesh said:

"But this is close to an accusation of murder. If the sender is traced, I imagine your lawyer would advise that it's actionable."

"Actionable, yes, I imagine so."

Dalgliesh thought that whoever had composed the message hadn't been uneducated. The punctuation was careful, the prose had a certain rhythm. He or she had taken trouble over the arrangement of the facts and in getting in as much relevant information as possible. It was certainly a cut above the usual filth and drivel which dropped unsigned into a Minister's postbag, and it was the more dangerous for that.

He handed it back and said:

"This isn't the original, of course. It's been photocopied. Are you the only person to receive it, Minister, or don't you know?"

"He sent it to the press, at least to one paper, the *Paternoster Review*. This is in today's edition. I've only just seen it."

He opened his desk drawer, took out the journal and handed it to Dalgliesh. There was a folded marker at page eight. Dalgliesh let his eyes slide down the page. The paper had been running a series of articles on junior members of the Government and it was Berowne's turn. The first part of the article was innocuous, factual, hardly original. It briefly reviewed Berowne's previous career as a barrister, his first unsuccessful attempt to enter Parliament, his success at the 1979 election, his phenomenal rise to junior ministerial rank, his probable standing with the Prime Minister. It mentioned that he lived with his mother, Lady Ursula Berowne, and his second wife in one of the few extant houses built by Sir John Soane and that he had one child by his first marriage, twenty-four-year-old Sarah Berowne, who was active in left-wing politics and who was thought to be estranged from her father. It was unpleasantly snide about the circumstances of his second marriage. His elder brother, Major Sir Hugo Berowne, had been killed in Northern Ireland and Paul Berowne had married his brother's fiancée within five months of the car accident which had killed his wife. "It was, perhaps, appropriate that the bereaved fiancée and husband should find mutual consolation although no one who has seen the beautiful Barbara Berowne could suppose that the marriage was merely a matter of fraternal duty." It went on to prognosticate with some insight but little charity about his political future. But much of that was little more than lobby gossip.

The sting lay in the final paragraph and its origin was unmistakable. "He is a man who is known to like women; certainly most find him attractive. But those women closest to him have been singularly unlucky. His first wife died in a car smash while he was driving. A young nurse, Theresa Nolan, who nursed his mother, Lady Ursula Berowne, killed herself after an abortion, and it was Berowne who found the body. Four weeks ago a girl who worked for him, Diana Travers, was found drowned following a party given for his wife on her birthday, a party at which he was expected to be present. Bad luck is as lethal for a politician as halitosis. It could yet follow him into his political career. It could be the sour smell of misfortune rather than the suspicion that he doesn't know what he really wants which could mock the prediction that here is the next Conservative Prime Minister but one."

Berowne said:

"The *Paternoster Review* isn't circulated in the Department. Perhaps it should be. Judging from this, we might be missing entertainment if not instruction. I read it occasionally at the club, mainly for the literary reviews. Do you know anything about the paper?"

He could, thought Dalgliesh, have asked the Department's own public relations people. It was interesting that apparently he hadn't chosen to. He said:

"I've known Conrad Ackroyd for some years. He owns and edits the *Paternoster*. His father and grandfather had it before him. In those days it was printed in Pater Noster Place in the City. Ackroyd doesn't make money out of it. Papa left him reasonably well provided for through more orthodox investments, but I imagine it just about breaks even. He likes to print gossip occasionally, but the paper isn't a second *Private Eye*. Ackroyd hasn't the guts, for one thing. I don't think he has ever risked being sued in the history of the paper. It makes it less audacious and less entertaining than the *Eye*, of course, except for the literary and dramatic reviews. They have an enjoyable perversity." Only the *Paternoster*, he recalled, would have described a revival of Priestley's *An Inspector Calls* as a play about a very tiresome girl who caused a great deal of trouble to a respectable family. He added: "The facts will be accurate as far as they go. This will have been checked. But it's surprisingly vicious for the *Paternoster*."

Berowne said:

"Oh yes, the facts are accurate." He made the statement calmly, almost sadly, without explanation and apparently without the intention of offering any.

Dalgliesh wanted to say "Which facts? The facts in this journal or the facts in the original communication?" But he decided against the question. This wasn't yet a case for the police, least of all for him. For the present, anyway, the initiative must lie with Berowne. He said:

"I remember the Theresa Nolan inquest. This Diana Travers drowning is new to me."

Berowne said:

"It didn't make the national press. There was a line or two in the local paper reporting the inquest. It made no mention of my wife. Diana Travers wasn't a member of her birthday party, but they did dine at the same restaurant, the Black Swan on the river at Cookham. The authorities seem to have adopted that slogan of the insurance company: Why make a drama out of a crisis?"

So there had been a cover-up, of sorts anyway, and Berowne had known it. The death by drowning of a girl who worked for a Minister of the Crown and who died after dining at the restaurant where that Minister's wife was also dining, whether or not he himself was present, would normally have justified at least a brief paragraph in one of the national papers. Dalgliesh asked:

"What do you want me to do, Minister?"

Berowne smiled.

"Do you know, I'm not exactly sure. Keep a watching brief, I suppose. I'm not expecting you to take this on personally. That would obviously be ridiculous. But if it does develop into open scandal, I suppose someone eventually will have to deal with it. At this stage I wanted to put you in the picture."

But that was precisely what he hadn't done. With any other man Dalgliesh would have pointed this out and with some asperity. The fact that he felt no temptation to do so with Berowne interested him. He thought, There'll be reports on both the inquests. I can get most of the facts from official sources. For the rest, if it does blow up into an open accusation,

he'll have to come clean. And if that happened, whether it became a matter
for him personally and for the proposed new squad would depend on how
great the scandal, how real the suspicion and of what precisely. He wondered what Berowne was expecting him to do, find a potential blackmailer
or investigate him for double murder? But it seemed likely that a scandal
of some sort would eventually break. If the communication had been sent
to the *Paternoster Review*, it had almost certainly been sent to other papers
or journals, possibly to some of the nationals. They might at present be
choosing to hold their fire, but that didn't mean they'd have thrown the
communication into their wastepaper baskets. They had probably spiked
it while they checked with their lawyers. In the meantime, to wait and
watch was probably the wisest option. But there would be no harm in
having a word with Conrad Ackroyd. Ackroyd was one of the greatest gossips
in London. Half an hour spent in his wife's elegant and comfortable drawing
room was usually more productive and a great deal more entertaining than
hours spent beavering through official files.

Berowne said:

"I'm meeting a party of constituents at the House. They want to be
shown round. Perhaps if you've time you could walk over with me." Again
the request was a command.

But when they left the building he turned without explanation to the
left and down the steps to Birdcage Walk. So they were to walk to the
House the longest way, along the fringe of St. James's Park. Dalgliesh
wondered if there were things his companion wished to confide which
could more easily be said out of the office. The twenty square acres of
entrancing if formalized beauty of the park, crossed by paths so convenient
that they might have been purposefully designed to lead from one centre
of power to another, must, he thought, have heard more secrets than any
other part of London.

But if that was Berowne's intention, it was destined to be thwarted.
They had hardly crossed Birdcage Walk when they were hailed by a cheerful
shout, and Jerome Mapleton trotted up beside them, rubicund, sweaty-
faced, a little out of breath. He was the Member for a South London constituency, a safe seat which he nevertheless hardly ever left, as if fearing
that even a week's absence might put it in jeopardy. Twenty years in the
House still hadn't dampened his extraordinary enthusiasm for the job and
his not unappealing surprise that he should actually be there. Talkative,
gregarious and insensitive, he attached himself as if by magnetic force
to any group larger or more important than the one he was actually in.

Law and order was his chief interest, a concern popular with his prosperous middle-class constituents cowering behind their security locks and decorative window bars. Adapting his subject to his captive audience, he plunged at once into parliamentary small talk about the newly appointed committee, bobbing up and down between Berowne and Dalgliesh like a small craft on bumpy water.

"This committee, 'Policing a Free Society: The Next Decade,' isn't that what it's called? Or is it 'Policing in a Free Society: The Next Decade'? Didn't you spend the first session deciding whether to include that little preposition? So typical. You're looking at policy as well as technical resources, aren't you? Isn't that a tall order? It's made the committee larger than is usually thought effective, hasn't it? Wasn't the original idea to look again at the application of science and technology to policing? The committee seems to have enlarged its terms of reference."

Dalgliesh said:

"The difficulty is that technical resources and policy aren't easily separated, not when you get to practical policing."

"Oh, I know, I know. I quite appreciate that, my dear Commander. This proposal to monitor vehicle movements on the motorways, for example. You can do it, of course. The question is, should you do it? Similarly with surveillance. Can you examine advanced scientific methods divorced from the policy and ethics of their actual use? That's the question, my dear Commander. You know it, we all know it. And, come to that, can we any longer rely on the received doctrine that it's for the chief constable to decide on the allocation of resources?"

Berowne said:

"You aren't, of course, about to utter heresy—that we ought to have a national force?" He spoke without apparent interest, his eyes fixed ahead. It was as if he were thinking: Since we're lumbered with this bore, let's throw him a predictable subject and hear his predictable views.

"No. But it might be better to have one by will and intention than by default. De jure, Minister, not de facto. Well, you'll have plenty to keep you busy, Commander, and given the membership of the working party, it won't be dull." He spoke wistfully. Dalgliesh suspected that he had hoped to be a member. He heard him add: "I suppose that's the attraction of the job for the sort of man you are."

What sort of man, thought Dalgliesh. The poet who no longer writes poetry. The lover who substitutes technique for commitment. The policeman disillusioned with policing. He doubted whether Mapleton intended his words to be offensive. The man was as insensitive to language as he was to people.

He said:

"I've never been quite sure what the attraction is except that the job isn't boring and it gives me a private life."

Berowne spoke with sudden bitterness:

"It's a job with less hypocrisy than most. A politician is required to listen to humbug, talk humbug, condone humbug. The most we can hope for is that we don't actually believe it." The voice rather than the words disconcerted Mapleton. Then he decided to treat it as a joke and giggled. He turned to Dalgliesh.

"So what now for you personally, Commander? Apart from the working party, of course?"

"A week of lectures to Senior Command Course at Bramshill. Then back here to set up the new squad."

"Well, that should keep you busy. What happens if I murder the Member for Chesterfield West when the working party is actually sitting?" He giggled again at his own audacity.

"I hope you'll resist the temptation, sir."

"Yes, I must try. The committee is too important to have the senior police detective interest represented on a part-time basis. And by the way, talking of murder, there's a very odd paragraph about you, Berowne, in today's *Paternoster Review*. Not altogether friendly, I thought."

"Yes," said Berowne shortly. "I've seen it." He increased his pace so that Mapleton, already out of breath, had to choose between talking or using his energy to keep up. When they reached the Treasury, he obviously decided that the reward was no longer worth the effort and with a valedictory wave disappeared up Parliament Street. But if Berowne had been seeking a moment for further confidences it had disappeared. The pedestrian signal had turned to green. No pedestrian, seeing the lights in his favour at Parliament Square, hesitates. Berowne gave him a rueful glance as if to say: "See how even the lights conspire against me," and walked briskly across. Dalgliesh watched as he crossed Bridge Street, acknowledged the salute of the policeman on duty and disappeared into New Palace Yard. It had been a brief and unsatisfactory encounter. He had the feeling that Berowne was in some trouble deeper and more subtly disturbing than poison pen messages. He turned back to the Yard telling himself that if Berowne wanted to confide he would do it in his own good time.

But that time had never come. And it had been on his drive back from Bramshill a week later that he had turned on his radio and heard the news of Berowne's resignation of his ministerial post. The details had been sparse. Berowne's only explanation had been that he felt it was time for his life to take a new direction. The Prime Minister's letter, printed in the next day's *Times*, had been conventionally appreciative but brief. The great British public, most of whom would have been hard pressed to name three members of the Cabinet of this or any administration, were preoccupied with chasing the sun in one of the rainiest summers in recent years and took the loss of a junior Minister with equanimity. Those parliamentary gossips still in London enduring the boredom of the silly season waited in happy expectation for the scandal to break. Dalgliesh waited with them. But there was, apparently, to be no scandal. Berowne's resignation remained mysterious.

Dalgliesh had already sent while at Bramshill for the reports of the inquests on Theresa Nolan and Diana Travers. On the face of it there was no cause for concern. Theresa Nolan, after having a medical termination on psychiatric grounds, had left a suicide note for her grandparents which they had confirmed was in her handwriting and which made her intention to kill herself plain beyond any doubt. And Diana Travers, after drinking and eating unwisely, had apparently herself dived into the Thames to swim out to her companions who were messing about in a punt. Dalgliesh had been left with an uneasy feeling that neither case was as straightforward as the reports made it appear, but certainly there was no prima facie evidence of foul play in connection with either of the two deaths. He was uncertain how much further he was expected to probe or whether, in the light of Berowne's resignation, there was any point in his probing. He had decided to do nothing further for the present and to leave it to Berowne to make the first move.

And now Berowne, the harbinger of death, was himself dead, by his hand or another's. Whatever secret he had been hoping to confide on that short walk to the House would remain forever unspoken. But if he had, indeed, been murdered, then the secrets would be told; through his dead body, through the intimate detritus of his life, through the mouths, truthful, treacherous, faltering, reluctant, of his family, his enemies, his friends. Murder was the first destroyer of privacy as it was of so much else. And it seemed to Dalgliesh an ironic twist of fate that it should be he, whom Berowne had shown a disposition to trust, who should now be travelling to begin that inexorable process of violation.

4
⊠

They were almost at the church before he wrenched his mind back to the present. Massingham had driven in, for him, an unusual silence as if sensing that his chief was grateful for this small hiatus between knowledge and discovery. And he had no need to enquire the way. As always, he had mapped his route before setting out. They were driving up the Harrow Road and had just passed the complex of St. Mary's Hospital when the campanile of St. Matthew's came suddenly into view on their left. With its crossed bands of stone, its high arched windows and copper cupola, it reminded Dalgliesh of the brick towers he had laboriously erected as a child, brick on precarious brick, until they toppled in noisy disorder on the nursery floor. It held for him some of the same hubristic impermanence and, even as he gazed, he half expected it to bend and sway. Without speaking, Massingham took the next turning to the left and drove towards it down a narrow road bordered on each side by a terrace of small houses. They were identical, with their small upper windows, narrow porches and square bays, but it was obvious that the road was coming up in the world. Some few still showed the tell-tale signs of multiple occupation: dishevelled lawns, peeling paint and drawn secretive curtains. But these were succeeded by bright little bandboxes of social aspiration: newly painted doors, carriage lamps, an occasional hanging basket, the front garden paved to provide standing for the car. At the end of the road the huge bulk of the church with its soaring walls of smoke-blackened brick looked as much out of keeping as it was out of scale with this small domestic self-sufficiency.

The huge north door, large enough for a cathedral, was closed. Beside it a grime-encrusted board gave the name and address of the parish priest and the time of services, but there was nothing else to suggest that the door was ever opened. They drove slowly down a narrow asphalt drive between the southern wall of the church and the railing bordering the canal, but still there was no sign of life. It was obvious that the news of a murder hadn't yet spread. There were only two cars parked outside the south porch. One, he guessed, belonged to Detective Sergeant Robins and the red Metro to Kate Miskin. He wasn't surprised that she was there before them. She opened the door before Massingham had time to ring, her handsome, shield-shaped face composed under the light brown fringe, and looking in her shirt, slacks and leather jerkin as elegantly informal as if she had just come in from a country walk. She said:

"The DI's compliments, sir, but he had to get back to the station. They've got a homicide at Royal Oak. He left as soon as Sergeant Robins and I arrived. He'll be available from midday if you need him. The bodies are here, sir. They call it the Little Vestry."

It was typical of Glyn Morgan not to have disturbed the scene. Dalgliesh had a respect for Morgan as a man and a detective but was grateful that either duty, tact or a mixture of both had taken him away. It was a relief not to have to soothe and propitiate an experienced detective who could hardly be expected to welcome a commander from the new C1 squad intruding on his patch.

Kate Miskin pushed open the first door on the left and stood aside for Dalgliesh and Massingham to enter. The Little Vestry was as garishly lit as a film set. Under the glare of the fluorescent light the whole bizarre scene, Berowne's sprawled body and severed throat, the clotted blood, the tramp propped like a stringless marionette against the wall, looked for a moment unreal, A Grand Guignol tableau too overdone and too contrived to be convincing. Hardly glancing at Berowne's body, Dalgliesh picked his way across the carpet to Harry Mack and squatted beside him. Without turning his head, he asked:

"Were the lights on when Miss Wharton found the bodies?"

"Not in the passage, sir. But she says this light was on. The boy confirms it."

"Where are they now?"

"In the church, sir. Father Barnes is with them."

"Have a word with them, will you, John? Tell them I'll speak to them as soon as I'm free. And try to contact the boy's mother. We ought to get him away from here as soon as possible. Then I want you here."

Harry looked as derelict in death as he must have done in life. If it hadn't been for the breastplate of blood, he could have been asleep, legs stuck out, head slumped forward, his woollen cap slipped over his right eye. Dalgliesh put his hand under the chin and gently lifted the head. He had the sensation that it would come apart from the body and roll over into his hands. He saw what he had expected to find, the single slash across the throat, apparently from left to right, cutting through the trachea to the vertebrae. Rigor mortis was already well established and the skin was ice cold and goosefleshed as the arrector muscles of the hairs contracted with the onset of rigor. Whatever concatenation of chance or desire had brought Harry Mack to this place, there was no mystery about the cause of death.

He was wearing old plaid trousers, over-large and loose as pantaloons, and tied at the ankles with string. Above them, as far as it was possible to see for the blood, he wore a striped knitted pullover over a navy jumper. A malodorous checked jacket, stiff with grime, was unbuttoned, the left flap lying open. Dalgliesh raised it with careful fingers, touching only the extreme edge of the cloth, and saw underneath a smudge of blood on the carpet about two centimetres long and thicker at the right end than at the left. Peering closer, he thought he could see a smear roughly the same length on the jacket pocket, but the cloth was too dirty for him to be sure. But the implication of the smear on the carpet was plain enough. One or more drops of blood must have fallen or been spilt from the weapon before Harry fell and had then been smeared along the carpet as the body was dragged against the wall. But whose blood? If it proved to be Harry's, the discovery was of small significance. But suppose it was Berowne's? Dalgliesh felt impatient for the arrival of the forensic biologist, although he knew he couldn't hope for the answer, not yet. Samples of both victims' blood would be taken from the bodies at the post-mortem, but it would be three days at least before he could expect to get the result of the analysis.

He wasn't sure what impulse had made him go first to Harry Mack's body. But now he trod carefully across the carpet to the bed and stood silently looking down at the body of Berowne. Even as a fifteen-year-old boy, standing at the side of the bed of his dead mother, he hadn't felt the need to think, far less to utter, the word good-bye. You couldn't speak to someone who was no longer there. He thought: We can vulgarize everything, but not this. The body in its stiff ungainliness, beginning already, or so it seemed to his over-sensitive nose, to emit the first sour-sweet stink of decay, yet had an inalienable dignity because it once had been a man.

But he knew, none better, how quickly this spurious humanity would drain away. Even before the pathologist had finished at the scene and the head was wrapped, the hands mittened in their plastic bags, even before Doc Kynaston got to work with his scalpels, the corpse would be an exhibit, more important, more cumbersome and more difficult to preserve than other exhibits in the case, but still an exhibit, tagged, documented, dehumanized, invoking only interest, curiosity or disgust. But not yet. He thought: I knew this man, not well, but I knew him. I liked him. Surely he deserves better of me than to gaze at him with my policeman's eyes.

He lay head towards the door and at an angle of forty-five degrees from the bed, his shoes touching the end. The left hand was flung out, the right lay closer to the body. The bed had been covered with a blanket of hand-knitted squares of bright wool. It looked as if Berowne had clutched it as he fell, half-pulling it from the bed, so that it lay partly bunched at his right side. An open razor, the blade thick with clotted blood, lay on top of it, a few inches from his right hand. It was extraordinary how many details simultaneously impressed themselves on Dalgliesh's mind. A thin wedge of what looked like mud caked between the heel and the sole of the left shoe; the pattern of blood stiffening the fine fawn cashmere of the sweater; the half-open mouth fixed in a rictus between a smile and a sneer; the dead eyes seeming as he watched to shrink into their sockets; the left hand with its long pale fingers, curved and delicate as a girl's; the palm of the right hand thick with blood. But the whole picture struck him as wrong, and he knew why. Berowne couldn't both have held the razor in his right hand and clutched at the blanket as he fell. But if he had first dropped the razor, why should it be lying on top of the blanket and so conveniently close to his hand, as if it had slipped from the opening fingers? And why should the palm be so thickly clotted, almost as if another's hand had lifted it and smeared it into the blood at the throat? If Berowne himself had wielded the razor, surely the palm which had clutched it would have been less bloodied.

He was aware of a small noise at his side and looked round to see Detective Inspector Kate Miskin looking, not at the corpse, but at him. She quickly turned her eyes away but not before he had detected, to his discomfort, a look of grave, almost maternal solicitude. He said roughly:

"Well, Inspector?"

"It looks obvious, sir, murder followed by suicide. The classical pattern of self-inflicted wounds—three cuts, two tentative, the third cutting through the trachea."

She added:

"It could be used as an illustration in a textbook of forensic medicine."

He said:

"There's no difficulty in recognizing the obvious. One should be slower to believe it. I want you to break the news to his family. The address is 62 Campden Hill Square. There is a wife and an elderly mother, Lady Ursula Berowne, and a housekeeper of sorts. Use your discretion about which is best able to take it. And take a DC. When the news breaks they may be pestered and need protection."

"Yes, sir."

She showed no resentment at being ordered from the scene. She knew that the job of breaking the news wasn't a routine chore, that she hadn't been chosen merely because she was the only woman in his team and he saw this as a woman's job. She would break the news with tact, discretion, even with compassion. God knew she had had enough practice in ten years of policing. But she would still be a traitor to grief, watching and listening, even as she spoke the formal words of condolence, for the flicker of an eyelid, the tensing of hands and face muscles, for the unwise word, for any sign that for someone in that waiting house in Campden Hill Square this might not be news at all.

5

⊠

Before he concentrated on the actual scene of the crime, Dalgliesh always liked to make a cursory survey of the surroundings to orientate himself and, as it were, to set the scene of murder. That exercise had its practical value, but he recognized that, in some obscure way, it fulfilled a psychological need. Just so in boyhood he would explore a country church by first walking slowly round it before, with a frisson of awe and excitement, pushing open the door and beginning his planned progress of discovery to the central mystery. And now, in these few remaining minutes, before the photographer, the fingerprint officers, the forensic biologists arrived at the scene, he had the place almost to himself. Moving into the passage, he wondered whether this quiet air tinctured with the scent of incense, candles and the more solidly Anglican smell of musty prayer books, metal polish and flowers had held for Berowne also the promise of discovery, of a scene already set, a task inevitable and inescapable.

The brightly lit passage with its floor of encaustic tiles and its white-painted walls ran the whole west end of the church. The Little Vestry was the first room on the left. Next to it and with a connecting door was a small kitchen about ten feet by eight. Then came a narrow lavatory with an old-fashioned bowl of decorated porcelain and a mahogany seat with, above it, a hanging chain set under a single high window. Lastly an open door showed him a high square room, almost certainly set under the campanile, which was obviously both the vestry proper and the bell room. Opposite it the passage was separated from the body of the church by a ten-foot-long grille in delicate wrought iron which gave a view up the

nave to the cavernous glitter of the apse and the Lady Chapel on the right.
A central door in the grille topped with figures of two trumpeting angels
gave entry to the church for the processing priest and choir. To the right
a padlocked wooden box was fixed to the grille. Behind it, but within reach
of stretching hands, stood a branching candlestand, also in wrought iron,
with a box of matches in a brass holder attached to it with a chain, and
a tray containing a few small candles. Presumably this was to enable people
who had business in the vestry to light a candle when the grille door to
the church was locked. Judging from the cleanness of the candleholders,
it was a facility of which they seldom, if ever, took advantage. There was
only one candle in place, stuck upright like a pale wax finger, and this
had never been lit. Two of the brass chandeliers suspended above the
nave gave a gentle diffused light, but the church looked dimly mysterious
compared with the glare of the passage, and the figures of Massingham
and the detective sergeant quietly conferring, of Miss Wharton and the
boy patiently sitting like hump-backed dwarfs on low chairs in what must
be the children's corner, seemed as distanced and insubstantial as if they
moved in a different dimension of time. As he stood watching, Massingham
looked up, caught his eye, and moved down the nave towards him.

He returned to the Little Vestry and, standing in the doorway, drew
on his latex gloves. It always surprised him a little that it was possible
to fix the attention on the room itself, its furniture and objects, even before
the bodies had been packaged and taken away, as if in their fixed and
silent decrepitude they had for a moment become part of the room's artefacts, as significant as any other physical clue, no more and no less.
As he moved into the room he was aware of Massingham behind him,
alert, already drawing on his gloves, but, for him, unnaturally subservient,
pacing quietly behind his chief like a recently qualified houseman def-
erentially attendant on the consultant. Dalgliesh thought: Why is he behaving as if I need tactful handling, as if I'm suffering from a private
grief? This is a job like any other. It promises to be difficult enough without John and Kate treating me as if I'm a sensitive convalescent.

Henry James, he remembered, had said of his approaching death,
"So here it is at last, the distinguished thing!" If Berowne had thought
in these terms, then this was an incongruous place in which to receive
so honoured a visitation. The room was about twelve feet square and lit
by a fluorescent tube running almost the full length of the ceiling. The
only natural light came from two high curved windows. They were covered
outside by a protective mesh which looked like chicken wire on which

the dirt of decades had accumulated, so that the panes were honeycombs of greenish grime. The furniture, too, looked as if it had been gradually acquired over the years: gifts, rejects, the unregarded remnants of long-forgotten jumble sales. Opposite the door and set under the windows was an ancient oak desk with three right-hand drawers, one without handles. On its top was a simple oak cross, a much used blotter in a leather pad, and an old-fashioned black telephone, the receiver off the rest and lying on its side.

Massingham said:

"Looks as if he took it off. Who wants the telephone to ring just when he's concentrating on slitting his jugular?"

"Or his killer was taking no chances on the bodies being discovered too soon. If Father Barnes took it into his head to ring and got no reply, he'd probably come round to see if Berowne was all right. If he continued to get the engaged sound, he'd probably assume that Berowne was having an evening of telephoning and let it go."

"We might get a palm print, sir."

"Unlikely, John. If this is murder, we're not dealing with a fool."

He continued his exploration. With his gloved hands, he pulled open the top drawer and found a stack of white writing paper, of cheap quality, headed with the name of the church, and a box of envelopes. Apart from these, the desk held nothing of interest. Against the left-hand wall was an assortment of canvas and metal chairs neatly stacked, presumably for the occasional use of the parochial church council. Beside them was a five-drawer metal filing cabinet, and next to it a small glass-fronted bookcase. He slipped the catch and saw that it contained an assortment of old prayer books, missals, devotional pamphlets, and a pile of booklets about the history of the church. There were only two easy chairs, one set on each side of the fireplace: a compact brown chair in torn leather with a patchwork cushion, and a grubby, more modern chair with fitted pads. One of the stacked chairs had been uprighted. A white towel hung over its back and on the seat rested a brown canvas bag, its zip open. Massingham rummaged gently inside and said:

"A pair of pyjamas, a spare pair of socks, and a table napkin wrapped round half a sliced loaf, wholemeal, and a piece of cheese. Roquefort, by the look of it. And there's an apple. A Cox, if that's relevant."

"Hardly. Is that all, John?"

"Yes, sir. No wine. Whatever he thought he was doing here, it doesn't look like an assignation, not with a woman anyway. And why choose this place with the whole of London open to him? Bed too narrow. No comfort."

"Whatever he was looking for, I don't think it was comfort."

Dalgliesh had moved over to the fireplace, a plain wooden overmantel with an iron surround patterned with grapes and convolvulus set in the middle of the right-hand wall. It must, he thought, have been decades since a fire was lit in it for warmth. In front of the grate was a tall electric fire with artificial coals, a high curved back and a triple set of burners. He moved it gently forward and saw that the grate had, in fact, been recently used; someone had tried to burn a diary. It lay open in the fire-basket, its leaves curled and blackened. Some pages had apparently been torn out and separately burnt; the brittle fragments of black ash had floated down to lie on top of the debris under the grate, old twisted match ends, coal dust, carpet fluff, the accumulated grit of years. The blue cover of the diary with the year clearly printed had been more resistant to the flames; one corner only was slightly scorched. Whoever had burnt it had evidently been in a hurry, unless, of course, he had been concerned only to destroy certain pages. Dalgliesh made no attempt to touch it. This was a job for Ferris, the scene-of-crime officer, already hovering impatiently in the passage. The Ferret was never happy when anyone other than himself was examining a scene of crime and it seemed to Dalgliesh that his impatience to get on with the job came through the wall as a palpable force. He crouched low and peered into the debris under the grate. Among the fragments of blackened paper he saw a used safety match, the unburnt half of the stem clean and white as if it had only recently been struck. He said:

"He could have used this to burn the diary. But, if so, where is the box? Have a look in the jacket pockets, will you, John."

Massingham walked over to Berowne's jacket hanging on a hook at the back of the door and felt in the two outer and one inner pockets. He said:

"A wallet, sir, a Parker fountain pen and a set of keys. No lighter and no matches."

And there were none, either, visible in the room.

With mounting excitement which neither betrayed, they moved over to the desk and peered intently at the blotter. It, too, must have been there for years. The pink blotting paper tattered at the edges was marked with a criss-cross of different inks blodged with faded blots. It wasn't, thought Dalgliesh, surprising; most people now use ball-points rather than ink. But peering more closely he could see that someone had recently been writing with a fountain pen. Superimposed on the older markings were more recent blottings, a pattern of broken lines and half curves in black ink extending over some six inches of the blotter. Their newness was obvious. He went over to Berowne's jacket and brought out the fountain pen. It was elegantly slim, one of the newest models, and filled, he saw, with black ink. It should be possible for the lab to match the ink even if the letters couldn't be deciphered. But if Berowne had been writing and had blotted the paper at the desk, where was it now? Had he himself disposed of it, torn it up, flushed it down the lavatory, burnt it among the debris of the diary pages? Or had someone else found it, perhaps even come specifically to find it, and either destroyed it or taken it away?

Lastly, he and Massingham passed through the open door to the right of the fireplace, careful not to brush against Harry's body, and explored the kitchen. There was a gas boiler, comparatively modern, mounted above a deep square porcelain sink much stained and with a clean but crumpled tea towel hanging on a hook beside it. Dalgliesh peeled off his gloves and felt the towel. It was slightly damp, not in patches but all over, as if it had been soaked in water then wrung out and left to dry through the night. He handed it to Massingham, who took off his own gloves and ran it through his hand. He said:

"Even if the murderer was naked, or half-naked, he would have needed to wash his hands and arms. He could have used this. Berowne's towel is presumably the one hanging on the chair, and that looked dry enough."

Massingham went out to check while Dalgliesh continued his exploration. On the right was a cupboard with a Formica top, brown with tea stains, on which stood one large kettle, one smaller more modern kettle and two teapots. There was also a chipped enamel mug, stained almost black inside and smelling of spirits. Opening the cupboard he saw that it held a collection of unmatched crockery and two folded clean tea towels, both dry, and on the bottom shelf an assortment of flower vases, a battered cane basket containing folded dusters, and tins of metal and furniture polish. Here presumably Miss Wharton and her fellow helpers would arrange the flowers, wash out their dusters, refresh themselves with tea.

Attached to the pipe of the gas boiler by a brass chain was a box of safety matches in a brass holder, similar to the one chained to the candlestand, hinged at the top to allow insertion of a fresh box. There had been a similar holder and brass chain in the parish room of his father's Norfolk church, but he couldn't remember seeing one since. They were clumsy to use, the striking surface barely adequate. It was difficult to believe

that the boxes had been removed, then replaced, and even more difficult
to credit that a match from either of the chained boxes had been struck,
then carried lit and precariously flickering into the Little Vestry and used
to burn the diary.

Massingham was back beside him. He said:

"The towel next door is perfectly dry and only slightly dirtied. It looks
as if Berowne could have washed his hands when he arrived and that's
all. It's odd that he didn't leave it in here, except that there's nowhere
convenient to hang it. Odder, though, that the killer, assuming there is
a killer, didn't use it to dry himself rather than the smaller tea towel."

Dalgliesh said:

"If he remembered to take it out with him to the kitchen. If he didn't,
he'd hardly want to go back for it. Too much blood, too much risk of leaving
a clue. Better to use what he found to hand."

It was apparent that the kitchen was the only room with water and
a sink; hand washing as well as washing up must be done here, if at
all. Above the sink was a mirror composed of glass tiles stuck to the wall,
and under it a simple glass shelf. Upon this was a sponge bag, its zip
open, containing a toothbrush and a tube of paste, a dry face flannel and
a used bar of soap. Beside this was a more interesting find, a narrow leather
case with the initials PSB stamped on it in faded gold. With his gloved
hands Dalgliesh lifted the lid and found what he had expected to see,
the twin to the cut-throat razor lying so incriminatingly close to Berowne's
right hand. On the satin lining of the lid was a sticker with the maker's
name in old-fashioned twirls, P. J. Bellingham, and the Jermyn Street
address. Bellingham, the most expensive and prestigious barber in London
and supplier still of razors to those clients who had never adjusted to the
shaving habits of the twentieth century.

There was nothing of apparent interest in the lavatory, and they made
their way into the robing vestry. It was obvious that this was where Harry
Mack had settled himself for the night. What looked like an old army
blanket, frayed at the edges and stiff with dirt, had been loosely spread
in a corner, its fumous stink mingling with the smell of incense to produce
an incongruous amalgam of piety and squalor. Beside it was an overturned
bottle, a length of grubby cord and a sheet of newspaper on which lay
a crust of brown loaf, the core of an apple and some crumbs of cheese.
Massingham picked them up and rubbed them between his palms and
thumbs and sniffed. He said:

"Roquefort, sir. Hardly a cheese which Harry would have provided for himself."

There was no evidence that Berowne had started his own meal—that in itself might be of some help in deciding on the approximate time of death—but he had apparently either cajoled Harry into the church with the promise of a meal or, more likely, had supplied an obvious and immediate need before he was ready for his own share of the supper.

The vestry itself was so familiar from childhood memories that Dalgliesh could have taken one quick glance, shut his eyes and spoken aloud an inventory of high church piety: the packets of incense on top of the cupboard; the incense holder and censer; the crucifix; and behind the faded red serge curtain, the lace-trimmed vestments and the short starched supplices of the choir. But now his mind was on Harry Mack. What had roused him from his half-drunken sleep: a scream, the sound of a quarrel, a falling body? But could he have heard it from this room? As if echoing his thoughts, Massingham said:

"He could have been roused by thirst, gone to the kitchen for a drink of water and stumbled into the crime. That enamel mug looked as if it might be his. Father Barnes will know whether it belongs to the church and with luck there may be prints. Or he could have gone to the lavatory, but I doubt whether he would have heard anything from there."

And, thought Dalgliesh, he was unlikely to have gone afterwards into the kitchen to wash. Massingham was probably right. Harry had settled himself for the night and then felt the need for a drink of water. But for that fatal thirst, he might still be quietly sleeping.

Outside in the passage Ferris was prancing gently on his toes like a runner limbering for a race.

Massingham said:

"The blotter, the enamel mug, the tea towel and the diary are all important and there's what looks like a recently struck match in the grate; we need that. But we shall want all the debris in the fireplace and the S-bends in the pipes. The probability is that the murderer washed himself in the kitchen."

None of it really needed saying, least of all to Charlie Ferris. He was the most expert of the Met's scene-of-crime officers and the one Dalgliesh always hoped would be available when he began a new case. It was inevitable that he should be nicknamed the Ferret, although seldom in his hearing. He was very small, sandy-haired, sharp-featured and with his

sense of smell so well developed that it was rumoured that he had sniffed
out a suicide in Epping Forest even before the animal predators got to
it. In his spare time he sang in one of the most famous of London's amateur
choirs. Dalgliesh, who had heard him at a police concert, never ceased
to be surprised that so narrow a chest and so slight a frame could produce
such a powerful organ-toned bass. He was fanatical about his job and
had even designed the most appropriate clothes for searching: white shorts
and a sweat shirt, a plastic swimming cap tight fitting to prevent the spilling
of hairs, latex gloves as fine as a surgeon's and rubber bathing shoes over
his bare feet. His creed was that no murderer ever left the scene of crime
without leaving some physical evidence of his crime behind him. If it was
there, Ferris would find it.

There were voices in the passage. The photographer and fingerprint
officers had arrived. Dalgliesh could hear George Matthews's booming voice
cursing the traffic in the Harrow Road and Sergeant Robins's quieter answer. Someone laughed. They were neither callous nor particularly insensitive, but neither were they undertakers, required to assume a professional
reverence in the face of death. The forensic biologist hadn't yet arrived.
Some of the most distinguished scientists at the Metropolitan Laboratory
were women, and Dalgliesh, recognizing in himself an old-fashioned sensitivity which he certainly wouldn't have confessed to them, was always
glad when it was possible to remove the more horrific bodies before they
arrived to track and photograph the bloodstains and supervise the collection
of samples. He left Massingham to greet and brief the new arrivals. It was
time to talk to Father Barnes. But first he wanted a word with Darren before
the boy was driven home.

6
⊠

Sergeant Robins said:

"He'd have been gone by now, sir, but the little devil's been playing us up. We couldn't get an address out of him, and when he did come up with one it was wrong, a non-existent road. Could have been a bloody waste of time. I think he's telling the truth now, but I had to threaten him with the Juvenile Bureau, the Welfare and God knows what before he did. And then he tried to give us the slip and run off. I was lucky to grab him."

Miss Wharton had already been driven back to Crowhurst Gardens by a woman police constable, there to be solaced no doubt with tea and sympathy. She had made gallant efforts to pull herself together but had still been confused about the precise sequence of events between arriving at the church and the moment when she had pushed open the door of the Little Vestry. The important fact for the police to ascertain was whether she or Darren had actually entered the room, with the risk that the scene had been contaminated. Both were adamant that they had not. Beyond this there was little of importance which she could tell, and Dalgliesh had briefly heard her story and let her go.

But it was irritating that Darren was still with them. If he needed to be questioned again it was right that it should be at home and with his parents present. Dalgliesh knew that his present insouciance in the face of death was no guarantee that the horror hadn't touched him. It wasn't always an obvious trauma which disturbed a child the most. And it was odd that the boy was so resistant to being driven home. Normally,

a ride in a car, even a police car, would be something of a treat for a
child, particularly now that a gratifying crowd was beginning to collect
to witness his notoriety, drawn by the yards of white tape which sealed
off the whole of the south part of the church and by the police cars and
the unmistakable black and sinister mortuary van parked between the
church wall and the canal. Dalgliesh went up to the car and opened the
door. He said:

"I'm Commander Dalgliesh. It's time we got you home, Darren. Your
mother will be worried." And surely the boy should be at school. The term
must have started. But that, thank God, was hardly his concern.

Darren, looking small and extremely disgruntled, was slumped in the
front left-hand seat. He was an odd-looking child with an engaging monkey-
like face, pale under the rash of freckles, snub-nosed and bright-eyed
beneath the spiked, almost colourless lashes. He and Sergeant Robins had
obviously tried each other's patience to the limits, but he cheered up at
the sight of Dalgliesh and enquired with childish belligerence:

"You the boss man round here?"

A little disconcerted, Dalgliesh replied cautiously:

"You could say that."

Darren looked round with bright suspicious eyes, then said:

"She never did it, Miss Wharton. She's innercent."

Dalgliesh said, seriously:

"No, we didn't think she did. You see, it needed more strength than
an elderly lady or a boy could have. You're both in the clear."

"Yeah, that's all right then."

Dalgliesh said:

"You're fond of her?"

"She's all right. She wants lookin' after, mind you. She's daft. She
hasn't got the sense she was born with. I keep an eye on her, like."

"I think she relies on you. It was lucky you were together when you
found the bodies. It must have been horrible for her."

"Turned her up proper. She don't like blood, you see. That's why she
won't have a coloured TV. She makes out she can't afford it. That's daft.
She's always buying flowers for that BVM."

"BVM?" said Dalgliesh, his mind scurrying after some unrecognized
make of car.

"That statue in the church. The lady in blue with the candles in front
of her. They're called BVMs. She's always puttin' flowers there and lightin'
candles. Ten pee, they are. Five pee for the small ones."

His eyes shifted as if he had been lured onto dangerous ground. He added quickly:

"I reckon she won't have a coloured TV 'cause she don't like the colour of blood."

Dalgliesh said:

"I think you're probably right. You've been very helpful to us, Darren. And you're quite sure that you didn't go into that room, either of you?"

"Naw, I told yer. I was behind 'er all the time." But the question had been unwelcome and for the first time some of his cockiness seemed to have been drained from him. He slumped back in his seat and stared resentfully through the windscreen.

Dalgliesh went back into the church and found Massingham.

"I want you to go home with Darren. I've a feeling there's something he's keeping back. It might not be important, but it would be helpful to have you there when he talks to his parents. You've got brothers, you know about small boys."

Massingham said, "You want me to go now, sir?"

"Obviously."

Dalgliesh knew that the order was unwelcome. Massingham hated to leave a scene of crime even temporarily while the body was still there, and he would go the more unwillingly because Kate Miskin, back now from Campden Hill Square, was to stay. But if he had to go he would go alone. He ordered the police driver out of the car with unusual curtness and drove off at a speed which suggested that Darren was about to enjoy a gratifyingly exciting ride.

Dalgliesh passed through the grille door into the body of the church, turning to close it gently behind him. But even so the soft clang rang sharply in the silence and echoed around him as he made his way down the nave. Behind him out of sight, but always present to the mind, was the apparatus of his trade: lights, cameras, equipment, a busy silence broken only by voices unhushed and confident in the presence of death. But here, guarded by the elegant whorls and bars of wrought iron, was another world as yet uncontaminated. The smell of incense strengthened and he saw ahead a haze of gold where the gleaming mosaics of the apse stained the air and the great figure of Christ in glory, his wounded hands stretched out, glared down the nave with cavernous eyes. Two more of the nave lights had been switched on, but the church was still dim compared with the harsh glare of the arc lights trained on the scene, and it took him a minute to locate Father Barnes, a dark shape at the end of the first row of chairs under the pulpit. He walked up to him, aware of the ring of his feet on the tiled floor, wondering whether they sounded as portentous to the priest as they did to him.

Father Barnes was sitting bolt upright on his chair, his eyes staring ahead at the gleaming curve of the apse, his body taut and contracted, like that of a patient expecting pain, willing himself to endure. He didn't turn his head as Dalgliesh approached. He had obviously been summoned in a hurry. His face was unshaved and the hands, rigidly clamped together in his lap, were grubby, as if he had gone to bed unwashed. The cassock, whose long black lines etiolated still further his lean body, was old and stained with what looked like gravy. One spot he had tried ineffectively to rub away. His black shoes were unpolished, the leather cracked at the sides, the toes scuffed into greyness. There came from him a smell, half musty, half disagreeably sweet, of old clothes and incense, overlaid with stale sweat, a smell which was a pitiable amalgam of failure and fear. As Dalgliesh eased his long limbs in the adjoining chair and rested his arm along its back, it seemed to him that his body encompassed and, by its own calm presence, gently eased a core of fear and tension in his companion, so strong that it was almost palpable. He felt a sudden compunction. The man would, of course, have come fasting to the first Mass of the day. He would be craving hot coffee and food. Normally someone at or near the scene would be brewing tea, but Dalgliesh had no intention of using the washroom even to boil a kettle until the scene-of-crime officer had done his work.

He said:

"I won't keep you long, Father. There are just a few questions and we'll let you go back to the vicarage. This must have been a horrible shock for you."

Father Barnes still didn't look at him. He said in a low voice:

"A shock. Yes, it was a shock. I shouldn't have let him have the key. I don't know really why I did. It isn't easy to explain." The voice was unexpected. It was low, with an agreeable trace of huskiness and with a hint of more power than the frail body would suggest—not an educated voice, but one on which education had imposed a discipline which hadn't quite obliterated the provincial, probably East Anglian, accent of childhood. He turned now to Dalgliesh and said again:

"They'll say I'm responsible. I shouldn't have let him have the key. I'm to blame."

Dalgliesh said:

"You aren't responsible. You know that perfectly well and so will they." The ubiquitous, frightening, judgemental "they." He thought, but did not say, that murder provided its own dreadful excitement for those who neither mourned nor were directly concerned and that people were commonly indulgent to those who helped provide the entertainment. Father Barnes would be surprised—agreeably or otherwise—by the size of next Sunday's congregation. He said:

"Could we start at the beginning? When did you first meet Sir Paul Berowne?"

"Last Monday, just over a week ago. He called at the vicarage at about half past two and asked if he could see the church. He'd come here first and found he couldn't get in. We'd like to keep the church open all the time, but you know how it is today. Vandals, people trying to break open the offertory box, stealing the candles. There's a note in the north porch saying that the key is at the vicarage."

"I suppose he didn't say what he was doing in Paddington?"

"Yes, he did, actually. He said that an old friend was in St. Mary's Hospital and he'd been to see him. But the patient was having treatment and couldn't see visitors, so he had an hour to spare. He said he'd always wanted to see St. Matthew's."

So that was how it had started. Berowne's life, like that of all busy men, was dominated by the clock. He had set aside an hour to visit an old friend. The hour had become unexpectedly available for a private indulgence. He was known to be interested in Victorian architecture. However fantastic the labyrinth into which that impulse had led him, his first visit to St. Matthew's at least had had the comforting stamp of normality and reason.

Dalgliesh said:

"Did you offer to accompany him?"

"Yes, I offered, but he said not to trouble. I didn't press it. I thought he might want to be alone." So, Father Barnes was not without sensitivity. Dalgliesh said:

"So you gave him the key. Which key?"

"The spare one. There are only three to the south porch. Miss Wharton has one and I keep the other two at the vicarage. There are two keys on each ring, one to the south door and a smaller key which opens the door in the grille. If Mr. Capstick or Mr. Pool want a key—they're our two churchwardens—they come to the vicarage. It's quite close, you see. There's only one key to the main north door. I always keep that in my study. I never lend it out in case it gets lost. It's too heavy, anyway, for general use. I told Sir Paul that he would find a booklet describing the church in the bookstand. It was written by Father Collins and we've always meant to revise it. It's over there on the table by the north porch. We only charge three pence." He turned his head painfully, like an arthritic patient, as if inviting Dalgliesh to buy a copy. The gesture was pathetic and rather appealing. He went on:

"I think he must have taken one because two days later I found a five-pound note in the box. Most people just put in three pence."

"Did he tell you who he was?"

"He said his name was Paul Berowne. I'm afraid it didn't mean anything to me at the time. He didn't say he was an MP or a baronet, nothing like that. Of course, after he'd resigned I knew who he was. It was in the papers and on the television."

Again there was a pause. Dalgliesh waited. After a few seconds the voice began again, stronger now and more resolute.

"I suppose he was away about an hour, perhaps less. Then he returned the key. He said he would like to sleep that night in the Little Vestry. Of course he didn't know it was called that. He said in the small room with the bed. The bed has been there since Father Collins's time, in the war. He used to sleep in the church during air raids so that he could put out the fire bombs. We've never taken it away. It's useful if people feel ill during services or if I want to rest before midnight Mass. It doesn't take up much room. It's only a narrow collapsible bed. Well, you've seen it."

"Yes. Did he give any reason?"

"No. He made it sound quite an ordinary request and I didn't like to ask why. He wasn't a man you could cross-question. I did say what about sheets, a pillowcase. He said he'd bring anything he needed."

He had brought one double sheet and had slept in it, doubled over. Otherwise he had used the existing old army blanket folded beneath him and on top the blanket of multicoloured woollen squares. The pillowcase on what was obviously a chair cushion was also presumably his.

Dalgliesh asked:

"Did he take the key away with him then or call back for it that night?"

"He called back for it. That must have been about eight o'clock or a little earlier. He was standing at the door of the vicarage carrying a grip. I don't think he came by car. I didn't see one. I gave him the key. I didn't see him again until next morning."

"Tell me about the next morning."

"I used the south door as usual. It was locked. The door to the Little Vestry was open and I could see that he wasn't there. The bed was made up very tidily. Everything was tidy. There was a sheet and a pillowcase folded on top. I looked through the grille into the church. The lights weren't on, but I could just see him. He was sitting in this row, a little further along. I went into the vestry and robed for the Mass, then through the grille door into the church. When he saw that Mass was to be in the Lady Chapel he moved across and sat in the back row. He didn't speak. No one else was there. It wasn't Miss Wharton's morning and Mr. Capstick, who likes to come to the nine-thirty Mass, had influenza. There were just the two of us. When I'd finished the first prayer and turned to face him, I saw that he was kneeling. He took Communion. Afterwards, we walked together to the Little Vestry. He handed me back the key, thanked me, picked up his grip and left."

"And that was all on that first occasion?"

Father Barnes turned and looked at him. In the dimness of the church his face looked lifeless. Dalgliesh saw in his eyes a mixture of entreaty, resolution and pain. There was something he feared to say yet needed to confide. Dalgliesh waited. He was used to waiting. At last Father Barnes spoke.

"No, there is something. When he lifted his hands and I placed the wafer in his palms—I thought I saw—" He paused, then went on: "There were marks, wounds. I thought I saw stigmata."

Dalgliesh fixed his eyes on the pulpit. The painted figure of a Pre-Raphaelite angel carrying a single lily, its yellow hair crimped under the wide halo, looked back at him with its bland, uncurious gaze. He asked:

"On his palms?"

"No. On his wrists. He was wearing a shirt and a pullover. The cuffs were a little loose. They slipped back. That's when I saw."

"Have you told anyone else about this?"

"No, only you."

For a full minute neither of them spoke. In all his career as a detective Dalgliesh couldn't remember a piece of information from a witness more unwelcome and—there was no other word—more shocking. His mind busied itself with images of what this news could do to his investigation if it ever became public: the newspaper headlines; the half-amused speculation of the cynics; the crowds of sightseers—the superstitious, the credulous, the genuine believers, thronging the church in search of . . . what?

A thrill, a new cult, hope, certainty? But his distaste went deeper than irritation at an unwelcome complication to his enquiry, at the bizarre intrusion of irrationality into a job so firmly rooted in the search for evidence which would stand up in court, documented, demonstrable, real. He was shaken, almost physically, by an emotion far stronger than distaste and one of which he was half-ashamed; it seemed to him both ignoble and in itself hardly more rational than the event itself. What he was feeling was a revulsion amounting almost to outrage. He said:

"I think you should continue to say nothing. It isn't relevant to Sir Paul's death. It isn't even necessary to include it in your statement. If you do feel the need to confide in anyone, tell your bishop."

Father Barnes said simply:

"I shan't tell anyone else. I think I did have a need to speak about it, to share it. I've told you."

Dalgliesh said:

"The church was dimly lit. You said the lights weren't on. You were fasting. You could have imagined it. Or it could have been a trick of the light. And you saw the marks only for a couple of seconds when he lifted his palms to receive the Host. You could have been mistaken."

He thought: Who am I trying to reassure, him or me?

And then came the question which against reason he had to ask: "How did he look? Different? Changed?"

The priest shook his head, then said, with great sadness:

"You don't understand. I wouldn't have recognized it, the difference, even if it had been there." Then he seemed to recover himself. He went on resolutely:

"Whatever it was I saw, if it was there, it didn't last long. And it's not so very unusual. It has been known before. The mind works on the body in strange ways; an intense experience, a powerful dream. And as you say, the light was very dim."

So Father Barnes didn't want to believe it either. He was arguing it away. Well that, thought Dalgliesh wryly, was better than a note in the parish magazine, a telephone call to the daily papers or a sermon next Sunday on the phenomenon of stigmata and the inscrutable wisdom of Providence. He was interested to find that they shared the same distrust, perhaps the same revulsion. Later there would be a time and a place to consider why this was so. But now there were more immediate concerns. Whatever had brought Berowne again to that vestry, it had been a human hand, his or another's, which had wielded that razor. He said:

"What about yesterday night? When did he ask you if he could come back?"

"In the morning. He rang shortly after nine. I said I'd be in any time after six that evening and he came for the key precisely on the hour."

"Are you sure of the time, Father?"

"Oh yes, I was watching the six o'clock news. It had only just started when he rang the bell."

"And again, no explanation?"

"No. He was carrying the same grip. I think he came by bus or underground or walked. I didn't see a car. I handed him the key at the door, the same key. He thanked me and left. I didn't come to the church last night, I had no reason to. The next I knew was when the boy came for me and told me that there were two dead bodies in the Little Vestry. You know the rest."

Dalgliesh said:

"Tell me about Harry Mack."

The change of subject was obviously welcome, and Father Barnes was voluble on the subject of Harry. Poor Harry was a problem for St. Matthew's. For some reason, no one knew why, he had for the last four months taken to sleeping in the south porch. He usually bedded down on newspapers and covered himself with an old blanket which he sometimes left in the porch, ready for the next night, and sometimes took away, rolled into a long wad and tied around his stomach with string. Father Barnes, when he found the blanket, hadn't liked to remove it. After all, it was Harry's only covering. But it wasn't really convenient to have the porch used as a shelter or as a storage for Harry's odd and rather smelly belongings. The Parochial Church Council had actually discussed whether they ought to install railings and a gate, but that had seemed uncharitable, and there were more important things to spend their money on. They had difficulty in meeting their diocesan quota as it was. They had all tried to help Harry, but he wasn't easy. He was known at the Wayfarers' Refuge in Cosway Street in St. Marylebone, an excellent place, where he usually got a midday meal and medical attention for minor ailments when he needed it. He was a little too fond of drink and would occasionally get into fights. St. Matthew's had liaised with the refuge about Harry, but they hadn't known what to suggest. They had tried to persuade Harry to have a bed in their dormitory, but he wouldn't agree. He couldn't bear the intimate contact with other people. He wouldn't even eat his dinner at the refuge. He'd put it between slabs of bread, then take it away to eat in the streets. The porch was his place, snug, south-facing, out of public view. Dalgliesh said:

"So he's not likely to have knocked on the door yesterday evening and asked Sir Paul to let him in."

"Oh no, Harry wouldn't have done that."

But somehow he had got in. Perhaps he'd already settled down under his blanket when Berowne arrived. Berowne had asked him in out of the cold to share his meal. But how had he persuaded Harry? He asked Father Barnes what he thought.

"It must have happened that way, I suppose. Harry could already have been here in the porch. He usually dosses down fairly early. And it was unexpectedly cold last night for September. But it's very odd. There must have been something about Sir Paul that gave him confidence. He wouldn't have done it for most people. Even the warden at the refuge, so experienced with the city's derelicts, couldn't persuade Harry to spend the night there. But they only have the dormitory, of course. It was sleeping or eating with other people Harry couldn't stand."

And here, thought Dalgliesh, he had had the larger vestry to himself. It could have been the assurance of that privacy and, perhaps, the promise of food which had persuaded him in from the cold. He asked:

"When were you last here in the church, Father? I'm talking about yesterday."

"From four thirty till about quarter past five, when I read Evensong in the Lady Chapel."

"And when you locked up after you, how certain could you be that there was no one here, perhaps hidden? Obviously you didn't search the church. Why should you? But if someone were hiding here, would you have been likely to see him?"

"I think so. You see how it is. We've no high pews, only the chairs. There's nowhere he could have hidden."

Dalgliesh said:

"Perhaps under the altar, the high altar or in the Lady Chapel? Or in the pulpit?"

"Under the altar? It's a horrible thought, sacrilege. But how could he have got in? I found the church locked when I arrived at four thirty."

"And no one had collected the keys during the day, not even the churchwardens?"

"No one."

And Miss Wharton had assured the police that her key hadn't left her handbag. He said:

"Could anyone have got in during Evensong? Perhaps while you were praying? Were you alone in the Lady Chapel?"

"Yes. I came in by the south door as usual and locked both it and the door in the grille after me. Then I unlocked the main door. That would be the natural way in for any stranger wanting to attend a service. My people know that I always unlock the main door for Evensong and it's very heavy. It squeaks dreadfully. We're always meaning to oil it. I don't think anyone could have entered without my hearing."

"Did you tell any other person that Sir Paul was spending the night here yesterday?"

"Oh no. There wasn't anyone to tell. And I wouldn't have said anything. He didn't ask for secrecy; he didn't ask for anything. But I don't think he would have liked another person to know. No one else knew anything about him, not until this morning."

Dalgliesh went on to question him about the blotter and the spent match. Father Barnes said that the Little Vestry had last been used two days ago, on Monday the sixteenth, when the Parochial Church Council had met as usual at five thirty, immediately after Evensong. He had presided, sitting at the desk, but hadn't used the blotter. He always wrote with a Biro. He hadn't been aware of any recent marks, but then, he wasn't very clever at noticing that kind of detail. He was sure that the match couldn't have been left there by anyone in the PCC. Only George Capstick smoked and he used a pipe, which he lit with a lighter. But he hadn't been at the PCC because of recovering, still, from the flu. People had remarked how pleasant it was not to be enveloped in smoke.

Dalgliesh said:

"These are small details and probably of no importance. But I would be grateful if you would keep them to yourself. And I'd like you to have a look at the blotter and see whether you can remember what it looked like on Monday. And we've found a rather dirty enamel mug. It would be helpful to know if that belonged to Harry."

Seeing Father Barnes's face, he added:

"You won't need to go back into the Little Vestry. When the photographer has finished we'll bring out the items to you. And then I expect you'll be glad to get back to the vicarage. We shall need a statement later, but that can wait."

They sat for a minute in silence as if what had passed between them needed to be assimilated in peace. So here, thought Dalgliesh, lay the secret of Berowne's quixotic decision to give up his job. It had been something more profound, less explicable, than disillusionment, midlife restlessness, the fear of a threatened scandal. Whatever had happened to him on that first night in St. Matthew's vestry had led him, the next day, to change the whole direction of his life. Had it also led him to his death?

As they both got up they heard the clang of the grille door. Inspector Miskin was walking down the aisle. When she came up to them she said:

"The pathologist has arrived, sir."

7
⊠

Lady Ursula Berowne sat immobile in her sitting room on the third floor of 62 Campden Hill Square and gazed out over the top boughs of the plane trees as if at some far distant unseeable vista. It seemed to her that her mind was like an overfilled glass which only she could hold steady. One jerk, one shudder, one small loss of control and it would spill over into a chaos so terrible that it could end only in death. It was strange, she thought, that her physical response to shock should be the same now as it had been after Hugo was killed, so that to her present grief was added a grief for him as keen, as new as when she had first heard that he was dead. And the physical symptoms had been the same: a raging thirst, her body parched and shrivelled, her mouth dry and sour as if infected with her own breath. Mattie had brewed her pot after pot of strong coffee which she had gulped down scalding hot, black, unaware of its oversweetness. Afterwards she had said:

"I would like something to eat, something salty. Anchovy toast." She had thought: I'm like a woman pregnant with grief, subject to odd fancies.

But that was over now. Mattie had wanted to put a shawl over her shoulders, but she had shrugged it off and demanded to be left alone. She thought: There is a world outside this body, this pain. I shall take hold of it again. I shall survive. I must survive. Seven years, ten at the most, that's all I need. Now she waited, husbanding strength for the first of many visitors. But this was someone she herself had summoned. There were things which had to be said to him and there might not be much time.

Shortly after eleven she heard the doorbell ring, then the groaning of the lift and a soft clatter as the grille door closed. The door of her sitting room opened and Stephen Lampart came quietly in.

It seemed to her important that she should meet him standing. But she couldn't restrain the grimace of pain as her arthritic hip took the weight, and she knew that the hand grasping the knob of her cane was trembling. Immediately he was at her side. He said:

"Oh no. Please, you mustn't."

With one firm hand on her arm he solicitously helped her back into the chair. She disliked casual touching, the assumption of acquaintances or strangers that her disablement entitled them to handle her, as if her body were a despised encumbrance which it was proper gently to push and pull into place. She wanted to shrug off his firm, proprietorial grasp, but managed to resist. But she couldn't prevent the tightening of her muscles at his touch and she knew that he hadn't missed this instinctive revulsion. When he had settled her, gently and with professional competence, he seated himself in the chair opposite. They were separated by a low table. A circle of polished rosewood established his dominance; strength against weakness, youth against age, doctor and subservient patient. Except that she wasn't his patient. He said:

"I believe you're waiting for a hip replacement." It was Barbara, of course, who had told him, but he wouldn't be the first one to mention her name.

"Yes, I'm on the list of the orthopaedic hospital."

"Forgive me, but why not go private? Aren't you suffering unnecessarily?"

It was, she thought, an almost indecently incongruous remark with which to begin a visit of condolence; or was this his way of confronting her grief and stoicism, by taking refuge on professional ground, the only one on which he felt confident and could speak with authority?

She said:

"I prefer to be treated as a National Health patient. I enjoy my privileges, but that is one I don't happen to want."

He smiled gently, humouring a child.

"It seems a little masochistic."

"Possibly. But I haven't called you here for a professional opinion."

"Which as an obstetrician I wouldn't, in any case, be competent to give. Lady Ursula, this news about Paul is horrifying, unbelievable. Shouldn't you have sent for your own doctor? Or a friend? You should have someone with you. It's wrong for you to be alone at a time like this."

"I have Mattie if I need the usual palliatives—coffee, alcohol, warmth. At eighty-two, the few people one might wish to see are all dead. I have outlived both my sons. That is the worst thing that can happen to a human being. I have to endure it. But I don't have to talk about it." She could have added: "Least of all with you," and it seemed to her that the words, unspoken, hung on the air between them.

He was for a moment silent as if considering them, accepting their justice. Then he said:

"I would, of course, have called on you later even if you hadn't telephoned. But I wasn't sure that you'd want to see anyone so soon. You got my letter?"

He must have written it as soon as Barbara had telephoned the news and had sent it round by one of his nurses who, in a hurry to get home after night duty, hadn't even stopped to hand it in but had slipped it through the letter box. He had used all the obvious adjectives. He hadn't needed a thesaurus to decide on the appropriate response. Murder, after all, was appalling, terrible, horrific, unbelievable, an outrage. But the letter, a social obligation too promptly performed, had lacked conviction. And he should have known better than to have his secretary type it. But that, she thought, was typical. Scrape away the carefully acquired patina of professional success, prestige, orthodox good manners, and the real man was there: ambitious, a little vulgar, sensitive only when sensitivity paid. But much of this, she knew, was prejudice, and prejudice was dangerous. She must be careful to betray it as little as possible if the interview was to go the way she wanted. And it was hardly fair to criticize the letter. Dictating condolences to the mother of a murdered husband whom you've been busily cuckolding for the last three years would take more than his limited social vocabulary.

She hadn't seen him for nearly three months and she was struck anew by his good looks. He had been an attractive youth, tall, rather ungainly, with a thatch of black hair. But now the gangling figure had been smoothed and tailored by success, he carried his height with easy assurance and the grey eyes—which he knew so well how to use—held a basic wariness. His hair, frosted now with grey, was still thick with an unruliness that expensive cutting hadn't completely disciplined. It added to his attractiveness, hinting at an untamed individuality which was far removed from the tedium of conventional male good looks.

He leaned forward and looked across at her intently, his grey eyes softened with sympathy. She found herself resenting his easy assumption of professional concern. But he did it very well. She almost expected him to say, "We did all we could, all that was humanly possible." Then she told herself that the concern could be genuine. She had to resist the temptation to underrate him, to stereotype him as the handsome, experienced seducer of cheap fiction. Whatever he was, he wasn't as uncomplicated as that. No human being could be. And he was, after all, acknowledged as a fine gynaecologist. He worked hard, he knew his job.

When Hugo was at Balliol, Stephen Lampart had been his closest friend. She had liked him in those days and some of that liking still remained, resented, only half-acknowledged, but bound up with memories of sunlit walks in Port meadow, luncheon and laughter in Hugo's rooms, with the years of hope and promise. He had been the clever, handsome, ambitious boy from a lower-middle-class home, likeable, amusing, buying himself into the company he wanted by looks and wit, clever at concealing the itch of ambition. Hugo had been the privileged one, his mother an earl's daughter, his father a baronet and a distinguished soldier, possessor of the Berowne name, inheritor of what remained of the Berowne money. For the first time she found herself wondering whether he had resented not only Hugo but all the family, and whether that subsequent betrayal could have had long roots in the soil of an old envy. She said:

"There are two things we have to discuss, and there may not be much time or another opportunity. Perhaps I ought to say first that I didn't ask you here to criticize my daughter-in-law for infidelity. I'm not in a position to criticize anyone's sexual life."

The grey eyes grew cautious. He said:

"How wise of you. Few of us are."

"But my son was murdered. The police will know that soon if they don't already. And I know it now."

He said:

"Forgive me, but can you be sure? All Barbara could tell me when she rang this morning was that the police had found Paul's body and that of a tramp"—he paused—"with injuries to their throats."

"Their throats were cut. Both their throats. And from the careful tact with which the news was broken, I imagine that the weapon was one of Paul's razors. I suppose Paul could have been capable of killing himself. Most of us are, given sufficient pain. But what he wasn't capable of was killing that tramp. My son was murdered, and that means that there are certain facts the police will make it their business to discover."

He asked calmly:

"What facts, Lady Ursula?"

"That you and Barbara are lovers."

The hands clasped loosely in his lap tightened, then relaxed. But he was still able to meet her eyes.

"I see. Was it Paul or Barbara who told you that?"

"Neither. But I've lived in the same house with my daughter-in-law for four years. I'm a woman. I may be crippled but I have the use of my eyes and my intelligence."

"How is she, Lady Ursula?"

"I don't know. But before you leave I suggest that you make it your business to find out. I've only seen my daughter-in-law for three minutes since I got the news. She is, apparently, too distressed to talk to visitors. It seems that I count as a visitor."

"Is that quite fair? Sometimes other people's grief is harder to bear, to face, than one's own."

"Particularly if one's own isn't acute?"

He leaned forward and said quietly:

"I don't think we have any right to assume that. Barbara's feelings may not be intense, but Paul was her husband. She cared for him, probably more than either of us understand. This is a horrible business for her, for all of us. Look, do we have to talk now? We're both in shock."

"We have to talk, and there isn't much time. Commander Adam Dalgliesh is coming to see me as soon as they've finished with whatever it is they're doing at the church. Presumably he'll want to interview Barbara, too. In time, probably sooner than later, they'll get round to you. I have to know what you propose to tell them."

"This Adam Dalgliesh, isn't he some kind of poet? An odd hobby for a policeman."

"If he's as good a detective as he is a poet, he's a dangerous man. Don't underestimate the police because of what you read in the upmarket papers."

He said:

"I don't underestimate the police, but I've no reason to fear them. I know that they combine a machismo enthusiasm for selective violence with a rigid adherence to middle-class morality, but you aren't seriously suggesting that they'll suspect me of cutting Paul's throat because I go to bed with his wife? They may be out of touch with social reality but, surely, not that much out of touch."

She thought: This is more like it, this is the real man.

She said calmly:

"I'm not saying they'll suspect you. I've no doubt you'll be able to provide a satisfactory alibi for last evening. But it will cause less trouble if neither of you lies about your relationship. I'd prefer not to have to lie about it myself. Naturally, I shan't volunteer the information. But it is possible that they will ask."

"And why should they, Lady Ursula?"

"Because Commander Dalgliesh will liaise with Special Branch. My son was a Minister of the Crown, however briefly. Do you suppose there's anything about a Minister's private life, particularly a Minister in that department, which isn't known to those people whose business it is to discover and document this kind of potential scandal? What sort of world do you think we're living in?"

He got up and began slowly pacing in front of her. He said:

"I suppose I ought to have thought of that. I would have thought of it, given time. Paul's death has been such an appalling shock. I don't think my mind is working properly yet."

"Then I suggest that it begin working. You and Barbara have to agree on your story. Better still, agree to tell the truth. I take it that Barbara was your mistress when you first introduced her to Hugo and that she remained your mistress after Hugo was killed and she married Paul."

He stopped and turned to her.

"Believe me, Lady Ursula, it wasn't intended, it wasn't like that."

"You mean that she and you graciously decided to abstain from your sexual liaison, at least until the honeymoon was over?"

He came and stood in front of her and looked down.

"I think there's something I ought to say, but I'm afraid it isn't, well, gentlemanly." She thought but did not speak: That word is meaningless now. With you it probably always was. Before 1914, one could talk like that without sounding false or ridiculous, but not now. That word and the world it represented had gone forever, trodden into the mud of Flanders. She said:

"My son's throat was cut. In the light of that brutality, I don't think we need concern ourselves about gentility, spurious or otherwise. It's about Barbara, of course."

"Yes. There's something you ought to understand if you don't already. I may be her lover, but she doesn't love me. She certainly doesn't want to marry me. She's as satisfied with me as she can be with any man. That's because I understand her needs and I don't make demands. Not many demands. We all make some. And, of course, I'm in love with her as far as I'm capable of loving anyone. That's necessary to her. And she feels safe with me. But she wouldn't get rid of a perfectly good husband and a title to marry me. Not by divorce. Certainly not by conniving at murder. You have to believe that if you and she are going to go on living together."

She said:

"That at least was frank. You seem well suited to each other."

He accepted the subtle insult behind the irony.

"Oh yes," he said sadly, "we suit each other." He added, "I suspect she doesn't even feel particularly guilty. Less so than I do, oddly enough. It's difficult to take adultery seriously if you're not getting much pleasure out of it."

"Your role must be exhausting and hardly satisfying. I admire your self-sacrifice."

His smile was reminiscent, secretive.

"She's so beautiful. It's absolute, isn't it? It doesn't even depend on whether she's well or happy or not tired or on what she wears. It's always there. You can't blame me for trying."

"Oh yes," she said, "I can, and I do."

But she knew that she was being less than honest. All her life she had been beguiled by physical beauty in men and in women. It was what she had lived by. When, in 1918, with her brother and fiancé both killed, she, an earl's daughter, had gone on the stage in defiance of tradition, what else had she to offer? Not, she thought with wry honesty, any great dramatic talent. She had, almost casually and instinctively, demanded physical beauty in her lovers and had been unjealous and over-indulgent of it in her women friends. They had been the more surprised when, at the age of thirty-two, she had married Sir Henry Berowne, apparently for less obvious qualities, and had given him two sons. She thought now of her daughter-in-law as she had watched her many times, standing motionless in front of the glass in the hall. Barbara was incapable of passing a mirror without that moment of narcissistic stillness, that calm reflective gaze. What had she been watching for? That first droop from the corner of the eyes, the fading blue, the dry fold of skin, the first crêping of the neck which would show how transitory it was, this over-prized perfection.

He was still restlessly pacing, still talking.

"Barbara likes to feel that attention is being paid to her. You have to admit that about the sexual act. Attention, specific and intense, is certainly being paid. She needs men to desire her. She doesn't much want them actually to touch her. If she thought I had a hand in killing Paul, she wouldn't thank me. I don't think she'd forgive me. And she certainly wouldn't protect me. I'm sorry. I've been too frank. But I think it had to be said."

"Yes, it had to be said. Whom would she protect?"

"Her brother, possibly, but not, I should have thought, for long and certainly not at any risk to herself. They've never been particularly close."

She said drily:

"No sibling loyalty will be demanded of her. Dominic Swayne was here in this house with Mattie for the whole of yesterday evening."

"Is that his story or hers?"

"Are you accusing him of having a hand in my son's death?"

"Of course not. The idea is ridiculous. And if Mattie says he was with her, I've no doubt he was. We all know that Mattie is a model of rectitude. You asked me if there was anyone Barbara would protect. I can think of no one else."

He had stopped his pacing now and sat down again opposite to her. He said:

"Your reasons for telephoning me. You said there were two things we needed to discuss."

"Yes. I should like to be sure that the child Barbara is carrying is my grandchild, not your bastard."

His shoulders stiffened. For a moment, it could have been a second only, he sat rigidly gazing down at his clasped hands. In the silence she heard the ticking of the carriage clock. Then he looked up. He was still calm but she thought that his face was paler.

"Oh, there's no doubt about that. No possible doubt. I had a vasectomy three years ago. I'm not suited to fatherhood and I hadn't any wish to be made ridiculous by paternity suits. I can give you the name of my surgeon if you want proof. That's probably simpler than relying on blood tests once he's born."

"He?"

"Oh yes, it's a boy. Barbara had an amniocentesis. Your son wanted an heir and he's going to get an heir. Didn't you know?"

She sat for a moment in silence. Then she said:

"Isn't that a risky procedure for the foetus, particularly so early in the pregnancy?"

"Not with the new techniques and in expert hands. And I saw that she was in expert hands. No, not mine. I'm not that kind of fool."

She asked:

"Did Paul know about the child before he died?"

"Barbara hasn't said. I imagine not. After all, she's only just heard of it herself."

"The pregnancy? Surely not."

"No, the sex of the child. I rang and told her first thing yesterday morning. But Paul may have suspected that there was a child on the way. After all, he did go back to that church, presumably to ask his God for further and better instructions."

She was seized by an anger so intense that, for a moment, she couldn't speak. And when her voice did come it quavered like the voice of an old, impotent woman. But at least her words could sting. She said:

"You never could resist it, even as a boy, the temptation to combine vulgarity with what you imagined was wit. Whatever happened to my son in that church, and I don't pretend to understand it, in the end he died because of it. When next you're tempted to indulge in a cheap witticism, you might remember that."

His own voice was low and as cold as steel.

"I'm sorry. I thought from the beginning that this conversation was a mistake. We're both too shocked to be rational. And now, if you'll excuse me, I'll go down to see Barbara before the police descend on her. She's alone, I take it?"

"As far as I know she is. Anthony Farrell should be arriving soon. I sent for him to his private address as soon as I got the news, but he has to get up from Winchester."

"The family lawyer? Having him here when the police arrive—won't that look suspicious? Too like a necessary precaution?"

"He's a family friend as well as a lawyer. It's natural for both of us to want him here. But I'm glad you're seeing her before he arrives. Tell her to answer Dalgliesh's questions but not to volunteer information, any information. I've no reason to suppose the police will take an unnecessarily dramatic view of what, after all, was common adultery. But it isn't something they'll expect her to confide even if they know about it. Too much candour looks as suspicious as too little."

He asked:

"Were you with her when the police broke the news?"

"The police didn't break the news. I did. It seemed to me advisable in all the circumstances. A competent woman officer told me first, then I went down alone to see Barbara. She behaved very prettily. Barbara has always known what emotion it is appropriate for her to feel. And she's a good actress. She should be. She's had plenty of practice. Oh, and another thing. Tell her to say nothing about the child. That's important."

"If it's what you want, what you think is wise. But it could be helpful to mention the pregnancy. They'd be particularly gentle with her."

"They'll be gentle. They won't be sending a fool."

They were speaking like confederates, precariously allied in a conspiracy which neither would acknowledge. She felt a cold disgust as physical as nausea, and with it there swept over her a weakness which shrivelled her in her chair. Immediately, she was aware of him at her side, of his fingers, gentle, firm, pressing her wrist. She knew that she should have resented his touch, but now it comforted her. She lay back, her eyes closed, and her pulse strengthened under his fingers. He said:

"Lady Ursula, you really should see your doctor. Malcolm Hancock, isn't it? Let me ring him."

She shook her head.

"I'm all right. I can't cope with another person yet. Until the police arrive I need to be alone." It was a confession of weakness which she hadn't expected to make, not to him and not at such a moment. He walked to the door. When his hand was on the knob, she said:

"There's one more thing. What do you know about Theresa Nolan?"

He turned and looked at her gravely.

"No more than you, I imagine, probably less. She only worked at Pembroke Lodge for four weeks and I hardly set eyes on her. She nursed you, lived in this house, for over six. And when she came to me she was already pregnant."

"And Diana Travers?"

"Nothing, except that she was unwise enough to overeat, drink too much and then dive into the Thames. As you must know, Barbara and I had left the Black Swan before she drowned." He was silent for a moment and then said, gravely:

"I know what you're thinking about, that ludicrous article in the *Paternoster Review*. Lady Ursula, may I give you some advice? Paul's murder, if it is murder, is perfectly simple. He let someone into that church, a thief, another derelict, a psychopath, and that person killed him. Don't complicate his death, which, God knows, is horrible enough, with old, irrelevant tragedies. The police will have enough to get their teeth into without that."

"Are they both irrelevant?"

He didn't answer. Instead he said:

"Has Sarah been told?"

"Not yet. I tried to telephone her this morning at the flat but there was no reply. She was probably out getting a paper. I'll try again as soon as you leave."

"Would you like me to go round? She is Paul's daughter, after all. This will be a terrible shock to her. She oughtn't to learn it from the police or the television news."

"She won't. If necessary, I'll go round myself."

"But who will drive you? Isn't Wednesday Halliwell's day off?"

"There are taxis."

She resented the way in which he seemed to be taking over, insinuating himself into the family as cunningly as he once had in Oxford. And then, again, she reproached herself for unfairness. He had never lacked his measure of kindness. He said:

"She ought to have time for preparation before the police burst in on her."

Time for what? she wondered. To make a decent pretence that she cared? She didn't reply. Suddenly she wanted him gone so urgently that it was all she could do not to order him to get out. Instead she held out her hand. Bending, he took it in his and then raised it to his lips. The gesture, theatrical and ludicrously inappropriate, disconcerted but did not disgust her. After he had left, she found herself looking down at her thin, ring-encrusted fingers, at the age-mottled knuckles against which, briefly, his lips had rested. Was the gesture a tribute to an old woman facing with dignity and courage a last tragedy? Or had it been something more subtle, a pledge that, despite everything, they were allies, that he under-stood her priorities and would make them his?

8
⊠

Dalgliesh remembered a surgeon once telling him that Miles Kynaston had shown promise of becoming a brilliant diagnostician, but had given up general medicine for pathology at registrar level because he could no longer bear to watch human suffering. The surgeon had sounded a note of amused condescension as though he were betraying a colleague's unfortunate weakness, wryly observed, which a more prudent man would have detected before beginning his medical training, or at least would have come to terms with before his second year. It could, Dalgliesh thought, have been true. Kynaston had fulfilled his promise, but now he applied his diagnostic skills to the unrepining dead, whose eyes couldn't implore him to offer hope, whose mouths could no longer cry out. Certainly he had a taste for death. Nothing about it disconcerted him: its messiness, its smell, the most bizarre of its trappings. Unlike most doctors, he saw it not as the final enemy, but as a fascinating enigma, each cadaver, which he would gaze at with the same intent look as he must once have fixed on his living patients, a new piece of evidence which might, if rightly interpreted, bring him closer to its central mystery.

Dalgliesh respected him more than any other pathologist with whom he had worked. He came promptly when called and was equally prompt reporting on a post-mortem. He didn't indulge in the crude autopsy humour which some of his colleagues found necessary to bolster their social self-esteem; dinner guests could know themselves safe from distasteful anecdotes about carving knives or missing kidneys. Above all he was good in the witness box, too good for some people. Dalgliesh remembered the sour comment of a defending counsel after a verdict of guilty: "Kynaston's getting dangerously infallible with juries. We don't want another Spilsbury."

He never wasted time. Even as he greeted Dalgliesh he was taking off his jacket and was drawing his fine latex gloves over stubby-fingered hands which looked unnaturally white, almost bloodless. He was tall and solidly built, giving an impression of shambling clumsiness until one saw him working in a confined space, when he would seem physically to contract and become compact, even graceful, moving about the body with the lightness and precision of a cat. His face was fleshy, the dark hair receding from a high speckled forehead, the long upper lip as precisely curved as an arrowhead, and the full, heavily lidded eyes dark and very bright, giving his face a look of sardonic, humorous intelligence. Now he squatted, toad-like, by Berowne's body, his hands hanging loosely in front of him, palely disembodied. He gazed at the throat wounds with extraordinary concentration, but made no move to touch the body except to run his hand lightly over the back of the head, like a caress. Then he said:

"Who are they?"

"Sir Paul Berowne, late MP and junior Minister, and a tramp, Harry Mack."

"On the face of it, murder followed by suicide. The cuts are textbook: two fairly superficial from left to right, then one above, swift, deep, severing the artery. And the razor neatly to hand. As I say, on the face of it obvious. A little too obvious?"

Dalgliesh said:

"I thought so."

Kynaston stepped gingerly over the carpet to Harry, prancing on tiptoe like an inexpert dancer.

"One cut. Enough. Again from left to right. Which means that Berowne, if it was Berowne, stood behind him."

"So why isn't Berowne's right shirt sleeve soaked with blood? All right, it's heavily bloodstained, his own or Harry's blood or both. But if he killed Harry, wouldn't you expect a greater amount of soaking?"

"Not if he turned up his shirt sleeve first and took him from behind."

"And turned it down again before slitting his own throat? Unlikely, surely."

Kynaston said:

"Forensic should be able to identify Harry's blood, or what could be Harry's blood, on the shirt sleeve as well as Berowne's own. There seem to be no visible stains between the bodies."

Dalgliesh said:

"Forensic have been over the carpet with the fibre-optic lamp. They may get something. And there is one discernible smudge under Harry's jacket and a trace of what looks like blood on the jacket lining immediately above it."

He lifted the corner. Both of them looked at the stain on the carpet in silence. Dalgliesh said:

"It was under the jacket when we found it. That means it was there before Harry fell. And if it proves to be Berowne's blood, then he died first, unless, of course, he staggered across to Harry after making one or more of the superficial cuts in his own throat. As a theory, it strikes me as ludicrous. If he were in the very act of cutting his own throat, how could Harry have stopped him? So why bother to kill him? But is it possible, medically possible?"

Kynaston looked at him. Both knew the importance of the question. He said:

"After the first superficial cut, I'd say that it was."

"But would he still have had the strength to kill Harry?"

"With his own throat partly cut? Again, after that first superficial cut, I don't think one can rule it out. He'd be in a state of high excitement, remember. It's amazing what strength people do find. After all, we're supposing that he was interrupted in the act of suicide. Hardly the moment when a man is at his most rational. But I can't be certain. No one can. You're asking the impossible, Adam."

"I was afraid so. But it's too neat."

"Or you want to believe it's too neat. How do you see it?"

"From the position of the body I think he could have been sitting on the edge of the bed. Assuming he was murdered, assuming that the murderer went first into the kitchen, then he could have crept back silently and attacked Berowne from behind. A blow, a cord round the throat. Or he grabs him by the hair, drags back the head, makes the first deep cut. The others, the ones designed to look tentative, could have come afterwards. So we look for any mark under the cuts, or for a bump on the back of the head."

Kynaston said:

"There is a bump but it's small. It could have been caused by the body falling. But we'll know more at the pm."

"An alternative theory is that the killer knocked him out first, then went into the kitchen to strip and came back for the final throat-cutting before Berowne had a chance to come round. But that raises obvious objections. He'd have to judge the force of the blow very carefully, and you'd expect it to leave more than a slight bump."

Kynaston said:

"But it raises fewer objections than the first theory, that he came in half-naked and armed with a razor and yet there are no obvious signs that Berowne put up any resistance."

"He could have been taken by surprise. He could expect his visitor to come back through the door to the kitchen. It's possible that he tiptoed down the passage and came in by the main door. That's the most likely theory, given the position of the body."

Kynaston said:

"You're assuming premeditation then? That the killer knew he'd find a razor to hand?"

"Oh yes. If Berowne was murdered, then the killing was premeditated. But I'm theorizing in advance of the facts, the unforgivable sin. All the same, there's something contrived about it, Miles. It's too obvious, too neat."

Kynaston said:

"I'll finish the preliminary examination and then you can take them away. I would normally do the pm first thing tomorrow, but they aren't expecting me back at the hospital until Monday and the pm room is tied up until the afternoon. Three thirty is the earliest. Is that all right for your people?"

"I don't know about the lab. The sooner the better for us."

Something in his voice alerted Kynaston. He said:

"Did you know him?"

Dalgliesh thought: This is going to come up again and again. You knew him. You're emotionally involved. You don't want to see him as mad, a suicide, a killer. He said:

"Yes, I knew him slightly, mostly across a committee table."

The words seemed to him grudging, almost a small treachery. He said again:

"Yes, I knew him."

"What was he doing here?"

"He had some kind of religious quasi-mystical experience here in this room. He may have been hoping to recapture it. He'd arranged with the parish priest to stay the night here. He gave no explanation."

"And Harry?"

"It looks as if Berowne let him in. He may have found him sleeping in the porch. Apparently Harry couldn't tolerate being with other people. There's evidence that he was proposing to sleep further along the passage in the larger vestry."

Kynaston nodded and got down to his familiar routine. Dalgliesh left him to it and went out into the passage. Watching this violation of the body's orifices, preliminaries to the scientific brutality to follow, had always made him feel uncomfortably like a voyeur. He had often wondered why he found it more offensive and ghoulish than the autopsy itself. Was it, perhaps, because the body was so recently dead, sometimes hardly cold? A superstitious man might fear that the spirit, so recently released, hovered around to be outraged at this insult to the discarded, still vulnerable, flesh. There was nothing for him to do now until Kynaston had finished. He was surprised to find himself tired. He expected to be exhausted later in an investigation when he would be working a sixteen-hour day, but this early heaviness, the feeling that he was already spent in mind and body, was new to him. He wondered whether it was the beginning of age or one more sign that this case was going to be different.

He went back into the church, sat down in a chair in front of a statue of the Virgin. The huge nave was empty now. Father Barnes had gone, escorted home by a police constable. He had been readily helpful about the mug, identifying it as one Harry had often had with him when he was found sleeping in the porch. And he had tried to be helpful about the blotter, staring at it with almost painful intensity before saying that he thought that the black markings hadn't been there when he had last seen the blotter on Monday evening. But he couldn't be sure. He had taken a sheet of writing paper from the desk and used it to make notes during the meeting. This had covered the blotter so that he had really only seen it for a short time. But, as far as his memory went, the black markings were new.

Dalgliesh was grateful for these minutes of quiet contemplation. The scent of incense seemed to have intensified, but it smelt to him overlaid with a sickly, more sinister smell, and the silence wasn't absolute. At his back he could hear the ring of footsteps, an occasional raised voice, calm, confident and unhurried, as the unseen professionals went about their work behind the grille. The sounds seemed very far off and yet distinct, and he had the sensation of a secret, sinister busyness, like the scrabbling of mice behind the wainscot. Soon, he knew, the two bodies would be neatly parcelled in plastic sheeting. The rug would be carefully folded to preserve bloodstains, and in particular that one significant stain of dried blood. The scene-of-crime exhibits packed and tagged would be carried to the police car: the razor, the crumbs of bread and cheese from the larger room, the fibres from Harry's clothing, that single burnt match head. For the moment he would keep possession of the diary. He needed to have it with him when he went to Campden Hill Square.

At the foot of the statue of the Virgin and Child stood a wrought-iron candleholder bearing its triple row of clotted sockets, the tips of burnt wick deep in their rims of wax. On impulse he felt in his pocket for a tenpenny piece and dropped it in the box. The clatter was unnaturally loud. He half expected to hear Kate or Massingham moving up beside him to watch, unspeaking but with interested eyes, this untypical act of sentimental folly. There was a box of matches in a brass holder chained to the candlerack, similar to the one at the back of the church. He took one of the smaller candles and struck a match, holding it to the wick. It seemed to take an unduly long time before it took hold. Then the flame burnt steadily, a limpid, unflickering glow. He stuck the candle upright in a socket, then sat and gazed at the flame, letting it mesmerize him into memory.

9

⊠

It was over a year ago but it seemed even longer. They had both been attending a seminar on judicial sentencing at a northern university, Berowne to open it formally with a brief speech, Dalgliesh to represent the police interest; and they had travelled by rail in the same first-class compartment. For the first hour Berowne, with his private secretary, had dealt with official papers, while Dalgliesh, after a final perusal of the agenda, had settled down to re-read Trollope's *The Way We Live Now*. When the last file had been placed in the briefcase, Berowne had looked across at him and had seemed to want to talk. The young Principal, with a tact that would help ensure he remained a "high flyer," had suggested that he should take first luncheon if that were agreeable to the Minister, and had disappeared. And for a couple of hours they had talked.

Looking back on it, Dalgliesh was still amazed that Berowne should have been so frank. It was as if the train journey itself, the old-fashioned intimate compartment in which they had found themselves, the freedom from interruptions and the tyranny of the telephone, the sense of time visibly flying, annihilated under the pounding wheels, not to be accounted for, had released both of them from a carefulness which had become so much a part of living that they were no longer aware of its weight until they let it slip from their shoulders. Both were very private men. Neither needed the masculine camaraderie of club or golf course, pub or grouse moor, which so many of their colleagues found necessary to solace or sustain their over-busy lives.

Berowne had spoken at first spasmodically, then easily, and finally

intimately. From the ordinary subjects of casual conversation—books, recent plays, acquaintances they had in common—he had gone on to talk
about himself. Both had leaned forward, hands loosely clasped. To a casual
passenger, glancing in as he lurched down the corridor, they must, thought
Dalgliesh, have looked like two penitents in a private confessional absolving
each other. Berowne had seemed not to expect a reciprocal confidence,
indiscretion traded for indiscretion. He spoke; Dalgliesh listened. Dalgliesh
knew that no politician would have talked with such freedom unless he
had had absolute confidence in his listener's discretion. It was impossible
not to feel flattered. He had always respected Berowne; now he warmed
to him and was honest enough about his own reactions to know why.

Berowne had spoken of his family:

"We're not a distinguished family, merely an old one. My great-grandfather lost a fortune because he was fascinated by a subject for which
he had absolutely no talent—finance. Someone told him that the way to
make money was to buy when the shares were low and sell when they
were high. A simple enough rule which struck his rather undeveloped
mind with the force of divine inspiration. He had absolutely no difficulty
in following the first precept. The problem was that he never had the
opportunity to follow the second. He had a positive genius for picking
losers. So had his father. In his case the losers were on four legs. But
I feel grateful to Great-grandfather nevertheless. Before he lost his money
he had the good sense to commission John Soane to design the Campden
Hill Square house. You're interested in architecture, aren't you? I'd like
you to see it when you can spare a couple of hours. It needs at least that.
In my view it's even more interesting than the Soane Museum in Lincoln's
Inn Fields; a perverse neo-classicism, I suppose you'd call it. I find it
satisfying, architecturally anyway. But I'm not sure that it isn't a house
to admire rather than to live in."

Dalgliesh had wondered how Berowne knew about his fondness for
architecture. It could only have been because he read his poetry. A poet
may heartily dislike having to talk about his verse, but the knowledge that
someone has actually read it is never unwelcome.

And now, sitting legs stretched, on a chair too low comfortably to
accommodate his six feet two inches, eyes fixed on that single taper, unflickering in the incense-heavy stillness, he could hear again the tone,
taut with self-disgust, in which Berowne had explained why he had given
up the law:

"Such odd things determine why and when one makes that kind of decision. I suppose I had persuaded myself that sending men to prison wasn't something I cared to do for the rest of my life. And appearing only for the defence has always seemed too easy an option. I was never really good at pretending that I could assume my client to be innocent because I or my instructing solicitor had been careful to ensure that he didn't actually confess. By the time you've seen your third rapist walk free because you've been cleverer than the prosecuting counsel, you lose the taste for that particular victory. But that's just the easy explanation. I suspect it wouldn't have happened if I hadn't lost an important case, important to me, anyway. You won't remember it—Percy Matlock. He killed his wife's lover. It wasn't a particularly difficult case, and we were confident we'd get it reduced to manslaughter. Even with that lesser verdict there was plenty of mitigation. But I didn't prepare carefully enough. I suppose I thought I didn't need to. I was pretty arrogant in those days. But it wasn't only that. At the time I was very much in love, one of those adventures which seem of overwhelming importance at the time but, afterwards, leave one wondering if it wasn't a kind of sickness. But I just wasn't giving the case what it needed. Matlock was convicted of murder and died in prison. He had one child, a daughter. Her father's conviction unhinged what precarious stability she'd managed to maintain. After she came out of the psychiatric hospital, she got in touch with me, and I gave her a job. She still keeps house for my mother. I don't think she's otherwise employable, poor girl. So I live with a constant and uncomely reminder of folly and failure, and no doubt it does me good. The fact that she's actually grateful to me, 'devoted' is the word people use, doesn't make it easier."

He had gone on to talk of his brother, killed five years earlier in Northern Ireland:

"The title came to me through his death. Most of the things I expected to value in life have come to me through death."

Not, Dalgliesh remembered, the "things I value." The "things I expected to value."

He could smell above the all-pervading redolence of incense the faint acrid smoke of the candle. Getting up from his chair, he left it burning, the pale flame staining the air, and moved down the nave through the grille and into the back of the church.

In the bell room Ferris had set up his metal exhibits table and had neatly laid out his spoils, each tagged and shrouded in its plastic envelope. Now he was standing back regarding them with the faintly anxious proprietorial air of a stallholder at a church bazaar wondering whether he has set out his wares to best advantage. And indeed, thus dignified and labelled, these diverse and ordinary objects had assumed an almost ritualistic significance: the shoes, one with its wedge of mud behind the heel, the stained beaker, the blotter with its criss-cross of dead marks made by dead hands, the diary, the remains of Harry Mack's last meal, the closed razor case and, occupying the centre of the table, the prize exhibit, the open cut-throat razor, its blade and bone handle gummy with blood.

Dalgliesh asked:

"Anything interesting?"

"The diary, sir." He made a move as if to take it out of its packet. Dalgliesh said:

"Leave it. Just tell me."

"It's the last page. It looks as if he tore out the entries for the last two months and burned those pages separately, then chucked the book open on the flames. The cover is only singed. The last page is the one which sets out the summary of the calendars for last year and next. There's no sign even of singeing, but the top half is missing. Someone has torn the page in two." He added:

"I suppose he could have folded it and used it as a spill to get a light from the pilot on the gas water heater."

Dalgliesh picked up the bag containing the shoes. He said:

"It's possible."

But it struck him as unlikely. For a murderer in a hurry, and this murderer had been in a hurry, it would have been a tedious and uncertain way to get a light. If he'd come without a lighter or matches, surely the obvious thing would have been to remove the box from the chained brass holder attached to the heater. He turned the shoes over in his hands and said:

"Handmade. There are some extravagances it's difficult to forgo. The toes are still polished, the sides and heels dull and slightly smeared. It looks as if they've been washed. And there are still traces of mud at the sides as well as under the left heel. The lab will probably find scrape marks."

They were hardly, he thought, the shoes you'd expect to find on a man who had spent the day in London unless he had walked in the parks or along the towpath of the canal. But he could hardly have walked to

St. Matthew's that way; there were no signs that he had cleaned his shoes anywhere in the church. But this, again, was theorizing in advance of the facts. They could hope to learn later where Berowne had spent his last day on earth.

Kate Miskin appeared in the doorway. She said:

"Doc Kynaston has finished, sir. They're ready to remove the bodies."

10

⊠

Massingham had expected that Darren would live in one of the high-rise local authority housing estates in Paddington. Instead the address which he had at last been persuaded to give was in a short and narrow street off the Edgware Road, an enclave of cheap, unsmart cafés chiefly Goan and Indian. As they turned into it Massingham realized that it wasn't strange to him, he had been here before. It was surely in this street that he and old George Percival had picked up two excellent vegetarian take-aways when they were both detective sergeants on division. Even the names, exotic, until now almost forgotten, came back to him: Alu Ghobi, Sag Bhajee. It had changed little since then, a street where people minded their own business, principally that of supplying their own kind with meals remarkable for value and cheapness. Although it was morning and the quietest time of the day, the air was already pungent with the smell of curry and spices, reminding Massingham that it was some hours since breakfast and that there was no certainty when he would get his lunch.

There was only one pub, a high narrow Victorian building squeezed between a Chinese take-away and a Tandoori café, darkly uninviting, with a painted scrawl on the window advertising with defiant Englishness: BANGERS AND MASH, BANGERS AND BUBBLE-AND-SQUEAK and TOAD-IN-THE-HOLE. Between the pub and the café was a small door with a single bell and a card with the one name: ARLENE. Darren stooped, took a key from the side of his canvas trainer shoes, then tiptoeing, inserted it in the lock. Massingham followed him up the narrow uncarpeted stairs. At the top he said:

"Where's your ma?"

Still without speaking, the boy pointed to the door on the left. Massingham knocked gently, then, getting no reply, pushed it open.

The curtains were drawn but they were thin and unlined, and even in the subdued light he could see that the room was spectacularly untidy. There was a woman lying on the bed. He moved over and, putting out his hand, found the switch of the bedside light. As it clicked on she gave a small grunt but didn't move. She was lying on her back, naked except for a short wrapover dressing gown from which one blue-veined breast had escaped and lay like a quivering jellyfish against the pink satin. A thin line of lipstick outlined the moistly open mouth from which a bleb of mucus ballooned and fell. She was snorting gently, small guttural sounds as if there were phlegm in her throat. Her eyebrows had been plucked in the manner of the thirties, leaving thin arches high above the natural line of the brow. They gave the face, even in sleep, a look of clownish surprise, enhanced by the circles of rouge on both cheeks. On a chair beside the bed was a large jar of Vaseline, the lid open, a single fly gummed to the rim. The back of the chair and the floor were strewn with clothes and the top of a chest of drawers which served as a dressing table under an oval mirror was crowded with bottles, dirty glasses, jars of make-up and packets of tissue. Set incongruously amid the mess was a jam jar with a bunch of freesias, still bound with a rubber band, whose delicate sweetness was lost in the stink of sex, scent and whisky. He said:

"Is this your ma?"

He wanted to ask "Is she often like this?" but instead he drew the boy out and closed the door. He had never liked questioning a child about its parents and he didn't propose to do it now. It was a common enough tragedy, but it was a job for the Juvenile Bureau, not for him, and the sooner one of their officers arrived the better. He was fretted by the thought of Kate, back at the scene of crime by now, and he felt a spurt of resentment against Dalgliesh, who had involved him in this irrelevant mess. He asked:

"Where do you sleep, Darren?"

The boy pointed to a back bedroom and Massingham pushed him gently before him.

It was very small, hardly more than a box room with a single high window. Under the window was a narrow bed covered with a brown army blanket, beside it a chair with a collection of objects neatly arranged. There was a model of a fire engine; a glass dome which shaken would produce a miniature snowstorm; two models of racing cars; three large veined marbles; and another jam jar, this one holding a bunch of roses, whose heads were already bending on their high thornless stems. An old chest of drawers, the only other furniture, was piled with an incongruous collection of objects, shirts still in their transparent packets, women's underwear, silk scarves, tins of salmon, baked beans, soup, a packet of ham and one of tongue, three model kits for making boats, a couple of lipsticks, a box of model soldiers, three packets of cheap scent.

Massingham had been a policeman too long to be easily moved. Some offences, cruelty to children or animals, violent crime against the vulnerable old, could still produce a flare of spectacular Massingham temper, which had resulted in more than one of his forebears facing a duel or a court-martial. But even this he had learned to discipline. But now, viewing with angry eyes this childish room with its pathetic neatness, its evidence of small self-sufficiency, the single jar of flowers which he guessed the boy himself had arranged, he was seized with an impotent anger against the drunken slut next door. He said:

"Did you steal these things, Darren?"

Darren didn't reply, then he nodded.

"Matey, you're in trouble."

The boy sat on the edge of the bed. Two tears rolled down his cheeks, followed by sniffs and heaves of the narrow chest. Suddenly he shouted:

"I ain't going to one of them council homes, I ain't! I ain't!"

"Stop crying," said Massingham urgently, hating the tears, wanting to get away. Christ, why had AD let him in for this? What was he supposed to be, a childminder? Torn between pity, anger and his impatience to be back on his proper job, he said more roughly:

"Stop crying!"

There must have been something urgent in his voice. Darren's gulps were immediately checked, although the tears flowed on. Massingham said more gently:

"Who said anything about a home? Look, I'm going to ring the Juvenile Bureau. Someone will come to look after you. It will probably be a WPC, you'll like her."

Darren's face expressed an immediate and lively scepticism which in other circumstances Massingham would have found amusing. The boy looked up and asked:

"Why can't I go 'ome with Miss Wharton?"

Why not, indeed, thought Massingham. The poor little bugger seemed to be attached to her. Two waifs supporting each other. He said:

"I don't really think that's on. Wait here, I'll be back."

He looked at his watch. He would have to stay, of course, until the WPC arrived, but she shouldn't be too long and at least AD would have an answer to his question. He knew now what had been worrying Darren, what he had been concealing. One small mystery, at least, was solved. AD could relax and get on with the enquiry. And so, with luck, could he.

11

⊠

Even Father Barnes's predecessor, Father Kendrick, hadn't been able to do much with St. Matthew's vicarage. It occupied the corner of St. Matthew's Court, an undistinguished three-storey, red brick block of flats bordering the Harrow Road. After the war, the Church Commissioners had finally decided that the existing huge Victorian house was unmanageable and uneconomic, and had sold the site to a developer on the understanding that a maisonette on the ground and first floors should be made over, in perpetuity, to house the parish priest. It was the only maisonette in the block but was otherwise indistinguishable from the flats, with their mean windows and small, badly proportioned rooms. At first the flats had been let to carefully chosen tenants and an attempt made to preserve the modest amenities: the square of lawn bordering the road, the two rose beds, the hanging windowboxes on each of the balconies. But the block, like most of its kind, had had a chequered history. The first property company had gone into liquidation, and the building had been sold to a second and then a third. The rents were raised, to general dissatisfaction, but were still inadequate to cover the maintenance costs of a poorly constructed building, and there were the usual acrimonious disputes between the tenants and the landlords. Only the church maisonette was well maintained, its two storeys of white windows an incongruous badge of respectability amid the peeling paint and disintegrating windowboxes.

The original tenants had been replaced by the transients of the city, the peripatetic young, sharing three to a room; unmarried mothers on social

security; foreign students—a racial mix which, like some human kaleidoscope, was continually being shaken into new and brighter colours. Those
few who did attend church found a congenial home with Father Donovan
at St. Anthony's with its steel bands, carnival processions, and general
inter-racial bonhomie. None of them ever knocked on Father Barnes's door.
They saw, with watchful and expressionless eyes, his almost furtive comings and goings. But he was as much an anachronism at St. Matthew's
Court as was the church he represented.

He had been escorted back to the vicarage by a plainclothes officer,
not the one who had been working most closely with Commander Dalgliesh,
but an older man, broad-shouldered, stolid, reassuringly calm, who had
spoken to him in a soft country accent which he couldn't recognize but
was most certainly not local. He said he was from the Harrow Road Station
but had only recently been transferred there from West End Central. He
waited while Father Barnes unlocked the front door, then followed him
in and offered to make a cup of tea, the British specific against disaster,
grief and shock. If he was surprised by the grubbiness of the ill-equipped
vicarage kitchen he concealed it. He had made tea in worse places. When
Father Barnes reiterated that he was perfectly all right and that Mrs. McBride
who did for him was due at ten thirty, he didn't persist. Before he left
he handed Father Barnes a card with a number on it.

"That's the number Commander Dalgliesh said you were to ring if
you need anything. If you're worried like. Or if anything new occurs to
you. Just give a ring. It'll be no trouble. And when the press come bothering,
just tell them as little as you need. No speculating. No use in speculating,
is there? Just tell it how it was. A lady from your congregation and a boy
found the bodies and the boy fetched you. Better not give any names unless
you have to. You saw that they were dead and rang for the police. No
need to say more. That's all there is to it."

The statement, stupendous in its over-simplification, opened a new
abyss before Father Barnes's horrified eyes. He had forgotten about the
press. How soon would they arrive? Would they want to take photographs?
Ought he to call an emergency meeting of the PCC? What would the
bishop say? Ought he to ring the archdeacon at once and leave it to him?
Yes, that would be the best plan. The archdeacon would know what ought
to be done. The archdeacon was capable of coping with the press, the
bishop, the police and the Parochial Church Council. Even so, he feared
that St. Matthew's was fated to be the centre of a dreadful attention.

He always went to Mass fasting and, for the first time that morning, he was aware of feeling weak, even paradoxically a little sick. He sank down onto one of the two wooden chairs at the kitchen table and looked rather helplessly at the card with its seven clearly written digits, then glanced round as if seeking inspiration where to put it for safekeeping. Finally, he dug in his cassock pocket for his wallet and slipped it in with his bank card and single credit card. He let his eyes roam round the kitchen, seeing it as that pleasant policeman must have seen it, in all its sad decrepitude. The plate from which he had eaten his hamburgers and frozen green beans, which had been last night's supper, still unrinsed in the sink; the splatter of grease marks above the ancient gas stove; the viscous mess of grime gumming the narrow gap between stove and cupboard; the soiled and smelly teacloth hanging from its hook at the side of the sink; last year's calendar askew on its nail; the two open shelves jammed with a conglomeration of half-used cereal packets, jars of stale jam, cracked mugs, packets of detergent; the cheap, unstable table with its two chairs, their backs grubby from numerous clutching hands; the linoleum curling at the wall where it had become unstuck; the general air of discomfort, uncaring, negligence, dirt. And the rest of the flat wasn't much better. Mrs. McBride took no pride in it because there was nothing to take a pride in. She didn't care because he didn't. Like him, she had probably ceased to notice the slow accretion of dirt over their lives.

After thirty years of marriage to Tom McBride, Beryl McBride sounded more Irish than did her husband. Sometimes, indeed, Father Barnes suspected that the brogue was less acquired than assumed, a music hall stereotype of Irishness adopted either out of marital togetherness or from some less recognizable need. He had noticed that in rare moments of stress she was apt to revert to her original Cockney. She was employed by the parish for twelve hours a week and her nominal duties were to come in on Mondays, Wednesdays and Fridays, clean the flat, wash and spin-dry any linen or articles in the soiled-linen basket, and prepare and leave for him a simple lunch on a tray. On the other weekdays and at weekends, Father Barnes was expected to look after himself. There had never been a job description. Mrs. McBride and the current incumbent were expected to work out a mutually agreed arrangement of hours and duties.

Twelve hours a week had been an adequate, even generous allocation of time when young Father Kendrick had been priest-in-charge. He was married to the prototype of an ideal parson's wife, a capable and buxom physiotherapist, well able to run her part-time hospital job and the parish simultaneously and to pound Mrs. McBride into shape as vigorously as, no doubt, she did her patients. No one, of course, had expected Father Kendrick to stay. He had only been a stop-gap, to fill in after Father Collins's twenty-five-year ministry until the appointment of a permanent successor, if there was to be a successor. St. Matthew's, as the archdeacon was never tired of pointing out, was surplus to the Church's pastoral ministry in inner London. With two other Anglican churches within a three-mile radius, both with vigorous young clergy and enough parochial organizations to provide serious competition for the social services department, St. Matthew's, with its small and ageing population, was an uncomfortable reminder of the declining authority of the Established Church in the inner cities. But as the archdeacon said, "Your people are remarkably loyal. It's a pity they aren't also rich. The parish is a drain on resources, no doubt about it. But we can hardly sell it. The building is supposed to be of some importance, architecturally. I can never see it myself. That extraordinary campanile. Hardly English, is it? One isn't, after all, on the Venetian Lido, whatever the architect thought." For the archdeacon, who had, in fact, never seen the Venetian Lido, had been reared in the Close at Salisbury and, making some allowance for scale, had known from childhood exactly what a church should look like.

Before Father Kendrick had set off for his new city parish—racial mix, boys' club, mothers' union, young people's fellowship; the proper challenge for a mildly high church, ambitious young priest with one eye on a mitre— he had had a brief word about Beryl McBride.

"Frankly, she terrifies me. I keep well out of her way. But Susan seems able to manage her. Better have a word with her about the domestic arrangements. I wish Mrs. McBride had taken her husband's religion instead of his accent. That way St. Anthony's would have had the benefit of her cooking. I did hint to Father Donovan that here was a brand ready for plucking, but Michael knows when to leave well alone. Now, if you can seduce his housekeeper, Mrs. Kelly, into Anglicanism, you'll be in clover."

Susan Kendrick, expertly wrapping china in newspaper and ankle-deep in shavings from her packing cases, had been briskly informative but hardly more reassuring.

"She needs watching. Her plain cooking is quite good, although the repertoire is a bit limited. But she isn't so dependable when it comes to housework. You need to begin as you mean to go on. If you set the right standards and she knows that she can't fool you, you'll be all right. She's been here a long time, of course, from Father Collins's days. She wouldn't be easy to dislodge. And she's a very loyal member of the congregation. St. Matthew's seems to suit her for some reason. As I said, just begin as you mean to go on. Oh, and watch the sherry. There's no real dishonesty. You can leave anything out, money, your watch, food. It's just that she likes the odd nip. Better offer her one occasionally. That way there's less temptation. You can hardly lock the stuff up."

"No, of course not," he had said. "No, I quite see that."

But it had been Mrs. McBride who had started as she meant to go on. It had been hopeless from the start. He still recalled, with a flush of shame, that first, all-important interview. He had sat in front of her, in the square little room which was used as a study, as if he were the suppliant, and had seen her sharp little eyes, black as currants, move round the room, noting the gaps in the shelves where Father Kendrick's leatherbound volumes had been stacked, the meagre rug in front of the gas fire, his few prints stacked against the wall. And that wasn't all she had taken in. She had had him summed up, all right. She had seen his timidity, his ignorance of housekeeping, his lack of authority as a man or a priest. And he suspected that she had known more intimate secrets. His virginity, his half-shameful fear of her close, warm-smelling, overwhelming femaleness, his social insecurity, born in that small, terraced house near the river at Ely, where he had lived with his widowed mother, nurtured by the desperate contrivings, the small deceptions of respectable poverty, the deprivation that was so much more humiliating than the real poverty of the inner cities. He could imagine the words in which she would later report to her husband.

"He's not really a gentleman, not like Father Kendrick. You can see that. Father Kendrick's father was a bishop, after all, and Mrs. Kendrick is the niece of Lady Nichols, when all's said and done. There's no knowing where this one comes from." Sometimes he suspected that she had even known how diminished was his remaining store of faith, that it was this essential lack and not his general inadequacy which was at the core of her disdain.

His most recent library book had been a Barbara Pym. He had read with envious disbelief the gentle and ironic story of a village parish where the curates were entertained, fed and generally spoilt by the female members of the congregation. Mrs. McBride, he thought, would soon put a stop to anything like that at St. Matthew's. Indeed, she *had* put a stop to it. During his first week, Mrs. Jordan had visited him with a homemade fruitcake. She had seen it on the table on her Wednesday visit and had said:

"One of Ethel Jordan's, is it? You want to watch her, Father, an unmarried priest like you." The words had hung on the air, heavy with innuendo, and an act of simple kindness had been spoiled. Eating the cake, he had felt it like tasteless dough in his mouth, every mouthful an act of shared indecency.

She arrived on time. Whatever her other negligences, Mrs. McBride was a stickler for punctuality. He heard her key in the door and a minute later she was in the kitchen. She didn't seem surprised to see him sitting there still in his cloak and obviously only just returned from Mass, and he knew at once that she had been told about the murders. He watched while she carefully removed her headscarf to reveal the upswept waves of unnaturally dark hair, hung up her coat in the hall cupboard, donned her overall from its hook behind the kitchen door, took off her outdoor shoes and eased her feet into her house slippers. It wasn't until she had put on the kettle for their morning coffee that she spoke.

"Well, here's a nice thing for the parish, Father. Two of 'em dead, so Billy Crawford was saying in the newsagent's. And one of 'em old Harry Mack."

"I'm afraid so, Mrs. McBride. One of them was Harry."

"And who would the other be? Or aren't the police knowing yet?"

"I think we'll have to wait until they notify the next of kin before they release that information."

"But you saw him, Father. Wasn't it with your own eyes now? And were you not recognizing him?"

"You really mustn't ask me that, Mrs. McBride. We must wait for the police."

"And who'd be wantin' to kill Harry? Sure, he wouldn't be killed for anything he had on him, the poor soul. It wasn't suicide, was it, Father? One of those suicide pacts? Or do the police think Harry did it?"

"They don't know what happened yet. We really ought not to speculate."

"Well, I don't believe it. Harry Mack's no murderer. As well believe that the other chap, the one you're keeping so quiet about, the one you're not telling about, did in Harry. Harry was a nasty, thieving, foul-mouthed old devil, God rest him, but he was harmless enough. The police have no call to be pinning it on Harry."

"I'm sure they won't try to. It could have been anyone, someone who broke in to steal. Or someone Sir Paul Berowne himself let in. Anyone. The door of the vestry was open when Miss Wharton arrived this morning."

He turned towards the stove so that she shouldn't see the flush of shame and dismay that he had let slip Berowne's name. And she hadn't missed it, not she. And why had he told her about that unlocked door? Was he trying to reassure her, or himself? But what did it matter? The details would be out soon enough and it would look odd if he were too reticent, odd and suspicious. But why suspicious? Surely no one, not even Mrs. McBride, was going to suspect him. He recognized, with a familiar confusion of self-disgust and hopelessness, that he was telling more than he ought in his usual attempt to propitiate her, to get her on his side. It had never worked and it wouldn't now. She didn't pick up the name Berowne although he knew that it was safely stowed in her mind. Sitting across from her, he saw the triumph in her cunning little eyes, heard in her voice the note of ghoulish relish.

"Bloody murder, is it then? That's a nice thing for the parish. You'll be needing to get the church fumigated, Father."

"Fumigated?"

"Well, sprinkled with holy water, that sort of thing. Maybe my Tom had better to speak to Father Donovan. He could let us have some from St. Anthony's."

"We have our own holy water, Mrs. McBride."

"In a case like this, you can't take chances. Better get some from Father Donovan. Be on the safe side. My Tom can bring it along after Mass on Sunday. Here's your coffee, Father. I've made it extra strong. You've had a nasty shock and that's the truth of it."

The coffee, as always, was the cheapest kind of bottled grains. It was even less palatable now that its strength made the taste discernible. On the brown surface a few globules of half-sour milk swam and coalesced. There was a smear of what looked like lipstick on the rim of the cup and he turned it away from him slowly, so that she shouldn't notice. He knew that he could have carried the coffee into the comparative serenity of his study, but he hadn't the courage to get to his feet. And to leave before both cups had been drained would only offend her. She had said, on her first morning with him, "Mrs. Kendrick and me always had a cup of coffee together before I got started, nice and friendly like." He had had no way of knowing whether this was the truth, but the pattern of spurious intimacy had been established.

"That Paul Berowne, he was an MP, wasn't he? Resigned or something. I remember reading about him in the *Standard*."

"Yes, he was an MP."

"And a Sir, too, didn't you say?"

"A baronet, Mrs. McBride."

"What was he doing in the Little Vestry, then? I never knew we had any baronets attending St. Matthew's."

It was too late now to take refuge in discretion.

"He didn't. He was just someone I knew. I gave him the key. He wanted to spend some time quietly in the church," he added, in a vain hope that a confidence so dangerously close to intimacy, to his job as priest, might flatter her, might even silence curiosity. "He wanted somewhere quiet to think, to pray."

"In the Little Vestry? A funny place to choose. Why wasn't he on his knees in a pew? Why wasn't he in the Lady Chapel in front of the Blessed Sacrament? That's the proper place to be praying, for them who can't wait till Sunday." Her voice with its note of aggrieved disapproval suggested that both the place and the praying were equally reprehensible.

"He could hardly sleep in the church, Mrs. McBride."

"And why should he want to be sleeping? Hadn't he his own bed to be going home to?"

Father Barnes's hands had begun to shake again. The coffee cup lurched in his fingers and he felt two scalding drops on his hand. Carefully, he replaced the cup in its saucer, willing the dreadful shaking to stop. He almost lost her next words.

"Well, if he did kill himself, he died clean, I'll say that for him."

"Died clean, Mrs. McBride?"

"Wasn't he washing himself when Tom and I passed by last night just after eight o'clock? Him or Harry Mack. And you can't be telling me that Harry went near running water if he could help it. Fairly gushing out of the drainpipe it was. 'Course we thought you were there. 'Father Barnes is having a stripwash in the vestry kitchen.' That's what I said to Tom. 'Perhaps he's saving on the gas bill back at the vicarage.' We had a laugh about it."

"When exactly was this, Mrs. McBride?"

"I told you, Father, just after eight. We were on our way to the Three Feathers. We wouldn't have been passing the church except that we called in to collect Maggie Sullivan and it's a shortcut from her place to the Feathers."

"But the police ought to know. This could be important information. They'll be interested in anyone who was near St. Matthew's last night."

"Interested? Is that what they'll be? And what are you getting at then, Father? You're saying that Tom and old Maggie Sullivan and I cut his throat for him?"

"Of course not, Mrs. McBride. That's ridiculous. But you could be important witnesses. That gushing water. It means that Sir Paul was alive at eight o'clock."

"Someone was alive in there at eight and that's for sure. And a fine rush of water he was using."

Father Barnes was struck with a terrible possibility and, without thinking, gave it voice:

"Did you notice what colour it was?"

"And what would I be doing peering down drains? Of course I didn't notice what colour it was. What colour would it be? But it was running away, fast and furious, that's for sure."

Suddenly, she pushed her face over the table towards him. Her huge breasts, so much at odds with the thin face and the bony arms, were pushed into great half moons by the table edge. Her coffee cup clattered in the saucer. The sharp little eyes widened. She whispered with alliterative relish:

"Father, are you saying that it would be running red?"

He said weakly:

"I suppose it's possible."

"You think he was in there, do you, Father, washing his bloody hands? Oh, my God! Suppose he had come out and seen us. We could have been murdered on the spot, Tom and Maggie and me. He could have slit our throats for us then and there and thrown us in the canal, likely as not. Holy Mother of God!"

The conversation had become bizarre, unreal, totally uncontrollable. He had been told by the police to say as little as possible to anyone. He had meant to say nothing. But now she knew the names of the victims, she knew who had found them, she knew that the door had been unlocked, she knew how they had died, although surely he hadn't mentioned the slitting of throats. But that could have been guesswork. A knife was, after all, a more likely weapon in London than a gun. She knew all that and, more, she had actually been passing at the time. He gazed back at her across the stained table with appalled eyes, linked to her by that blood-stained gurgle of water which was gushing through both their minds, sharing the same dreadful imagining of that silently emerging figure, the raised and bloody knife. And he was aware of something else. Horrible as was the deed that bound them in a fascinated confederacy of blood, they were, for the first time, having a conversation. The eyes, which met his across the table top, were bright with horror and with an excitement which was too close to relish to be comfortable. But the familiar glance of insolence and contempt had gone. He could almost deceive himself that she was confiding in him. The relief was so great that he found that his hand was creeping across the table towards hers in some gesture of mutual comfort. Ashamed, he quickly drew it back.

She said:

"Father, what shall we do?" It was the first time she had ever asked him that question. He was surprised at the confidence in his voice.

"The police have given me a special telephone number. I think we ought to ring now, at once. They'll send someone round, either here or to your house. After all, you and Tom and Maggie are very important witnesses. And then when we've done that, I shall need to be undisturbed in the study. I wasn't able to say Mass. I shall read Morning Prayer."

"Yes, Father," she said, her voice almost meek. And there was something else he ought to do. Strange that the thought hadn't occurred to him before. Surely it must be his duty to call in the next day or so on Paul Berowne's wife and his family. Now that he knew what had to be done, it was remarkable how different he felt. A biblical phrase dropped into his mind, "Doing evil that good may come." But he quickly put it away from him. It was too close to blasphemy to be comfortable.

BOOK TWO

Next
of Kin

1
⊠

After leaving the church Dalgliesh went briefly back to the Yard to pick up his file on Theresa Nolan and Diana Travers, and it was after midday before he arrived at 62 Campden Hill Square. He had brought Kate with him, leaving Massingham to supervise what remained to be done at the church. Kate had told him that at present there were only women in the house, and it seemed sensible that he should have a woman with him, particularly as it was Kate who had first broken the news. It was not a decision he had expected Massingham to welcome, and nor had he. These first interviews with the next of kin were crucial and Massingham wanted to be there. He would work with Kate Miskin loyally and conscientiously because he respected her as a detective and that was what he was required to do. But Dalgliesh knew that Massingham still half-regretted the days when women police officers were content to find lost children, search female prisoners, reform prostitutes, comfort the bereaved and, if they hankered for the excitement of criminal investigation, were suitably occupied coping with the peccadillos of juvenile delinquents. And, as Dalgliesh had heard him argue, for all their demands for equality of status and opportunity, putting them in the front line behind the riot shields, taking the petrol bombs, the hurled stones and, now, the bullets, only made the job of their male colleagues even more onerous. In Massingham's view the instinct to protect a woman in moments of high danger was deep-seated and in-eradicable, and the world would be a worse place if it weren't. He had, as Dalgliesh knew, grudgingly respected Kate's ability to look down at the butchered bodies in St. Matthew's vestry and not be sick, but he hadn't liked her the better for it.

He knew that he would find no police officer at the house. Lady Ursula had gently but firmly rejected the suggestion that someone should stay. Kate had reported her words:

"You are not, presumably, expecting this murderer, if he exists, to turn his attention to the rest of the family. That being so, I hardly see the need for police protection. You, I am sure, have a better use for your manpower and I would prefer not to have an officer sitting in the hall like a bailiff."

She had, too, insisted on herself breaking the news to her daughter-in-law and the housekeeper. Kate was given no opportunity to observe the reaction of anyone other than Lady Ursula to Paul Berowne's death.

Campden Hill Square lay in its midday calm, an urban oasis of greenery and Georgian elegance rising from the ceaseless grind and roar of Holland Park Avenue. An early-morning mist had cleared and a fugitive sun glinted on leaves which were only now beginning to yellow and which hung in heavy swathes, almost motionless in the still air. Dalgliesh couldn't re-member when he had last seen the Berowne house. Living as he did high above the Thames on the fringe of the city, this wasn't his part of London. But the house, one of the rare examples of Sir John Soane's domestic architecture, was pictured in so many books on the capital's buildings that its elegant eccentricity was as familiar to him as if he commonly walked these streets and squares. The conventional Georgian houses each side of it were as high, but its neo-classical facade in Portland stone and brick dominated the terrace and the whole square, inalienably a part of them, yet looking almost arrogantly unique.

He stood for a minute looking up at it, Kate unspeaking at his side. On the second floor rose three very high, curved windows, originally, he suspected, an open loggia but now glazed and fronted with a low stone balustrade. Between the windows, mounted on incongruous corbels which looked more Gothic than neo-classical, were stone caryatids, whose flowing lines reenforced by the typically Soanian pilasters at the corners of the house drew the eye upwards, past the square windows of the third storey to an attic storey faced in brick and, finally, to the stone balustrade with its row of curved shells echoing the curve of the lower windows. As he stood contemplating it, as if hesitating to violate its calm, there was a moment of extraordinary silence in which even the muted roar of the traffic in the avenue was stilled and in which it seemed to him that two images, the shining facade of the house and that dusty blood-boltered room in Paddington, were held suspended out of time, then fused so that the stones were blood-splattered, the caryatids dripped red. And then the traffic lights released the stream of cars, time moved on, the house lay uncontaminated in its pale pristine silence. But he had no sense that they were being watched, that somewhere behind these walls and the windows glinting in the transitory sun there were people waiting for him in anxiety, grief, perhaps in fear. Even when he rang the doorbell it was a full two minutes before the door was opened and he faced a woman who he knew must be Evelyn Matlock.

She was, he guessed, in her late thirties, and was uncompromisingly plain in a way it struck him few women nowadays were. A small sharp nose was imbedded between pudgy cheeks on which the threads of broken veins were emphasized rather than disguised by a thin crust of make-up. She had a primly censorious mouth above a slightly receding chin already showing the first slackness of a dewlap. Her hair, which looked as if it had been inexpertly permed, was pulled back at the sides but frizzed over the high forehead rather in the poodle-like fashion of an Edwardian. But as she stood aside to let them enter he saw that her wrists and ankles were slim and delicate, curiously at odds with the sturdy body, heavy-busted, almost voluptuous, under the high-necked blouse. He remembered what Paul Berowne had said of her. Here was the woman whose father he had unsuccessfully defended, to whom he had given a home and a job, who was supposed to be devoted to him. If that was true, she was concealing her grief at his death with remarkable stoicism. A police officer, he thought, is like a visiting doctor. One is greeted with no ordinary emotions. He was used to seeing relief, apprehension, dislike, even hatred; but now, for a moment, he saw in her eyes naked fear. It passed almost at once and gave place to what seemed to him an assumed and slightly truculent indifference, but it had been there. She turned her back on them, saying:

"Lady Ursula is expecting you, Commander. Will you please follow me."

The words, spoken in a high, rather forced voice, had the repressive authority of a nurse-receptionist greeting a patient from whom she expects nothing but trouble. They passed through the outer vestibule, then under the fluted dome of the inner hall. To their left, the finely wrought balustrade

of a stone cantilevered staircase rose like a border of black lace. Miss Matlock
opened the double door to the right and stood back to let them enter. She
said:

"If you will wait here I will let Lady Ursula know that you have arrived."

The room in which they found themselves ran the whole width of
the house and was obviously both the formal dining room and library.
It was full of light. At the front, two high curved windows gave a view
of the square garden while at the rear one huge expanse of glass looked
out over a stone wall with three niches, each containing a marble statue:
Venus, naked, one hand delicately shielding the mons veneris, one pointing
at her left nipple; a second female figure, half robed and wearing a wreath
of flowers; and between them, Apollo with his lyre, laurel-crowned. The
two sections of the room were divided by projecting piers formed of mahogany glass-fronted bookcases from which sprang a canopy of three semi-
circular arches decorated and painted in green and gold. High bookcases
lined the library walls and stood between the windows, each topped with
a marble bust. The volumes, bound in green leather and tooled in gold,
were identical in size and fitted the bookshelves so precisely that the effect
was more of an artist's trompe l'oeil than of a working library. Between
the shelves and in the recesses over them were mirrors so that the rich
splendour of the room seemed to be endlessly reflected, a vista of painted
ceilings, leather books, of marble, gleaming mahogany and glass. It was
difficult to imagine the room being used for dining, or indeed, for any
purpose other than the admiring contemplation of the architect's romantic
obsession with spatial surprise. The oval dining table stood before the rear
window, but it held in the middle a model of the house on a low plinth
as if it were a museum exhibit, and the eight high-backed dining chairs
had been set back against the walls. Over the marble fireplace was a portrait,
presumably of the baronet who had commissioned the house. Here the
delicate fastidiousness of the painting in the National Portrait Gallery was
metamorphosed into a sturdier nineteenth-century elegance, but with the
unmistakable Berowne features still arrogantly confident above the fault-
lessly tied cravat. Looking up at it, Dalgliesh said:

"Lady Ursula Berowne, remind me of what she said, Kate."

"She said: 'After the first death there is no other.' It sounded like
a quotation."

"It is a quotation." He added without explanation, "Her elder son was
killed in Northern Ireland. Do you like this room?"

"If I wanted to settle down for a quiet read I'd prefer the Kensington public library. It's for show rather than use, isn't it? Odd idea, having a library and dining room in one." She added: "But I suppose it's splendid in its way. Not exactly cosy, though. I wonder if anyone has ever been murdered for a house."

It was a long speech for Kate.

Dalgliesh said:

"I can't say that I remember a case. It might be a more rational motive than murdering for a person; less risk of subsequent disenchantment."

"Less chance of betrayal, too, sir."

Miss Matlock appeared in the doorway and said with cold formality: "Lady Ursula is ready to see you now. Her sitting room is on the top floor, but there is a lift. Would you please follow me."

They could have been a couple of unpromising applicants for a minor domestic job. The lift was an elegant gilded birdcage in which they were borne slowly upwards in a repressive silence. When it jerked to a stop they were led out into a narrow carpeted passage. Miss Matlock opened a door immediately opposite and announced:

"Commander Dalgliesh and Miss Miskin are here, Lady Ursula." Then without waiting for them to step into the room, she turned and left.

And now, as he entered Lady Ursula Berowne's sitting room, Dalgliesh felt for the first time that he was in a private house, that this was a room which the owner had made peculiarly her own. The two high, beautifully proportioned windows with their twelve panes gave a view of sky delicately laced with the top boughs of the trees, and the long narrow room was full of light. Lady Ursula was sitting very upright to the right of the fireplace, her back to the window.

There was an ebony cane with a gold knob leaning against her chair. She did not rise when they came in but held out her hand as Kate introduced Dalgliesh. Her clasp, quickly released, was surprisingly strong, but it was still like holding briefly a disconnected set of bones loosely enclosed in dry suede. She gave Kate a quick appraising glance and a nod which could have been acknowledgement or approval and said:

"Please sit down. If Inspector Miskin is required to make notes, then she may find that chair by the window convenient. Perhaps you will sit opposite me, Commander."

The voice, with its timbre of upper-class arrogance, an arrogance of which its owner so often seems unaware, was exactly as he would have expected. It seemed artificially produced as if, in an attempt to control any quavering, she had had to gather both breath and energy to produce the measured cadences. But it was still a beautiful voice. As she sat facing him, rigidly upright, he saw that her chair was one designed for the disabled, with a button in the armrest to raise the seat when she wanted help in rising. Its functional modernity struck a discordant note in a room which was otherwise cluttered with eighteenth-century furniture; two chairs with embroidered seats, a Pembroke table, a bureau, each a fine example of its period, were strategically placed to provide an island of support if she needed to make her painful progress to the door, so that the room looked rather like an antique shop with its treasures ineptly displayed. It was an old woman's room, and above the smell of beeswax and the faint summer scent from a bowl of pot-pourri on the Pembroke table, his sensitive nose could detect a whiff of the sour smell of old age. Their eyes met and held. Hers were still remarkable, immense, well spaced and heavily lidded. They must once have been the focus of her beauty, and although they were sunken now, he could still see the glint of intelligence behind them. Her skin was cleft with deep lines running from the jaw to the high jutting cheekbones. It was as if two palms had been placed against the frail skin and forced it upwards, so that he saw with a shock of premonitory recognition the shine of the skull beneath the skin. The scrolls of the ears flat against the sides of the skull were so large that they looked like abnormal excrescences. In youth she would have dressed her hair to cover them. Her face was devoid of make-up and, with the hair drawn back tightly and twisted into a high roll, it looked naked, a face stripped for action. She was wearing black trousers topped with a belted tunic in thin grey wool, high-buttoned almost to the chin, and deep-cuffed. Her feet were lodged in wide, black-barred shoes, and in their immobility gave the impression of being clamped to the carpet. There was a paperback on the round table to the right of her chair. Dalgliesh saw that it was Philip Larkin's *Required Writing*. She put out her hand and laid it on the book, then said:

"Mr. Larkin writes here that it is always true that the idea for a poem and a snatch or line of it come simultaneously. Do you agree, Commander?"

"Yes, Lady Ursula, I think I do. A poem begins with poetry, not with an idea for poetry."

He betrayed no surprise at the question. He knew that shock, grief, trauma took people in different ways, and if this bizarre opening was helping her, he could conceal his impatience. She said:

"To be a poet and a librarian, even if unusual, has a certain appropriateness, but to be a poet and a policeman seems to me eccentric, even perverse."

Dalgliesh said:

"Do you see the poetry as inimical to the detection, or the detection to the poetry?"

"Oh, the latter, surely. What happens if the muse strikes—no, that is hardly the appropriate word—if the muse visits you in the middle of a case? Although if I remember, Commander, your muse in recent years has been somewhat fugitive." She added with a note of delicate irony: "To our great loss."

Dalgliesh said:

"It hasn't so far happened. Perhaps the human mind can deal with only one intense experience at a time."

"And poetry is, of course, an intense experience."

"One of the most intense there is."

Suddenly she smiled at him. It lit up her face with the intimacy of a shared confidence, as if they were old sparring partners.

"You must excuse me. Being interrogated by a detective is a new experience for me. If there is an appropriate dialogue for this occasion, I haven't yet found it. Thank you, anyway, for not burdening me with your condolences. I have received too many official condolences in my time. They have always seemed to me either embarrassing or insincere."

Dalgliesh wondered what she would reply if he said: "I knew your son. Not well, but I did know him. I accept that you don't want my condolences, but if I had been able to speak the right words, they would not have been insincere."

She said:

"Inspector Miskin broke the news to me with tact and consideration. I am grateful. But she was, of course, unable or unwilling to tell me much more than that my son was dead, and that there were certain wounds. How did he die, Commander?"

"His throat was cut, Lady Ursula."

There was no way of softening that brutal reality. He added:

"The tramp with him, Harry Mack, died the same way."

He wondered why he had felt it important to speak Harry's name. Poor Harry, so incongruously yoked in the forced democracy of death, whose stiffening body would receive far more attention in its dissolution than it had ever received in life. She said:

"And the weapon?"

"A bloodstained razor, his apparently, was close to your son's right hand. There are a number of forensic tests to be carried out, but I expect to find that the razor was the weapon."

"And the door to the church—the vestry, or wherever he was—that was open?"

"Miss Wharton, who with a young boy discovered the bodies, says that she found it unlocked."

"Are you treating this as suicide?"

"The tramp, Harry Mack, didn't kill himself. My preliminary view is that neither did your son. It's too early to say more until we get the results of the post-mortem examination and the forensic tests. Meantime I am treating it as a double murder."

"I see. Thank you for being so frank."

Dalgliesh said:

"There are questions I need to ask. If you would rather wait I could come back later, but it is, of course, important to lose as little time as possible."

"I would prefer to lose none, Commander. And two of your questions I can anticipate. I have no reason to believe that my son was contemplating ending his life and he had to my knowledge no enemies."

"As a politician that makes him unusual, surely."

"He had political enemies, obviously. Some few from his own party, no doubt. But none as far as I know is a homicidal maniac. And terrorists, surely, use bombs and guns, not their victim's razor. Forgive me, Commander, if I'm stating the obvious, but isn't it most likely that someone unknown to him, a tramp, a psychopath, a casual thief, killed both him and this Harry Mack?"

"It is one of the theories we have to consider, Lady Ursula." He asked: "When did you last see your son?"

"At eight o'clock yesterday morning, when he carried up my breakfast tray. That was his usual practice. He wished to reassure himself, no doubt, that I had survived the night."

"Did he tell you then or at any time that he intended returning to St. Matthew's?"

"No. We didn't discuss his plans for the day, only mine, and those I presume are hardly of interest to you."

Dalgliesh said:

"It could be important to know who was here in the house during the day and at what time. Your own timetable could help us to that."

He gave no further explanation and she asked for none.

"My chiropodist, Mrs. Beamish, arrived at ten thirty. She always comes to the house. I was with her for about an hour. Then I was driven to a luncheon engagement with Mrs. Charles Blaney at her club, the University Women's. After luncheon we went to look at some watercolours in which she is interested at Agnew's, in Bond Street. We had tea at the Savoy together and dropped Mrs. Blaney at her Chelsea house before returning here at about half past five. I asked Miss Matlock to bring me up a thermos of soup and a plate of smoked salmon sandwiches at six o'clock. She did so and I told her I preferred not to be disturbed again that evening. The luncheon and exhibition had been more tiring than I had expected. I spent the evening reading, and rang for Miss Matlock to help me to bed shortly before eleven."

"Did you see any other members of the household during the day apart from your son, Miss Matlock and the chauffeur?"

"I saw my daughter-in-law briefly when I had occasion to go into the library. That was some time during the early part of the morning. I presume that this is relevant, Commander?"

"Until we know how your son died it is difficult to be sure what is or is not relevant. Did any other member of the household know that Sir Paul intended revisiting St. Matthew's yesterday evening?"

"I have had no opportunity to ask them. I can't believe it likely that they did. No doubt you will enquire. We have only a small staff. Evelyn Matlock, whom you have met, is the housekeeper. Then there is Gordon Halliwell. He is an ex-sergeant in the Guards, who served with my elder son. He, I suppose, would describe himself as a chauffeur-handyman. He came here just over five years ago, before Hugo was killed, and has stayed on."

"He drove your son?"

"Rarely. Paul, of course, had the use of his ministerial car before he resigned; otherwise he drove himself. Halliwell drives me almost daily, and occasionally my daughter-in-law. He has a flat over the garage. You will have to wait, Commander, to hear anything he may disclose. Today is his day off."

"When did he leave, Lady Ursula?"

"Either very late last night or early this morning. That is his usual practice. I have no idea where he is. I don't question my servants about their private lives. If the news of my son's death is broadcast this evening, as I expect it will be, no doubt he will return early. In any case he is normally back before eleven. Incidentally, I spoke to him by house telephone yesterday evening shortly after eight o'clock and, again, at about nine fifteen. Apart from Halliwell, there is now only one other member of the staff, Mrs. Iris Minns, who comes here four days a week to do general housework. Miss Matlock can give you her address."

Dalgliesh asked:

"This experience of your son's in the vestry of St. Matthew's, did he talk to you about it?"

"No. It was not a subject with which he would expect me to sympathize. I have not since 1918 been a religious woman. I doubt if I ever was in any real sense. Mysticism, in particular, is as meaningless to me as music must be to the tone deaf. I accept, of course, that people do have these experiences. I would expect the causes to be physical and psychological; overwork, the ennui of middle age, or a need to find some meaning to existence. That to me has always been a fruitless quest."

"Did your son find it fruitless?"

"Until this happened, I would have described him as a conventional Anglican. I suspect that he used the offices of his religion as a reminder of fundamental decencies, an affirmation of identity, a brief breathing space when he could think without fear of interruption. Like most upper-class Anglicans, he would have found the incarnation more understandable if God had chosen to visit His creation as an eighteenth-century English gentleman. But like most of his class, he got over that little difficulty by more or less refashioning Him in the guise of an eighteenth-century English gentleman. His experience—his alleged experience—in that church is inexplicable, and to do him justice, he didn't attempt to explain it, at least not to me. I hope you won't expect me to discuss it. The subject is unwelcome, and it can surely have had nothing to do with his death."

It was a long speech, and he could see that it had tired her. And she could not, thought Dalgliesh, be as naive as that; he was surprised that she could expect him to believe that she was. He said:

"When a man changes the whole direction of his life and is dead—possibly murdered—within a week of that decision, it must be relevant, at least to our investigation."

"Oh yes, it's relevant to that, I've no doubt. There will be very few privacies in this family which won't be relevant to your investigation, Commander."

He saw that in the last few seconds she had been overcome with exhaustion. Her body looked diminished, almost shrivelled, in the huge chair, and the gnarled hands on the arms began very gently to shake. But he controlled his compassion as she was controlling her grief. There were questions he still needed to ask and it wouldn't be the first time that he had taken advantage of tiredness or grief. He bent and took from his case the half-burnt diary still in its protective transparent wrapping. He said:

"It's been examined for fingerprints. We shall need in time to check which belong to people who had a right to handle the diary—Sir Paul, yourself, members of the household. I wanted you to confirm that it is in fact his. It would be helpful if you could do that without unwrapping it."

She took the package and it lay for a moment in her lap while she stared down at it. He had a sense that she was unwilling to meet his eyes. She sat with extraordinary stillness, then she said:

"Yes, this is his. But it's unimportant surely. A mere record of engagements. He wasn't a diarist."

"It's odd, in that case, that he should wish to burn it—if he did burn it. And there's another oddity; the top half of the last page has been torn away. It's the page setting out last year's calendar and the calendar for 1986. Can you recall what else, if anything, was on that page, Lady Ursula?"

"I can't remember that I ever saw that page."

"Can you recall when and where you last saw the diary?"

"I'm afraid that's the kind of detail it's impossible for me to remember. Is there anything else, Commander? If there is, and it isn't urgent, perhaps it could wait until you are sure that you are, in fact, investigating murder."

Dalgliesh said:

"We know that already, Lady Ursula. Harry Mack was murdered."

She didn't reply, and for about a minute they sat in silence, facing each other. Then she lifted her great eyes to his and he thought he detected a mixture of fleeting emotions: resolution, appeal, defiance. He said:

"I am afraid I've kept you too long and tired you. There is really only one more matter. Is there anything you can tell me about the two young women who died after they had been working in this house, Theresa Nolan and Diana Travers?"

The production of the half-burnt diary had shocked her deeply, but this question she took in her stride. She said calmly:

"Very little, I'm afraid. I've no doubt you know most of it already. Theresa Nolan was a gentle, considerate nurse and a competent, but not,

I think, very intelligent, young woman. She came as night nurse on the second of May, when I had a bad attack of sciatica, and left on the fourteenth of June. She had a room in this house but was on duty only at night. She went, as I expect you know, to a maternity nursing home in Hampstead. I accept that she probably became pregnant while she was working here, but I can assure you that no one in this house was responsible. Pregnancy is not an occupational hazard of nursing an eighty-two-year-old arthritic woman. I know even less of Diana Travers. She was apparently an un-employed actress who was doing domestic work while she was 'resting'— I think that's the euphemism they use. She came to the house in response to a card Miss Matlock had placed in a local newsagent's window, and Miss Matlock took her on to replace a cleaning woman who had recently left."

"After consulting you, Lady Ursula?"

"It was hardly a matter on which she needed to consult me and, in fact, she did not. I know, of course, why you are enquiring about both women. One or two of my friends made it their business to send me the cutting from the *Paternoster Review*. I'm surprised that the police should trouble themselves with what is surely no more than cheap journalistic spite. It can hardly be relevant to my son's murder. If that is all, Commander, perhaps you would like to see my daughter-in-law now. No, don't bother to ring. I prefer to take you down myself. And I can manage perfectly well without your help."

She pressed the knob in the arm of her chair and the seat slowly rose. It took her a moment to establish her balance. Then she said:

"Before you meet my daughter-in-law there is something I should perhaps say. You may find her less apparently distressed than you expect. That is because she has no imagination. Had she found my son's body she would have been disconsolate, certainly too shocked and distressed to talk to you now. But what her eyes don't actually see she finds it difficult to imagine. I say this only in justice to both of you."

Dalgliesh nodded but didn't reply. It was, he thought, the first mistake she had made. The implication of her words was obvious, but it would have been wiser of her to have left them unspoken.

2

He watched while she braced herself for the first step, steeling herself
for the expected gripe of pain. He made no move to help her; he knew
that the gesture would be as presumptuous as it was unwelcome and Kate,
sensitive as always to unspoken commands, closed her notebook, then
waited in watchful silence. Slowly Lady Ursula made her way to the door,
steadying herself with her cane. Her hand shook on the gold knob, the
veins starting out like blue cords. They followed her slowly down the carpeted corridor and into the lift. There was barely room in its elegantly
curved interior for three, and Dalgliesh's arm was against hers. Even through
the tweed of his sleeve he could sense its brittleness and could feel its
gentle, perpetual shaking. He was aware that she was under intense strain,
and he wondered how much it would take to break her and whether it
would be his job to see that she did break. As the lift ground slowly down
the two floors he knew that she was as aware of him as he was of her,
and that she saw him as the enemy.

They followed her into the drawing room. This room, too, Paul Berowne
would have shown him, and for a moment he had the illusion that it was
the dead man, not his mother, who stood at his side. Three tall curved
windows, ornately curtained, gave a view of the garden trees. They looked
unreal, a one-dimensional woven tapestry in an infinite variety of green
and gold. Under the elaborately enriched ceiling with its curious mixture
of the classic and Gothic, the room was sparsely furnished, and the air
had the melancholy, unbreathed atmosphere of a seldom-visited country
house drawing room, an amalgam of pot-pourri and wax polish. Almost

he expected to see a white looped cord marking off the area where tourists' feet were forbidden to tread.

The bereaved mother had received him alone, presumably by choice. The widow had thought it prudent to be solaced and protected by her doctor and her lawyer. Lady Ursula briefly introduced them, then immediately went out, and Dalgliesh and Kate were left to walk alone across the carpet to a scene which looked as contrived as a tableau. Barbara Berowne was sitting in a high-backed armchair to the right of the fire. Opposite her, and leaning forward in his chair, was her lawyer, Anthony Farrell. Standing beside her with his hand on her wrist was her doctor, George Piggott. It was he who spoke first:

"I'll leave you now, Lady Berowne, but I'll look in again this evening, about six o'clock if that is convenient, and we'll try to do something to help you sleep tonight. If you need me earlier, get Miss Matlock to ring. Try to eat a little supper if you can. Get her to make you something light. You won't feel like food, I know, but I want you to try. Will you?"

She nodded and held out her hand. He held it for a moment, then turned his gaze on Dalgliesh, shifted his eyes and muttered:

"Appalling, appalling."

As Dalgliesh made no response, he said:

"I think Lady Berowne is strong enough to talk to you now, Commander, but I hope it won't take long."

He spoke like an amateur actor in a murder play, predictable dialogue predictably delivered. It surprised Dalgliesh that a doctor, presumably not unused to tragedy, should be more ill at ease than his patient. When he reached the door, Dalgliesh asked quietly:

"Were you also Sir Paul's physician?"

"Yes, but only recently. He was a private patient of Dr. Gillespie, who died last year. Sir Paul and Lady Berowne then registered with me under the National Health Service. I now have his medical records, but he has never consulted me professionally. He was a very healthy man."

So part of the unease was explained. Here was no old and valued family physician but an overworked local general practitioner, understandably anxious to get back to a crowded surgery or his round of visits, perhaps unhappily aware that the situation required a social skill and concentrated attention which he hadn't the time to give, but trying, not very convincingly, to play the part of a family friend in a drawing room which he probably had not entered until that moment. Dalgliesh wondered whether Paul Berowne's decision to register as a National Health patient had been a matter of political expedience, conviction or economy, or of all three. There was a rectangle of faded wallpaper above the carved marble fireplace. It was half-obscured by a not particularly distinguished family portrait, but Dalgliesh suspected that a more valuable oil had once hung there. Barbara Berowne said:

"Please sit down, Commander."

She waved vaguely towards a sofa set against the wall. It was inconveniently placed and looked too insubstantial for use, but Kate went over to it, sat down and unobtrusively took out her notebook. Dalgliesh walked over to one of the upright chairs, carried it across to the fireplace and set it down to the right of Anthony Farrell. He said:

"We are sorry to have to bother you at a time like this, Lady Berowne, but I'm sure you'll understand that it is necessary."

But Barbara Berowne was gazing after Dr. Piggott. She said resentfully:

"What a funny little man! Paul and I only registered with him last June. His hands are sweaty."

She gave a little moue of distaste and rubbed her fingers stiffly together. Dalgliesh said:

"Do you feel able to answer some questions?"

She looked across at Farrell rather like a child expecting guidance. He said in his smooth professional voice:

"I'm afraid, my dear Barbara, that in a murder investigation the usual civilized conventions have to go. Delay is a luxury the police can't afford. I know that the Commander will make it as short as possible, and you'll be brave and make it as easy for him as you can."

Before she had a chance to reply, he said to Dalgliesh:

"I'm here as Lady Berowne's friend as well as her lawyer. The firm has looked after the family for three generations. I had a great personal regard for Sir Paul. I've lost a friend as well as a client. That's partly why I'm here. Lady Berowne is very much alone. Her mother and stepfather are both in California."

Dalgliesh wondered what Farrell would say if he replied: "But her mother-in-law is only a couple of floors away." He wondered if the implication of their separateness at a time when the family would naturally seek support, if not comfort, from each other was lost on them, or on Farrell, or whether they were so used to living their lives under one roof but apart that even in a moment of high tragedy neither could cross the psychological barrier represented by that caged lift, those two floors.

Barbara Berowne turned her remarkable violet-blue eyes on Dalgliesh

and he was for a second disconcerted. After the first fleeting glimmer of
curiosity the glance was deadened, almost lifeless, as if he were looking
into coloured contact lenses. Perhaps after a lifetime of seeing the effect
of her gaze she no longer needed to animate it with any expression other
than a casual interest. He had known that she was beautiful, how he
couldn't remember, probably it was an accumulation of casually dropped
comments when her husband was talked of, of press photographs. But
it wasn't a beauty to stir his heart. It would have given him pleasure to
sit unnoticed and look at her as he might at a picture, to note with dis-
passionate admiration the delicate, perfectly curved arch above the slanting
eyes, at the curve of the upper lip, the shadowed hollow between the
cheekbone and the jaw, the rise of the slim throat. He could look and
admire and leave without regret. For him this blond loveliness was too
exquisite, too orthodox, too perfect. What he loved was a more individual
and eccentric beauty, vulnerability allied to intelligence. He doubted whether Barbara Berowne was intelligent, but he didn't underrate her. Nothing
in police work was more dangerous than to make superficial judgements
about human beings. But he wondered briefly whether here now was a
woman for whom a man would kill. He had known three such women
in his career; none would have been described as beautiful.

She was sitting in her chair with a still, relaxed elegance. Above her
skirt of light grey, finely pleated wool, she wore a silk shirt of pale blue
with a grey cashmere cardigan slung loosely over her shoulders. Her only
jewellery was a couple of gold chains and small gold stud earrings. Her
hair, with its strands of pale and darker corn yellow, was drawn back and
hung over her shoulder in a single thick plait fastened at the end with
a tortoiseshell clamp. Nothing, he thought, could have been more discreetly
fitting. Black, particularly in so recent a widow, would have been osten-
tatious, theatrical, even vulgar. This gentle arrangement of grey and blue
was entirely appropriate. Kate had, he knew, arrived with her news before
Lady Berowne had dressed. She had been told that her husband was dead
with his throat cut, and she had still been able to take trouble with her
dressing. And why not? He was too old a hand to assume grief wasn't
genuine because it was appropriately clad. There were women whose self-
respect demanded perpetual attention to detail no matter how violent events,
others for whom it was a matter of confidence, of routine, or of defiance.
In a man such punctiliousness was normally regarded as commendable.
Why not, then, in a woman? Or was it merely that her appearance had
for over twenty years been the major preoccupation of her life and she

couldn't change that habit merely because someone had slit her husband's throat? But he couldn't help noticing the details, the intricate buckle at the side of the shoes, the lipstick meticulously applied and precisely matching the pink of her nail varnish, the trace of eye shadow. Her hands at least had been steady. When she spoke her voice was high and, to him, unpleasing. It would, he thought, easily degenerate into a childish whine. She said:

"Of course I want to help, but I don't know how I can. I mean, it's all so incredible. Who could have wanted to kill Paul? He hadn't any enemies. Everyone liked him. He was very popular."

The banal, inadequate tribute in that high, slightly jarring tone must have struck even her as gauche. There was a short silence which Farrell thought it prudent to break. He said:

"Lady Berowne is, of course, deeply shocked. We were hoping, Commander, that you would be able to give us more information than we have at present. We gather that the weapon was some kind of knife and that there were injuries to the throat."

And that, thought Dalgliesh, was as tactful a way of saying that Sir Paul's throat had been slit as even the most skilled lawyer could devise. He said:

"Both Sir Paul and the tramp were apparently killed in the same way."

"Was the weapon at the scene?"

"A possible weapon was at the scene. They may both have been killed with Sir Paul's razor."

"And that was left by the murderer in the room?"

"We found it there, yes."

The implication of Dalgliesh's careful words wasn't lost on Farrell. For his part he wouldn't use the word "suicide," but it lay between them with all its implications. Farrell went on:

"And the church door. Had that been forced?"

"It was unlocked when Miss Wharton, the church worker, found the bodies this morning."

"So anyone could have got in and someone, presumably, did?"

"Certainly. You will understand that the investigation is still in its early stages. We can be sure of nothing until we have the result of the autopsy and the forensic reports."

"Of course. I ask because Lady Berowne prefers to know the facts, or as many of them as are available. And she has a right, of course, to be kept fully informed."

Dalgliesh made no reply, nor did he need to; they understood each other perfectly. Farrell would be polite, studiously so, but not affable. His carefully controlled demeanour, so much a part of his professional life that it no longer seemed assumed, was saying: We're both professionals with something of a reputation in our jobs. We both know what we're about. You will excuse a certain lack of amiability, but we may be required to be on different sides.

The truth was that they were already on different sides and both knew it. It was as if Farrell emanated an ambiguous ectoplasm which folded Barbara Berowne in its comforting aura, saying: Here I am, I'm on your side, leave this to me. There's nothing to worry about. It came to Dalgliesh as a subtle, masculine understanding, close to conspiracy, from which she was excluded. He did it very well.

His city firm of Torrington, Farrell and Penge, with its many ramifications, had enjoyed an unsullied legal reputation for over two hundred years. Its criminal department had represented some of the most ingenious villains in London. Some were holidaying in their Riviera villas, some on their yachts. Very few were behind bars. Dalgliesh had a sudden picture of a prison van which two days previously he had driven past on his way to the Yard, of the row of anonymous, hostile eyes gazing out through the slots as if they were expecting to see nothing more. The ability to pay for a couple of hours of Farrell's time at a crucial stage of their misfortunes would have made all the difference.

Barbara Berowne said peevishly:

"I don't see why I have to be bothered. Paul didn't even tell me he was going to spend the night in that church. Dossing down with a tramp. I mean, it was all so silly."

Dalgliesh said:

"When did you last see him?"

"At about nine fifteen yesterday morning. He came up to see me just before Mattie brought up my breakfast tray. He didn't stay long. About fifteen minutes."

"How did he seem, Lady Berowne?"

"He seemed himself. He didn't say very much. He never did. I think I told him how I was going to spend the day."

"And how was that?"

"I had a hair appointment at Michael and John in Bond Street at eleven. Then I lunched in Knightsbridge with an old school friend and we did some shopping in Harvey Nichols. I got home here at teatime and by then he'd left. I never saw him after nine fifteen."

"And, as far as you know, he didn't return to the house?"

"I don't think so, but I wouldn't have seen him anyway. After I got back I changed and then took a taxi to Pembroke Lodge. That's my cousin's nursing home in Hampstead. He's an obstetrician, Mr. Stephen Lampart. I was with him until midnight, when he brought me home. We drove to Cookham to have dinner at the Black Swan. We left Pembroke Lodge at seven forty and drove straight to the Black Swan, I mean, we didn't stop on the way."

It was, he thought, remarkably pat. He had expected her to come out with an alibi sooner or later, but hardly so soon and in such detail. He asked:

"And when you last saw Sir Paul at breakfast time, he didn't tell you how he proposed to spend the day?"

"No. But couldn't you look in his diary? He keeps it in his desk drawer in the study."

"We found part of his diary in the vestry. It had been burnt."

He was watching her face closely as he spoke. The blue eyes flickered, grew wary, but he could have sworn that this was news to her. She turned again to Farrell:

"But this is extraordinary! Why should Paul burn his diary?"

Dalgliesh said:

"We don't know that he did. But the diary was there in the grate. A number of pages were burnt and the final page torn in half."

Farrell's eyes met Dalgliesh's. Neither spoke. Then Dalgliesh said:

"So we need to try to establish his movements some other way. I had hoped you might be able to help."

"But does it matter? I mean, if someone broke in and killed him, how does it help to know that he went to the estate agent a few hours earlier?"

"And did he?"

"He said he had an appointment."

"Did he say with which one?"

"No, and I didn't ask. I suppose God told him to sell the house. I don't think He told him which estate agent to use."

The words were as shocking as an indecency. Dalgliesh felt Farrell's dismayed surprise as clearly as if the man had gasped. He could detect neither bitterness nor irony in that high, slightly petulant voice. She could have been a mischievous child, daring in the presence of adults to say the unpardonable thing and half-surprised by her own temerity. Anthony Farrell decided that the time had come to intervene. He said smoothly:

"I myself was expecting to see Sir Paul yesterday afternoon. He had made an appointment at two thirty with me and two of my colleagues on the financial side of the firm to discuss certain arrangements made necessary, I understand, by his decision to give up his parliamentary career. But he rang yesterday shortly before ten to cancel the appointment and to make a new appointment for the same time today. I hadn't myself arrived at the office when he telephoned, but he left a message with my clerk. If you are able to prove that his death was murder, then I naturally accept that every detail of his affairs will properly come under scrutiny. Both Lady Ursula and Lady Berowne would wish that they should."

He might be a pompous ass, thought Dalgliesh, but he was no fool. He knew or guessed that most of these questions were premature. He was prepared to allow them, but he could stop them when he chose. Barbara Berowne turned on him her remarkable eyes.

"But there isn't anything to discuss. Paul left everything to me. He told me he had after we were married. The house too. It's quite straightforward. I'm his widow. It's all mine—well, nearly all."

Farrell said smoothly:

"Perfectly straightforward, my dear. But it's hardly necessary to discuss it now."

Dalgliesh took from his wallet a copy of the poison pen letter and handed it to her.

He said:

"I expect you saw this."

She shook her head and gave it to Farrell, who read it, taking his time, his face expressionless. If he had seen it before, he certainly wasn't admitting to the knowledge.

He said:

"That on the face of it is a malicious and possibly actionable attack on Sir Paul's character."

"It may have nothing to do with his death but, obviously, we should like to clear it out of the way."

He turned again to Barbara Berowne.

"Are you sure that your husband didn't show it to you?"

"No, why should he? Paul didn't believe in worrying me with things

I couldn't do anything about. Isn't it the usual kind of poison pen letter? I mean, politicians get them all the time."

"You mean, this wasn't unusual, that your husband had received similar communications?"

"No, I don't know, I don't think he did. He never said so. I meant that anyone in public—"

Farrell broke in, smoothly professional:

"Lady Berowne means, of course, that anyone in public life and particularly in politics has to expect a certain amount of this kind of malice and unpleasantness."

Dalgliesh said:

"But not quite as specific as this, surely. There was a subsequent article, obviously based on this, in the *Paternoster Review*. Did you see that, Lady Berowne?"

She shook her head.

Farrell said:

"I suppose this has to be relevant, but do we need to talk about it now?"

Dalgliesh said:

"Not if Lady Berowne finds it too distressing."

The implication was plain and Farrell didn't like it. His client helped him. She turned to him with a look in which appeal, surprise and distress were beautifully mingled.

"But I don't understand. I've told the Commander all I know. I've tried to help, but how can I? I don't know anything about Diana Travers. Miss Matlock, Mattie, looks after the house. I think this girl answered an advertisement and Mattie took her on."

Dalgliesh said:

"Wasn't that rather unusual for these days? Young people don't often want to do housework."

"Mattie said that she was an actress who only wanted to work a few hours each week. It suited her."

"Did Miss Matlock consult you before taking on the girl?"

"No. I expect she asked my mother-in-law. They look after the house between them. They don't bother me with it."

"And the other dead girl, Theresa Nolan. Did you have anything to do with her?"

"She was my mother-in-law's nurse, nothing to do with me. I hardly saw her."

She turned to Anthony Farrell:

"Do I have to answer all these questions? I want to help, but how can I? If Paul did have enemies, I don't know about them. We didn't really talk about politics, things like that."

The sudden blaze of blue conveyed that no man would wish to burden her with matters so irrelevant to the essential fact about her.

She added:

"It's too dreadful. Paul dead, murdered—I can't believe it. I haven't really taken it in. I don't want to go on talking about it. I just want to be left alone and to go to my room. I want Mattie."

The words were a piteous appeal for sympathy, for understanding, but the voice was that of a querulous child.

Farrell went over to the fireplace and pulled on the bell cord. He said:

"I'm afraid that one of the dreadful facts about murder is that the police are obliged to intrude on grief. It's their job. They have to be sure that there is nothing your husband said to you which could give them a clue to suggest that he had an enemy. Someone who might know that he would be in St. Matthew's Church that night, someone who had a grudge against him, might want him out of the way. It seems most likely that Paul was killed by a casual intruder, but the police have to exclude other possibilities."

If Anthony Farrell thought that he was going to conduct the interview on his terms, he was mistaken. But before Dalgliesh could speak, the door burst open and a young man flung himself across the room to Barbara Berowne. He cried:

"Barbie darling! Mattie rang me with the news. It's awful, unbelievable. I'd have come earlier only she couldn't reach me until eleven. Darling, how are you? Are you all right?"

She said rather faintly:

"This is my brother, Dominic Swayne."

He nodded at them as if their presence were an intrusion and turned again to his sister.

"But what happened, Barbie? Who did it? D'you know?"

Dalgliesh thought, this isn't genuine, he's acting. And then he told himself that the judgement was certainly premature and possibly unjust. One thing policing taught you was that in moments of shock and grief, even the most articulate could sound platitudinous. If Swayne was overacting the part of a devoted consoling brother, that didn't necessarily mean that he wasn't both genuinely devoted and anxious to console. But Dalgliesh hadn't missed Barbara Berowne's small shudder as his arms went round her shoulders. It could, of course, have been a small manifestation of shock, but Dalgliesh wondered if it hadn't also been one of mild revulsion.

He wouldn't have known at first that they were brother and sister. True, Swayne had the same corn-yellow hair, but his, either by nature or art, was tightly curled above a round pale forehead. The eyes, too, were alike, the same remarkable violet blue under the curved brows. But there the resemblance ended. He had none of his sister's classical, heart-catching beauty. But his face, delicately featured, wasn't without a certain puckish charm with its well-formed, rather petulant mouth, ears as tiny as a child's, milk white and slightly jutting like incipient wings. He was short, little more than five foot three, but broad-shouldered and with long arms. This simian strength grafted onto the delicate head and face was so discordant that the first impression was of a minor physical deformity.

But Miss Matlock had answered the bell and was standing in the doorway. Without saying good-bye and with a little moan, Barbara Berowne half-stumbled over to her. The woman gazed first at her, then at the men in the room impassively, then, placing an arm across her shoulder, guided her out. There was a moment of silence, then Dalgliesh turned to Dominic Swayne.

"As you are here, perhaps you would answer one or two questions. It's possible you may be able to help us. When did you last see Sir Paul?"

"My revered brother-in-law? Do you know, I can't remember. Not for some weeks anyway. Actually I was in this house all yesterday evening, but we didn't meet. Evelyn, Miss Matlock, wasn't expecting him back for dinner. She said that he had left after breakfast and no one knew where he had gone."

Kate asked from her seat by the wall:

"When did you arrive, sir?"

He turned to look at her, the blue eyes amused, frankly appraising, as if signalling a sexual invitation.

"Just before seven. The neighbour was coming out of his door and saw me arrive, so he'll be able to confirm the time if it's important. I can't see why it should be. Miss Matlock too, of course. I stayed until just before ten thirty, then went over to the local pub, the Raj, for a last drink. They'll remember me there. I was one of the last to leave."

Kate asked:

"And you were here the whole time?"

"Yes. But what's it got to do with Paul's death? I mean, is it important?"

He couldn't, thought Dalgliesh, be as naive as that. He said:

"It could be helpful in tracing Sir Paul's movements yesterday. Could he have returned to the house while you were here?"

"I suppose so, but it doesn't seem likely. I was having a bath for about an hour, that's principally why I came. He might have come back then, but I think that Miss Matlock would have mentioned it. I'm an actor, out of work at present. Just auditioning. They call it resting, God knows why. It seems more like feverish activity to me. I lodged here for a week or two in May, but Paul wasn't all that welcoming, so I moved in with Bruno Packard. He's a theatre designer. He has a small flat, a conversion, at Shepherds Bush. But what with his model sets and gear, there's not a lot of room. On top of that there isn't a bath, only a shower, and that's in the loo, so it isn't exactly convenient for anyone reasonably fastidious. I've taken to turning up here for an occasional bath and meal."

It was, thought Dalgliesh, almost suspiciously pat, as if the whole speech had been rehearsed. And he was certainly being unusually confiding for a man who hadn't even been asked to explain his movements, who could have no reason to suppose that this was a case of murder. But if the times were confirmed, it looked as if Swayne could be in the clear. Swayne said:

"Look, if there's nothing else you want, I'll go up to Barbie. This is an appalling shock for her. Mattie will give you Bruno's address if you want it."

After he had left, no one spoke for a moment, then Dalgliesh said:

"I am interested that Lady Berowne inherits the house. I would have expected it to be entailed."

Farrell took the question with professional calm.

"Yes, the situation is unusual. I have, of course, authority from both Lady Ursula and Lady Berowne to give you any information you need. The old Berowne property, the one in Hampshire, was entailed, but that has long since gone, together with most of the fortune. This house has always been willed from one baronet to the next. Sir Paul inherited it from his brother, but he had absolute discretion about its disposal. After his marriage he made a new will and left it to his wife absolutely. The will is quite straightforward. Lady Ursula has her own money, but there is a small bequest to her and a larger one to his only child, Miss Sarah Berowne. Halliwell and Miss Matlock get £10,000 each and he has left an oil painting, an Arthur Devis if I remember rightly, to the chairman of his local party. There are other minor bequests. But the house, its contents, and an adequate provision go to his wife."

And the house alone, thought Dalgliesh, must be worth at least three-quarters of a million, probably considerably more, given its position and unique architectural interest. He recalled as he so often did the words of an old detective sergeant when he, Dalgliesh, had been a newly appointed DC. "Love, Lust, Loathing, Lucre, the four L's of murder, laddie. And the greatest of these is lucre."

3

⊠

Their last interview that afternoon at Campden Hill Square was with Miss Matlock. Dalgliesh had asked to be shown where Berowne had kept his diary, and she had led them into the ground floor study. It was, he knew, architecturally one of the most eccentric rooms in the house, and the one, perhaps, most typical of Soane's style. It was octagonal, each wall fitted from floor to ceiling with glass-fronted bookcases between which fluted pilasters rose to a dome topped by an octagonal lantern decorated with richly coloured glass. It was, he thought, an exercise in the clever organization of limited space, an eminently successful example of the architect's peculiar genius. But it was still a room to wonder at rather than to live in, to work in or to enjoy.

Solidly placed in the centre of the room was Berowne's mahogany desk. Dalgliesh and Kate moved over to it while Miss Matlock stood in the doorway and watched them, her eyes fixed on Dalgliesh's face, as if a momentary lapse of concentration might cause him to spring at her. Dalgliesh said:

"Could you show me, please, exactly where the diary was kept?"

She moved forward and, without speaking, pulled open the top right-hand drawer. It was empty now except for a box of writing paper and one of envelopes. He asked:

"Did Sir Paul work here?"

"He wrote letters. He kept his parliamentary papers in his office at the House and everything to do with his constituency at his office at Wrentham Green." She added:

"He liked things separate."

Dalgliesh thought: Separate, impersonal, under control. Again he had the sense that he was in a museum, that Berowne had sat in this richly ornamented cell like a stranger. He said:

"What about his private papers? Do you know where those are kept?"

"I suppose in the safe. It's concealed behind the books in the case to the right of the door."

If Berowne had, indeed, been murdered, the safe and its contents would have to be examined. But that, like much else, could wait.

He moved over to the bookcases. It was, of course, popular wisdom that personality could be diagnosed from the shelves of a private library. This revealed that Berowne had read more biography, history and poetry than he had fiction, and yet, scanning the shelves, it struck Dalgliesh that he could have been browsing in the library of a private club or a luxury cruise ship, although admittedly one where the object of the voyage was cultural enrichment rather than popular entertainment, and the fares high. Here, tidily shelved, was essentially the predictable, unexceptional choice of a well-educated, cultured Englishman who knew what it was proper to read. But he couldn't believe that Berowne was a man whose idea of choosing fiction was to order routinely the Booker shortlist. Again he had the sense of a personality escaping him, of even the room and its objects conspiring to hide from him the essential man. He asked:

"How many people had access to this room yesterday?"

The formal impersonality of the library must have affected him. The question sounded oddly phrased even to his own ears, and she made no attempt to hide the tone of contempt.

"Access? The study is part of a private house. We don't keep it locked. All the family and their friends have what you call access."

"And who did, in fact, come in here yesterday?"

"I can't be sure. I suppose Sir Paul must have done if you found his diary with him in the church. Mrs. Minns would have come in to dust. Mr. Frank Musgrave, who is chairman of the constituency party, was shown in here at lunchtime, but he didn't wait. Miss Sarah Berowne called in during the afternoon to see her grandmother, but I think she waited in the drawing room. She left before Lady Ursula returned."

Dalgliesh asked:

"Mr. Musgrave and Miss Berowne were let in by you?"

"I opened the door to them. There's no one else to do it." She paused, then added:

"Miss Berowne used to have her own keys to the front door, but she didn't take them with her when she left home."

"And when did you last see the diary?"

"I can't remember. I think it was about two weeks ago, when Sir Paul rang from his office in the Department and asked me to check on a dinner engagement."

"And when did you last see Sir Paul?"

"Just before ten o'clock yesterday. He came into the kitchen to collect some food for a picnic lunch."

"Then perhaps we could go to the kitchen now."

She led him along the tiled passage, down a couple of steps, then through a baize-covered door to the back of the house. Then she stood aside to let him in, and again stood at the door, hands clasped, the parody of a cook awaiting judgement on the cleanliness of the kitchen. And indeed there would be nothing to fault. Like the study, it was curiously impersonal, lacking cosiness without being actually uncomfortable or poorly equipped. There was a central table in well-scrubbed pine with four chairs and a large and very old gas cooker, in addition to a more modern solid-fuel stove. It was obvious that little money had been spent on the kitchen in recent years. From the low window he could see the back of the wall dividing the house from the mews garages, and the feet only of the marble statues in their niches. Thus truncated, a row of delicately carved toes, they seemed to emphasize the room's colourless deprivation. The only individual note was a pink geranium in a pot on the shelf over the sink, and beside it a second pot with a couple of cuttings. He said:

"You told me that Sir Paul collected his lunch. Did he do that himself or did you get it for him?"

"He did. He knew where things were kept. He was often in the kitchen when I prepared Lady Ursula's breakfast tray. He used to take it up to her."

"And what did he take away with him yesterday?"

"Half a loaf of bread, which he sliced ready to eat, a piece of Roquefort cheese, two apples." She added:

"He seemed preoccupied. I don't think he much minded what he was taking."

It was the first time she had volunteered any information, but when he went on to question her gently about Berowne's mood, what, if anything he had said, she seemed to regret the moment of confidence and became almost surly. Sir Paul had told her that he wouldn't be in to luncheon, but nothing else. She hadn't known that he was going to St. Matthew's Church, nor whether he would be back for dinner. Dalgliesh said:

"So you prepared dinner in the usual way and at the usual time?"

The question disconcerted her. She flushed and the clasped hands tightened. Then she said:

"No. No, not in the usual way. Lady Ursula asked me when she got back after her tea engagement to bring up a tray with a flask of soup and a plate of smoked salmon sandwiches in brown bread. She didn't want to be disturbed again that evening. I took it up shortly after six. And I knew that Lady Berowne was dining out. I decided to wait and see if Sir Paul actually came back. There were things I could cook quickly if he did. I had soup I could warm up. I could make him an omelette. There's always something." She sounded as defensive as if he had accused her of dereliction of duty.

He said:

"But it was, perhaps, a little inconsiderate of him not to let you know whether he would be in to dinner."

"Sir Paul was never inconsiderate."

"And to stay out all night without word was surely unusual? It must have been worrying for all the household."

"Not for me. It isn't my business what the family choose to do. He could have been staying in the constituency. At eleven o'clock I asked Lady Ursula if it was all right to go to bed and leave the front door unbolted. She said that I should. Lady Berowne knew that it was necessary to bolt it after her when she came in."

Dalgliesh changed the tack of his questions.

"Did Sir Paul take matches with him yesterday morning?"

Her surprise was obvious and, he thought, unfeigned.

"Matches? He didn't need matches. Sir Paul doesn't—he didn't—smoke. I didn't see him with any matches."

"If he had taken them, where would he have got them?"

"From here at the side of the stove. It isn't self-lighting. Or there is a packet of four boxes in the cupboard above."

She opened and showed him. The paper wrapping round the four boxes had been torn and one box taken, presumably that now lying at the side of the stove. She was gazing at him now with a fixed attention, her eyes very bright, her face a little flushed, as if she had a slight fever. His questions about the matches, which had first surprised her, now seemed to disconcert her. She was more on her guard, warier, much more tense.

He was too experienced and she too poor an actress for him to be deceived. Up to now she had answered his questions in the tone of a woman performing a necessary if disagreeable duty. But now the interview had become an ordeal. She wanted him gone. He said:

"We would like to see your sitting room, if you have no objection?"

"If you think it necessary. Lady Ursula said that you were to be given every facility."

Dalgliesh thought it unlikely that Lady Ursula had said any such thing, and certainly not in those words. He and Kate followed her across the passage and into the opposite room. It must, Dalgliesh thought, once have been the butler's or housekeeper's sanctum. As with the kitchen, there was no view except of the courtyard and the door leading through to the mews garages. But the furniture was comfortable enough: a chintz-covered sofa for two, a matching armchair, a gate-legged table and two dining chairs set against the wall, a bookcase filled with volumes of an identical size, obviously from a book club. The fireplace was of marble with a wide overmantel on which was crowded, with no attempt at arrangement, a collection of modern and prettily sentimental figurines—women in crinolines, a child hugging a puppy, shepherds and shepherdesses, a ballet dancer. These presumably belonged to Miss Matlock. The pictures were prints in modern frames, Constable's *Hay Wain* over the fireplace and Monet's *Women in a Field*. They and the furniture were innocuous, predictable, as if someone had said, "We need to employ a housekeeper, furnish a room for her." Even rejects from the rest of the house would have had more character than these impersonal objects. What again was missing was the sense that someone had impressed on this place her own personality. He thought: They live here their separate cabined lives. But only Lady Ursula is at home in this house. The rest are no more than squatters.

He asked her where she had spent the previous evening. She said:

"I was here or in the kitchen. Mr. Dominic Swayne came for a meal and a bath, and afterwards we played Scrabble. He arrived shortly before seven and left before eleven. Our neighbour, Mr. Swinglehurst, was garaging his car and saw Mr. Swayne arrive."

"Did anyone else in the house see him while he was here?"

"No, but he did take a telephone call at about twenty to nine. It was from Mrs. Hurrell, the wife of the last agent in the constituency. She wanted to try and contact Sir Paul. I told her that no one knew where he was."

"And Mr. Swayne, where did he bath?"

"Upstairs, in the main bathroom. Lady Ursula has her own bathroom, and there is a shower room down here, but Mr. Swayne wanted a proper bath."

"So you were either in this room or the kitchen and Mr. Swayne was upstairs for at least part of the evening. The back door, was it locked?"

"Locked and bolted. It always is after tea. The key is here on the keyboard in that cupboard."

She opened it and showed him the wall-mounted board with its rows of hooks and tagged keys. He asked:

"Could anyone have got out without your noticing, perhaps while you were in the kitchen?"

"No. I usually keep the door to the passage open. I should have seen or heard. No one left the house last night by that door." She seemed to rouse herself and said with sudden vigour:

"All these questions. What was I doing? Who was here? Who could have left without being seen? Anyone would think he was murdered."

Dalgliesh said:

"It is possible that Sir Paul was murdered."

She gazed at him, appalled, then sank down onto the chair. He saw that she was shaking. She said in a low voice:

"Murdered. No one said anything about murder. I thought . . ." Kate moved over to her, glanced at Dalgliesh, then placed her hand on Miss Matlock's shoulder. Dalgliesh asked:

"What did you think, Miss Matlock?"

She looked up at him and whispered so quietly that he had to bend his head to hear.

"I thought he might have done it himself."

"Had you any reason to suppose that?"

"No. No reason. Of course not. How could I? And Lady Berowne said . . . There was something about his razor. But murder . . . I don't want to answer any more questions, not tonight. I don't feel well. I don't want to be badgered. He's dead. That's terrible enough. But murder! I can't believe it's murder. I want to be left alone."

Looking down at her, Dalgliesh thought: The shock is real enough, but part of this is acting, and not very convincing acting at that. He said coolly:

"We're not allowed to badger a witness, Miss Matlock, and I don't think you really believe that we have been badgering you. You've been very helpful. I'm afraid we shall have to talk again, to ask you more questions, but it needn't be now. We can see ourselves out."

She got out of the chair as clumsily as an old woman and said:

"No one sees themselves out of this house. That's my job."

In the Rover Dalgliesh rang the Yard. He said to Massingham:

"We'll see Lampart as early as we can tomorrow. It would be helpful if we could fit that in before the pm at three thirty. Is there any news of Sarah Berowne?"

"Yes sir. She's a professional photographer, apparently, and has had sessions all today. She's got another booked for tomorrow afternoon, a writer who's due to leave for the States in the evening. It's rather important, so she hopes it won't be necessary to cancel. I told her we'd come along in the evening at six thirty. And Press Office want an urgent word. The news will break at one o'clock and they want to set up a press conference first thing tomorrow."

"That's premature. What on earth do they expect us to be able to say at this stage? Try to get it postponed, John."

If he could prove that Berowne had been murdered the whole investigation would take place against a background of feverish media interest. He knew that, although he didn't welcome it, but there was no reason why it should start yet. As Kate manoeuvred the Rover out of its restricted parking place and began to move slowly down the Square he looked back at the elegant facade of the house, at the windows like dead eyes. And then, on the top floor, he saw the twitch of a curtain and knew that Lady Ursula was watching them leave.

4
⊠

It was six twenty before Sarah Berowne managed to reach Ivor Garrod by telephone. She had been in her flat for most of the early part of the afternoon but hadn't dared ring from there. It was an absolute rule of his, born, she had sometimes felt, from his obsession with secrecy, that nothing important should ever be told over her own telephone. So the whole afternoon from the time her grandmother had left her had been dominated by the need to find a convenient public kiosk, to have sufficient coins ready. But he had always been unavailable and she hadn't liked to risk leaving a message, not even her name.

Her only appointment of the day had been to photograph a visiting writer staying with friends in Hertfordshire. She always worked with the minimum of equipment and had travelled by train. She couldn't remember very much of the short session. She had worked like an automaton, choosing the best setting, testing the light, fitting the lenses. She supposed it had gone reasonably well, the woman had seemed satisfied, but even as she worked she had been impatient to get away to find a public telephone, to try once again to reach Ivor.

She had jumped down from the train almost before it drew to a stop at King's Cross and had looked round with desperate eyes for the arrows pointing to the telephones. They were open instruments banked each side of a malodorous passageway leading from the main concourse, its walls scribbled with numbers and graffiti. The rush hour was in progress and it was a couple of minutes before an instrument was free. She almost snatched it, still warm, from the relinquishing hand. And this time she was lucky; he was in his office, it was his voice that answered. She gave a small sob of relief.

"It's Sarah. I've been trying to reach you all day. Can you talk?"

"Briefly. Where are you?"

"At King's Cross. You've heard?"

"Only now, on the six o'clock news. It hasn't made the evening papers."

"Ivor, I have to see you."

He said calmly:

"Naturally. There are things we need to talk about, but not tonight. That isn't possible. Have the police been in touch with you?"

"They've been trying to get me, but I told them that I was tied up all today and wouldn't be free until six thirty tomorrow."

"And are you?"

What does that matter, she thought. She said:

"I've got two appointments in the afternoon."

"Hardly being tied up all day. Never lie to the police unless you can be sure that they have no way of finding out. They only have to check with your diary."

"But I couldn't let them come until we'd spoken. There are things they might ask. About Theresa Nolan, about Diana. Ivor, we have to meet."

"We shall. And they won't ask about Diana. Your father killed himself, his final and most embarrassing folly. His life was a mess. The family will want it decently buried, not dragged out stinking into the daylight. How did you learn the news, by the way?"

"Grandmama. She rang me, then came round by taxi after the police had left her. She didn't tell me very much. I don't think she knew all the details. She doesn't believe that Daddy killed himself."

"Naturally. The Berownes are expected to put on uniform and kill other people, not themselves. But that, come to it, was apparently what he did, kill another person. I wonder how much sympathy Ursula Berowne will waste on that dead tramp."

A small burr of doubt caught at her mind. Could they possibly have said on the news that the second victim was a tramp? She said:

"But it isn't only Grandmama. The police, a Commander Dalgliesh, he doesn't seem to think that Daddy killed himself either."

The level of noise had risen. The narrow hallway was crowded with people needing to telephone before catching their trains. She felt the bodies thrusting against her. The air was a jabber of voices against the background thud of marching feet, the raucous, unintelligible litany of the station announcer. She bent her head more closely over the mouthpiece. She said:

"The police don't seem to think it was suicide."

There was a silence. She dared to speak more loudly against the noise.

"Ivor, the police don't think—"

He cut in:

"I heard you. Look, stay where you are. I'll come now. We can only have half an hour but you're right, we ought to talk. And don't worry, I'll be with you in the flat when they arrive tomorrow. It's important you don't see them alone. And, Sarah . . ."

"Yes, I'm here."

"We were together the whole of yesterday evening. We were together from six o'clock when I arrived from work. We stayed together all night. We ate in the flat. Get that into your mind. Start concentrating on it now. And stay where you are. I'll be there in about forty minutes."

She replaced the receiver and stood for a moment motionless, her head against the cold metal of the instrument. A furious female voice said: "Do you mind. Some of us have trains to catch," and she felt herself pushed aside. She fought her way out of the hall and leaned against the wall. Small waves of faintness and nausea flowed over her, each leaving her more desolate, but there was nowhere to sit, no privacy, no peace. She could go to the coffee bar, but he might get there early. Suppose she became disorientated, lost track of time. He had said "stay where you are," and obeying him had become a habit. She leaned back and closed her eyes. She had to obey him now, rely on his strength, rely on him to tell her what to do. She had no one else.

He hadn't once said he was sorry that her father was dead, but he wasn't sorry and he didn't expect her to be. He had always been brutally unsentimental; that was what he meant by honesty. She wondered what he would do if she said: "He was my father and he's dead. I loved him once. I need to mourn for him, for myself. I need to be comforted. I'm lost, I'm frightened. I need to feel your arms around me. I need to be told that it wasn't my fault."

The marching horde flowed past her, a phalanx of grey intent faces, eyes staring ahead. They were like a flood of refugees from a stricken city or a retreating army, still disciplined, but dangerously on the edge of panic. She closed her eyes and let the tramp of their feet engulf her. And, suddenly, she was in another station, another crowd. But then she had been six years old and the station had been Victoria. What were they doing there, she and her father? Probably meeting her grandmother, re-turning by overland and by boat from her house rising out of the Seine at Les Andelys. For one moment she and her father had been parted. He had paused to greet an acquaintance and she had momentarily slipped his hand and run to look at the brightly coloured poster of a seaside town. Looking round, she saw with panic that he was no longer there. She was alone, menaced by a moving forest of endless, tramping, terrifying legs. They could have been parted only for seconds, but the terror had been so dreadful that, recalling it now, eighteen years later, she felt the same loss, the same engulfing terror, the same absolute despair. But suddenly he had been there, striding towards her, his long tweed coat flapping open, smiling, her father, her safety, her god. Not crying, but shuddering with terror and relief, she had run into his outstretched arms and felt herself lifted high, had heard his voice: "It's all right, my darling, it's all right, it's all right." And she had felt the dreadful shaking dissolving in his strong clasp.

She opened her eyes and, blinking away the smarting tears, she saw the drab blacks and greys of the marching army fudge, dissolve, then whirl into a kaleidoscope shot through with flashes of bright colour. It seemed to her that the moving feet were pounding over and through her, that she had become invisible, a brittle, empty shell. But suddenly the mass parted and he was there, still in that long tweed coat, moving towards her, smiling, so that she had to restrain herself from crying "Daddy, Daddy" and running into his arms. But the hallucination passed. This wasn't he, this was a hurrying stranger with a briefcase who glanced with momentary curiosity at her eager face and outstretched arms, then looked through her and passed on. She shrank back, wedging herself more firmly against the wall, and began her long, patient wait for Ivor.

5

It was just before ten o'clock and they were thinking of locking up their papers for the night when Lady Ursula rang. Gordon Halliwell had returned and she would be grateful if the police could see him now. He himself would prefer it. Tomorrow was going to be a busy day for both of them, and she couldn't say when they would be available. Dalgliesh knew that Massingham, if in charge, would have said firmly that they would arrive next morning, if only to demonstrate that they worked at their own convenience, not that of Lady Ursula. Dalgliesh, who was anxious to question Gordon Halliwell and who had never felt the need to bolster either his own authority or his self-esteem, said that they would arrive as soon as possible.

The door of number sixty-two was opened by Miss Matlock, who gazed at them for a couple of seconds with tired, resentful eyes before standing to one side to let them in. Dalgliesh could see that her skin was grey with weariness, the set of her shoulders a little too rigid to be natural. She was wearing a long dressing-gown in flowered nylon, strained across the breast, the belt doubly knotted as if she were afraid they would tear it off. She made a clumsy flutter of her hands towards it and said peevishly:

"I'm not dressed for visitors. We were hoping to get an early bed. I wasn't expecting you to come back tonight."

Dalgliesh said:

"I'm sorry to have to disturb you again. If you want to go to bed, perhaps Mr. Halliwell could let us out."

"It isn't his job. He's only the chauffeur. Locking up the house is my responsibility. Lady Ursula has asked him to take the telephone calls tomorrow, but it isn't suitable, it isn't right. We've had no peace since the six o'clock news. This will kill her if it goes on."

It was, thought Dalgliesh, likely to go on for a very long time, but he doubted whether it would kill Lady Ursula.

Their footsteps rang on the marble floor as Miss Matlock led them down the passage past the octagonal study, then through the baize door to the back of the house and finally down three stairs to the outside door. The house was very quiet but portentously expectant like an empty theatre. He had the sense, as he often did in the house of the recently murdered, of a thin denuded air, a voiceless presence. She drew the locks and they found themselves in the rear courtyard. The three statues in their niches were subtly lit with concealed lighting and seemed to float, gently gleaming, in the still air. The night was surprisingly balmy for autumn, and there came from some nearby garden the transitory smell of cypress so that he felt for a moment displaced, disorientated, as if transported to Italy. It seemed to him inappropriate that the statues should be lit, the beauty of the house still celebrated when Berowne lay frozen like a carcass of meat in his plastic shroud, and he found himself instinctively putting out his hand for a switch before following Miss Matlock through a second door which led to the old mews and the garages.

The rear of the wall with the statues was unadorned; the spoils of the eighteenth-century grand tour were not for the eyes of the footmen or coachmen who once must have inhabited the mews. The yard was cobbled and led to two large garages. The double doors on the left were open and in the glare of two long tubes of fluorescent light they saw that the entrance to the flat was by way of a wrought-iron staircase leading up the side of the garage wall. Miss Matlock merely pointed to the door at the top and said:

"You'll find Mr. Halliwell there." And then, as if to justify the formal use of his name, she said: "He used to be a sergeant in the late Sir Hugo's regiment. He's been decorated for bravery, the Distinguished Service Medal. I expect Lady Ursula told you. He isn't the usual kind of chauffeur-handyman."

And what in these egalitarian, servantless days, thought Dalgliesh, did she suppose the usual kind of chauffeur-handyman to be?

The garage was large enough comfortably to hold the black Rover with its A registration and a white Golf, both of which were neatly parked, with room for a third car. Making their way down the side of the Rover through a strong smell of petrol, they saw that the garage was obviously also used as a workshop. Under a high, long window at the rear was a wooden bench with fitted drawers, and on the wall above, a pegboard on which tools were neatly displayed. Propped against the right-hand wall was a man's bicycle.

They had hardly set foot on the bottom step of the staircase when the door above opened and the figure of a man stood stockily silhouetted against the light. As they came up to him Dalgliesh saw that he was both older and shorter than he had expected, surely only just the statutory height for a soldier, but broad-shouldered and giving an immediate impression of disciplined strength. He was very dark, almost swarthy, and the straight hair, longer than it would have been in his Army days, fell across his forehead almost touching eyebrows straight as black gashes above the deep-set eyes. His nose was short, with slightly flared nostrils, the mouth uncompromising above a square chin. He was wearing well-cut fawn slacks and a woollen checked shirt, open-necked, and gave no sign of tiredness, seeming as fresh as if this were a morning visit. He looked at them with keen but untroubled eyes, eyes that had seen worse things than a couple of CID officers arriving at night. Standing aside to let them in, he said in a voice which held only a trace of roughness:

"I'm just making coffee, or there's whisky if you'd prefer it."

They accepted the coffee, and he went through a door at the back of the room from which presently they heard the noise of running water, the clatter of a kettle lid. The sitting room was long but narrow and ran almost the whole length of the garage, its low windows looking out on the blank rear of the wall. Soane, as a good architect, would have ensured that the privacy of the family was protected; the mews would be unseen from all but the top windows of the house. At the far end of the room a door stood open and Dalgliesh could glimpse the end of a single bed. At the back was a small, delicately wrought Victorian fireplace with a carved wooden surround and an elegant fire-basket reminding him of the grate in St. Matthew's Church. A modern three-bar electric fire was plugged into a socket at its side.

A pine table with four chairs occupied the middle of the room and two rather battered armchairs stood each side of the fireplace. Between the windows was a worktop with, above it, a pegboard of tools, smaller and more delicate than those in the garage. They saw that Halliwell's hobby was wood carving and that he was working on a Noah's Ark with a set of animals. The ark was beautifully constructed with dovetail joints and an elegant clapboard roof; the completed animals, pairs of lions, tigers and giraffes, were more crudely carved but instantly recognizable and with a certain vigorous life.

The far wall was fitted with a bookshelf from floor to ceiling. Dalgliesh moved across to it and saw with interest that Halliwell owned what looked like a complete set of the *Notable British Trials*. And there was one other volume even more interesting: he drew out and leafed through the eighth edition of Keith Simpson's *Textbook on Forensic Medicine*. Replacing it and glancing round the room, he was struck with its tidiness, with its self-containment. It was the room of a man who had organized his living space and probably his life to fulfil his needs, who knew his own nature and was at peace with it. Unlike Paul Berowne's study, this was the room of a man who felt he had a right to be there.

Halliwell came in carrying a tray with three stoneware mugs, a bottle of milk and one of Bell's whisky. He motioned towards the whisky and when Dalgliesh and Massingham shook their heads added a generous measure to his own black coffee. They sat round the table.

Dalgliesh said:

"I see you've got what looks like a complete set of the *Notable British Trials*. That must be comparatively rare."

Halliwell said:

"It's an interest of mine. I could have fancied being a criminal lawyer if things had been different."

He spoke without resentment. It was a statement of fact; but there was no need to ask which things. The law was still a privileged profession. It was rare for a working-class boy to end up eating his dinners in the Inns of Court.

He added:

"It's the trials I find interesting, not the defendants. Most murderers seem pretty stupid and commonplace when you see them in the dock. Same will be true of this chap, no doubt, when you get your hands on him. But maybe a caged animal is always less interesting than one running wild, especially when you've glimpsed his spoor."

Massingham said:

"So you're assuming it's murder."

"I'm assuming that a commander and a chief inspector of the CID wouldn't come here after ten at night to discuss why Sir Paul Berowne should want to slit his throat."

Massingham leaned across to reach the milk bottle. Stirring his coffee, he asked:

"When did you hear of Sir Paul's death?"

"On the six o'clock news. I rang Lady Ursula and said I'd drive back at once. She said I wasn't to hurry. There was nothing I could do here and she wouldn't be wanting the car. She said the police had asked to see me, but that you'd have plenty to occupy yourselves until I got back."

Massingham asked:

"How much has Lady Ursula told you?"

"As much as she knows, which isn't a great deal. She said that their throats were cut and that Sir Paul's razor had been the weapon."

Dalgliesh had asked Massingham to do most of the questioning. This apparent reversal of role and status was often disconcerting to a suspect, but not to this one. Halliwell was either too confident or too unworried to be troubled by such niceties. Dalgliesh had the impression that, of the two, it was Massingham who was, unaccountably, the less at ease. Halliwell, who answered his questions with what seemed deliberate slowness, had an odd and disconcerting trick of fixing his dark eyes intently on the questioner, as if it were he who was the interrogator, he who was seeking to fathom an unknown, elusive personality.

He admitted that he had known that Sir Paul used a cut-throat razor; anyone in the house would know that. He knew that the diary was kept in the top right-hand drawer. It wasn't private. Sir Paul might ring and ask whoever answered the telephone to check on the time of an engagement. There was a key to the drawer, kept usually in the lock or in the drawer itself. Occasionally Sir Paul had been known to lock the drawer and take the key with him, but that wasn't usual. These were the sort of details you got to know if you lived or worked in a house. But he couldn't remember when he had last seen the razors or the diary, and he hadn't been told that Sir Paul would be visiting the church that previous evening. He couldn't say whether anyone else in the house had known; no one had mentioned the matter to him.

Asked for his movements during the day, he said that he had got up at about half past six and had gone for a half-hour jog in Holland Park before boiling an egg for his breakfast. At eight thirty he had gone over to the house to see if there were any odd jobs Miss Matlock had which needed doing. She had given him a table lamp to mend and an electric kettle. He had then driven to collect Mrs. Beamish, Lady Ursula's chi-

ropodist, who lived in Parsons Green and who no longer ran a car. That
was a regular arrangement on the third Tuesday in the month. Mrs. Beamish was over seventy, and Lady Ursula was the only patient she now saw.
The session was over by eleven thirty, and he had then driven Mrs. Beamish
home and returned to take Lady Ursula to a luncheon engagement with
a friend, Mrs. Charles Blaney, at the University Women's Club. He had
parked the car near the club, gone for a solitary pub lunch and returned
at two forty-five to drive both ladies to an exhibition of watercolours at
Agnew's. Afterwards he had driven them to the Savoy for afternoon tea,
then returned to Campden Hill Square by way of Chelsea, where he had
dropped Mrs. Blaney at her Chelsea house. He and Lady Ursula were
back at number sixty-two by five thirty-three. He could remember the
time exactly because he had looked at the car clock. He was used to organizing his life by time. He had helped Lady Ursula into the house, had
then garaged the Rover and had spent the rest of the evening in his flat
until leaving for the country just after ten o'clock. Massingham said:

"I believe Lady Ursula telephoned you twice during the evening. Can
you remember when that was?"

"Yes. Once at about eight, and once again at nine fifteen. She wanted
to discuss next week's arrangements and to remind me that she had said
I could take the Rover. I drive one of the early Cortinas, but it's having
its MOT test."

Massingham asked:

"When the cars are garaged, the Rover, your own and the Golf, is
the garage kept locked?"

"It's kept locked whether or not the cars are garaged. The outer gate
is, of course, always secure, so there isn't much risk of theft, but it's possible that kids from the comprehensive school could climb over the wall,
perhaps as a dare. There are dangerous tools in the larger garage, and Lady
Ursula thinks it wiser always to keep it locked. I didn't bother to lock it
tonight because I knew you were coming."

"And yesterday evening?"

"It was locked after five forty."

"Who has the keys except yourself?"

"Sir Paul and Lady Berowne both have a set and there's a spare bunch
on the keyboard in Miss Matlock's sitting room. Lady Ursula wouldn't
need them. She relies on me to drive her."

"And you were here in this flat all yesterday evening?"

"From five forty. That's right."

"Is there any chance that someone from the house or from outside could have taken out a car or the bicycle without your knowing?"

Halliwell paused, then he said:

"I don't see how that would be possible."

Dalgliesh interposed quietly:

"I'd like you to be more definite than that, Mr. Halliwell, if you can be. Could they or couldn't they?"

Halliwell looked at him.

"No, sir, they couldn't. I must have heard the garage being unlocked. I've got sharp ears."

Dalgliesh went on:

"So last night from about five forty until you left for the country shortly after ten you were here alone in this flat and the garage door was bolted?"

"Yes, sir."

"Is it usual for you to keep the doors bolted when you're in the flat?"

"If I know I'm not going out, it is. I rely on the garage door for my security. The flat lock is only a Yale. It's become a habit to bolt the doors."

Massingham asked:

"And where did you go when you left here?"

"Into the country. To Suffolk, to see a friend. It's a two-hour drive. I arrived about midnight. It's the widow of one of my mates killed in the Falklands. There's a boy. He doesn't miss his dad, he was killed before he was born, but his mother reckons that it's good for him to have a man about the place occasionally."

Massingham asked:

"So you went to see the boy?"

The smouldering eyes were fixed on him. Halliwell answered simply:

"No. I went to see his mother."

Massingham said:

"Your private life is your affair, but we need confirmation about when you arrived at your friend's house. That means we need to know her address."

"Maybe, sir, but I don't see why I need to give it. She's had enough to put up with in the last three years without the police bothering her. I left here just after ten. If Sir Paul was dead before then, what I did later that night isn't relevant. Maybe you know when he died, maybe not, but when you get the autopsy report you'll get a clearer idea. If I need to give you her name and address then, OK, I'll give it. But I'll wait until you convince me that it's necessary."

Massingham said:

"We shan't bother her. She merely has to answer one simple question."

"A question about murder. She's had enough of death and dying. Look, I left here shortly after ten and I arrived almost exactly at midnight. If you do ask her, she'll say the same, and if it's relevant, if I had anything to do with Sir Paul's death, then I'll have fixed a time with her anyway, won't I?"

Massingham asked:

"Why did you start out so late? Today was your day off. Why hang about until ten before starting on a two-hour journey?"

"I prefer driving when the worst of the traffic is over, and I had some jobs I wanted to get finished first, a plug to fix on the table lamp, the electric kettle to mend. They're on the side if you want to check on the work. Then I bathed, changed, cooked myself a meal."

The words, if not the voice, were on the edge of insolence, but Massingham held his temper. Dalgliesh, his own well under control, thought he knew why. Halliwell was a soldier, decorated, a hero. Massingham would have dealt less gently with any man for whom he felt less instinctive respect. If Halliwell had murdered Paul Berowne then the Victoria Cross wouldn't save him, but Dalgliesh knew that Massingham would prefer almost any other suspect to be guilty. Massingham asked:

"Are you married?"

"I had a wife and a daughter. They're both dead."

He turned and looked directly at Dalgliesh. He said:

"What about you, sir? Are you married?"

Dalgliesh had reached out behind him and taken up one of the carved lions. Now he turned it gently in his hands. He said:

"I had a wife and a son. They, too, are dead."

Halliwell turned again to Massingham and bent on him his dark, unsmiling eyes.

"And if that question was none of my business, neither are my wife and daughter any of yours."

Massingham said:

"Nothing is irrelevant when it comes to murder. This lady you visited yesterday night, are you engaged to her?"

"No. She's not ready for that. After what happened to her husband, I don't know that she ever will be. That's why I don't want to give you her address. She's not ready for that kind of question from the police, or for any other question."

Massingham rarely made that kind of mistake and he didn't compound it by explanation or excuse. Dalgliesh didn't press the matter. The important hour was eight o'clock. If Halliwell had an alibi for the hours until ten, he was in the clear and was entitled to his privacy for the following day. If he was trying with difficulty to build up a relationship with a bereaved and vulnerable woman, it was understandable that he didn't want the police arriving with unnecessary questions, however tactful. He said:

"How long have you been working here?"

"Five years three months, sir. I took the job when Major Hugo was alive. After he was killed, Lady Ursula asked me to stay on. I stayed. The money suits, the place suits, you could say Lady Ursula suits. Apparently I suit her. I like living in London and I haven't decided yet what to do with my gratuity."

"Who pays your wages? Who actually employs you?"

"Lady Ursula. It's my job to drive her mostly. Sir Paul used to drive himself or use the ministerial car. Occasionally I'd drive him and her young ladyship if they were out in the evening. There wasn't much of that. They weren't a social couple."

"What sort of couple were they?" Massingham's voice was carefully uninterested.

"They didn't hold hands in the back of the car, if that's what you mean." He paused, then added: "I think that she was a bit afraid of him."

"With reason?"

"Not that I could see, but I wouldn't describe him as an easy man. Nor a happy one, come to that. If you can't cope with guilt, best avoid doing things that make you feel guilty."

"Guilt?"

"He killed his first wife, didn't he? All right, it was an accident; wet road, bad visibility, a notorious bend. That all came out at the inquest. But he was the one driving. I've seen it before. They never quite forgive themselves. Something here"—he gave his chest a gentle thump—"keeps asking them whether it really was an accident."

"There's no evidence that it wasn't, and he was as likely to kill himself as his wife."

"Maybe that wouldn't have worried him that much. Still, he didn't die, did he? She did. And then, five months later, he married again. He got his brother's fiancée, his brother's house, his brother's money, his brother's title."

"But not his brother's chauffeur?"

"No. He didn't take over me."

Dalgliesh asked:

"Did the title matter to him? I shouldn't have thought so."

"Oh, it mattered all right, sir. It wasn't much, I suppose, a baronetcy, but it was old—1642. He liked it, all right, the sense of continuity, his little bit of vicarious immortality."

Massingham said:

"Well, we can all hope for that. You don't sound as if you much liked him."

"Liking didn't come into it between him and me. I drove his mother, she paid me. And if he disliked me he didn't show it. But I reckon I reminded him of things he'd rather forget."

Massingham said:

"And now it's all gone, ended with him, even the title."

"Maybe. Time will show. I think I'd wait nine months before I was sure of that."

It was a hint of a possibility Dalgliesh had already suspected, but he didn't pursue it. Instead he asked:

"When Sir Paul gave up his ministerial job and then his parliamentary seat, what was the feeling in the house among the staff?"

"Miss Matlock didn't discuss it. This isn't the sort of house where the staff sit in the kitchen drinking tea and gossiping about the family. We leave Upstairs, Downstairs to the telly. Mrs. Minns and I thought we might be in for a scandal."

"What sort of a scandal?"

"Sexual, I suppose. That's the kind it usually is."

"Had you any reason to suspect that?"

"None, except that bit of dirt in the *Paternoster Review*. I've no evidence. You asked me what I thought, sir. That was what I thought most likely. Turns out I was wrong. It was more complicated apparently. But then he was a complicated man."

Massingham went on to ask him about the two dead women.

Halliwell said:

"I hardly saw Theresa Nolan. She had a room here, but she either stayed in it most of the time or went out. Kept herself to herself. She was employed as a night nurse and wasn't supposed to be on duty until seven. Miss Matlock nursed Lady Ursula during the day. Theresa seemed a quiet, rather shy girl. A bit timid for a nurse, I thought. Lady Ursula had no complaints as far as I know. You'd better ask her."

"You know that she got pregnant while she was working here?"

"Maybe, but she didn't get pregnant in this flat, nor in the house, for all I know. There's no law which says you can only have sex between seven at night and seven next morning."

"And Diana Travers?"

Halliwell smiled.

"A different girl altogether. Lively. Very bright, I'd say. I saw more of her, although she only worked the two days, Monday and Friday. Odd sort of job for a girl like that to take, I thought. And a bit of a coincidence, seeing Miss Matlock's advert just when she was looking for a part-time job. Those cards usually stick in the windows until they get too brown and faded to be read."

Massingham said:

"Apparently Lady Berowne's brother, Mr. Swayne, was here last evening. Did you see him?"

"No."

"Is he often here?"

"More often than Sir Paul liked. Or other people, for that matter."

"Including you?"

"Me and his sister, I reckon. He has a habit of turning up for a bath or a meal when it suits him, but he's harmless. Spiteful, but about as dangerous as a wasp."

It was, Dalgliesh thought, too facile a judgement.

Suddenly all three men, keen-eared, raised their heads and listened. Someone was coming through the garage. There was a rush of footfalls, soft-soled, on the iron staircase, the door was almost flung open, and Dominic Swayne stood in the entrance. Halliwell must have left the latch of the Yale up. It was, thought Dalgliesh, a curious oversight unless, of course, he had been half-expecting this sudden intrusion. But he made no sign, merely fixing on Swayne his dark unwelcoming gaze before turning again to his mug of coffee and whisky. Swayne must have known that they were there since, presumably, Miss Matlock had let him into the house, but his start of surprise and the tentative embarrassed smile were nicely judged.

"Oh, my God! Sorry, sorry! I seem to have an unlucky habit of bursting in when the police are doing their stuff. Well, I'll leave you to the third degree."

Halliwell said coldly:

"Why not try knocking first?"

But it was to Dalgliesh that Swayne turned:

"I only wanted to tell Halliwell that my sister says I can borrow the Golf tomorrow."

Halliwell said, without moving from his seat:

"You can borrow the Golf without prior notice. You usually do."

Swayne kept his eyes on Dalgliesh.

"That's OK then. Look, I'm here. Is there anything you want to ask me? If so, go ahead."

Massingham had got up from the table and had picked up one of the carved elephants. His voice was carefully devoid of emphasis.

"Just to confirm again that you were here in the house the whole of last evening from the time you arrived, just before seven, till you left for the Raj at half past ten?"

"That's right, Inspector. Clever of you to remember."

"And during that time you didn't leave number sixty-two?"

"Right again. Look, I'm hardly everyone's favourite brother-in-law, I admit, but I had nothing to do with Paul's death. And I don't see why Paul should have resented me so much, unless I reminded him of someone he'd rather not be reminded of. I mean, I don't drug unless someone else is paying, which they so rarely do. I'm comparatively sober. I work when there's work to be had. I admit I bath and eat at his expense occasionally, but I don't see why he should resent that—he's hardly on the bread line— or my having a game of Scrabble with poor Evelyn. No one else bothers to. And I didn't slit his throat for him. I'm not in the least bloodthirsty. I don't think I've got the nerve. I'm not like Halliwell, trained to creep about among the rocks with my face blacked and a knife between my teeth. That's not my idea of amusement."

Massingham put the elephant down. It was like a rejection.

He said:

"You prefer an evening's Scrabble with your lady friend? Who won?"

"Oh, Evelyn won, she usually does. Yesterday she got 'zephyr' on a treble, clever girl. Three hundred and eighty-two points to my two hundred. It's extraordinary how often she picks the high numbers. If she weren't so depressingly honest, I'd suspect her of cheating."

Massingham said:

" 'Zig-zag' would have scored even higher."

"Ah, but there aren't two Zs in Scrabble. I can see that you aren't an addict. You should try it sometime, Inspector. It's excellent for sharpening the wits. Well, if that's all, I'll be off."

Dalgliesh said:

"Not quite all. Tell us about Diana Travers."

Swayne stood for a couple of seconds very still, the bright eyes rapidly blinking. But the shock, if it was shock, was quickly mastered. Dalgliesh could see the muscles of his hands and shoulders relaxing. He said:

"What about her? She's dead."

"We know that. She drowned after a dinner party given by you at the Black Swan. You were there when she died. Tell us about it."

"There's nothing to tell. I mean, you must have read the report of the inquest. And I don't see what it's got to do with Paul. She wasn't his girl or anything like that."

"We didn't suppose that she was."

He shrugged and held out his palms in a parody of resigned reasonableness.

"Well, what do you want to know?"

"Why not begin by telling us why you invited her to the Black Swan."

"No particular reason. Call it a generous impulse. I knew my dear sister was having what she would describe as an intimate dinner party for her birthday, too intimate to invite me, apparently. So I thought I'd organize a little celebration of my own. I was here bringing Barbara my birthday present, and I saw Diana dusting the hall as I left. So I asked her to come along. I picked her up outside Holland Park tube at six thirty and drove her to meet the gang at the Black Swan."

"Where you had dinner."

"Where we had dinner. Do you want the details of the menu?"

"Not unless it's relevant. Suppose you go on from there."

"After dinner we went out to the riverbank and found this punt moored downstream. The rest of the party thought it would be amusing to mess about on the river. Diana and I decided that it would be even more amusing to mess about on the bank. She was pretty high. Drink, not drugs. Then we thought it would be fun to swim out to the punt and bob up beside them."

"Having first taken off your clothes."

"They were already off. Sorry if I shock you."

"And you dived in first."

"Not dived, waded. I never dive into unknown water. Anyway, I struck out with my usual elegant crawl and reached the punt. Then I looked back for Diana. I couldn't see her on the bank, but then, there are quite a few bushes at that spot, Jean Paul trying to make some sort of a garden I suppose, and I thought she might have changed her mind and be dressing. I suppose I was a bit worried, but not frantically worried, if you see what I mean. But I thought I'd better go back and check. And the whole idea of the swim was losing its charm. The water was icy cold and very dark, and the chums hadn't greeted me with quite the enthusiasm I expected. So I let go of the punt and struck back towards the bank. She wasn't there, but her clothes were. So then I really was scared. I called out to the party in the punt but they were rocking about, giggling, and I don't think they heard me. And then they found her. They struck the body with the punt pole just as she surfaced. Pretty ghastly for the girls. They managed to hold her head above water and paddled to the bank, nearly upsetting the punt in the process. I helped drag her out and we tried the usual mouth-to-mouth. It was a god-awful mess. The girls crying and trying to get some clothes on her. Me dripping wet and shivering. Tony forcing his breath into her mouth as if he were pumping up a balloon. Diana lying there, eyes staring, with the water running off her hair and the weeds wrapped round her neck like a green scarf. They made her look decapitated. Erotic in a horrible way. And then one of the girls ran to the restaurant for help and that chef chap came out and took over. He seemed to know what he was doing. But no good. End of Diana. End of jolly evening. End of story."

There was a scrape of wood as Halliwell violently pushed himself up from the table and disappeared swiftly into the kitchen. Swayne looked after him.

"What's he upset about? I was the one who had to look at her. You'd think he'd heard worse things than that."

Neither Dalgliesh nor Massingham spoke and almost immediately Halliwell was back. He was carrying another half bottle of Scotch and set it down. It seemed to Dalgliesh that his face was paler, but he poured himself another tot of whisky with a perfectly steady hand. Swayne glanced at the bottle as if wondering why he wasn't invited to drink, then turned again to Dalgliesh.

"I'll tell you one thing about Diana Travers. She wasn't an actress. I found that out on our drive to the Black Swan. No Equity card. No drama school. No theatrical jargon. No agent. No parts."

"Did she say what her job really was?"

"She said she wanted to be a writer and was collecting material. It was easier to tell people you were on the stage. That way, they never asked why you wanted a temporary job. I can't say I cared one way or the other. I mean, I was taking the girl out to dinner, I wasn't proposing to shack up with her."

"And during the time you were with her on the riverbank, before the swim and when you went back to find her, did you see or hear any other person?"

The blue eyes widened and became so like his sister's that the resemblance was uncanny. He said:

"I don't think so. We were a bit preoccupied, if you get me. You mean, a peeping Tom, someone spying on us? The thought didn't occur to me."

"Let it occur to you now. Were you absolutely alone?"

"We must have been, mustn't we? I mean, who else would be there?"

"Think back. Did you see or hear anything suspicious?"

"I can't say that I did, but then there was all the jolly girlish screaming from the punt. And I don't think I would have seen or heard anything very clearly once I'd waded in and begun swimming. I do seem to remember that I heard Diana diving in after me, but that's what I expected her to do so maybe I imagined it. And there could have been someone watching us, I suppose. In the bushes, maybe. But I didn't see him. Sorry if that's the wrong answer. And sorry for barging in. Oh, by the way, I'll be staying here in the house if you want me. Brotherly consolation for the widow."

He gave a shrug and a smile which seemed bestowed on the room generally rather than anyone in it. Then he was gone. They heard the soft thud of his descending footsteps on the iron staircase. No one made any comment. As they rose to go, Massingham asked his last question. He said:

"We can't be certain yet how Sir Paul and Harry Mack died, but we think the probability is that both were murdered. Have you seen or heard anything in this house or outside it which would give you a suspicion of who might be responsible?"

It was the question they always asked, expected, formal, almost crudely direct. Because of this, it was often the one least likely to elicit the truth.

Halliwell poured himself another whisky. It looked as if he were settling in for a night's hard drinking. Without looking up he said:

"I didn't slit his throat for him. If I knew who had, I'd probably tell you."

Massingham persevered:

"Sir Paul had no enemies as far as you are aware?"

"Enemies?"

Halliwell's smile was nearer a grin. It transformed his swarthy good looks into a mask at once sinister and sardonic, giving force to Swayne's description of him creeping black-faced among the rocks.

"He must have had, mustn't he, sir, being a politician? But that's all over now. Done with. Finished. Like the Major, he's moved out of the gunshot now."

And with that echo of Bunyan, which Dalgliesh suspected might have been a deliberate half-quotation, the interview was at an end.

Halliwell went down with them through the garage and dragged the heavy doors shut behind them. They heard the rasp of the two bolts. The lights in the niches had been switched off and the cobbled yard was in darkness except for twin wall-mounted lights at each end of the garage wall. In the half-darkness the smell of cypress had strengthened, but was overlaid with a scent sicklier and funereal, as if somewhere close was a dustbin of dead and rotting flowers. As they approached the back door to the house the figure of Miss Matlock stepped noiselessly out of the shadows. In the folds of the long dressing-gown she seemed taller, hier-archic, almost graceful in her watching stillness. Dalgliesh wondered how long she had stood silently waiting for them.

He and Massingham followed her in silence through the quiet house. As she turned the key and drew back the bolts of the front door Massingham said:

"That game of Scrabble you played last night with Mr. Swayne. Who won?"

The ploy was deliberately naive, the trap obvious. But her reaction was surprising. In the subdued light of the hall they watched the flush mottle her throat then flare up to crimson her face.

"I did. I got three hundred and eighty-two points in case you should be interested. That game was played, Inspector. You may be used to talking to liars. I'm not one of them."

Her body was rigid with fury, but the clasped hands shook as if they were palsied. Dalgliesh said gently:

"No one is suggesting that you are, Miss Matlock. Thank you for waiting up for us. Good night."

Outside as he unlocked the Rover, Massingham said:

"Now, why should that simple question shake her? Literally."

Dalgliesh had met with it before, the clumsy aggression of women who were both shy and insecure. He wished that he could feel more sorry for her. He said:

"It wasn't particularly subtle, John."

"No sir, it wasn't meant to be. She played that game of Scrabble, all right. The question is, when?"

Dalgliesh took the wheel. He drove away from the house, then drew into a vacant space halfway down Campden Hill Square and rang the Yard. Kate Miskin's answering voice sounded as strong and lively as it had in the early hours of the enquiry.

"I've traced and seen Mrs. Hurrell, sir. She confirms that she did ring the Campden Hill Square house just before eight forty-five to ask for Sir Paul. A man answered. He said: 'Swayne speaking.' Then when she told him what she wanted he handed her over to Miss Matlock. Miss Matlock said that she didn't know where Sir Paul was, and nor did anyone else in the house."

It was, thought Dalgliesh, an odd way for Swayne to answer the telephone when in someone else's house. One might almost believe that he wanted to establish that he was there. He asked:

"Anything from the door-to-door enquiries?"

"Nothing yet, sir, but I've spoken again to the McBrides and Maggie Sullivan. All three are definite about the gush of water from the church drain. Someone was using the sink in the washroom just after eight o'clock. They all agree about the time."

"And the lab?"

"I've had a word with the senior biologist. If they can get the blood samples immediately after the pm, say by late afternoon, they'll set up the electrophoresis overnight. The director has agreed that they can work over the weekend. We should know about the bloodstains by Monday morning."

"No news from the document examiner yet, I suppose. And what about the match end?"

"The document examiner hasn't been able to start on the blotter yet, but he'll give it priority. The usual problems with the match, sir. They'll do an analysis with the SEM and look for print marks, but they're unlikely to be able to say more than that the wood is the usual poplar. They couldn't possibly say that it was from a particular box, and it's too short for a length comparison."

"Right, Kate. We'll call it a day. Better get home. Good night."

"Good night, sir."

As the car slid down Campden Hill Square and turned into Holland Park Avenue Dalgliesh said:

"Halliwell has expensive tastes. That set of the *Notable British Trials* must have cost close on a thousand pounds, unless he collected them volume by volume over the years."

"Not as expensive as Swayne, though, sir. That's a Fellucini jacket he was wearing, silk and linen, silver-crested buttons. They sell for four fifty."

"I'll take your word for it. I wonder why he burst in like that. It was an unconvincing performance. Probably hoping to find out how much Halliwell was telling. It's significant, though, that he did burst in and as if he made a habit of it. And when Halliwell isn't there, he'd have no problem in getting hold of a key or even manipulating the Yale if necessary."

"Is it important, sir, whether he could get into the mews flat?"

"I think so. This murderer was aiming at verisimilitude. There's a copy of Simpson's *Textbook on Forensic Medicine* in Halliwell's bookcase. It's all set out there in Chapter Five with the writer's usual clarity, a table showing the distinction between suicidal and homicidal cuts of the throat. Swayne could have seen it at any time, browsed through it, remembered it. So, too, could anyone else at Campden Hill Square with access to the garage flat, and most easily, of course, Halliwell himself. Whoever slit Berowne's throat knew exactly what effect he was aiming to produce."

Massingham asked:

"But would Halliwell have left the Simpson there for us to find?"

"If other people knew of its existence, to destroy it would be more incriminating than to leave it on the shelf. But Halliwell has to be in the clear if Lady Ursula is telling the truth about those two telephone calls, and I can't see her giving Halliwell an alibi for the murder of her son. Or any other suspect, for that matter."

Massingham said:

"Or Halliwell giving Swayne an alibi unless he had to. There's no love lost there. He despises the man. Incidentally, I knew I'd seen Swayne somewhere before. I've remembered now. He was in that play at the Coningsby Theatre in Camden Town a year ago. *The Garage.* The cast actually constructed a garage on the stage. In the first act they put it up, in the second they knocked it down."

"I thought it was a wedding tent."

"Wrong play, sir. Swayne played the local psychopath, one of the gang who pulled it down. So he must have an Equity card."

"How did he strike you as an actor?"

"Energetic but unsubtle. Not that I'm much of a judge. I prefer films. I only went because Emma was going through her cultural stage. The play was highly symbolic. The garage was supposed to represent Britain, or capitalism, or imperialism, or, maybe, the class struggle. I'm not sure the author knew. You could tell that it was going to be a great critical success. No one spoke a literate line and a week later I couldn't remember a word of the dialogue. There was some fairly energetic fighting in the second act. Swayne knows how to handle himself. Still, kicking in a garage wall isn't the most suitable training for slitting a throat. I can't see Swayne as a killer, not this killer, anyway."

They were both experienced detectives, they knew the importance at this stage of keeping the detection rational, of concentrating on the physical, ascertainable facts. Which of the suspects has the means, the opportunity, the knowledge, the physical strength, the motive? It was unproductive so early in the investigation to begin asking: Has this man the ruthlessness, the nerve, the desperation, the psychological make-up to commit this particular crime? And yet, seduced by the fascination of human personality, they nearly always did.

6
⊠

In the small back bedroom on the second floor of 49 Crowhurst Gardens, Miss Wharton lay rigidly awake and stared into the darkness. Her body, pressed into the hard mattress, felt unnaturally hot and heavy as if weighted with lead. Even to turn in search of greater comfort was too great an effort. She hadn't expected to sleep soundly, but she had gone through her nightly routine with a dogged hope that adhering to these small and comforting rituals would deceive her body into slumber or at least into quietude; the chapter of Scripture prescribed in her book of devotions, the hot milk, the one digestive biscuit, final indulgence of the day. None had worked. The passage from St. Luke's Gospel had been the parable of the good shepherd. It was one of her favourites, but tonight she had read it with a sharpened, perversely questioning mind. What, after all, was a shepherd's job? Only to care for the sheep, to make sure they didn't escape so that they could be branded, sheared and then slaughtered. Without the need for their wool, their flesh, there would be no job for the shepherd.

Long after she had closed her Bible she lay rigid for what seemed an endless night, her mind burrowing and scurrying like a tormented animal. Where was Darren? How was he? Who was making sure that he wasn't lying uncomforted or distressed? He hadn't seemed too affected by the horror of that awful scene, but with a child one never knew. And it was her fault that they were cut off from each other. She should have insisted on knowing where he lived, meeting his mother. He had never spoken of his mother, and when she had asked him he had shrugged and not replied. She hadn't liked to press it. Perhaps she could reach him through the police. But ought she to worry Commander Dalgliesh when he had two murders to solve?

And the word "murder" brought on a new anxiety. There was something she ought to remember but couldn't; something she ought to have told Commander Dalgliesh. He had questioned her briefly, gently, sitting beside her on one of the small chairs in the children's corner of the church, as if uncaring, even unaware, how oddly it suited his tall figure. She had tried to be calm, accurate, matter-of-fact, but she knew there were gaps in her memory, that there was something the horror of the scene had blotted out. Yet what could it be? It was something small, possibly insignificant, but he had said she must tell him every detail, however trivial.

But now another and more immediate worry surfaced. She needed to go to the lavatory. She switched on her bedside light, fumbled for her spectacles and peered at the carriage clock ticking gently on her bedside table. It was only ten past two. There was no hope of waiting until morning. Although she had her own sitting room, bedroom and kitchen, Miss Wharton shared the bathroom with the McGraths in the flat below. The plumbing was old-fashioned, and if she had to use the lavatory in the night, Mrs. McGrath would complain next morning. The alternative was to use her chamber pot, but that had to be emptied and the whole morning would be dominated by her anxious listenings to know when it would be safe to carry it down to the lavatory without meeting Mrs. McGrath's bold, contemptuous eyes. Once she had bumped into Billy McGrath on the stairs with the covered pot in her hand. The memory of it still burned her cheeks. But she would have to use it. The night was still so quiet she couldn't face creeping down to shatter its peace with cascades of swirling water, those long-drawn-out shakes and grumbles of the pipes.

Miss Wharton didn't know why the McGraths disliked her so much, why her inoffensive gentility should be so provocative to them. She tried to keep out of their way, although this wasn't easy when they shared the same front door, the same narrow entrance passage. She had explained Darren to them on his first visit to her room by telling them that his mother worked at St. Matthew's. The lie, blurted out in panic, had seemed to satisfy them, and she had subsequently put it resolutely out of her mind since she could hardly include it in her weekly confession and Darren was so swift in his comings and goings that there was little risk they would question him. It was as if he sensed that the McGraths were enemies, better avoided than encountered. She attempted to propitiate Mrs. McGrath with a desperate over-politeness and even by small acts of kindness: taking her milk bottles in out of the sun in summer, leaving a jar of homemade jam or chutney on her doorstep when she came home from St. Matthew's Christmas Fair. But these signs of weakness seemed only to increase their enmity, and she knew in her heart that there was nothing to be done about it. People, like countries, needed someone weaker and more vulnerable than themselves to bully and despise. This was what the world was like. As she gently dragged the chamber pot from under the bed and crouched over it, muscles tense, trying to regulate and quieten the flow, she thought again how much she would have liked to have a cat. But the garden, twenty yards of unmown grass, hummocky as a field, surrounded by an almost obliterated border of overgrown rose bushes and torn, unflowering shrubs, belonged to the bottom flat. The McGraths would never let her have use of it, and it wouldn't be fair to keep a cat cooped up all night and day in her own two small rooms.

Miss Wharton had been taught to fear in her childhood, and it isn't a lesson children can ever unlearn. Her father, a schoolmaster in an elementary school, had managed to maintain a precarious tolerance in the classroom by a compensating tyranny in his own home. His wife and three children were all afraid of him. But shared fear hadn't brought the children closer. When, with his usual irrationality, he would single out one child for his displeasure, the siblings would see in each other's shamed eyes their relief at this reprieve. They learned to lie to protect themselves, and were beaten for lying. They learned to be afraid, and were punished for cowardice. And yet, Miss Wharton kept on her side table a silver-framed photograph of both her parents. She never blamed her father for past or present unhappiness. She had learned her lesson well. She blamed herself.

She was now virtually alone in the world. Her younger brother, John, to whom she had been closest, more psychologically robust than his siblings, had fared best. But John had been burnt alive in the rear gun turret of his Lancaster bomber the day before his nineteenth birthday. Miss Wharton, mercifully ignorant of the steel-bound inferno in which John had screamed away his life, had been able to prettify his death into the peaceful picture of the single German bullet finding the heart, the young, pale-faced warrior being gently wafted earthwards, his hands still resting on his gun. Her older brother, Edmund, had emigrated to Canada after the war and now, divorced and childless, worked as a clerk in some small northern town whose name she could never remember since he so seldom wrote.

She slid the chamber pot back under the bed, then put on her dressing-gown and padded on naked feet across the narrow hall and into her front sitting room to the single window. The house was very quiet. Under the lights the street shone ebony black between the banks of parked cars. Even with her window closed she could hear the muted roar of night traffic along the Harrow Road. It was a night of low cloud, stained red with the glare of the restless city. Sometimes it seemed to Miss Wharton, looking out into that eerie half-darkness, that London was built on coal and was perpetually smouldering, that Hell, unrecognized, was all around her. To the right, silhouetted against the hectic glow, was the campanile of St. Matthew's. Usually it gave her comfort. Here was a place where she was known, valued for the small services she could give, kept busily occupied, solaced, shriven and at home. But now the thin, alien tower, stark against the ruddy sky, was a symbol of horror and death. And her twice-weekly walk to St. Matthew's along the towpath: how could she face that now? The path had seemed to her mysteriously exempt from the terrors of the city streets, except for those brief stretches of dark tunnel. Even on the darkest mornings she had walked there in blessed freedom from fear. And in recent months she had had Darren. But now Darren was gone, safety was gone, the towpath would always be slippery with imagined blood. As she crept back to bed her mind journeyed across the roofs to the Little Vestry. It would be empty now, of course. The police would have taken the bodies away. The black windowless van had been parked there ready even before she had left. There would be nothing now but the bloodstains browning on the carpet—or would that, too, have been taken away? Nothing but emptiness and darkness and the smell of death, except in the Lady Chapel, where the sanctuary light would still be gleaming. Was she to lose even this? she wondered. Was this what murder did to the innocent? Took away the people they loved, loaded their minds with terror, left them bereft and unfriended under a smouldering sky.

7

⊠

It was after eleven thirty when Kate Miskin clanged the lift door behind her and unlocked the security lock of her flat. She had wanted to wait at the Yard until Dalgliesh and Massingham had returned from seeing Halliwell. But AD had suggested that it was time she called it a day and there was little more that she or anyone could do until the morning. If AD was right, and Berowne and Harry Mack had both been murdered, she and Massingham could be regularly working a sixteen-hour day, sometimes longer. It wasn't a possibility she feared; she had done it before. As she switched on the light and double-locked the door behind her, it struck her as odd, perhaps even reprehensible, that she should be hoping that AD was right. Then almost immediately she absolved herself with the universal and comforting platitude. Both Berowne and Harry were dead; nothing could bring them back. And if Sir Paul Berowne hadn't slit his own throat, then the case promised to be fascinating as well as important, and not only to her personally, to her chance of promotion. There had been a certain amount of opposition to the setting up in C1 of a special squad to investigate serious crimes which were thought to be politically or socially sensitive, and she could name a number of senior officers who wouldn't be sorry if this, their first case, collapsed into a commonplace tragedy of murder followed by suicide.

She entered her flat, as always, with a sense of satisfaction, of coming home. She had lived in Charles Shannon House for just over two years; buying the flat on a carefully calculated mortgage had been the first step in a planned upward progress, even eventually to one of the converted warehouses on the Thames—wide windows overlooking the river, huge rooms with their bare rafters, a distant view of Tower Bridge. But this was a beginning. She rejoiced in it and sometimes had to prevent herself from prowling round, touching the walls, the furniture, to reassure herself of its reality.

The flat, a long sitting room with a narrow iron balcony running its whole width, two small bedrooms, a kitchen and a bathroom and separate lavatory, was on the top floor of a Victorian block just off Holland Park Avenue. It had been built in the early 1860s to provide studios for artists and designers in the growing arts and crafts movement, and a couple of blue commemorative plaques over the door testified to its historic interest. But architecturally it was without merit, an aberration of yellowish London brick set amidst the surrounding Regency elegance, immensely tall, castellated and incongruous as a Victorian castle. The soaring walls, broken by numerous carved and oddly proportioned windows and criss-crossed with iron fire escapes, rose to a roof topped with rows of chimney pots between which sprouted a variety of television aerials, some long defunct.

It was the only place she had ever thought of as home. She was illegitimate and had been brought up by her maternal grandmother, who had been nearly sixty when she was born. Her unmarried mother had died within days of her birth and was known to her only as a thin, serious face in the front row of a school photograph, a face in which she could recognize none of her own strong features. Her grandmother had never spoken of her father, and she had assumed that her mother had never divulged his identity. She was fatherless even in name, but it had long ceased to worry her if it ever had. Apart from the inevitable fantasies of early childhood when she had pictured her father seeking her out, she hadn't known any urgent need to discover her roots. Two half-remembered lines of Shakespeare which had met her eyes when she had casually opened the book in the school library had become for her the philosophy by which she intended to live.

What matters it what went before or after,
Now with myself I will begin and end.

She hadn't chosen to furnish her flat in a period style. She had little feeling for the past; all her life had been a striving to struggle free of it, to make a future fashioned to her own need for order, security, success. So she had lived for a couple of months with nothing but a folding table, one chair and a mattress on the floor, until she had saved the money to buy the austere, well-designed modern furniture she liked: the sofa and two easy chairs in real leather, the dining table and four chairs in polished elm, the fitted bookcase completely covering one wall, the sleek, professionally designed kitchen which held the minimum of necessary utensils and crockery but nothing superfluous. The flat was her private world kept inviolate from colleagues in the police. Only her lover was admitted, and when Alan had first stepped through the door, uncurious, unthreatening, carrying as always his plastic bag of books, even his gentle presence had seemed for a moment a dangerous intrusion.

She poured herself an inch of whisky, mixed it with water, then unlocked the security lock of the narrow door which led from the sitting room to the iron balcony. The air rushed in, fresh and clean. She closed the door, then stood, glass in hand, leaning back against the brickwork and staring out eastward over London. A low bank of heavy cloud had absorbed the glare of the city's lights and lay, palely crimson, like a colourwash carefully laid against the richer blue-black of night. There was a light breeze, just strong enough to stir the branches of the great limes lining Holland Park Avenue and to twitch the television aerials which sprouted like frail exotic fetishes from the patterned roofs fifty feet below. To the south the trees of Holland Park were a black curdle against the sky, and ahead the spire of St. John's Church gleamed like some distant mirage. It was one of the pleasures of these moments, seeing how the spire appeared to move, sometimes so close that she felt that she would only have to stretch out a hand to feel its harshly textured stones, sometimes, like tonight, as distant and insubstantial as a vision. Far below to her right under the high arc lights the avenue ran due west, greasy as a molten river, bearing its unending cargo of cars, trucks and red buses. This, she knew, had once been the old Roman road leading westward straight out of Londinium; its constant grinding roar came to her only faintly, like the surge of a distant sea.

Whatever the time of year, except in the worst of winter weather, this was her nightly routine. She would pour one whisky, Bell's, and take out the glass for these minutes of contemplation, rather, she thought, like a caged prisoner reassuring herself that the city was still there. But her small flat was no prison, rather the physical affirmation of a freedom hard won and jealously maintained. She had escaped from the estate, from her grandmother, from that meanly proportioned, dirty, noisy flat on the seventh floor of a post-war tower block, Ellison Fairweather House, monument to a local councillor passionately dedicated, like most of his kind, to the destruction of small neighbourhood streets and the erection of twelve-storey monuments to civic pride and sociological theory. She had escaped from the shouting, the graffiti, the broken lifts, the stink of urine. She remembered the first evening of her escape, the eighth of June over two years ago. She had stood where she stood now and poured her whisky like a libation, seeing the momentary arc of liquid light as it fell between the grating, saying aloud "Sod you, Councillor Bloody Fairweather. Welcome, freedom."

And now she was really on her way. If she made a success of this new job, anything—well, almost anything—was possible. It was perhaps not surprising that AD would choose at least one woman for his squad. But he wasn't the man to make routine gestures to feminism, or to any other fashionable causes, come to that. He had selected her because he needed a woman in the squad and because he knew her record, knew that he could rely on her to do a good job. Looking out over London, she felt confidence surge through her veins strong and sweet as the first conscious breath of morning. The world stretched out below her was one she was at home in, part of that dense, exciting conglomerate of urban villages which made up the Metropolitan Police district. She pictured it stretching away over Notting Hill Gate, over Hyde Park and the curve of the river, past the towers of Westminster and Big Ben, briefly over that anomaly the patch of the City of London Police, then on to the eastern suburbs to the boundary with the Essex Constabulary. She knew almost to a yard where that boundary lay. This was how she saw the capital, patterned in police areas, districts, divisions and sub-divisions. And immediately below her lay Notting Hill, that tough, diverse, richly cosmopolitan village where she had been posted after leaving the preliminary training school. She could remember every sound, colour, smell as strongly as on that torrid August night eight years ago when it had happened, the moment she knew that her choice had been right and that this was her job.

She had been on foot patrol in Notting Hill with Terry Read on the hottest August night in living memory. A boy, almost squealing with excitement, had rushed at them and, gibbering, had pointed to a nearby tenement. She saw it again: the huddle of frightened neighbours at the foot of the stairs, faces gleaming with sweat, stained shirts stuck to steaming bodies, a smell of hot, unwashed humanity. And above the whispers a raucous voice from upstairs shouting its unintelligible protest. The boy said:

"He got a knife, miss. George tried to get it but he threatened him. That's right, ain't it, George?"

George, white, small, weasel-like in the corner:

"Yeah, that's right."

"And he's got Mabelle in with him, Mabelle and the kid."

A woman whispered:

"Blessed Jesus, he's got the kid in there."

They had fallen back to let her through, herself and Terry. She asked:

"What's his name?"

"Leroy."

"His other name?"

"Price. Leroy Price."

The hallway was dark, the room itself, unlocked since the lock was smashed, was even darker. The harsh glare filtered through a torn piece of carpet nailed over the window. She could see dimly the stained double mattress on the floor, a folding table, two chairs, one on its side. There was a smell of vomit, of sweat, of beer overlaid with the strong oily smell of fish and chips. Against the wall cowered a woman, a child in her arms.

She said gently:

"It's all right, Mr. Price. I'll have that knife. You don't mean to hurt them. She's your kid. You wouldn't want to hurt either of them. I know what it is, it's too hot, and you've had enough. We all have."

She had seen it before on the estate as well as on the beat, that moment when the burden of frustration, hopelessness and misery suddenly became too heavy and the mind exploded into an anarchy of protest. He had indeed had too much. Too many unpaid, unpayable bills, too much worry, too many demands, too much frustration and, of course, too much drink. She had walked up to him not speaking, calmly meeting his eyes, holding out her hand for the knife. She wasn't aware of fear, only the fear that Terry might come crashing in. There was no sound; the group at the foot of the stairs was frozen into silence, the street outside stilled in one of those strange moments of quietness which sometimes fall on even the rowdiest quarters of London. She could hear only her own quiet breathing and his harsh grating breaths. Then with a wild sob he had dropped the knife and flung himself towards her. She had held him, murmuring as she might to a child, and it was over.

She had overplayed Terry's part in the affair, and he had let her. But old Moll Green, never absent when there was a chance of excitement and the hope of bloodshed, had been one of those waiting, bright-eyed, at the foot of the stairs. The following Tuesday Terry had busted her for carrying hash, admittedly with small provocation, but he was behind with his self-imposed weekly quota of arrests. Moll, motivated either by an unexpected surge of female solidarity or by a revulsion against men in general and Terry in particular, had given her own version of the incident to the station sergeant. Little was subsequently said to Kate, but enough to make it plain that the truth was known, and that her reticence had done her no harm. Now she wondered briefly what had happened to that man, to Mabelle, to the child. For the first time it struck her as odd that, the incident over, her report made, she had never given any of them another thought.

She came in, closed the door and drew the heavy linen curtains, then went to telephone Alan. They had planned to see a film the following night, but this would no longer be possible. It was pointless to make any plans until the case was finished. He took the news calmly, as he always did when she had to break a date. One of the many things she liked about him was that he never fussed.

He said:

"It looks then as if dinner next Thursday may not be possible either."

"We may be through by then, but it's unlikely. Still, keep it free and if I have to I'll ring and cancel."

"Well, good luck with the case. I hope it won't be love's labour's lost."

"What?"

"Sorry. Berowne is the name of an attendant lord in Shakespeare. It's an unusual and interesting name."

"It was an unusual and interesting death. See you next Thursday at about eight."

"Unless you find it necessary to cancel. Good-bye, Kate."

She thought that she detected a trace of irony in his voice, then decided that tiredness had made her imaginative. It was the first time he had wished her good luck with a case, but he had still asked no questions. He was, she thought, as punctiliously discreet about her job as she was herself. Or was it merely that he didn't care? Before he put the receiver down she said quickly:

"That attendant lord, what happened to him?"

"He loved a woman called Rosalind, but she told him to go and nurse the sick. So he went off to jest a twelvemonth in a hospital."

There was hardly, she thought, much inspiration to be gained from that. She smiled as she put down the receiver. It was a pity about next Thursday's dinner. But there would be other dinners, other evenings. He would come when she rang and asked him. He always did.

She suspected that she had met Alan Scully just in time. Her early sexual education in the concrete underpasses of the high-rise flats and behind the bicycle sheds of her north London comprehensive school, the mixture of excitement, danger and disgust, had been a good preparation for life but a poor preparation for loving. Most of the boys had been less intelligent than she. This might not have mattered to her if they had had looks or some wit. She was amused, but also a little dismayed, to realize by the time she was eighteen that she was thinking of men as they were alleged so often to regard women, an occasional sexual or social diversion, but too unimportant to be allowed to interfere with the serious business of life: passing her A-levels, planning her career, getting away from Ellison Fairweather buildings. She found that she could enjoy sex while despising the source of her pleasure. It wasn't, she knew, an honest basis for any relationship. And then, two years ago, she had met Alan. His flat in a narrow street behind the British Museum had been burgled, and it was she who had arrived with the fingerprint and scene-of-crime officers. He told her that he worked in a theological library in Bloomsbury and that he was an amateur collector of books of early Victorian sermons—it seemed to her an extraordinary choice—and that two of the most valuable volumes had been taken. They had never been recovered, and she sensed from the calm resignation with which he answered her questions that he had hardly expected that they would be. His flat, small, cluttered, a repository for books rather than a space for living, was unlike any place she had ever seen, as he was unlike any man. She had had to make a return visit, and they had spent about an hour chatting over coffee. He had then asked her, simply, to go with him to see a Shakespearean production at the National Theatre.

It was less than a month after that evening that they first went to bed together and he had demolished one of her firmly held assumptions, that intellectuals weren't interested in sex. He was both interested in and very good at it. They had settled into a comfortable, apparently mutually satisfactory, loving friendship in which each saw the other's job, without resentment or envy, as foreign territory, its speech and mores so far removed from any possibility of comprehension that they rarely spoke of it. Kate knew that he was intrigued, not so much by her lack of religious faith as by the fact that she apparently had no intellectual curiosity about its diverse and fascinating manifestations. She sensed, too, although he never said so, that he thought that her literary education had been neglected. She could, if challenged, quote angry modern verse about unemployed youth in the inner cities and the subjection of the blacks in South Africa, but this he saw as a poor substitute for Donne, Shakespeare, Keats or Eliot. She, for her part, saw him as innocent, so deficient in the skills necessary for survival in the urban jungle that it amazed her that he should walk with such apparent indifference through its perils. Apart from the burglary, which remained mysterious, nothing untoward ever seemed to happen to him or, if it did, he failed to notice. It amused her to ask him to recommend books, and she persevered with those which, diffidently, he produced for her. At present her bedtime reading was Elizabeth Bowen. The life of her heroines, their private incomes, their charming houses in St. John's Wood, their uniformed parlourmaids and formidable aunts, above all the delicate sensitivity of their emotions amazed her. "Not enough washing up, that's their trouble," she told Allen, having in mind the author as well as her characters. But it interested her that she needed to go on reading.

And now it was close to midnight. She was both too excited and too tired to feel much hunger, but she supposed that she ought to cook something light, perhaps an omelette, before she went to bed. But first she switched on the answerphone. And with the first sound of the familiar voice, euphoria died to be replaced by a confusion of guilt, resentment and depression. It was her grandmother's social worker. There were three messages, at two-hour intervals, controlled professional patience gradually giving way to frustration and, finally, an irritation that was close to hostility. Her grandmother, weary of incarceration in her seventh-floor flat, had gone out to the post office to collect her pension and had come back to find that the window had been smashed and an attempt made to force the door. It was the third such incident in less than a month. Mrs. Miskin was now too apprehensive to go out. Would Kate please ring the local authority social services department as soon as she got in, or, if it was after five thirty, ring her grandmother direct. It was urgent.

It always was, she thought wearily. And this was a ridiculously late hour at which to ring. But it couldn't wait until morning. Her grandmother wouldn't sleep until she had rung. Her call was answered after the first burr, and she guessed that the old lady had been sitting waiting by the telephone.

"Oh, there you are. Fine time to ring. Nearly bloody midnight. Mrs. Mason's been trying to get you."

"I know. Are you all right, Gran?"

"Course I'm not all right. Bloody hell, I'm not. When are you coming round?"

"I'll try to look in some time tomorrow, but it won't be easy. I'm in the middle of a case."

"Better come at three o'clock. Mrs. Mason said she'll look in at three. She wants to see you 'specially. Three o'clock, mind."

"Gran, that's just not possible."

"How'm I goin' to get my shopping, then? I'm not leaving this flat alone, I tell you that."

"There should be enough in the freezer for at least another four days."

"I don't fancy that made-up muck. I told you before."

"Can't you ask Mrs. Khan? She's always so helpful."

"No I can't. She don't go out now, not unless her husband's with her, not since that lot from the National Front were up this way. Besides, it's not fair. More than enough trouble luggin' up her own stuff. The kids have broken the bloody lift again, in case you didn't know."

"Gran, is the window mended?"

"Oh, they've been and mended the window." Her grandmother's voice suggested that this was no more than an unimportant detail. She added: "You gotta get me out of this place."

"I'm trying, Gran. You're on the waiting list for a one-person flat in one of those blocks with a warden, sheltered housing. You know that."

"I don't need any bloody warden. I ought to be with my own kith and kin. See you tomorrow then at three o'clock. Mind you come. Mrs. Mason wants to see you."

She put down the receiver.

Kate thought: Oh God, I can't cope with this again, not now, not just at the beginning of a new case.

She told herself, with angry self-justification, that she wasn't irresponsible, that she did what she could. She had bought her grandmother a new refrigerator topped with a small freezer and visited every Sunday to stock it with meals for the week ahead, only, more often than not, to be met with the familiar complaint:

"I can't eat that fancy stuff. I want to do my own shopping. I want to get out of here."

She had paid for a telephone to be installed and had taught her grandmother not to be afraid of it. She had liaised with the local authority and arranged for a weekly visit from a home help to clean the flat. She would willingly have cleaned it herself if her grandmother would have tolerated the interference. She would take any trouble, spend any money, to avoid taking her grandmother to live with her in Charles Shannon House. But that, she knew, was what the old lady, in alliance with her social worker, was inexorably pressing her to accept. And she couldn't do it. She couldn't give up her freedom, Alan's visits, the spare room where she did her painting, her privacy and peace at the end of the day for an old woman's impedimenta, the ceaseless noise of her television, the mess, the smell of old age, of failure, the smell of Ellison Fairweather House, of childhood, of the past. And now, more than ever, it was impossible. Now, with her first case with the new squad, she needed to be free.

She was seized with a spurt of envy and resentment against Massingham. Even if he had a dozen difficult and demanding relatives, no one would expect him to have to cope. And if she did have to take time off from the job, he would be the first to point out that, when the going got really tough, you couldn't rely on a woman.

8
⊠

In her bedroom on the second floor Barbara Berowne lay back on her bank of pillows and stared ahead at the television screen mounted on the wall opposite her uncurtained four-poster. She was waiting for the late-night movie, but had switched on the set as soon as she had got into bed, and was now tuned to the last ten minutes of a political discussion. She had turned down the sound so low that she could hear nothing, but she still gazed intently at the restless mouths as if she were lip-reading. She remembered how Paul's mouth had tightened with disapproval when he had first seen the television set, mounted on its swivel, obtrusively overlarge, spoiling the wall and dwarfing into insignificance the two Cotman watercolours of Norwich Cathedral each side of it. But he had said nothing, and she had told herself defiantly that she didn't care. But now she could watch the late film without being uneasily aware that he was there in the next room, perhaps lying sleepless in rigid disapproval, hearing the muted screams and gunfire like the noisy manifestations of their own subtler, undeclared warfare.

He had disliked, too, her untidiness, an unconscious protest against the impersonality, the obsessive neatness of the rest of the house. In the light of her bedside lamp she gazed untroubled over the muddle in the room, the clothes strewn where she had dropped them—the sheen of her satin dressing-gown thrown across the foot of the bed, the grey skirt splayed fan-like over a chair, her pants lying like a pale shadow on the carpet, her brassiere hanging by one strap from the dressing table. What an indecent, silly garment it looked, thus casually discarded; so precisely shaped and moulded and looking surgical, for all its lace and delicacy. But Mattie would tidy up her things in the morning, gather up her underclothes for washing, hang jackets and skirts in the wardrobe. And she would lie with the breakfast tray on her knees and watch; then get up, bath, dress and face the world, as always immaculate.

It had been Anne Berowne's room and Barbara had moved into it after their marriage. Paul had suggested that they might change bedrooms, but she hadn't seen why she should sleep in a smaller, inferior room, deprived of the view of the square garden, simply because this had been Anne's bed. First it had been Anne's room, then it was Paul's and hers, then it was hers alone, but always with the knowledge that he was sleeping next door. And now it was hers absolutely. She remembered the afternoon when they had first stood in the bedroom together after their marriage, his voice so formal that she had hardly recognized it. He could have been showing round a prospective purchaser.

"You may care to choose different pictures; there are some in the small salon. Anne liked watercolours and the light here is good for them, but you don't have to keep them."

She hadn't cared about the pictures, which had seemed to her rather dull, insignificant English landscapes by painters Paul seemed to think she ought to recognize. She still didn't care, not even enough to change them. But the bedroom had, from her first possession, taken on a different personality: softer, more luxurious, scented and feminine. And gradually it had become as cluttered as an indiscriminately stocked antique shop. She had gone round the house and moved up to her room the items of furniture, the oddly assorted objects which had taken her fancy, as if obsessively raping the house, leaving no space for those rejected but insidious ghosts. A Regency two-handled vase under a glass dome filled with multicoloured flowers intricately devised from shells, a gilt-bronze Tudor wood cabinet decorated with porcelain ovals of shepherds and shepherdesses, a bust of John Soane on a marble pedestal, a collection of eighteenth-century snuff boxes, taken from their showcase and now casually littering her dressing table. But there were still ghosts, living ghosts, voices on the air which no object, however desired, had power to exorcise. Propped against the scented pillows she was back in her childhood bed, a twelve-year-old lying rigid and sleepless, hands clutching the bedclothes. Snatches of endless argument half-heard over weeks and months, then only partly understood, had come together into a coherent whole, refined by her imagination and now unforgettable. First her mother's voice:

"I thought you'd want custody of the children. You're their father."

"And leave you free of responsibility to enjoy yourself in California? Oh no, my dear, you were the one who wanted children, you take them. I suppose Frank didn't bargain for two stepchildren? Well, he's got them. I hope he likes them."

"They're English. Their place is here."

"What did you tell him? That you were coming without encumbrances? A little shop-soiled, darling, but unencumbered? Their place is with their mother. Even a bitch has some maternal instincts. You take them or I fight the divorce."

"My God, they're your children. Don't you care? Don't you love them?"

"I might have done if you'd let me and if they'd been less like you. As it is, I'm frankly indifferent. You want freedom, so do I."

"All right, we'll share. I'll take Barbie, you have Dicco. A boy's place is with his father."

"Then we're in a difficulty. You'd better consult the father—that is, if you know which one it was. By all means let him have Dicco. I won't stand in his way. If there was anything of me in that boy I'd have recognized it. He's grotesque."

"My God, Donald, you bastard!"

"Oh no, my dear, I'm not the bastard in this family."

She thought: I won't listen, I won't remember, I won't think about it, and pressed the volume button, letting the rancorous voices batter at her ears. She didn't hear the door open, but suddenly there was an oblong of pale light and Dicco stood there, wrapped in his knee-length dressing-gown, his springing hair a tangled halo. He stood watching her in silence, then moved barefooted across the room, and the bedsprings bounced as he settled himself close against her. He said:

"Can't you sleep?"

She turned off the set, feeling the familiar twinge of guilt.

"I was thinking about Sylvia and Father."

"Which one? We've had so many."

"The first. Our proper father."

"Our proper father? Our improper father. I wonder if he's dead yet. Cancer was too good for him. Don't think about them, think about the money. That's always a comfort. Think about being free, your own person. Think how well you always look in black. You aren't frightened, are you?"

"No, of course not. There's nothing to be frightened about. Dicco, go back to bed."

"His bed. You knew that, didn't you? You know where I'm sleeping. In his bed."

"Mattie won't like that, nor will Lady Ursula. Why couldn't you sleep in the spare room? Or go back to Bruno?"

"Bruno doesn't want me in the flat. He never did. There isn't room. And I wasn't comfortable. You want me to be comfortable, surely? And I'm getting a little tired of Bruno. My place is here. I'm your brother. This is your house now. You're not being very welcoming, Barbie. I thought you'd want me near you, in case you wanted to talk in the night, confide, confess. Come on, Barbie, confess. Who do you think killed them?"

"How do I know? Someone broke in, I suppose, a thief, another tramp, someone who wanted to steal the church collection. I don't want to talk about it."

"Is that what the police think?"

"I suppose so. I don't know what they think."

"Then I can tell you. They think it was an odd church for a thief to choose. I mean, what was there worth stealing?"

"There are things on the altar, aren't there? Candlesticks, a cross. There were in the church where I was married."

"I wasn't there when you were married, Barbie. You didn't invite me, remember."

"Paul wanted a quiet wedding, Dicco. What does it matter?"

And that, she thought, was another thing Paul had cheated her out of. She had imagined a grand wedding, herself floating up the aisle of St. Margaret's Westminster, the sheen of white satin, a veil like a cloud, the flowers, the crowds, the photographers. Instead he had suggested a registrar's office and when she had protested had insisted on their local parish church and the quietest of ceremonies, almost as if the wedding were something to be ashamed of, something furtive and indecent.

Dicco's voice came to her in a low insinuating whisper:

"But they don't keep them on the altar any more, not at night. Crosses and candlesticks, they lock them away. Churches are dark, empty. No silver, no gold, no lights. Nothing. Do you suppose that's when their God comes down from His cross and walks about, goes up to the altar and finds that it's only a wooden table with a piece of fancy cloth pinned round it?"

She wriggled under the bedclothes.

"Don't be silly, Dicco. Go to bed."

He leaned forward, and the face so like hers and yet so different gleamed within inches of her eyes, so that she could actually see the sheen of sweat on his brow and smell the wine on his breath.

"That nurse, Theresa Nolan, the one who killed herself. Was Paul the father of her baby?"

"Of course not. Why does everyone go on about Theresa Nolan?"

"Who goes on about her? Did the police ask about her?"

"I can't remember. I think they asked why she left. Something like that. I don't want to think about it."

His soft, indulgent laugh was like a conspiracy.

"Barbie, you've got to think. You can't go through life not thinking about things just because they're inconvenient or unpleasant. It was his child, wasn't it? That's what your husband was up to while you were cavorting with your lover, fucking his mother's nurse. And that other girl, Diana Travers, the one who drowned. What was she doing in this house?"

"You know what she was doing. Helping Mattie."

"A dangerous occupation, though, isn't it, working for your husband? Look, if someone did murder Paul, it was someone very clever and cunning; someone who knew he was there in that church; someone who knew he would find a cut-throat razor ready to hand; someone with the nerve to take one enormous risk; someone used to cutting human flesh. Do you know someone like that, Barbie? Do you? It's lucky, isn't it, that you and Stephen have an alibi."

"You have an alibi, too."

"And Mattie, of course. And Lady Ursula. And Halliwell. It's a bit suspicious, all these iron-clad alibis. What about Sarah?"

"I haven't spoken to her."

"Well, let's hope she hasn't an alibi too, otherwise the police will begin to scent conspiracy. When you rang to tell me that he was going to chuck you, I said that it would be all right. Well, it is all right. I said not to worry about the money. Well, you don't have to worry. It's all yours."

"Not so very much."

"Come off it, Barbie, enough. The house to begin with, that must be worth a cool million. And he was insured, wasn't he? Was there a suicide clause? That would be awkward."

"Mr. Farrell said that there wasn't. I asked."

Again that soft inward laugh, something between a grunt and a giggle:

"So you actually got round to asking about the insurance! You don't waste time, do you? And that's what the lawyers think, is it? That Paul killed himself?"

"Lawyers never say. Mr. Farrell told me not to talk to the police unless he was there."

"The family won't want it to be suicide; they'd rather he was murdered. And perhaps he was. If he'd wanted to kill himself, why didn't he use the gun? His brother's gun. A man doesn't cut his throat if he's got a gun. And he had ammo, too, didn't he?"

"Ammo?"

"Bullets. Where is the gun? Still in his safe?"

"No. I don't know where it is."

"What do you mean you don't know? Have you looked?"

"Yesterday after he'd left. Not for the gun, I wanted to look for some papers, his will. I opened the safe and it wasn't there."

"Are you sure?"

"Of course I'm sure. It's a very small safe."

"And you didn't tell the police, naturally. It wouldn't be easy to explain why you wanted to take a look at your husband's will just a few hours before he so conveniently died."

"I haven't told anyone. How did you know about the gun, anyway?"

"My God, Barbie, you are extraordinary! Your husband has his throat slit, his gun is missing and you tell no one."

"I expect he got rid of it. Anyway, what does it matter? He didn't shoot himself. Dicco, go to bed. I'm tired."

"But you aren't frightened? It's because you know who's taken it, don't you? You know, or you suspect. Who was it, Lady Ursula, Halliwell, Sarah, your lover?"

"Of course I don't know! Dicco, leave me alone. I'm tired. I don't want to talk any more. I want to sleep."

Her eyes brimmed with tears. It was unfair of him to upset her like this. She felt an immense sorrow for herself, widowed, alone, vulnerable. And pregnant. Lady Ursula didn't want her to tell anyone about the baby yet, not the police, not Dicco. But he would have to know sometime. Everyone would. And they ought to know so that they could look after her, see that she wasn't worried. Paul would have looked after her, but Paul wasn't here. And she had only told him about the baby yesterday morning. Yesterday. But she wouldn't think about yesterday, not now, not ever again. And the film was due to begin, a Hitchcock revival, and she had always liked Hitchcock. It wasn't fair of Dicco to come in, badgering her, making her remember.

He smiled and patted her on the head as he would a dog, and then he was gone. She waited until the door was closed and she could be certain he wouldn't reappear, then she pressed the TV button. The screen glowed into light and the credits for the previous programme began to roll. She was in time. She settled more comfortably against her pillows, keeping the sound low so that he shouldn't hear.

9
⊠

Massingham had hung about at the Yard longer than was strictly necessary and it was a minute to midnight by the time he drove up to the villa in St. Petersburgh Place. But the downstairs light was still on; his father hadn't yet gone up to bed. He turned the key in the lock as quietly as possible and pushed open the door as stealthily as if he were making an illegal entrance. But it was no good. His father must have been waiting for the noise of the car. Almost at once the door of the small front sitting room opened and Lord Dungannon shuffled out. The words "slippered pantaloon" fell into Massingham's mind, bringing with them the familiar dragging weight of pity, irritation and guilt.

His father said:

"Oh, here you are then, my dear boy. Purves has just brought in the grog tray. Would you care to join me?"

His father never used to call him my dear boy. The words sounded false, over-rehearsed, ridiculous. And his answering voice struck the same note of embarrassed insincerity.

"No thank you, Father. I'd better get up. It's been a tiring day. We're working on the Berowne case."

"Of course. Berowne. She was Lady Ursula Stollard before she married. Your Aunt Margaret was presented in the same year. But she must be over eighty. It can't have been unexpected."

"It's not Lady Ursula who's dead, Father. It's her son."

"But I thought Hugo Berowne was killed in Northern Ireland."

"Not Hugo, Father. Paul."

"Paul." His father seemed to contemplate the word, then said:

"Then I must, of course, write to Lady Ursula. Poor woman. If you're sure you won't come in . . ." His voice, which since April had become the quaver of an old man, broke off. But Massingham was already bounding up the stairs. Halfway along the landing he paused and glanced down over the banisters expecting to see his father shuffling back into the sitting room to his solitude and his whisky. But the old man was still there, gazing up at him with what seemed almost indecent longing. In the strong light from the hall lamp he saw clearly what the last five months had done to the craggy Massingham features. The flesh seemed to have slipped from the bones so that the beaked nose cleft the skin sharp as a knife edge while the jowls hung in slack, mottled pouches like the flesh of a plucked fowl. The flaming Massingham hair was bleached and faded now to the colour and texture of straw. He thought: He looks as archaic as a Rowlandson drawing. Old age makes caricatures of us all. No wonder we dread it.

Mounting the short flight of stairs to his flat, he was caught in the same old muddle. It really was becoming intolerable. He had to get away and soon. But how? Apart from a brief spell in the Section House, he had lived in his separate rooms in his parents' house ever since he had joined the police. While his mother had been alive, the arrangement had suited him admirably. His parents, absorbed in each other as they had been ever since his father's late marriage in his mid-forties, had left him alone, hardly noticing whether he was in or out. The shared front door had been an inconvenience but nothing more. He had lived comfortably, paid a nominal rent, saved money, told himself that he would buy his own flat when he was ready. He had even found it possible to conduct his love affairs in privacy, while at the same time being able to call on his mother's depleted staff if he wanted a meal cooked, his clothes washed, his rooms cleaned, his parcels taken in.

But with his mother's death in April, all that had changed. While the House of Lords was sitting his father managed to get through his days, padding out with his bus pass to catch the number 12 or the 88 to Westminster, lunching at the House, occasionally sleeping through the evening debates. But at the weekends, even more in the parliamentary recess, he had become as clinging as a possessive woman, watching his son's comings and goings with almost obsessive interest, listening for his key in the lock, making his quiet but desperate pleas for companionship. Massingham's two youngest brothers were still at school and escaped from their father's grief during the holidays by staying with friends. His only sister was married to a diplomat and lived in Rome. His younger brother was at Sandhurst. The burden fell almost entirely on him. And now he knew that even the rent he paid had become a necessary contribution, almost as important to his father's dwindling resources as the daily attendance payment at the Lords.

Suddenly repentant, he thought: I could have spared him ten minutes. Ten minutes of embarrassing non-communication, of small talk about his job, which, until now, his father had never thought worthy of interest. Ten minutes of boredom only partly alleviated by alcohol and setting a precedent for nights of boredom to come.

Closing the door of his flat behind him, he thought of Kate Miskin, less than a couple of miles to the west, relaxing in her flat, pouring herself a drink, free of responsibility, free of guilt, and felt a surge of envy and irrational resentment so strong that he could almost persuade himself that it was all her fault.

BOOK THREE

Helping with Enquiries

1
⊠

The message from Pembroke Lodge was polite but unambiguous. Mr. Lampart would be operating all morning but would be happy to see Commander Dalgliesh when he was free. That would be at about one o'clock or a little later, depending on the length of his list. Translated, this meant that Lampart was a busy man concerned with saving life and alleviating pain, who could legitimately claim that these benign activities took precedence over the sordid preoccupations of a policeman, however distinguished. And the time of the appointment was nicely judged, too. Dalgliesh could hardly complain about going without his lunch since Lampart, more importantly occupied, was obviously unconcerned about his.

He took Kate with him and asked her to drive. She slid into the right-hand seat without fuss and drove as she always did, competently and strictly according to the book, with none of Massingham's occasional impatience or sudden spurts of speed. When they had climbed Haverstock Hill and were passing the Round Pond he said:

"Pembroke Lodge is about a half mile after the Spaniards. The entrance could be easy to miss." She slowed down, but even so they saw it only just in time, a wide, white-painted gate, set well back from the road and screened with horse chestnuts. A wide gravel drive curved to the left, then divided to circle an immaculate lawn fronting the house. They saw a low elegant Edwardian villa set on the edge of the heath, obviously built when a rich man could indulge his fancy for fresh air, an open view and convenient proximity to London without being thwarted by planning authorities or conservationists concerned about encroachment on public land.

As the Rover crunched slowly over the gravel Dalgliesh saw that the former stables to the right of the house had been converted to garages, but little other architectural change was apparent, as least outwardly. He wondered how many beds the nursing home could accommodate. Probably not more than thirty at most. But Stephen Lampart's activities wouldn't be restricted to his private facilities here. He was, as Dalgliesh had already checked, on the staff of two major London teaching hospitals, and no doubt operated at private clinics other than Pembroke Lodge. But this was his personal domain, and Dalgliesh had no doubt that it was a highly profitable one.

The outer door was open. It led into an oval and elegant vestibule with a pair of ornate doors and a notice inviting visitors to enter. They found themselves in an entrance hall, square and very light. The staircase, with its delicate carved balustrade, was lit by a huge stained-glass window. To the left was a carved fireplace in veined marble. Above it hung an oil painting in the manner of a late Gainsborough, a young mother, serious-faced, her white arms encircling her two daughters in folds of blue satin and lace. To the right was a desk in polished mahogany, decorative rather than utilitarian, complete with its bowl of roses and presided over by a white-coated receptionist.

The smell of disinfectant was discernible, but overlaid with a heavier scent of flowers. It was apparent that a consignment had recently been delivered. Great sheaves of roses and gladioli, formal arrangements in beribboned baskets and more outré examples of the florist's ingenuity were piled by the door awaiting distribution. The aura of pampered femininity was almost overwhelming. It was not a place in which a man could feel at home, yet Dalgliesh sensed that it was Kate who felt the more ill at ease. He saw her give a glance of fascinated disgust at one of the more bizarre offerings of conjugal congratulations: a baby's cot, over two feet long, tightly covered with the wired heads of rosebuds, dyed blue, with a pillow and coverlet of white carnations similarly decapitated, the whole monstrosity embellished with a huge blue bow. As they moved to the reception desk across a carpet thick enough to drag at their feet, a trolley of coloured bottles, nail varnishes and assorted jars was pushed across the hall by an elegant older woman in a pale pink trousersuit, obviously the beautician. Dalgliesh was reminded of a conversation overheard at a dinner party some months earlier. "But darling, the place is divine. One is pampered from the moment one arrives. Hairdresser, facials, cordon bleu menu, champagne instead of Valium for the blues. The lot. The thing is, though, that I'm not sure they don't overdo it. One feels absolutely

outraged when labour starts and one realizes that there are some humiliations and discomforts that even dear Stephen can't do much about."
Dalgliesh wondered suddenly and irrelevantly whether Lampart's patients ever died on him. Probably not, not here anyway. Those at risk would be admitted elsewhere. The place had its own subtle aura of bad taste, but the ultimate bad taste of death and failure would be rigorously excluded.

The receptionist, like the decor, had been carefully chosen to reassure, not to threaten. She was middle-aged, pleasant-looking rather than beautiful, well-groomed, immaculately coiffured. They were, of course, expected. Mr. Lampart wouldn't keep the Commander more than a few minutes. Would they care for some coffee? No? Then perhaps they wouldn't mind waiting in the drawing room.

Dalgliesh looked at his watch. He estimated that Lampart would arrive in about five minutes, a nicely calculated delay, long enough to demonstrate lack of anxiety but short enough not to antagonize a man who was, after all, a senior officer of the Yard.

The drawing room into which they were shown was large and high-ceilinged, with a central bay window and two flanking smaller ones overlooking the lawn and giving a distant view of the heath. Something of its Edwardian formality and plush comfort remained in the Axminster carpet, the heavy sofas set at right angles to the fire, and the open fire itself, in which synthetic nuggets were roasting under the carved overmantel. Stephen Lampart had resisted any temptation to combine the room's domesticity with a consulting room. There was no couch tactfully secreted behind screens, no washbasin. This was a room where clinical realities could be, for a moment, forgotten. Only the mahogany desk reminded the visitor that it was also a room for business.

Dalgliesh glanced at the pictures. There was a Frith over the fireplace, and he walked over to study more closely its meticulous romanticizing of Victorian life. It showed, at a London railway terminus, uniformed heroes returning from some colonial adventure. The first-class carriages were in the foreground. Richly mantled and beribboned ladies, with their decorously pantalooned daughters, decorously greeted their returning menfolk, while the more unrestrained welcomes of the common soldiery occupied the periphery of the canvas. On the opposite wall was a bank of stage designs, drawings and costumes for what looked like Shakespearean productions. Dalgliesh supposed that the stage provided some of Lampart's most notable patients and that these were a thank-offering for services rendered. A side table was covered with signed photographs in silver frames. Two, flamboyantly signed, were from minor European ex-royalty. The rest were of impeccably groomed mothers, wistful, sentimental, triumphant or reluctant, who displayed their babies in unpractised arms. There was the unmistakable aura of nanny in the background. This phalanx of maternity in a room which otherwise was essentially male struck an incongruous note. But at least, thought Dalgliesh, the man hadn't displayed his medical diplomas over the sideboard.

Dalgliesh left Kate studying the Frith and walked over to the windows. The huge horse chestnut in the middle of the lawn was still heavy with its summer foliage, but the screen of beech trees which partly hid the heath was already showing the first bronze of autumn. The morning light was diffused through a sky which had at first been as opaque as thin milk but which had now lightened into silver. There was no sun, but he was aware that it shone above the gauze of clouds and the air was light. Along the path two figures were slowly walking, a nurse wearing a white cap and cloak and a woman with a helmet of yellow hair and a ponderous fur coat which looked far too heavy for a day in early autumn.

It was six minutes precisely before Stephen Lampart arrived. He came in without hurry, apologized for the delay and greeted them with calm courtesy as if this were a social call. If he was surprised to find Dalgliesh accompanied by a woman detective, he concealed it admirably. But, as Dalgliesh introduced them and they shook hands, he caught Lampart's sharp appraising glance. He could have been greeting a prospective patient, assessing from long experience, in this their first meeting, whether he was likely to have trouble with her.

He was expensively but not formally dressed. The dark grey tweed with its almost invisible stripe and the immaculate blue shirt were, no doubt, designed to distance him from the more intimidating orthodoxy of the successful consultant. He could, thought Dalgliesh, have been a merchant banker, an academic, a politician. But whatever the job, he would have been good at it. His face, his clothes, the confident gaze, all bore the unmistakable imprint of success.

Dalgliesh had expected him to seat himself at the desk with the advantage of dominance which this would give. Instead, he motioned them to the low sofa and sat opposite them in a higher and straight-backed armchair. It gave him a more subtle advantage, while reducing the interview to the level of an intimate, even cosy, discussion of a mutual problem. He said:

"I know, of course, why you're here. This is an appalling business.

I still find it difficult to believe. I suppose relations and friends all tell you that. Brutal murder is the sort of thing that happens to strangers, not to the people one knows."

Dalgliesh said:

"How did you learn about it?"

"Lady Berowne telephoned me soon after your people brought the news, and as soon as I was free I called in at the house. I wanted to offer any help I could to her and Lady Ursula. I still don't have any details. Are you any clearer yet what exactly happened?"

"Both their throats were cut. We don't yet know why or by whom."

"I understood that much from the press and television, but the reports seemed almost wilfully uncommunicative. I take it you're treating it as murder."

Dalgliesh said drily:

"There's no evidence to suggest that it was a suicide pact."

"And the church door, the one leading to this vestry or wherever it was where the bodies were found, may I ask whether you found it open, or is that the sort of question that you're not supposed to answer?"

"It was unlocked."

He said:

"Well, that at least will reassure Lady Ursula." He didn't elucidate. But then, he didn't need to. After a pause he asked:

"What do you want of me, Commander?"

"I'd like you to talk to us about him. This murder could be what at first sight it appears. He let someone in and that person, a stranger, killed them both. But if it isn't as simple as that, then we need to know as much about him as we can get."

Lampart said:

"Including who could have known where he was yesterday night and who hated him enough to cut his throat."

"Including anything you can tell us which could be even remotely relevant."

Lampart paused as if to collect and marshal his thoughts. It was unnecessary. Both of them knew that his thoughts had been marshalled long before. Then he said:

"I don't think I can give much help. Nothing I know or could guess about Paul Berowne is remotely relevant to his death. If you ask about his enemies, I suppose he must have had them, political enemies. But I should suppose that Paul had fewer than most people in government and, anyway, they're not the sort to go in for murder. The idea that this could be a political crime is absurd. Unless, of course"—again he paused and Dalgliesh waited—"unless someone on the extreme left had a personal animosity. But it seems unlikely. More than unlikely, ridiculous. Sarah, his daughter, strongly disliked his politics. But I've no reason to suppose that the set she's mixed up with or even her Marxist boyfriend goes in for razor slashing."

"What set is that?"

"Oh, some minor revolutionary outfit on the extreme left. I don't suppose Labour would have them. I'd have thought you would already have known. Don't Special Branch make it their business to keep track of these people?" His gaze was open and mildly enquiring, but Dalgliesh caught the bite of contempt and dislike in the careful voice and wondered if Kate had heard it too. He asked:

"Who is the boyfriend?"

"Oh really, Commander, I'm not accusing him. I'm not accusing anyone." Dalgliesh didn't speak. He wondered what length of silence Lampart would think convincing before he came across with the information. After a pause he said: "He's Ivor Garrod. Banner carrier for all the fashionable shibboleths. I've only met him once. Sarah brought him to dinner at Campden Hill Square about five months ago, principally, I imagine, to annoy Papa. It was a meal I prefer to forget. From the talk then, the violence he advocates is on a somewhat grander scale than merely cutting the throat of a single Tory ex-Minister."

Dalgliesh asked quietly:

"When did you last see Sir Paul Berowne?" The change of questioning almost disconcerted Lampart, but he answered calmly enough:

"About six weeks ago. We're not as friendly as we used to be. Actually I was proposing to telephone him today and ask if he could have dinner with me tonight or tomorrow, unless, of course, religious conversion had destroyed his taste for good food and wine."

"Why did you want to see him?"

"I wanted to ask him what he intended to do about his wife. You know, of course, that he'd recently resigned his seat as well as his job as junior Minister, and you probably know as much as I do why. He was proposing apparently to drop out of public life. I wanted to know if that included dropping out of his marriage. There was the question of financial provision for Lady Berowne, for Barbara. She is my cousin, I've known her since childhood. I have an interest."

"How strong an interest?"

Lampart looked sideways over his shoulder at the fair-haired woman and her nurse still patiently circling the lawn. He seemed momentarily to transfer his interest to them, then recollected himself, a little too obviously, and turned again to Dalgliesh.

"I'm sorry. How strong an interest? I don't want to marry her, if that's what you're implying, but I am concerned about her. For the past three years I've been her lover as well as her cousin. You could call that a strong interest, I suppose."

"Did her husband know that you and she were lovers?"

"I've no idea. Husbands usually do get to know these things. Paul and I didn't see each other often enough to make it an embarrassment. We're both busy men with little in common now. Except Barbara, of course. Anyway, he was hardly in a position to object, morally speaking. He had a mistress, as I've no doubt you've discovered. Or haven't you grubbed out that piece of dirt yet?"

Dalgliesh said:

"I'm interested in knowing how you managed to grub it out."

"Barbara told me. She guessed, or rather she knew. She employed a private detective about eighteen months ago and had him followed. To be accurate, she told me of her suspicions, and I got hold of a suitably discreet man on her behalf. I don't think it bothered her particularly, the infidelity. It was just that she liked to know. I don't think she saw the woman as a serious rival. Actually, I suspect she was quite pleased. It amused her, and it gave her something to hold over Paul if the need arose. And, of course, freed her from the disagreeable necessity of sleeping with him, at least on an inconveniently regular basis. But she didn't lock her door. Barbara liked an occasional assurance that he was still suitably enthralled."

He was, thought Dalgliesh, being remarkably candid, unnecessarily so. He wondered whether this apparently naive willingness to confide his own and other people's more intimate emotions arose from over-confidence, arrogance and vanity, or whether there was a more sinister motive. Lampart wouldn't be the first murderer to argue that if you told the police details they had no particular right to demand they would be less likely to suspect other, more dangerous secrets.

He asked:

"And was he still suitably enthralled?"

"I imagine so. What a pity he isn't here to be asked." With a quick and surprisingly clumsy gesture he got up from the desk and walked to the window as if seized by restlessness. Dalgliesh turned in his chair and watched him. Suddenly he strode over to the desk, picked up the telephone and dialled. He said:

"Sister, I think Mrs. Steiner has had enough outdoor exercise. It's too cold this morning for slow walking. Tell her I'll be along to see her again in"—he glanced at his watch—"in about fifteen minutes. Thank you." He put down the receiver, came back to his chair and said almost roughly: "Let's get down to it, shall we? What you want from me, I suppose, is some sort of statement. Where was I, what was I doing, who was I with when Paul got himself killed? If it was murder, I'm not naive enough to deceive myself that I'm not a suspect."

"It isn't a question of suspicion. We have to ask those questions of anyone who was closely connected with Sir Paul."

He laughed, a sudden explosion of sound, harsh and mirthless.

"Closely connected! You could say that, I suppose. And it's all just a matter of routine. Isn't that what you usually tell your victims?"

Dalgliesh didn't reply. The silence seemed to irritate Lampart. He said:

"Where do I make it, this statement? Here, or at the local police station? Or are you operating from the Yard?"

"You could make it there, in my office, if that's convenient for you. Perhaps you could come in this evening. Or it could be taken at the local station, if that would save time. But it would be helpful to have the gist of it now."

Lampart said:

"You've noticed, I suppose, that I haven't asked to have my solicitor present. That shows rather a touching confidence in the police, wouldn't you say?"

"If you want him to be present, that, of course, is your right."

"I don't want him. I don't need him. I hope you won't be disappointed, Commander, but I think I have an alibi. That is, if Berowne died between seven and midnight."

Still Dalgliesh didn't speak. Lampart went on:

"I was with Barbara for the whole of that time as, no doubt, you already know. You must have seen her. Earlier, from two o'clock until five, I was here operating. The list is available and theatre sister and the anaesthetist can corroborate. I know I was gloved, gowned and masked, but I can assure you that my staff recognize my work even if they don't actually see my face. But, of course, they did see it, before I gowned up. I mention that in case you had some fanciful idea that I might have persuaded a colleague to stand in for me."

Dalgliesh said:

"That might work in fiction, but hardly in real life."

"And afterwards, Barbara and I had tea in this room, then spent some time in my private flat, upstairs. Then I changed, and we left here together at about seven forty. The night porter saw us go and can probably confirm the time. We drove to the Black Swan at Cookham, where we had dinner together. I wasn't particularly noticing the time, but I suppose we got there at about eight thirty. I drive a red Porsche, in case that's significant. The table was booked for eight forty-five. Jean Paul Higgins is the manager. He'll be able to confirm it. No doubt he'll also confirm that it was after eleven when we left. But I'd be grateful for a little tact. I'm not over-sensitive about reputation, but I can't afford to have half of fashionable London gossiping about my private life. And while some of my patients have their little foibles, like giving birth under water or squatting on the drawing room carpet, being delivered by a murder suspect isn't everyone's fancy."

"We'll be discreet. When did Lady Berowne arrive here? Or did you call for her earlier at Campden Hill Square?"

"No. I haven't been inside number sixty-two for weeks. Barbara came by cab. She arrived shortly after four, I suppose. She was in the theatre watching me operate from about four fifteen until I finished. Did I mention that?"

"She was with you the whole time?"

"Most of the time. I think she slipped out for a few minutes after I'd completed the third caesarean."

"And she was masked and gowned too?"

"Of course. But of what possible relevance is that? He couldn't have died, surely, before the evening."

"Is that something she often does? Watch you operate?"

"It isn't uncommon. It's a fancy she has . . ." He paused and added: "From time to time."

They were both silent. There were some things, thought Dalgliesh, that even Stephen Lampart, with his pose of ironic detachment and contempt for reticence, couldn't bring himself actually to say. So that was how she got her kicks. That was what turned her on: watching, masked and gowned, while his hands cut into another woman's body. The erotic charge of the medical priesthood. The attendant nurses moving in patterned ceremony about him. The grey eyes meeting the blue above the mask. And afterwards, watching, while he peeled off his gloves, held out his arms in a parody of benediction while an acolyte lifted the gown from his shoulders. The heady mixture of power, mystery, ruthlessness. The rituals of knife and blood. Where, he wondered, had they made love—his bedroom, a private sitting room? It was surprising that they didn't couple on the operating table. Perhaps they did.

The telephone on the desk rang. With a muttered apology, Lampart picked up the receiver. The conversation, apparently with a colleague, was highly clinical and one-sided, with Lampart doing most of the listening. But he made no attempt to cut it short. Dalgliesh gazed out over the garden while his mind busied itself with its preliminary assessment. If they had left Pembroke Lodge at seven forty it would need fast driving to get to the Black Swan by eight thirty. Time to take in a murder on the way? It was feasible, provided he could make an excuse to leave her in the car. No man in his senses would take her with him into the church on such a bloody mission, even if she knew or guessed what he had in mind. So there would have be an excuse. Someone he had briefly to see. Some business to be transacted. The car would have to be parked close to the church. That in itself would be risky. A red Porsche was conspicuous. And then what? The knock on the church door. Berowne letting him in. The rehearsed excuse for calling. How long for these preliminaries? Less than a minute perhaps. The sudden blow to knock Berowne out. Then to the washroom for the razor, which he could be sure he would find, the quick stripping off of jacket and shirt and back to the vestry, razor in hand. The careful tentative cuts followed by the final slash to the bone. He must have done some forensic medicine when a student, if not since. He would know better than any other suspect how to simulate a suicide.

And then the disaster. Harry appears, stumbling, probably half-drunk, half-asleep, but not so asleep that he couldn't see, couldn't remember. And now, there would be no time for finesse and none needed. And afterwards: the quick wash; the razor placed near Berowne's hand; the rapid glance to left and right; the covering darkness; the door left unlocked since he couldn't take away the key; the unhurried return to the car. He would have to depend on her silence, of course. He would need to be certain that she would stick to their story and say that they had driven straight to the Black Swan. But it was an easy lie, no complicated fabrication, no difficult details of timing to remember. She would say what in fact she had in effect already said. "We drove straight there. No, I can't remember the route. I wasn't noticing. But we didn't stop." He would have to fabricate a good reason for asking her to lie. "I needed to see one of my patients, a woman." But why not tell the police that? There's nothing wrong about a quick professional visit. The need to stop would have to be faintly disreputable. Either that or something he had suddenly remembered. A telephone call which had been unanswered. Too quick. He would need longer than that. And why not wait and make it from the Black Swan? But, of course, there was the obvious ploy. He would say he had called at the church, spoken to Berowne, left him alive and well. That way, she would back up his alibi in her own interest as well as his. And if, in the end, she didn't, he would still have his story. "I called to talk to Berowne about his wife. I only stayed for ten minutes at the most. The discussion was perfectly amicable. I saw no one but Berowne and I left him alive and well."

Lampart replaced the receiver. He said:

"Sorry about that. Where were we, Commander? At the Black Swan?"

But Dalgliesh changed the tack of the questioning. He said:

"You knew Sir Paul Berowne intimately once, even if you weren't particularly close at the end. No two men share a woman without being interested in each other." He could have added, "sometimes obsessed with each other." He went on: "You're a doctor. I'm wondering what you make of it, this experience he had in the vestry at St. Matthew's." The flattery was hardly subtle and Lampart was too clever a man to miss it. But he wouldn't be able to resist it. He was used to being asked his opinion, to being listened to with deference. It was partly what he lived by. He said:

"I'm an obstetrician, not a psychiatrist. But I shouldn't have thought the psychology of it was particularly complicated. The usual story. It's only the manifestations that are a little bizarre. Call it the mid-life crisis. I don't like the expression 'male menopause.' It's inaccurate anyway. The two things are fundamentally different. I think he looked at his life, what he'd achieved, what he could hope for, and didn't much care for it. He'd tried law and politics and neither satisfied him. He had a wife he lusted after but didn't love. A daughter who didn't love him. A job which constrained any hope he might have of breaking out into spectacular or exuberant protest. All right; he'd got himself a mistress. That's the easy expedient. I haven't seen the lady, but from what Barbara told me it's more a question of comfort and cocoa, a bit of mild office gossip on the side rather than any breaking of the straitjacket he'd got himself strapped into. So he needed an excuse for chucking it all. What better one than proclaiming that God himself has told you you're on the wrong tack? I don't think it would be my way out. But you can argue that it's preferable to a nervous breakdown, alcoholism or cancer."

When Dalgliesh didn't speak he went on quickly, with a kind of nervous sincerity which was almost convincing.

"I see it all the time. The husbands. They sit where you're sitting now. Ostensibly, they come to talk to me about their wives. But they're the ones with the problem. They can't win. It's the tyranny of success. They spend most of their youth working to qualify, most of their young manhood building up success—the right wife, the right house, the right schools for the children, the right clubs. For what? For some money, more comfort, a bigger house, a faster car, more taxation. And they don't even get much of a kick out of it. And there's another twenty years to be got through. And it isn't much better for those who aren't disillusioned, who find their niche, who actually enjoy what they do. Their fear is the prospect of retirement. Overnight you're nobody. The walking dead. Haven't you seen those dreadful old men, trawling for a committee, angling for a royal commission, a job, any kind of a job, as long as it gives them the illusion that they're still important?"

Dalgliesh said:

"Yes, I've seen them."

"Christ, they practically go down on their knees and slaver for it."

"I think that's true enough, but it didn't apply to him. He was still only a junior Minister. His success was ahead. He was still at the striving stage."

"Oh yes, I know. The next Tory Prime Minister but one. Do you think that was a serious possibility? I don't. He hadn't the fire in the belly, not for politics anyway. Not even one little smouldering coal."

He spoke with a kind of triumphant bitterness. He said:

"I'm all right, Jack. I'm one of the lucky ones. No hostages to fortune. The job gives me what I need. And when I'm ready for the scrapheap, I've got the *Mayflower*, a sloop, fifty feet. She's berthed at Chichester. I don't get much time for her now. But once retired, I'll provision her and be off. And you, Commander? No *Mayflower*?"

"No *Mayflower*."

"But you've your poetry, of course. I was forgetting." He spoke the word as if it were an insult. As if he were saying 'you've got your woodwork, your stamp collection, your embroidery.' Worse, he spoke it as if he knew there hadn't been a poem for four years, that there might never be one again. Dalgliesh said:

"For someone who wasn't intimate, you know a lot about him."

"He interested me. And at Oxford his elder brother and I were friends. I dined at Campden Hill Square fairly often when he was alive, and the three of us used to sail together. To Cherbourg specifically, in 1978. You get to know a man when you've survived a ten-force gale together. Actually, Paul saved my life. I went overboard and he got me back."

"But isn't yours a rather superficial assessment, the obvious explanation?"

"It's surprising how often the obvious explanation is the correct one. If you were a diagnostician, you'd know that."

Dalgliesh turned to Kate:

"Is there anything you wanted to ask, Inspector?" Lampart wasn't quite quick enough to restrain his momentary frown of surprise and discomfiture that a woman he had taken to be no more than Dalgliesh's helot, whose role was to take unobtrusive notes and sit as a meek and silent witness, was apparently licensed to question him. He turned on her a half-smiling over-attentive gaze, but his eyes were wary.

Kate said:

"This dinner at the Black Swan . . . is that a favourite place of yours? Do you and Lady Berowne go there often?"

"Fairly often in summer. Less so in winter. The ambience is agreeable. It's a convenient distance from London, and now that Higgins has changed his chef the food is good. If you're asking for a recommendation for a quiet dinner, yes, I can recommend it." The sarcasm was unsubtle and he had made his resentment too obvious. The question, innocuous enough, if apparently irrelevant, had rattled him. Kate said:

"And you were there, both of you, on the evening of the seventh of August, when Diana Travers was drowned?"

He said drily:

"You obviously already know that we were there, so there seems little point in asking. It was Lady Berowne's twenty-seventh birthday party. She was born on the seventh of August."

"And you escorted her, not her husband?"

"Sir Paul Berowne was otherwise engaged. I gave the party for Lady Berowne. He was expected to join us later, but rang to say that he couldn't make it. Since you know that we were there, you obviously know, too, that we left before the tragedy."

"And the other tragedy, sir, Theresa Nolan? You were not, of course, present when that happened either?" Careful, Kate, thought Dalgliesh. But he didn't interfere, and he wasn't anxious.

"If you mean did I sit by her side in Holland Park when she swallowed a bottle of distalgesic tablets and washed them down with cooking sherry, no I wasn't. If I had been, obviously I should have stopped her."

"She left a note making it plain that she'd killed herself because of guilt over her abortion. A perfectly legal abortion. She was one of your nurses here. I wonder why she didn't have the operation at Pembroke Lodge."

"She didn't ask. And if she had, I wouldn't have done it. I prefer not to operate on my own staff. If there appear to be medical reasons for termination, I refer them to a fellow gynaecologist. Actually, I can't see how her death or that of Diana Travers has anything to do with the business that brings you here this morning. Ought we to be wasting time with irrelevant questions?"

Dalgliesh said:

"Not irrelevant. Sir Paul received letters suggesting, obliquely but fairly unmistakably, that he was somehow connected with those two deaths. Anything that happened to him during the last weeks of his life has to be relevant. The letters were probably the usual malicious nonsense that politicians expose themselves to, but it's as well to clear them out of the way."

Lampart turned his gaze from Kate to Dalgliesh.

"I see. I'm sorry if I sounded uncooperative, but I know absolutely nothing of the Travers girl except that she worked at Campden Hill Square as a part-time domestic and that she was at the Black Swan on the night of the birthday party. Theresa Nolan came here from Campden Hill Square, where she'd been nursing Lady Ursula, who was laid low with sciatica. I understand they got her from a nursing agency. When Lady Ursula no longer needed a night nurse, she suggested to the girl that she apply here. She had a midwifery qualification. She was perfectly satisfactory. She must have got pregnant when she was working at Campden Hill Square. But I didn't ask by whom and I don't think she ever said."

Dalgliesh said:

"Did it occur to you that the child could have been Sir Paul Berowne's?"

"Yes. It occurred to me. I imagine it occurred to quite a number of people."

He said no more and Dalgliesh didn't press him. He asked:

"What happened when she discovered she was pregnant?"

"She came to me and said that she couldn't face having a baby and wanted a termination. I referred her to a psychiatrist and left him to make the necessary arrangements."

"Did you think that the girl's condition at the time, I mean her mental condition, was such that she was likely to qualify legally for an abortion?"

"I didn't examine her. I didn't discuss it with her. And it wasn't a medical decision I was qualified to make. As I said, I referred her to a psychiatric colleague. I told her that she could have leave with pay until a decision was made. She only came back here for a week after the operation. And the rest you know."

Suddenly he got to his feet and began restlessly pacing. Then he turned to Dalgliesh.

"I've given some thought to this business of Paul Berowne. Man is an animal, and he lives most at ease with himself and the world when he remembers that. Admittedly he's the cleverest and most dangerous of animals, but he's still an animal. The philosophers, and poets too, for all I know, make it all too complicated. It isn't. Our basic needs are pretty straightforward—food, shelter, warmth, sex, prestige, in that order. The happiest people go after them and are satisfied with them. Berowne wasn't. God knows what unattainable intangibles he thought he'd a right to. Eternal life, probably."

Dalgliesh said:

"So you believe the probability is that he killed himself?"

"I haven't enough evidence. But let's say that if you finally decide it was suicide, then I for one won't be surprised."

"And the tramp? There were two deaths."

"That's more difficult. Did he kill Paul or did Paul kill him? Obviously the family won't want to believe the latter. Lady Ursula will never accept that explanation, whatever the final verdict."

"But you . . ."

"Oh, I feel that if a man has sufficient violence in him to slit his own throat, he's certainly capable of slitting another's. And now, perhaps you'll excuse me." He glanced at Kate. "Both of you. I have a patient waiting. I'll call in at the Yard between eight and nine thirty and sign my statement." He added, rising: "Perhaps by then I shall manage to think of something else to help you. But don't be too sanguine." He made it sound like a threat.

2
⊠

There was an almost unbroken stream of traffic past the front gate and Kate had to wait for over a minute before it was safe to filter in. She thought: I wonder just how he does it. The interview was all there in her notebook in her neat, unorthodox shorthand, but she had the gift of almost perfect verbal recall and she could have typed most of it out without reference to the hieroglyphics. She let her mind slide over each question and response and she still couldn't see where AD had been so clever.

He had said very little, his questions short and sometimes apparently unrelated to the line of enquiry. But Lampart, and that after all was the intention, had been seduced into saying a great deal too much. And all that guff about the male mid-life crisis—popular psychology which you could have sent to you in a plain envelope if you wrote to the agony aunties enquiring what was wrong with your old man. He could be right, of course. But, after all, medically speaking, varieties of the male menopause weren't Stephen Lampart's field. He'd been asked for his opinion and he'd given it, but you'd expect a man as fond of his own voice as he was to be even more forthcoming about the psychological problems of pregnancy and abortion. But when it came to Theresa Nolan, what had they got? A brush-off, the keep-off signs clearly posted. He hadn't even wanted to think about her, let alone talk about her. And it wasn't just because she, Kate, had been the one to do the questioning and had done it with that undeferential over-politeness which she had known would be more offensive to his vanity than rudeness or open antagonism. She had hoped that, with luck, it might goad him into an indiscretion, but it wouldn't have worked if there had been nothing to conceal. She heard AD's voice:

"That touching detail, about Sir Paul saving his life. Did you believe it?"

"No sir. Not as he told it. I think something of the sort probably happened. He went overboard and his friend yanked him back. He wouldn't have mentioned it if there weren't some corroboration. But I think he was really saying, 'Look, I might have pinched his wife, but I wouldn't have killed him, would I? He saved my life.' " She added: "It wasn't very subtle, the way he fingered Garrod." She glanced at him quickly. He smiled with wry distaste as he sometimes did when a colleague used an Americanism. But he let it pass, merely saying:

"Nothing about him was subtle."

Suddenly she felt a surge of optimism, heady, intoxicating and dangerously close to the euphoria which always came when a case was going well but which she had learned to distrust and subdue. If this goes all right, if we get him, whoever he is, and we will, then I'm on my way. I'm really on my way. But the elation went deeper than mere ambition or the satisfaction of a test passed, a job well done. She had enjoyed herself. Every minute of her brief confrontation with that self-satisfied poseur had been deeply pleasurable. She thought of her first months with the CID, the plugging, conscientious, door-to-door enquiries which had made up her day, the pathetic victims, the even more pathetic villains. How much more satisfying was this sophisticated manhunt: the knowledge that they were up against a killer with the intelligence to think and plan, who wasn't an ignorant, feckless victim of circumstance or passion. She had learned facial control long before she had joined the police. She drove carefully, her face calmly set on the road ahead. But something of what she was feeling must have communicated itself to her companion. He said:

"Did you enjoy yourself, Inspector?" The question and the rare use of her rank jolted her, but she decided to answer it honestly, knowing that she had no option. She had done her homework. She knew his reputation, and when colleagues had spoken about him she had made it her business to listen. They had said: "He's a bastard, but a just bastard." She knew that there were some inadequacies he could forgive and some foibles he could tolerate. But dishonesty wasn't among them. She said:

"Yes, sir. I liked the sense of being in control, that we were getting somewhere." Then she added, knowing as she spoke that this was dangerous territory, but hell, she thought, why should he get away with it:

"Was the question meant as a criticism, sir?"

"No. No one joins the police without getting some enjoyment out of exercising power. No one joins the murder squad who hasn't a taste for death. The danger begins when the pleasure becomes an end in itself. That's when it's time to think about another job."

She wanted to ask: "Have you ever thought of another job, sir?" But she knew the temptation was illusory. There were some senior officers of whom one could ask that question after a couple of whiskies in the senior officers' mess, but he wasn't among them. She remembered the moment when she had told Alan that Dalgliesh had chosen her for the new squad. He had said, smiling: "So isn't it about time you tried reading his verse?" and she had replied: "I'd better come to terms with the man before I try coming to terms with his poetry." She wasn't sure that she had succeeded. Now she said:

"Lampart spoke about razor slashing. We deliberately didn't tell him how Sir Paul died. So why should he have mentioned a razor?"

Dalgliesh said:

"Reasonably enough. He was an old friend, one of the people who would know how Berowne shaved. He must have guessed what weapon was used. It's interesting that he couldn't bring himself to ask us outright if it was. Incidentally, we'll have to check that timing fairly quickly. It's a job for Saunders, I think. He'd better make three runs, the same time, the same make of car, the same night of the week, and, with luck, the same weather conditions. And we'll need to know everything possible about Pembroke Lodge. Who owns the freehold, who holds shares, how the business operates, what its reputation is." She couldn't make a written note of his instructions. But then, she didn't need to.

"Yes, sir."

Dalgliesh went on:

"He had the means, he had the knowledge, he had the motive. I don't think he wanted marriage with the lady, but he certainly didn't want an impoverished mistress who might begin thinking in terms of divorce. But if he wanted Berowne dead, and dead before he threw away his money on some half-baked scheme for housing derelicts, he didn't need to slit his throat. He's a doctor. There are more subtle methods. This murderer didn't kill merely from expediency. There had been hatred in that room. Hate isn't an easy emotion to hide. I didn't see it in Stephen Lampart.

Arrogance, aggression, sexual jealousy of the man in possession. But not hate."

Kate had never lacked courage and she didn't now. After all, he'd selected her for the team. Presumably he thought her opinion worth having. He wasn't looking for a female subordinate to massage his ego. She said:

"But couldn't it have been expediency rather than hate, sir? Killing without arousing suspicion isn't easy even for a doctor. He wasn't Sir Paul's general practitioner. And this, if he could pull it off, would be the perfect murder, one that isn't even suspected as murder. It was Harry Mack who did for him. Without that second killing, wouldn't we have taken it at its face value . . . suicide?"

Dalgliesh said:

"Followed by the usual euphemistic verdict 'while the balance of his mind was disturbed.' Perhaps. If he hadn't made the mistake of taking away the matches and of half-burning the diary. That was an unnecessary refinement. In some ways, the clue of that half-burnt match is the most interesting in the case."

Suddenly she felt at ease with him, almost companionable. She was no longer thinking of the impression she might be making but of the case. She did what she would have done with Massingham. With her eyes fixed on the road ahead, she thought it through aloud:

"Once the killer decided to burn the diary, he'd know he needed to take the matches with him to the church. Berowne didn't smoke, so there wouldn't be a lighter on the body and he couldn't be sure he'd find matches in the vestry. And when he did, they were chained, and it was easier and quicker to use the box he'd brought with him. Time was vital. So we get back to someone who knew Sir Paul, knew his habits, knew where he was on Tuesday night, but who wasn't familiar with the church. But he'd hardly be carrying the diary in his hand when he arrived. So he was wearing a jacket or coat with largish pockets. Or he had a bag of some kind, a carrier, a tote bag, a briefcase, a medical bag."

Dalgliesh said:

"Or he could have carried it folded inside an evening paper."

Kate went on:

"He rings. Sir Paul lets him in. He asks to go to the washroom. He leaves his bag there together with the matches and the diary. He strips. Perhaps he strips naked. Then it's back to the Little Vestry. But this is getting bizarre, sir. His victim isn't going to sit there quietly waiting for it. Not confronted by a man stark naked with an open razor in his hand. Paul Berowne wasn't old or sick or weak. He would have defended himself. It couldn't have happened that way."

"Concentrate on the matches."

"But he must have been naked when he killed. Naked to the waist anyway. He must have known that it would be a bloody business. He couldn't have risked getting his clothes splashed. But of course! He knocks out his victim first. Then he goes for the razor, strips, does the fancy bit. Then back to the washroom. He has a quick but thorough sluice down and gets back into his clothes. Then, last of all, he burns the diary. That way he can be sure there's no blood on the cover or in the grate. It must have happened in that order. Finally, perhaps a matter of habit, he slips the matchbox in his jacket pocket. That suggests he was used to carrying matches. A smoker, perhaps. It must have given him a shock when he put his hands in his pocket later and found them and realized that he should have left them at the scene. Why didn't he go back? Too late, perhaps. Or perhaps he couldn't face the shambles."

Dalgliesh said:

"Or he knew that a second visit would add to the risk of being seen, or leaving some trace of himself in the vestry. But let's assume that the killer took his own box away on purpose. What does that suggest?"

"That the box he used could be traced to him. But that's unlikely, surely. He'd use an ordinary brand, one of a million similar boxes. And he couldn't have known that we'd find that half-burnt match. Perhaps he took it away because it was a box someone might miss. Perhaps he always planned to return it. And that means he didn't go to the church from his own home. Logically, he came from Campden Hill Square, where he'd helped himself both to the diary and to the box of matches. But if so, if the matchbox came from Berowne's own home, why not leave it at the scene? Even if the box were traced, it would only lead us back to Berowne himself. So we get back to a simple mistake. A matter of habit. He slipped the box into his pocket."

Dalgliesh said:

"If he did, it might not have worried him too much after the first shock of discovery. He'd tell himself that we'd assume Berowne used the matches from the chained box, or that we'd think that the matches had been burnt with the diary. Or perhaps we'd argue that he could have used a match from one of those packets you can pick up in hotels and restaurants, small enough to burn away without a trace. Admittedly, Berowne wasn't a man likely to collect restaurant matches, but defence counsel could argue that it happened that way. This isn't exactly a propitious time to ask for a conviction on forensic evidence alone, certainly not on one inch of a half-burnt match."

Kate asked:

"How do you think it happened, sir?"

"Possibly much as you've described. If Sir Paul had been faced with a naked and armed assailant, I doubt if we'd have found what we did find at the scene. There was no sign of a struggle. That suggests that he must have been knocked out first. That done, the killer got to work swiftly, expertly, knowing just what he was about. And he didn't need much time. A couple of minutes to strip and lay his hands on the razor. Less than ten seconds to do the killing. So the knockout blow need not have been heavy. In fact, it would have had to be nicely judged if it weren't to leave a suspiciously large bruise. But there's another possibility. He could have slipped something over Berowne's head and dragged him down. Something soft, a scarf, a towel, his own shirt. Or a noose, a cord, a handkerchief."

Kate said:

"But he'd have to be careful not to pull it too tight, not to throttle his victim. The cause of death had to be the slit throat. And wouldn't a scarf or handkerchief leave a mark?"

Dalgliesh said:

"Not necessarily. Not when he'd finished his butchery. But we may get something from this afternoon's pm."

And suddenly she was back in the Little Vestry, looking down again at that half-severed head, seeing the whole picture, vivid, clear-edged, bright as a coloured print. And this time there was no blessed moment of preparation, no chance to compose her mind and muscles for what she knew she would have to face. Her hands, white-knuckled, tightened on the wheel. For a moment she imagined the car had stalled, that she had stepped on the brake. But they were still riding smoothly, down the Finchley Road. How strange, she thought, that the horror, briefly recalled, should be more terrible than reality. But her companion was speaking. She must have lost a few seconds of what he was saying. But now she heard him talking about the time of the post-mortem, saying that she might like to watch. Normally the suggestion, which she translated as an order, would have pleased her. She would have welcomed it as one more affirmation that she was really part of his team. But now for the first time she felt a spasm of distaste, almost a revulsion. She would be there, of course. This wouldn't be her first autopsy. She had no fear of disgracing herself. She could gaze and not be sick. In detective training school, she had seen her male colleagues topple in the pm room while she had stood firm. It was important to be present at the pm if the pathologist would allow it. You could learn a lot, and she was eager to learn. Her grandmother and the social worker would be waiting for her at three o'clock, but they would have to wait. She had tried, but not too hard, to find a moment in the day to ring and say that she couldn't be there. But she told herself that it wasn't necessary; her grandmother knew that already. She would try to drop in at the end of the day if it wasn't too late. But for her, now at this moment, the dead had to take priority over the living. But for the first time since she had joined the CID, a small treacherous voice, whispering in self-distrust, asked her what exactly it was that her job was doing to her.

She had chosen to be a police officer deliberately, knowing that the job was right for her. But she had never, even from the first, had any illusions about it. It was a job where people, when they needed you, demanded that you should be there at once, unquestionably, effectively, and when they didn't, preferred to forget you existed. It was a job where you were sometimes required to work with people you'd rather not work with and show respect for senior officers for whom you felt little or none; where you could find yourself allied to men you despised and against some for whom, more often than you'd bargained for, more often than was comfortable, you felt sympathy, even pity. She knew the comfortable orthodoxies, that law and order were the norms, crime the aberration, that policing in a free society could be done only with the consent of the policed, even presumably in those areas where the police had always been seen as the enemy and had now been elevated into convenient stereotypes of oppression. But she had her own credo. You kept sane by knowing that hypocrisy might be politically necessary, but that you didn't have to believe it. You kept honest; there was no point in the job otherwise. You did the job so that your male colleagues had to respect you even if it was too much to expect that they would like you. You kept your private life private, unmessy. There were men enough in the world without being trapped by propinquity into sexual entanglement with your colleagues. You didn't fall into the easy habit of obscenity; you had heard enough of that in Ellison Fairweather buildings. You knew how far you could reasonably hope to rise and how you proposed to get there. You made no unnecessary enemies; it was hard enough for a woman to climb without getting kicked in the ankles on the way up. Every job, after all, had its disadvantages. Nurses got used to the smell of dressings and bedpans, unwashed bodies, other people's pain, the smell of death. She had made her choice. And now, more than ever, she had no regrets.

3
⊠

The hospital where Miles Kynaston held his appointment as consultant pathologist had needed a new pm room for years, but facilities for the living patients had taken priority over accommodation for the dead. Kynaston grumbled, but Dalgliesh suspected that he didn't really care. He had the equipment he needed, and the pm room in which he worked was sparse, familiar territory in which he felt as comfortably at home as he might in an old dressing-gown. He had no real wish to be banished to some larger, more remote and more impersonal quarters, and his occasional complaints were no more than ritual noises made to remind the medical committee that the Forensic Pathology Department existed.

But there was, inevitably, always something of a squash. Dalgliesh and his officers were there primarily from interest rather than necessity, but the exhibits sergeant, the fingerprint officer, the scene-of-crime and exhibit officers with their envelopes, bottles and tubes took up necessary room. Kynaston's secretary, a plump, middle-aged woman, as cheerfully efficient as a president of the Women's Institute, sat in her twin-set and tweeds, squashed in the corner with a bulging bag at her feet. Dalgliesh always expected her to take out her knitting. Kynaston had always disliked using a tape recorder, and from time to time he turned towards her and dictated his findings in low, staccato sentences which she seemed to understand. He always worked to music, often Baroque and sometimes a string quartet, Mozart, Vivaldi, Haydn. This afternoon's recording was one Dalgliesh immediately recognized since he, too, owned it: Neville Marriner conducting Telemann's Viola Concerto in G. Dalgliesh wondered if its enigmatic, richly melancholy tone provided Kynaston with a necessary catharsis; whether it was his way of attempting to dramatize the routine indignities of death; or whether, like house painters or others less singularly employed, he simply liked music while he worked.

Dalgliesh noted with a mixture of interest and irritation that Massingham and Kate kept their eyes fixed on Kynaston's hands with an attention which suggested that they were afraid to shift their gaze in case inadvertently they should happen to meet his eyes. He wondered how they could possibly suppose that he saw this ritual disembowelment as having anything to do with Berowne. The detachment, which had become second nature to him, was helped by the matter-of-fact efficiency with which the organs were drawn out, examined, bottled and labelled. He felt exactly as he had when, as a young probationer, he had watched his first autopsy: a surprise at the bright colours of the coils and pouches dangling in the pathologist's gloved and bloody hands, and an almost childish wonder that so small a cavity should be capable of accommodating such a large and diverse collection of organs.

Afterwards, as they scrubbed their hands in the washroom, Kynaston from necessity, Dalgliesh from a fastidiousness which he would have found difficult to explain, he asked:

"What about the time of death?"

"No reason to alter the estimate I made at the scene. Seven o'clock would be the earliest. Say between seven and nine. I may be able to be a little more precise when the stomach contents have been analysed. There were no signs of a struggle. And if Berowne was attacked, he made no attempt to protect himself. There are no cuts across the gripping aspect of Berowne's palm. Well, you saw that for yourself. The blood on his right palm came from the razor, not from defensive cuts."

Dalgliesh said:

"From the razor or from the blood on his throat?"

"That's possible. The palm was certainly more thickly coated than one might expect. Nothing complicated about the cause of death in either case. In both, it's a classical fine cut, through the thyro-hyoid ligament, severing everything from the skin to the spine. Berowne was healthy, no reason why he shouldn't have lived to a good old age if someone hadn't cut his throat for him. And Harry Mack was in better shape, medically speaking, than I expected. Liver not too good, but it could have stood a few more years' abuse before it actually gave out on him. The lab will get the throat tissue under the microscope, but I don't think you'll get any joy. There is no obvious sign of a ligature at the edge of the wound. The bump on the back of Berowne's head is superficial, probably made when he fell."

Dalgliesh said:

"Or was pulled down."

"Or was pulled down. You'll have to wait for the lab report on the blood smear before you can go much further, Adam."

Dalgliesh said:

"And even if that smear isn't Harry Mack's blood, you still aren't prepared to say that Berowne wasn't capable of stumbling across to Harry even with those two superficial cuts in his throat."

Kynaston said:

"I could say it was improbable. I couldn't say that it was impossible. And we're not just talking about the superficial cuts. Remember that case quoted by Simpson? The suicide practically severed his head, yet remained conscious long enough to kick the ambulance man downstairs."

"But if Berowne killed Harry, why move back to the bed to finish himself off?"

"A natural association, bed, sleep, death. If he had decided to die on his bed, why should he change his mind because it was necessary to kill Harry first?"

"It wasn't necessary. I doubt whether Harry could have reached him in time to stop that final cut. It offends against common sense."

"Or it offends against your idea of Paul Berowne."

"Both. This was double murder, Miles."

"I believe you, but it's going to be the devil to prove, and I don't think my report will be much help. Suicide is the most private and mysterious of acts, inexplicable because the chief actor is never there to explain it."

Dalgliesh said:

"Unless, of course, he leaves his testimony behind. If Berowne did decide to kill himself, I'd have expected to find some kind of note, an attempt at explanation."

Kynaston said enigmatically:

"The fact that you didn't find it doesn't necessarily mean that he didn't write it."

He drew on a fresh pair of gloves and pulled his face mask over his mouth and nose. Already a new cadaver was being wheeled in. Dalgliesh looked at his watch. Massingham and Kate could drive back to the Yard and get on with the paperwork. He had another appointment. After the frustrations of the day he needed a little light relief, even a little cosseting. He proposed to extract information by more agreeable ways than a police interrogation. He had earlier that morning telephoned Conrad Ackroyd and had been invited to take a civilized afternoon tea with the owner and editor of the *Paternoster Review*.

4

⊠

Conrad and Nellie Ackroyd lived in a gleamingly neat stucco Edwardian villa in St. John's Wood with a garden running down to the canal, a house reputedly built by Edward VII for one of his mistresses and inherited by Nellie Ackroyd from a bachelor uncle. Ackroyd had moved into it from his city flat above the *Paternoster* office three years previously, following his marriage, and had happily accommodated his books, his belongings and his life to Nellie's taste for comfort and domesticity. Now, although they had a servant, he himself welcomed Dalgliesh at the door, his black eyes as brightly expectant as a child's.

"Come in, come in. We know what you're here for, dear boy. It's about my little piece in the *Review*. I'm glad you haven't felt it necessary to come in pairs. We're quite prepared to help the police with their enquiries, as you so tactfully put it when you've caught your man and he's having his arms twisted in a little back room, but I draw the line at giving afternoon tea to some oversized minion who wears out the springs in my sofa and eats my cucumber sandwiches with one hand while taking down everything I say with the other."

"Be serious, Conrad. We're talking about murder."

"Are we? There was a rumour—just a rumour, of course—that Paul Berowne could have made his own quietus. I'm glad it isn't true. Murder is more interesting and far less depressing. It's inconsiderate of one's friends to commit suicide; too like setting a good example. But all that can wait. Tea first."

He called up the stairs:

"Nellie, darling, Adam is here."

Looking at him as he led the way into the drawing room, Dalgliesh thought that he never seemed a day older than when they had first met. He gave the impression of plumpness, perhaps because of his almost round face and the chubbiness of his marsupial cheeks. But he was firm-fleshed, active, moving with the nimble grace of a dancer. His eyes were small and upward-slanting. When he was amused he would narrow them into twin creases of flesh. The most remarkable thing about his face was the restless mobility of his small, delicately formed mouth, which he used as a moist focus of emotion. He would press it in disapproval, turn it down like a child's in disappointment or disgust, lengthen and curve it when he smiled. It seemed never the same shape. Even in repose he would munch with it, as if relishing the taste of his tongue.

Nellie Ackroyd, in contrast, was slim where he was plumpish, fair where he was dark, and topped him by three inches. She wore her long blond hair twined in a plait round her head in the fashion of the twenties. Her tweed skirts were well cut but longer than had been fashionable for half a century and topped invariably by a loose cardigan. Her shoes were pointed and laced. Dalgliesh remembered one of his father's Sunday school teachers who could have been her double. As she came into the room, he was for a moment back in that village church hall, sitting in a circle with the other children on the low wooden chairs and waiting for Miss Mainwaring to hand out that Sunday's stamp, a coloured biblical picture which he would lick and stick with infinite care on that week's space on his card. He had liked Miss Mainwaring—dead now for over twenty years, of cancer, and buried in that distant Norfolk churchyard—and he liked Nellie Ackroyd.

The Ackroyds' marriage had astounded their friends and been a source of prurient speculation to their few enemies. But whenever he was with them, Dalgliesh never doubted that they were genuinely happy together and he marvelled anew at the infinite variety of marriage, that relationship at once so private and public, so hedged with convention and yet so anarchical. In his private life Ackroyd was reputed to be one of the kindest men in London. His victims pointed out that he could afford to be: one issue of the *Paternoster Review* commonly contained sufficient spleen to satisfy a normal life span. The reviews of new books and plays were always clever and entertaining, sometimes perceptive and occasionally cruel, and were a form of fortnightly entertainment cherished by all except the victims. Even when the *Times Literary Supplement* changed its practice, the

Paternoster continued to preserve the anonymity of its reviewers. Ackroyd took the view that no reviewer, not even the most scrupulous or disinterested, could be completely honest if his copy were signed, and he preserved the confidence of his contributors with all the high-minded zeal of an editor who knows that he is hardly likely to be presented with a court injunction. Dalgliesh suspected that the most vicious reviews were written by Ackroyd himself, abetted by his wife, and indulged a private picture of Conrad and Nellie sitting up in their separate beds and calling their happier inspirations through the open communicating door.

Whenever he was with them he was struck anew by the self-sufficiency amounting to conspiracy of their connubial felicity. If ever there were a marriage of convenience, this was it. She was a superb cook. He loved food. She liked nursing, and he suffered each winter from a mild recurrent bronchitis and from attacks of sinus headache which exacerbated his mild hypochondria and which kept her happily busy with chest rubs and inhalations. Dalgliesh, although the least prurient of men about the sex lives of his friends, couldn't resist wondering occasionally whether the marriage had ever been consummated. On the whole he thought that it had. Ackroyd was a stickler for legality, and on one honeymoon night at least he must have closed his eyes and thought of England. After which necessary sacrifice to legal and theological requirements, they had both settled down to the more important aspects of matrimony, the decoration of their house and the state of Conrad's bronchial tubes.

Dalgliesh hadn't come empty-handed. His hostess was a passionate collector of 1920s and 1930s girls' school stories, her series of early Angela Brazil being particularly notable. The shelves of her sitting room were witness to her addiction for this potent nostalgia: stories in which a succession of sloping-bosomed heroines, bloused and booted, called Dorothy or Madge, Marjorie or Elspeth, whacked hockey sticks with vigour, exposed the cheat in the upper fourth or were instrumental in unmasking German spies. Dalgliesh had found his first edition some months earlier in a second-hand bookshop in Marylebone. The fact that he couldn't recall precisely when or where reminded him how long it had been since he had last seen the Ackroyds. He suspected that they were most often visited by people who, like himself, wanted something, usually information. Dalgliesh reflected again on the oddness of human relationships in which people could describe themselves as friends who were content not to see each other for years, yet when they did meet could resume their intimacy as if there had been no interval of neglect. But their mutual liking was genuine enough. Dalgliesh might call only when there was something he needed. But he was never less than glad to sit in Nellie Ackroyd's elegant sitting room and gaze out through the Edwardian conservatory to the shimmer of the canal. Resting his eyes on it now, he found it difficult to believe that this light-dappled water seen through hanging baskets of variegated ivy and pink geraniums was the same which, a couple of miles upstream, slid like a liquid menace through the dark tunnels and flowed sluggishly past the south door of St. Matthew's Church.

He handed over his offering with the customary chaste kiss which seemed to have become a social convention even among comparatively recent acquaintances.

"For you," he said. "I think it's called *Dulcy on the Game*."

Nellie Ackroyd unwrapped it with a little squeak of pleasure.

"Don't be naughty, Adam. *Dulcy Plays the Game*. How lovely! And it's in perfect condition. Where did you find it?"

"In Church Street, I think. I'm glad you haven't got it already."

"I've been looking for it for years. This completes my pre-1930 Brazils. Conrad, darling, look what Adam has brought."

"Very civil of you, dear boy. Ah, here comes tea."

It was brought in by an elderly maid and set down in front of Nellie Ackroyd with almost ritual care. The tea was substantial. Thin crustless bread and butter, a plate of cucumber sandwiches, homemade scones with cream and jam, a fruitcake. It reminded him of childhood rectory teas, of visiting clergy and parish workers balancing their wide-brimmed cups in his mother's shabby but comfortable drawing room, of himself, carefully schooled, handing round plates. It was odd, he thought, that the sight of a coloured plate of thinly cut bread and butter could still evoke a momentary but sharp pain of grief and nostalgia. Watching Nellie as she carefully aligned the handles, he guessed that all their life was governed by small diurnal rituals: early-morning tea, the cocoa or milk last thing at night, beds carefully turned down, nightdress and pyjamas laid out. And now it was five fifteen, the autumn day would soon be darkening into evening and this small, very English tea ceremony was designed to propitiate the afternoon furies. Order, routine, habit, imposed on a disorderly world. He wasn't sure that he would like to live with it, but as a visitor he found it soothing and he didn't despise it. He had, after all, his own contrivances for keeping reality at bay. He said:

"This piece in the *Review*. I hope you're not thinking of turning the paper into a new gossip magazine."

"Not at all, dear boy. But people like an occasional titbit. I'm thinking of including you in our new column, 'What They Find to Talk About.' Incongruous people seen dining together. Adam Dalgliesh, poet-detective, with Cordelia Gray at Mon Plaisir, for example."

"Your readers must lead very dull lives if they can find vicarious excitement in a young woman and myself virtuously eating duck à l'orange."

"A beautiful young woman dining with a man over twenty years her senior is always interesting to our readers. It gives them hope. And you're looking very well, Adam. The new adventure obviously suits you. All right, I meant the new job, of course. Aren't you in charge of the sensitive crime squad?"

"It doesn't exist."

"No, that's my name for it. The Met probably call it C3A or something equally boring. But we know about it. If the Prime Minister and the leader of the Social Democrats imbibe arsenic while secretly dining together to plan a coalition and the Cardinal Archbishop of Westminster and His Grace of Canterbury are seen tiptoeing mysteriously from the scene, we don't want the local CID charging in to dirty the carpets with their size twelves. Isn't that rather the idea?"

"A fascinating if unlikely scenario. What about the editor of a literary review found battered to death and a senior detective observed tiptoeing from the scene? Your piece about Paul Berowne, Conrad, what started it off?"

"An anonymous communication. And you needn't assume a look of pained disgust. We all know that your people sit in pubs paying out tax-payers' money to the most sordid ex-cons for information received, most of it no doubt of highly dubious accuracy. I know all about snouts. And I didn't even have to pay for this. It came through the post, free and gratis."

"Who else had it, do you know?"

"It went to three of the dailies, to the gossip writers. They decided to wait and see before using it."

"Very prudent. You checked it."

"Naturally I checked it. At least, Winifred did."

Winifred Forsythe was nominally Ackroyd's editorial assistant, but there were few jobs connected with the *Review* that she couldn't turn her hand to, and there were those who claimed that it was Winifred's financial nous that kept the journal afloat. She had the appearance, dress and voice of a Victorian governess, an intimidating woman who was accustomed to getting her own way. Perhaps because of some atavistic fear of female authority, few people stood up to her, and when Winifred asked a question she expected to get an answer. There were times when Dalgliesh wished that he had her on his staff.

"She began by telephoning the Campden Hill Square house and asking for Diana Travers. A woman answered, not Lady Berowne or Lady Ursula. Either a servant or housekeeper—Winifred said she didn't sound like a secretary, not authoritative enough, not that competent kind of voice. Anyway, Berowne never had a living-in secretary. It was probably the housekeeper. When she heard the question there was a silence and she gave a kind of gasp. Then she said: 'Miss Travers isn't here, she's left.' Winifred asked if they had an address and she said 'No' and put down the receiver rather sharply. It wasn't well handled. If they wanted to conceal the fact that Travers had worked there, they should have schooled the woman more efficiently. There was no mention at the inquest that the girl had worked for Berowne, and no one else seems to have caught on to it. But it looked as if our poison pen was right in at least one of his facts. Travers was certainly known at Campden Hill Square."

Dalgliesh asked:

"And after that?"

"Winifred went down to the Black Swan. I have to admit her cover story wasn't particularly convincing. She told them that we were thinking of doing an article on drowning accidents in the Thames. We could confidently expect that no one would have heard of the *Paternoster Review*, so that the essential incongruity of it wouldn't be apparent. Even so, everyone was remarkably cagey. The proprietor—what's his name, some Frenchman?—wasn't there when Winifred called, but the people she did talk to had been well rehearsed. After all, no restaurant owner wants a death on the premises. In the midst of life we are in death, but not, one hopes, in the midst of dinner. Dropping unfortunate live lobsters into boiling water is one thing—really, how can people believe that they don't feel it?—but a drowned customer on the premises is quite another. Not that the Thames exactly counts as his premises, but the general theory holds. Much too close to be comfortable. From the moment one of the party she was with came dripping in to say the girl was dead, he and his staff took up their defensive positions, and I must say they seemed to have carried it off very neatly."

Dalgliesh didn't say that he had already studied the local police reports. He asked:

"What happened exactly? Did Winifred find out?"

"The girl, Diana Travers, came with a party of five friends. I gather they were mostly theatrical people, on the fringe anyway. No one well known. They got a little noisy after dinner and went out to the riverbank, where there was a certain amount of larking about. That isn't encouraged at the Black Swan, tolerated if you're a young viscount with the right connections no doubt, but this particular lot weren't rich enough, aristocratic enough or famous enough for that kind of licence. The owner was wondering whether to send someone out to remonstrate when the party moved further downstream and more or less out of earshot."

Dalgliesh said:

"Presumably they'd paid their bill by then."

"Oh yes, everything settled."

"Who paid?"

"Now, this may surprise you: Dominic Swayne, Barbara Berowne's brother. It was his party. He booked the table, he paid."

Dalgliesh said:

"The young man must have plenty of money if he could settle a bill for six at the Black Swan. Why wasn't he a member of his sister's birthday party?"

"Now, that wasn't a question Winifred thought it would be productive to ask. But it did occur to her that he might have held his own party on the same night to embarrass his sister or, of course, her escort."

It had also occurred to Dalgliesh. He recalled the police report. There had been six in the party: Diana Travers, Dominic Swayne, two female drama students whose names he couldn't recall, Anthony Baldwin, a stage designer, and Liza Galloway, who was taking a course in stage management at the City College. None had a criminal record, and it would have been a matter of mild surprise if they had. None had been investigated by the Thames Valley police, and that wasn't surprising either. There had been nothing suspicious, at least on the surface, about the Travers death. She had dived naked into the Thames and drowned with unspectacular efficiency in twelve feet of reed-infested water on a warm summer night.

Ackroyd went on with his story:

"Apparently the party had the good sense, from the restaurant's point of view, not to carry a dead and weed-wrapped body straight through the french windows into the dining room. Luckily the side door which leads to the kitchen quarters was the one closest. The girls rushed in bleating that one of their party had drowned, while Baldwin, who seems to have behaved with more good sense than the rest of them, was trying to give the girl the 'kiss of life,' not very efficiently. The chef ran out and took over with rather more expertise and worked on her until the ambulance arrived. By then she was dead by any criteria. She probably had been from the moment they brought her out. But you know all this. Don't tell me that you haven't studied the inquest report."

Dalgliesh said:

"Did Winifred ask whether Paul Berowne had been there that evening?"

"Yes, she did, with as much tact as she's capable of. Apparently he was expected. He had some business that prevented him joining the party for dinner, but he said that he would try to get there in time for coffee. Just before ten there was a telephone call to say that he had been delayed and couldn't make it. The interesting thing is that he was there . . . at least his car was."

"How did Winifred discover that?"

"Well, I must say, by a great deal of cleverness and even more good luck. You know the car park at the Black Swan presumably?"

Dalgliesh said:

"No, I've never been there, it's a pleasure to come. Tell me."

"Well, the proprietor dislikes the sound of cars arriving and leaving and I don't blame him, so the park is about fifty yards from the restaurant and surrounded by a high beech hedge. They haven't got valet parking, presumably that would be too expensive. People just have to walk the fifty yards, and if it's raining they drop their guests at the door first. So the car park is secluded and reasonably private. Even so, the doorman does keep an eye on it from time to time, and it occurred to Winifred that Berowne would hardly leave his car there if he were actually telephoning to say that he couldn't arrive. After all, any of the party might have taken it into their heads to leave soon afterwards and would have recognized it. So she made some enquiries further down the lane. There's a kind of lay-by just before you reach the A3 opposite a farm cottage lying a little back from the road. She enquired there."

Dalgliesh asked:

"On what pretext?"

"Oh, she just said that she was a private enquiry agent trying to trace a stolen car. People will answer almost anything as long as you ask with sufficient assurance. You should know that, my dear Adam."

Dalgliesh said:

"And she struck lucky."

"Indeed she did. A boy, he's fourteen, was doing his homework upstairs in his front bedroom in the cottage and saw a black Rover parked. Being a boy, he was naturally interested. He was quite definite about the make. It was there from about ten o'clock and was still there when he went to bed."

"Did he get the number?"

"No, that would have meant going out of the house, of course, and he wasn't sufficiently intrigued to take that kind of trouble. What interested him was that there was only one man in the car. He parked it, locked it and walked off towards the Black Swan. It's not unusual to have cars parked there, but they're usually courting couples and they stay in the car."

"Was he able to give a description?"

"Only a very general one, but as far as it went it corresponded more or less with Berowne. I'm satisfied myself that it was his car and that he was there. But I admit there's no proof. It was ten at night when the boy glimpsed him, and there are no lights in the lane. I couldn't be certain that he was at the Black Swan when Diana Travers drowned, and as you'll have noticed from my piece, I very carefully didn't say that he was."

"Did you check it with your lawyers before you printed it?"

"Indeed I did. They weren't exactly happy, but they had to admit that it wasn't libellous. After all, it was purely factual. Our gossip always is."

And gossip, thought Dalgliesh, was like any other commodity in the marketplace. You received it only if you had something of value to give. And Ackroyd, one of London's most notorious gossips, had a reputation for accuracy and value. He collected small titbits of information as other men hoarded screws and nails. They might not be wanted for the job on hand, but sooner or later they would come in useful. And he liked the sense of power which gossip gave him. Perhaps it reduced the vast amorphous city to manageable proportions for him, a few hundred people who counted in his world and who gave him the illusion of living in a private village, intimate but diverse and not unexciting. And he wasn't vicious. He liked people and he enjoyed pleasing his friends. Ackroyd crouched spider-like in his study and spun his web of mild intrigue. It was important to him that at least one thread connected him to a senior police officer as others, rather stronger, did to the parliamentary lobby, the theatre, Harley Street, the bar. Almost certainly he would have tapped his sources, ready to offer Dalgliesh a small bonus of information, if he could get it. Dalgliesh thought it was time he fished for it. He said:

"What do you know of Stephen Lampart?"

"Not a great deal, since nature has mercifully spared me the experience of childbirth. Two dear friends had their babies at his place in Hampstead, Pembroke Lodge. Everything went very well; an heir to a dukedom and a future merchant banker, both safely delivered and both boys, which, after a succession of girls, was what was wanted. He's reputedly a good gynaecologist."

"What about women?"

"Dear Adam, how prurient you are. Being a gynaecologist must present particular temptations. Women, after all, are so ready to show their gratitude in the only way some of the poor dears know. But he protects himself, and not only where his sex life is concerned. There was a libel case eight years ago. You may remember it. A journalist, Mickey Case, was so ill advised as to suggest that Lampart had carried out an illegal abortion at Pembroke Lodge. Things were a little less liberal in those days. Lampart sued and got exemplary damages. It ruined Mickey. There's not been a hint of scandal since. There's nothing like a reputation for being litigious to save you from slander. It is occasionally rumoured that he and Barbara Berowne are rather more than cousins, but I don't think anyone has actual proof. They've been remarkably discreet, and Barbara Berowne, of course, played the part of the MP's adoring and beautiful wife to perfection when called upon to do so, which wasn't so very often. Berowne was never a social chap. A small dinner party occasionally, the usual mild constituency beanfeasts, fund raising and so on. But otherwise, she wasn't required to exhibit herself in that particular role inconveniently often. The odd thing about Lampart is that he spends his life delivering babies, but he dislikes children intensely. But I rather agree with him. Up to four weeks they're quite enchanting. After that all one can say in favour of children is that they eventually grow up. He took his own precautions against procreation. He's had a vasectomy."

"How on earth did you get to know that, Conrad?"

"My dear boy, it isn't a secret. People used to boast about it. When he first had it done he used to wear one of those revolting ties advertising the fact. A little vulgar, I admit, but then there is a streak of vulgarity in Lampart. He keeps it under better control now—the vulgarity, I mean. The tie is folded away in a drawer along, no doubt, with other mementoes from his past."

And this indeed was a bonus, thought Dalgliesh. If Barbara Berowne was pregnant and Lampart wasn't the father, then who was? If it was Berowne himself and he had known of the fact, would he have been more or less likely to have killed himself? A jury would probably think less likely. To Dalgliesh, who had never believed the suicide theory, this wasn't particularly relevant. But it would be highly relevant to the prosecution if he caught his man and the case came to trial.

Ackroyd said:

"How did you get on with the formidable Lady Ursula? Had you met her before?"

"No. In my life, I don't often meet the daughter of an earl. Until now I haven't met one in my job either. What should I think of her? You tell me."

"What everyone wants to know about her—everyone of her generation, anyway—is why she married Sir Henry. Now, I happen to know the answer. I've thought it out all on my own. You may think my theory is obvious, but it's none the worse for that. It explains why so many beautiful women choose such ordinary men. It's because a beautiful woman—and I'm talking about beauty, not just prettiness—is so ambivalent about her beauty. With part of her mind she knows it's the most important thing about her. Well, of course, it is. But with another part she distrusts it. After all, she knows how transitory it is. She has to watch it fading. She wants to be loved for some other quality, usually one she doesn't possess. So when Lady Ursula got tired of all the importunate young men badgering and praising her, she chose dear old Henry, who had loved her devotedly for years, would obviously continue to love her until he died and seemed not to notice that he'd got himself the most admired beauty in England. Apparently it worked out very well. She gave him two sons and was faithful to him, well, more or less. And now, poor dear, she's left with nothing. Her father's title became extinct when her only brother was killed in 1917. And now this. Unless, of course, Barbara Berowne is pregnant with an heir, which, on the face of it, seems unlikely."

Dalgliesh asked:

"Isn't that the least important part of the tragedy, the extinction of the baronetcy?"

"Not necessarily. A title, particularly an old one, confers a comforting sense of family continuity, almost a kind of personal immortality. Lose it and you really begin to understand that all flesh is grass. I'll give you a word of advice, my dear Adam. Never underestimate Lady Ursula Berowne."

Dalgliesh said:

"I'm in no danger of that. Did you ever meet Paul Berowne?"

"Never. I knew his brother, but not well. We met when he was first engaged to Barbara Swayne. Hugo was an anachronism, more like a First World War hero than a modern soldier. You half-expected to see him slapping his cane against khaki breeches, carrying a sword. You expect his kind to get killed. They're born for it. If they didn't, what on earth would they do with themselves in old age? He was very much the favourite son, of course. He was the kind of man his mother understood, was brought up with, that mixture of physical beauty, recklessness and charm. I began to get interested in Paul Berowne when we decided to do that short feature, but I admit that most of my information about him is second hand. Part of Paul Berowne's private tragedy, admittedly a small one viewed sub specie aeternitatis, was neatly summed up by Jane Austen. 'His temper might, perhaps, be a little soured by finding, like many others of his sex, that through some unaccountable bias in favour of beauty he was the husband of a very silly woman.' *Pride and Prejudice*, Mr. Bennet."

"*Sense and Sensibility*, Mr. Palmer. And when one meets Barbara Berowne the bias doesn't seem so very unaccountable."

"*Sense and Sensibility*? Are you sure? Anyway, I'm glad that I'm immune to that particular enthrallment and the urge for possession that seems inseparable from it. Beauty suborns the critical faculty. God knows what Berowne thought he was getting, apart from a load of guilt. Probably the Holy Grail."

All in all, thought Dalgliesh, the visit to St. John's Wood had been even more fruitful than he had hoped. He took his time over finishing his tea. He owed his hostess at least the appearance of a decent civility, and he had no particular wish to hurry away. Soothed by Nellie Ackroyd's solicitous attention, comfortably ensconced in a gently rocking button-backed armchair whose arms and headrest seemed precisely designed to suit his body, and with his eyes soothed by the distant sheen of the canal seen through the light-filled conservatory, he had to make an effort to rouse himself to make his farewells and set off to drive back to the Yard, pick up Kate Miskin and take her with him to interview Berowne's only child.

5

Melvin Johns hadn't intended to make love. He had met Tracy at their usual place, the gate leading to the towpath, and they had walked together, her arm tucked under his, her thin body hugging against his until they came to their secret place, the patch of flattened grass behind the thick elderberries, the straight, dead stump of tree. And it had happened, as he knew it would. The brief, unsatisfactory spasm and what went before were no different than they had always been. The potent smell of loam and dead leaves, the soft earth under his feet, her eager body straining under his, the smell of her armpits, her fingers scratching at his scalp, the scrape of the bark of the tree against his cheek, the gleam of the canal seen through a thicket of leaves. All over. But afterwards the depression that always followed was worse than he had ever known. He wanted to sink into the earth and groan aloud. She whispered:

"Darling, we have to go to the police. We must tell them what we saw."

"It wasn't anything. Just a car parked outside the church."

"Outside the vestry door. Outside where it happened. The same night. And we know the time, about seven o'clock. It could be the murderer's car."

"It isn't likely he'd be driving a black Rover, and it isn't as if we noticed the number, even."

"But we have to tell. If they never find who did it, if he kills again, we'd never forgive ourselves."

The note of unctuous self-righteousness nauseated him. How was it, he wondered, that he'd never noticed before that perpetual whine in her voice. He said hopelessly:

"You said your dad would kill us if he knew we'd been meeting. The lies, telling him you were at evening classes. You said he'd kill us."

"But, darling, it's different now. He'll understand that. And we can get engaged. We'll tell them all that we were engaged."

Of course, he thought, suddenly enlightened. Dad, that respectable lay preacher, wouldn't mind as long as there was no scandal. Dad would enjoy the publicity, the sense of importance. They would have to marry. Dad, Mum, Tracy herself, would ensure that. It was as if his life were suddenly revealed to him in a slow unwinding reel of hopelessness, picture succeeding picture down the inescapable years. Moving into her parents' small house; where else could they afford to live? Waiting for a council flat. The first baby crying in the night. Her whining, accusing voice. The slow death, even of desire. A man was dead, an ex-Minister, a man he had never known, never seen, whose life and his had never until this moment touched. Someone, his murderer or an innocent motorist, had parked his Rover outside the church. The police would catch the killer, if there was a killer, and he would go to prison for life and in ten years he would be let out, free again. But *he* was only twenty-one and *his* life sentence would end only with his death. And what had he done to deserve his punishment? Such a little sin compared with murder. He almost groaned aloud with the injustice of it.

"All right," he said with dull resignation. "We'll go to the Harrow Road police station. We'll tell them about the car."

6

⊠

Sarah Berowne's flat was in a gaunt Victorian terrace of five-storey houses whose over-ornate and grimy facade was set back some thirty feet from the Cromwell Road behind a hedge of dusty laurel and spiky, almost leafless privet. Next to the entry phone was a bank of nine bells, the top one bearing only the single word BEROWNE. The door opened to their push as soon as they rang, and Dalgliesh and Kate passed through a vestibule into a narrow hall, the floor linoleum-covered, the walls painted the ubiquitous glossy cream, the only furniture a table for letters. The caged box of a lift was large enough only for two passengers. Its back wall was almost completely mirrored, but as it groaned slowly upwards the image of their two figures standing so close that he could smell the clean sweet scent of Kate's hair, could almost imagine that he could hear her heart beat, did nothing to dispel his incipient claustrophobia. They stopped with a jerk. As they stepped out into the corridor and Kate turned to close the lift grille, he saw Sarah Berowne was standing waiting for them at her open door.

The family resemblance was almost uncanny. She stood framed against the light from her flat like a frail feminine shadow of her father. Here were the same wide-spaced grey eyes, the same droop of the eyelid, the same finely boned distinction but devoid of the patina of masculine confidence and success. The fair hair, not layered in gold like Barbara Berowne's but darker, almost ginger, already showed its first grey and hung in dry lifeless strands framing the tapering Berowne face. She was, he knew, only in her early twenties, but she looked much older, the honey-coloured skin drained with weariness. She didn't even bother to glance at his warrant card, and he wondered whether she didn't care or was making a small gesture of contempt. She gave only a nod of acknowledgement as he introduced Kate, then stood aside and motioned them across the hall into the sitting room. A familiar figure rose to meet them and they found themselves facing Ivor Garrod.

Sarah Berowne introduced them but didn't explain his presence. But then there was no reason why she should; this was her flat, she could invite in whom she wished. It was Kate and he who were the interlopers, there at best by invitation or on sufferance, tolerated, seldom welcome.

After the dimness of the hall and the claustrophobic lift, they had walked into emptiness and light. The flat was a conversion from the mansard roof, the low sitting room running almost the whole length of the house, its northern wall composed entirely of glass, with sliding doors opening onto a narrow balustraded balcony. There was a door at the far end, presumably leading to the kitchen. The bedroom and bathroom would, he assumed, open from the entrance hall at the front of the house. Dalgliesh had developed a knack of taking in the salient features of a room without that preliminary frank appraisal which he himself would have found offensive from any stranger, let alone a policeman. It was odd, he sometimes thought, that a man morbidly sensitive about his own privacy should have chosen a job that required him to invade almost daily the privacy of others. But people's living space and the personal possessions with which they surrounded themselves were inevitably fascinating to a detective, an affirmation of identity, intriguing both in themselves and as a betrayal of character, interests, obsessions.

This room was obviously both her living room and her studio. It was sparsely but comfortably furnished. Two large and battered sofas sat against opposite walls with shelves over them for books, stereo and a drinks cupboard. Before the window there was a small round table with four dining chairs. The wall facing the window was covered with a cork board on which was pinned a collection of photographs. To the right were pictures of London and Londoners obviously designed to make a political point: couples over-dressed for a Palace garden party drifting across the grass of St. James's Park against the background of the bandstand; a group of blacks in Brixton staring resentfully into the lens; the Queen's Scholars of Westminster School filing decorously into the Abbey; an over-crowded Victorian playground with a thin, wistful-eyed child grasping the railings like an imprisoned waif; a woman with a face like a fox choosing a fur in Harrods; a couple of pensioners, gnarled hands curled in their laps, sitting stiff as Staffordshire figures one each side of their single-bar electric fire. The political message was, he thought, too facile to carry much weight but, as far as he was capable of judging, the pictures were technically clever; they were certainly well composed. The left of the board displayed what had probably been a more lucrative commission: a line of portraits of well-known writers. Some of the photographer's concern with social deprivation seemed to have infected even her work here. The men, unshaven, fashionably under-dressed in their tieless open-necked shirts, looked as if they had either just taken part in a literary discussion on Channel Four or were on their way to a 1930s labour exchange, while the women looked either haunted or defensive, except for a buxom grandmother, noted for her detective stories, who gazed mournfully at the camera as if deploring either the bloodiness of her craft or the size of her advance.

Sarah Berowne motioned them to the sofa to the right of the door and seated herself on the one opposite. It was hardly, thought Dalgliesh, a convenient arrangement for other than shouted conversation. Garrod perched himself on the arm of the sofa farthest from her as if purposely distancing himself from all three of them. In the last year he had, it seemed deliberately, moved out of the political limelight and was now less often heard propounding the views of the Workers' Revolutionary Campaign, concentrating, apparently, on his job as a community social worker, whatever that might mean. But he was immediately recognizable, a man who even in repose held himself as if well aware of the power of his physical presence but with that power under conscious control. He was wearing denim jeans with a white open-necked shirt and contrived to look both casual and elegant. He could, thought Dalgliesh, have stepped down from a portrait in the Uffizi with his long arrogant Florentine face, the generously curved mouth under the short upper lip, the high arched nose and tumble of dark hair, the eyes which gave nothing away. He said:

"Would you like something to drink? Wine, whisky or coffee?"

His tone was almost studiously polite, but neither sardonic nor provocatively obsequious. Dalgliesh knew his opinion of the Metropolitan Police; he had proclaimed it often enough. But he was playing this very carefully. They were all to be on the same side, at least for the present. Dalgliesh and Kate refused his offer of a drink, and there was a small silence broken by Sarah Berowne. She said:

"You're here about my father's death, of course. I don't think there's very much I can say to help. I haven't seen or spoken to him for over three months."

Dalgliesh said:

"But you were at 62 Campden Hill Square on Tuesday afternoon."

"Yes, to see my grandmother. I had an hour to spare between appointments, and I wanted to try to find out what was happening, my father's resignation, the rumour about his experience in that church. There was no one else to ask, to talk to. But she was out to tea. I didn't wait. I left at about four thirty."

"Did you go into the study?"

"The study?"

She looked surprised, then asked:

"I suppose you're thinking of his diary. Grandmama told me that you'd found it half-burnt in the church. I was in the study, but I didn't see it."

Dalgliesh said:

"But you knew where he kept it?"

"Of course. In the desk drawer. We all knew that. Why do you ask?"

Dalgliesh said:

"Just in the hope that you might have seen it. It would have been useful to know if the diary was there at four thirty. We can't trace your father's movements after he left the office of an estate agent in Kensington High Street at half past eleven. If you had happened to look in the drawer and seen the diary, then there is the possibility that he came back to the house unnoticed sometime during the afternoon."

That was only one possibility and Dalgliesh didn't deceive himself that Garrod, for one, was ignorant of the others. Now he said:

"We don't even know what happened, except what Sarah has learned from her grandmother, that Sir Paul and the tramp had their throats cut and that it looks as if his razor was the weapon. We were hoping you would be able to tell us more. Are you suggesting that it was murder?"

Dalgliesh said:

"Oh, I don't think there can be any doubt that this was murder."

He watched as the two bodies opposite seemed visibly to stiffen, then added calmly:

"The tramp, Harry Mack, certainly didn't slit his own throat. His death may not be of shattering social significance, but no doubt his life had some importance, at least to him."

He thought: If that doesn't provoke Garrod, then I wonder what would. But Garrod merely said:

"If you're asking us to provide an alibi for Harry Mack's murder, then we were here together from six o'clock on Tuesday until nine o'clock Wednesday morning. We had supper here. I bought a mushroom flan from Marks and Spencer's in Kensington High Street and we ate that. I could tell you what wine we drank with it, but I don't suppose that's relevant."

It was the first sign of irritation, but his voice was still mild, the gaze clear and unflustered. Sarah Berowne said:

"But Daddy! What happened to Daddy?"

Suddenly she sounded as frightened and helpless as a lost child. Dalgliesh said:

"We're treating it as a suspicious death. We can't say much more until we get the result of the post-mortem and the forensic tests."

Suddenly she got up and moved over to the window, staring out over the thirty yards of dishevelled autumnal garden. Garrod slid down from the arm of the sofa and went to the drinks cupboard, then poured a couple of glasses of red wine. He took one over to her and offered it silently, but she shook her head. He moved back to the sofa and sat holding his own glass, not drinking. He said:

"Look, Commander, this isn't exactly a visit of condolence, is it? And although it's reassuring to hear of your concern for Harry Mack, you're not here because of a dead tramp. If Harry's body had been the only one in that church vestry, it would have ranked a detective sergeant at best. I would have thought Miss Berowne had a right to know whether she's being questioned in a murder investigation or whether you're just curious to know why Paul Berowne should have slit his own throat. I mean, either he did or he didn't. Criminal investigation is your job, not mine, but I should have thought that, by now, it ought to be pretty clear-cut one way or the other."

Dalgliesh wondered whether the dreadful pun had been intentional. Either way, Garrod saw no reason to apologize for it. Watching that still figure by the window, Dalgliesh saw Sarah Berowne give a little shudder. Then, as if by an act of will, she turned from the window and faced him. He ignored Garrod and spoke directly to her.

"I should like to be more positive but, at the moment, that just isn't possible. Suicide is obviously one possibility. I was hoping that you might have seen your father recently and been able to say how he seemed to you, whether he said anything that could be relevant to his death. I know this is painful for you. I'm sorry that we have to ask these questions, that we have to be here."

She said:

"He did speak to me once about suicide, but not in the way you mean."

"Recently, Miss Berowne?"

"Oh no, we haven't spoken for years. Not really spoken, really talked to each other, as opposed to making sounds with our mouths. No, this was when I was home from Cambridge after my first term. One of my friends had killed himself, and my father and I talked about his death, about suicide generally. I've always remembered it. He said that some people thought of suicide as one of the options open to them. It wasn't. It was the end of all options. He quoted Schopenhauer: 'Suicide may be regarded as an experiment, a question which man puts to nature trying to force her to an answer. It is a clumsy experiment to make; for it involves the destruction of the very consciousness which puts the question and awaits the answer.' Daddy said that while we live there is always the possibility, the certainty of change. The only rational time for a man to kill himself is not when life is intolerable, but when he would prefer not to live it even if it became tolerable, even pleasant."

Dalgliesh said:

"That sounds like the ultimate despair."

"Yes. I suppose that's what he could have felt, ultimate despair."

Suddenly Garrod spoke. He said:

"He could more reasonably have quoted Nietzsche. 'The thought of suicide is a great consolation: by means of it one gets successfully through many a bad night.' "

Ignoring him, Dalgliesh still spoke directly to Sarah Berowne. He said:

"So your father didn't see you or write to you? He didn't explain what had happened in that church, why he was giving up his job, his parliamentary seat?"

He almost expected her to say: "What has that to do with this enquiry and what has it to do with you?" Instead she said:

"Oh no! I don't suppose he thought that I cared one way or the other. I only learned about it when his wife telephoned me. That was when he gave up his ministerial job. She seemed to think I might have some influence over him. It showed how little she understood either of us. If she hadn't telephoned, I should have had to learn about his resignation from the newspapers." Then she suddenly broke out:

"My God! He couldn't even get converted like an ordinary man. He had to be granted his own personal beatific vision. He couldn't even resign his job with decent reticence."

Dalgliesh said mildly:

"He seems to have acted with considerable reticence. He obviously felt that it was a private experience to be acted upon rather than discussed."

"Well, he could hardly splash it on the front pages of the Sunday heavies. Perhaps he realized that he'd only make himself ridiculous. Himself and the family."

Dalgliesh asked:

"Would that have mattered?"

"Not to me, but Grandmama would have minded—will mind now, I suppose. And his wife, of course. She thought she was marrying the next Prime Minister but one. She wouldn't relish being tied to a religious crank. Well, she's free of him now. And he's free of us, all of us."

She was silent for a moment, then said with sudden vehemence:

"I'm not going to pretend. Anyway, you know perfectly well that my father and I were—well, estranged. There's no secret about it. I didn't like his politics, I didn't like the way he treated my mother, I didn't like the way he treated me. I'm a Marxist, there's no secret about that either. Your people will have me on one of their little lists somewhere. And I care about my political beliefs. I don't believe he really did. He expected me to discuss politics as if we were chatting about a recent play we'd both seen, or a book we'd read, as if it were an intellectual diversion, something you could have what he would call a civilized argument about. He said that was one of the things he deplored about the loss of religion, it meant that people elevated politics into a religious faith and that was dangerous. Well, that's what politics are for me, a faith."

Dalgliesh said:

"Feeling as you do about him, his bequest to you must present you with a dilemma of conscience."

"Is that your tactful way of asking me if I killed my father for his money?"

"No, Miss Berowne. It's a not particularly tactful way of finding out what you feel about a not uncommon moral dilemma."

"I feel fine, just fine. There's no dilemma as far as I'm concerned. Anything I get will be put to good use for a change. It won't be much. Twenty thousand, isn't it? It's going to need more than twenty thousand pounds to change this world."

Suddenly she went back to the sofa, sat down, and they saw that she was crying. She said:

"I'm sorry, I'm sorry. This is ridiculous. It's only shock. And tiredness. I didn't sleep much last night. And I've had a busy day, things I couldn't cancel. Why should I cancel them, anyway? There's nothing I can do for him."

The phenomenon wasn't new to him. Other people's tears, other people's grief were inseparable from a murder enquiry. He had learned not to show surprise or embarrassment. The response varied, of course. A cup of hot, sweet tea if there was someone around to make it, a glass of sherry if the bottle was to hand, a slug of whisky. He had never been good at the comforting hand on the shoulder, and here, he knew, it wouldn't be welcome. He felt Kate stiffen at his side as if to make an instinctive move towards the girl. Then she looked at Garrod, but Garrod didn't move. They waited silently. The sobbing was quickly checked and Sarah Berowne again raised her face to them. She said:

"I'm sorry, I'm sorry. Please don't mind me. I'll be all right in a minute."

Garrod said:

"I don't think there's anything else we can usefully tell you, but if there is, perhaps it could wait until another time. Miss Berowne is upset."

Dalgliesh said:

"I can see that. If she wants us to go, of course we shall."

She looked up and said to Garrod:

"You go. I'm all right. You've said what you came to say. You were here with me on Tuesday night, all night. We were together. And there's nothing you can say about my father. You never knew him. So why don't you go?"

Dalgliesh was surprised by the sudden venom in her voice. Garrod could have hardly welcomed this curt dismissal, but he was too controlled and too astute to protest. He looked at her with what seemed detached interest rather than resentment and said:

"If you need me, just ring."

Dalgliesh waited until he was at the door, then said quietly:

"One moment. Diana Travers and Theresa Nolan. What do you know about them?"

Garrod was motionless for a second, then swung slowly round. He said:

"Only that they're both dead. I do occasionally see the *Paternoster Review.*"

"The recent article about Sir Paul in the *Review* was partly based on a scurrilous communication sent to him and to a number of papers. This communication."

He took it from his briefcase and handed it to Garrod. There was a silence while he read it. Then, his face devoid of expression, he handed it to Sarah Berowne. He said:

"You aren't, surely, suggesting that Berowne cut his throat because someone sent him an unkind letter? Wouldn't that be a little over-sensitive for a politician? And he was a barrister. If he thought it was actionable, he had his remedy."

"I'm not suggesting that it provides a motive for suicide. I was wondering whether you or Miss Berowne had any idea who could have sent it?"

The girl handed it back, merely shaking her head. But Dalgliesh saw that its production had been unwelcome. She was neither a good actress nor a good liar. Garrod said:

"I admit that I took it for granted that the child Theresa Nolan aborted was Berowne's, but I didn't feel called upon to do anything about it. If I had, I'd have done something more effective than this farrago of unsubstantiated spite. I only met the girl once, at an unfortunate dinner party at Campden Hill Square. Lady Ursula was convalescent; it was her first night down. The poor girl certainly didn't look happy. But then, Lady Ursula was brought up to know what room people are entitled to dine in and, of course, their proper placement at table. Nurse Nolan, poor child, was eating out of her station and was made to feel it."

Sarah Berowne said softly:

"Not intentionally."

"Oh, I didn't say it was intentional. Women like your grandmother are offensive merely by existing. Intention doesn't come into it."

Then, without touching Sarah Berowne, without even a glance at her, he said his good-byes to Kate and Dalgliesh as formally as if they had been fellow guests at a dinner party, and the door closed behind him. The girl tried to control herself, then broke into open sobbing. Kate got up, went through the opposite door and, after what seemed to Dalgliesh an unnecessarily long time, came back with a glass of water, then sat down beside Sarah Berowne and silently offered it. The girl drank it thirstily, then said:

"Thank you. This is silly. It's just that I can't believe he's dead, that I'll never see him again. I suppose I always thought that sometime, somehow, things would be right between us. I suppose I thought that there was plenty of time. All the time in the world. They're all gone now, Mummy, Daddy, Uncle Hugo. Oh, God, I feel so hopeless."

There were things that he would like to have asked, but now wasn't the time. They waited until she was calm again and then asked if she was sure she was all right before they left. The question struck him as insincere, a formal hypocrisy. She was as right as she would ever be when they were there.

As they drove away, Kate was for a time silent, then she said:

"It's an all-electric kitchen, sir. There's one wrapped packet of four boxes of Bryant and May matches in the cupboard, that's all. But that doesn't prove anything. They could have bought a single box and chucked it away afterwards."

Dalgliesh thought: She was fetching the glass of water showing genuine sympathy, genuine concern. But her mind was still on the evidence. And some of my officers think women are more sentimental than men. He said:

"We shan't get much joy trying to trace a single box of matches. A safety match is the easiest thing to lay hands on, the most difficult to identify."

"There's another thing, though, sir. I looked in the waste bin. I found the cardboard packet from the Marks and Spencer mushroom flan. They ate it all right, but it was two days past its last marked date of sale on Tuesday. He couldn't have bought it then. Since when have Marks and Spencer sold stale food? I wasn't sure whether you'd want the package or not."

Dalgliesh said:

"We haven't yet a right to take anything out of that flat. It's too early. You could argue that it's a clue in their favour. If they'd planned this crime I suspect Garrod would have bought the food on Tuesday morning and have made sure that the girl at the desk remembered him. And there's another thing, they've produced an alibi for the whole night. That suggests that they may not know the relevant time."

"But isn't Garrod too clever to fall into that trap?"

"Oh, he wouldn't produce an alibi neatly timed for eight o'clock, but the somewhat over-generous one he has produced to cover every hour from six to nine the next morning does suggest that he's playing safe."

And, like the other alibis, it wouldn't be an easy one to break. They had briefed themselves before this visit as they did before every interview.

They knew that Garrod lived alone in a single-bedroom mansion flat in Bloomsbury, a large, anonymous block, without a porter. If he claimed to have spent the night elsewhere it was difficult to see who could prove otherwise. Like everyone else concerned with the case whom they had interviewed to date, Sarah Berowne and her lover had produced an alibi. The police might not consider it a particularly convincing one, but Dalgliesh had too high an opinion of Garrod's intelligence to suppose that it could be easily broken and certainly not by a date stamp on the carton of a mushroom flan.

Back at the Yard, Dalgliesh had hardly entered his office before Massingham came in. He prided himself on his ability to control his excitement and his voice was carefully nonchalant.

"Harrow Road have just been on the phone, sir. There's an interesting development. A couple walked into the station ten minutes ago, a twenty-one-year-old and his girl. They say they were on the towpath on Tuesday evening, courting apparently. They passed through the turnstile by St. Matthew's just before seven. There was a black Rover parked outside the south door."

"Did they get the number?"

"No such luck. They can't even be sure of the make. But they are definite about the time. The girl was expected home by seven thirty and they looked at their watches just before leaving the towpath. And the boy, Melvin Johns, thinks that it could have been an A registration. Harrow Road think he's telling the truth. The poor kid seems petrified. He's certainly not a nut case looking for publicity. They've asked the couple to wait until I get over." He added:

"That parking lot by the church could be useful for anyone who knew it. But the local people obviously prefer to park their cars where they can keep an eye on them. And it isn't as if the area has a theatre, fashionable restaurants. For my money, there's only one black Rover one might expect to see parked outside that church."

Dalgliesh said:

"That's premature, John. It was getting dark, they were in a hurry. They can't even be sure of the make."

"You're depressing me, sir, I'd better get over there. It'll be just my luck to discover it was the local undertaker's hearse!"

7

⊠

She knew that Ivor would come back that night. He wouldn't telephone first, partly out of excessive caution, partly because he always expected her to be there waiting when she knew he was likely to arrive. For the first time since they had become lovers she found herself dreading his signal, the one long ring of the entry phone followed by the three short. Why couldn't he telephone, she thought resentfully, let her know when to expect him. She tried to settle to work on her newest project, the montage of two black-and-white photographs taken last winter in Richmond Park of the naked boughs of huge oak trees under a sky of tumbling clouds, and which she now planned to mount, one reversed under the other, so that the tangled boughs looked like roots reflected in water. But it seemed to her as she shifted the prints with increasing dissatisfaction that the device was meaningless, a cheap derivative effect, that this, like all her work, was symbolic of her life, thin, insubstantial, second-hand, pilfered from other people's experience, other people's ideas. Even the London pictures, cleverly composed, were without conviction, stereotypes seen through Ivor's eyes, not her own. She thought: I must learn to be my own person, however late, however much it hurts, I have to do it. And it seemed to her strange that it should have taken her father's death to show her what she was.

At eight o'clock she was aware of hunger and cooked herself scrambled eggs, stirring them carefully over a low heat, taking as much trouble as if Ivor had been there to share them. If he did arrive while she was eating, he could cook his own. She washed up and he still hadn't arrived. Walking out to the balcony, she gazed over the garden to the darkening bulk of the opposite terrace, whose windows were beginning to light up like signals from space. Those unknown people would be able to see her window, too, the huge expanse of lighted glass. Would the police call on them, ask them whether they had seen a light here on Tuesday night? Had Ivor, for all his cleverness, thought of that?

Gazing out over the darkness, she made herself think of her father. She could recall the precise moment at which things had changed between them. They had been living then in the Chelsea house, just her parents, herself and Mattie. It had been seven o'clock on a misty August morning and she had been alone in the dining room, pouring her first cup of coffee, when the call came. She answered the telephone from the hall and had been given the news just as her father came down the stairs. He had seen her face, stopped, his hand on the banister, and she had looked up at him.

"It's Uncle Hugo's colonel. He wanted to ring himself. Daddy, Hugo's dead." And then their eyes had met, had for a moment held, and she had seen it clearly: the mixture of exultation and wild hope, the knowledge that now he could have Barbara. It had lasted only a second. Time had moved on. And then he had taken the receiver from her and, without speaking, she had walked back into the dining room, through the French windows and into the enclosing greenness of the garden, shaking with the horror of it.

Nothing afterwards could ever be right between them. Everything that followed, the car accident, her mother's death, his marriage to Barbara less than five months later, had seemed only the inevitable consequence of that moment of realization, not willed by him, not even connived at, but accepted as inescapable. And even before the marriage the enormity of that mutual knowledge made it impossible for them to meet each other's eyes. He was ashamed that she knew. She was ashamed of knowing. And it seemed to her that when they moved into Hugo's house, the house which from their first moment of possession had seemed to resent and reject them, she carried her knowledge like a secret infection, that if Halliwell, Mattie, her grandmother knew, they had caught the knowledge from her.

At Campden Hill Square she and her father had been like fellow guests at a hotel who had met by chance, aware of a shared and shameful history, creeping down the passages in case the other should suddenly appear, planning to take meals at different times, harassed by the knowledge of the other's presence, the footstep in the hall, the key in the door. Ivor had been her escape and her revenge. She had been desperate for a cause, for an excuse to distance herself from her family, for love; but most of all for revenge. Ivor, whom she had met when he had commissioned a series of photographs, had provided them all. Before her father's marriage to Barbara she had moved out, borrowing against her modest legacy from her mother's will to put down a deposit on the Cromwell Road flat. She had tried by embracing with passion everything he most disliked or despised to free herself of her father. But now he was gone and she would never be free of him, never again.

One of the dining chairs was still pulled out from the table. Here, only yesterday, her grandmother had painfully seated herself and had told her the news in brutal monosyllables, the taxi meter ticking away outside. She had said:

"No one expects you to show much grief, but try, when the police arrive, as they will, to behave with reasonable discretion. If you have any influence over him, persuade your lover to do the same. And now perhaps you could help me with the lift door."

She had always been a little afraid of her grandmother, knowing from childhood that she was a disappointment, that she should have been a son. And she had none of the qualities her grandmother admired: beauty, intelligence, wit, not even courage. There was no comfort for her in that cluttered top-floor sitting room at Campden Hill Square, where the old lady had sat since Hugo's death like some archaic prophetess awaiting the inevitable doom. It was her father who had always come first with her, in her childhood and afterwards. It was her father who had been the more supportive when she had left Cambridge at the end of her first year and had gone to a London polytechnic to study photography. How much had she really cared about her mother's anguish when the infatuation with Barbara became obvious? Wasn't it just that she had hated the threat to her comfortable, ordered, conventional life, resented the fact that, entranced, her father no longer seemed even to notice her? Perhaps, she thought, the belated acknowledgement of that old jealousy was one small step towards becoming her own person.

It was after eleven before Ivor arrived, and she was very tired. He made no excuses and wasted no time on preliminaries. Throwing himself down on the sofa, he said:

"It wasn't very clever, was it? The idea of my being here was to have a witness. You let yourself be left alone with probably the most dangerous detective of the Yard and a female sidekick brought along to reassure you that he wasn't going to stop behaving like a gentleman."

She said:

"Don't worry. I didn't reveal the Boy Scout password. And they're human, I suppose. Inspector Miskin was rather kind."

"Don't be ridiculous. The girl's a fascist."

"Ivor, how can you say that? How can you know?"

"I make it my business to know. I suppose she held your hand, made you a nice cup of tea."

"She fetched me a drink of water."

"Which gave her an excuse to ferret around in the kitchen without the trouble of getting a search warrant."

She cried:

"It wasn't like that! She wasn't like that!"

"You haven't an idea what any of the police are like. The trouble with you middle-class liberals is that you're conditioned to see them as allies. You never accept the truth about them. You can't. To you they're always the avuncular Sergeant Dixon tugging his forelock and telling the kids the time. It's what you're brought up on. 'If you're ever in difficulty, darling, if a nasty man approaches you and wiggles his johnny at you, always find a policeman.' Look, Dalgliesh knows your politics, he knows about the legacy, he knows you've got a lover who's a committed Marxist and who might like to get his hands on the cash for the best or worst of reasons. So he's got a motive and a suspect, a very satisfactory suspect from his point of view, just what the Establishment are hoping for. Then he can get down to the business of fabricating the evidence."

"You don't really believe that."

"For Christ's sake, Sarah, there are precedents. You can't have lived for over twenty years with your eyes shut. Your grandmother prefers to believe that her son wasn't a murderer or a suicide. Fair enough. She may even persuade the police to play along with her fantasy. She's nearly in her dotage, but these old women still have extraordinary influence. But she's not making me the sacrificial victim to Berowne family pride. There's only one way to treat the police. Tell them nothing, nothing. Let the bastards find out the hard way. Make them do some work for their index-linked pensions."

She said:

"I suppose if it really comes to it, you'll let me tell them where I was Tuesday night?"

"If it comes to what? What are you talking about?"

"If they actually arrest me."

"For cutting your father's throat? Is it likely? Come to think of it, a woman could have done it. Given a razor, it wouldn't need much strength, only immense nerve. But it would have to be a woman he trusted, one who could get close to him. That could explain why there wasn't a struggle."

She said:

"How do you know that there wasn't a struggle, Ivor?"

"If there had been, the press and the police would have said so. It would have been one of the strongest indications that it wasn't suicide. You must have read the sort of thing they print: 'Sir Paul put up a desperate struggle for life. There were considerable signs of disorder in the room.' Your father killed himself, but that doesn't mean that the police won't use his death to make nuisances of themselves."

She said:

"Suppose I decide to tell?"

"Tell what? Give them the code names of eleven people whose addresses, whose real names you don't even know? Give them the address of a suburban terraced house where they'll find nothing incriminating? The moment a police officer sets foot in the safe house the cell is disbanded, re-formed, re-housed. We're not fools. There is a procedure for treachery."

"What procedure? Throwing me in the Thames? Slitting my throat?"

She saw the surprise in his eyes. Was it her imagination that it was tinged with respect? But he only said:

"Don't be ridiculous."

He unwound himself from the sofa and made for the door. But there was something she needed to ask. Once she would have been afraid. She was still a little afraid, but perhaps it was time to take a small step towards courage. She said:

"Ivor, where were you on Tuesday night? You've never been late for a cell meeting before, you've always been there before the rest of us. But it was after ten past nine before you arrived."

"I was with Cora at the bookshop and there was a hold-up on the tube. I explained at the time. I wasn't at St. Matthew's Church cutting your father's throat, if that's what you're implying. And until the police are forced to accept that he killed himself, we'd better not meet. If it's necessary, I'll be in touch in the usual way."

"And the police? Suppose they come back?"

"They'll come back. Stick to the alibi and don't try to be clever. Don't embroider. We were here together from six o'clock all night. We ate a mushroom flan, we drank a bottle of Riesling. All you have to do is to remember what we did on Sunday night and transpose it to Tuesday. Don't think you're doing me any great favour, it's yourself you need to protect."

And without touching her he was gone. So that, she thought wearily, was how love ended, with the slam of a grille door, the grind of the lift bearing him slowly downwards out of her life.

BOOK FOUR

Devices and Desires

1
⊠

The Black Swan, despite its name, didn't derive from a riverside pub but from an elegant two-storey villa built at the turn of the century by a prosperous Kensington painter seeking a weekend retreat with country quiet and a river view. After his death it had suffered the usual vicissitudes of a private residence too damp and inconveniently situated to be suitable as a permanent home and too large for a weekend cottage. It had been a restaurant of sorts for twenty years under its original name, but hadn't flourished until Jean Paul Higgins took it over in 1980, renamed it, built on a new dining room with wide windows overlooking the river and the far water meadows, employed a French chef, Italian waiters, and an English doorman, and set out to win his first modest mention in the *Good Food Guide*. Higgins's mother had been a Frenchwoman and he had obviously decided that, as a restaurateur, it was that half of his parentage he had better emphasize. His staff and customers called him Monsieur Jean Paul, and it was only his bank manager who, to his chagrin, insisted on greeting him with cheerful exuberance as Mr. Higgins. He and his bank manager were on excellent terms and for the best of reasons: Mr. Higgins was doing very well. In the summer it was necessary to book a table for luncheon or dinner at least three days in advance. In autumn and winter the place was less busy and the luncheon menu offered only three main dishes, but the standard of cooking and service never varied. The Black Swan was close enough to London to attract a number of city regulars willing to drive twenty-odd miles for the Black Swan's peculiar advantages: an attractive ambience, tables spaced at a reasonable distance, a low noise level, no piped music, unostentatious service, discretion and excellent food.

Monsieur Jean Paul was small and dark with melancholy eyes and a thin moustache which made him look like a stage Frenchman, an impression strengthened when he spoke. He himself greeted Dalgliesh and Kate at the door with unflurried courtesy as if there were nothing he had been looking forward to more than a visit from the police. But Dalgliesh noticed that despite the early hour and the quietness of the house, they were shown into his private office at the rear of the building with the minimum of delay. Higgins was of the school which believes, not without reason, that even when the police come visiting in plainclothes and don't actually kick down the door, they are always unmistakably the police. Dalgliesh didn't miss his quick glance of appraisal at Kate Miskin, the quickly suppressed look of surprise changing to modified approval. She was wearing slacks in fawn gabardine with a well-cut, unobtrusive checked jacket over a rollneck cashmere jumper and with her hair bound back in a short, thick plait. Dalgliesh wondered what Higgins expected a plainclothes police-woman to look like, an over-made-up harpy in black satin and a trench coat?

He offered refreshment, at first carefully ambiguous about the kind, and then more specific. Dalgliesh and Kate accepted coffee. It came quickly, served by a young waiter in a short white jacket, and it was excellent. When Dalgliesh had swallowed his first sip, Higgins gave a small sigh of relief as if his guest, now irrevocably compromised, had lost some of his power.

Dalgliesh said:

"As I expect you know, we are investigating the death of Sir Paul Berowne. You may have information which can help fill in some of the background."

Jean Paul spread his palms and launched into his voluble Frenchman act. But the melancholy eyes were wary.

"The death of Sir Paul, so terrible, so tragic. I ask myself what the world is coming to when such violence is possible. But how can I help the Commander? He was murdered in London, not here, thank God. If it was murder. There's a rumour that, maybe, Sir Paul himself . . . But that, too, would be terrible, more terrible for his wife than murder, perhaps."

"He came here regularly?"

"From time to time, not regularly. He was a busy man, of course."

"But Lady Berowne was here more often, usually with her cousin, I understand?"

"A delightful lady. She adorned my dining room. But, of course, one does not always notice who is dining with whom. We concentrate on the food and the service. We are not gossip writers, you understand."

"But presumably you can remember whether she was dining with her cousin, Stephen Lampart, on the Tuesday of this week, just three days ago?"

"On the seventeenth. That was so. They were seated at twenty minutes to nine. It is a little foible of mine, to note the time the customer is actually seated. The booking was for eight forty-five, but they were a little early. Monsieur may wish to inspect the book."

He opened his desk drawer and produced it. Obviously, thought Dalgliesh, he had been expecting a visit from the police and had placed the evidence to hand. The time against the name Lampart was written clearly and there was no sign that the figures had been altered.

He asked:

"When was the table booked?"

"That morning. At ten thirty, I believe. I cannot, I regret, be more precise."

"Then he was fortunate to get it."

"We can always find a table for an old and valued customer, but it is, of course, easier if a booking is made. The notice was sufficient."

"How did Mr. Lampart and Lady Berowne seem when they arrived?"

The dark eyes lifted reproachfully to his as if in silent protest at so tactless a question.

"How should they seem, Commander? Hungry." Then he added, as if fearing the answer had been imprudent:

"They were as usual. The lady is always gracious, most friendly. They were content that I was able to give them their usual table, in the corner by the window."

"What time did they leave?"

"At eleven or a little after. One does not hurry a good dinner."

"And during dinner? They talked, presumably."

"They talked, monsieur. It is a pleasure of dining, to share good food, good wine and good talk with a friend. But as for what they said, we are not eavesdroppers, Commander. We are not the police. These are good customers, you understand."

"Unlike some of the customers you had here on the night Diana Travers drowned. You had time to notice them, I suppose?"

Higgins showed no surprise at the sudden change in questioning. He spread his hands in a Gallic gesture of resignation.

"Alas, who could overlook them? They were not the kind of client we usually attract. At dinner they were quiet enough, but afterwards, well, it was not agreeable. I was relieved when they left the dining room."

"Sir Paul Berowne wasn't with his wife's party, I understand."

"That is so. When they arrived, Monsieur Lampart said that Sir Paul hoped to join them later, in time for coffee. But as you may know, he telephoned at ten o'clock, or a little later maybe, and said that it would not, after all, be possible."

"Who took the call?"

"My doorman, Henry. Sir Paul asked to speak to me, and I was called to the telephone."

"Did you recognize his voice?"

"As I have said, he was not here so very often, but I knew his voice. It was a voice, how you say, a distinctive voice, surprisingly like your own, Commander, if I may be permitted to say so. I cannot swear to these things, but I had no doubt at the time who was speaking."

"Have you any doubt now?"

"No, Commander, I cannot say that I have."

"The two parties for dinner, Mr. Lampart's and the young people, did they mix, greet each other?"

"They may have done, on arrival, but the tables were not close." He would have seen to that, thought Dalgliesh. If there had been the slightest sign of embarrassment on Barbara Berowne's part, or of insolence on her brother's, Higgins would have noticed it.

"And the members of Diana Travers's party, had you ever seen them here before?"

"Not that I remember, except for Mr. Dominic Swayne. He has dined here once or twice with his sister, but the last time was some months ago. But for the others, I cannot be sure."

"It was strange, surely, that Mr. Swayne wasn't included in Lady Berowne's birthday party?"

"Monsieur, it is not for me to dictate which guests my customers should invite. No doubt there were reasons. There were four only in the birthday group, an intimate party. The table was balanced."

"But would have become unbalanced if Sir Paul had arrived?"

"That is so, but then he was expected only for coffee, and he was, after all, the lady's husband."

Dalgliesh went on to ask Higgins about the events leading up to the drowning.

"As I have said, I was glad when the young people left the dining room and went out through the conservatory to the garden. They took two bottles of wine with them. It was not the best claret, but for them it was good enough. I do not like to see my wine swung about as if it were beer. There was much laughter and I was wondering whether to send Henry or Barry to deal with them, but they moved along the bank out of earshot. It was there that they found the punt. It was tied up, wedged you might say, in a small inlet about eighty yards downstream. Now, of course, it has been removed. Perhaps it should not have been there, but how can I blame myself? I cannot control what my patrons do when they are off the premises, nor indeed when they are here."

He used the word blame but the regret was perfunctory. No voice could have held less concern. Dalgliesh suspected that the only thing Higgins ever blamed himself for was a spoilt dinner or poor service. He went on:

"The next thing I know is the chef beckoning me from the door of the dining room. That was unusual, you understand. Immediately I could see something is wrong. I go quickly out. In the kitchen is one of the girls crying and saying that this other girl, Diana, is dead, drowned. We go out to the riverbank. The night is dark, you understand, the stars high and the moon not full. But there is some light from the car park, which is always brightly lit, and some from the kitchen wing of the house. But I take with me a torch. Monsieur may imagine the distress. The girls crying, one of the young men working on the body, Mr. Swayne standing there with his clothes dripping. Marcel takes over the respiration—he has many talents, that one—but it is of no use. I could see she was dead. The dead are not like the living, monsieur, never, never, never."

"And the girl was naked?"

"As you no doubt have been told. She had taken off all her clothes and dived in for a swim. It was a great folly."

There was a silence while he contemplated the folly. Then Dalgliesh put down his coffee cup. He said:

"It was convenient that Mr. Lampart should have been dining that night. It was natural, of course, to call on him for help."

The dark eyes, carefully expressionless, looked straight into his.

"That was my first thought, Commander. But it was too late. When I reached the dining room, I was told that Monsieur Lampart's party had only that moment left. I myself saw the Porsche as it turned out of the drive."

"So Mr. Lampart could have been fetching his car from the park shortly before you learned of the tragedy?"

"That is possible, certainly. I understand that the rest of his party waited at the door."

"Surely an early, and somewhat hurried, end to the evening?"

"As to hurried, that I cannot say. But the party had been seated early, shortly after seven. If Sir Paul had been able to join them, no doubt they would have stayed later."

Dalgliesh said:

"There has been a suggestion that Sir Paul may have arrived here that night after all."

"I have heard that, Commander. There was a woman who came to question my staff. It was not agreeable. I was not here at the time, but I would have dealt with her. No one saw Sir Paul on that night, I assure you. And his car was not seen in the parking lot. It may have been there, but it was not seen. And how can this concern his death, I ask myself."

Dalgliesh could usually tell when he wasn't getting the truth or was getting only part of it. It was less a matter of instinct than of experience. And Higgins was lying. Now he decided to take a chance. He said:

"But someone did see Sir Paul Berowne that night. Who was it?"

"Monsieur, I assure you . . ."

"I need to know and I'm quite prepared to hang around until I do. If you want to get rid of us, a perfectly reasonable wish on your part, you'll succeed most quickly by answering my questions. The verdict at the inquest was accidental death. No one, to my knowledge, has suggested that it was anything else. She had eaten too much, drunk too much, she got caught in the reeds and panicked. It is of academic interest whether she died of shock or was drowned. So what are you hiding and why?"

"We are hiding nothing, Commander, nothing. But as you have just said, the death was an accident. Why then make trouble? Why add to distress? And one cannot be sure. A figure quickly walking, glimpsed in the darkness, in the shadow of the hedge, who can tell who it was?"

"So who was it saw him? Henry?"

It was less a lucky guess than a reasonable assumption. Berowne almost certainly hadn't shown himself on the premises, and the doorman was the member of staff most likely to have been outside.

"It was Henry, yes." Higgins admitted the fact with a sad defeatism. The mournful eyes gazed reproachfully at Dalgliesh as if to say: "I have been helpful, I have given you information and coffee, and look where it has led me."

"Then perhaps you'll send for him. And I'd like to speak to him alone."

Higgins lifted the telephone receiver and dialled a single digit. It connected him to the front entrance. Henry answered it and was summoned. When he appeared, Higgins said:

"This is Commander Dalgliesh. Please tell him what you thought you saw the night that girl was drowned." Then he gave him a half-rueful glance, shrugged his shoulders and left. Henry, unruffled, stood at attention. Dalgliesh saw that he was older than his confident, upright figure would suggest, certainly nearer seventy than sixty.

He said:

"You're ex-Army, aren't you?"

"That's right, sir, the Gloucesters."

"How long have you been working here for Mr. Higgins, for Monsieur Jean Paul?"

"Five years, sir."

"You live in?"

"No, sir. The wife and I, we live at Cookham. This place is handy as places go." He added, as if hoping that a personal touch would demonstrate his willingness to cooperate frankly: "I've got my Army pension but a little extra never hurts."

And it wouldn't be so little, thought Dalgliesh. The tips would be good and most of them, given human frailty about the depredations of the Inland Revenue, would be tax free. Henry would want to keep his job.

He said:

"We're investigating the death of Sir Paul Berowne. We're interested in anything that happened to him during the last weeks of his life, however unimportant and irrelevant it might seem. Apparently he was here on the night of August seventh, and you saw him."

"Yes, sir, crossing the car park. One of our guests that night was leaving and I was fetching his Rolls. We haven't valet parking, sir, it would take me off the door too often. But occasionally guests like to have their cars parked and they hand me their keys on arrival. Antonio, he's one of the waiters, gave me the word that my party was ready to leave and

I went for the car. I was standing there putting the key in the lock when I saw Sir Paul cross the car park, walking along the line of the hedge and out through the gate leading to the river."

"How certain are you it was Sir Paul Berowne?"

"Pretty certain, sir. He isn't here often, but I've a good eye for faces."

"Do you know what car he drives?"

"A black Rover, I think. An A registration. I can't remember the number." Couldn't or wouldn't, thought Dalgliesh. A black Rover would be difficult to identify; a registration number was irrefutable evidence. He asked:

"And there was no black Rover parked that night?"

"Not that I noticed, sir, and I think I would have noticed."

"And you said he was walking briskly?"

"Very briskly, sir, purposefully you might say."

"When did you tell Monsieur Jean Paul about this?"

"The next morning, sir. He said that there was no need to tell the police. Sir Paul had a right to walk by the river if he chose. He said we had better wait until the inquest. If there had been marks on the body, any suggestion of foul play, that would be different. The police would want to know the names of anyone who had been here that night. But it was accidental death. The coroner was satisfied that the young lady had herself dived into the river. After that, Monsieur Jean Paul decided we should say nothing."

"Even after Sir Paul's death?"

"I don't think Monsieur thought the information would be helpful, sir. Sir Paul Berowne was dead. How could it matter if he'd taken a walk by the river six weeks earlier?"

"Have you told this story to anyone else? Anyone at all? Your wife, a member of the staff here?"

"To no one, sir. There was a lady came inquiring. I was off sick that day. But even if I'd been here, I would have said nothing, not unless Monsieur had told me it was all right."

"And about ten minutes after you saw him walking across the car park, Sir Paul rang to say he wouldn't be arriving after all?"

"Yes, sir."

"Did he say where he was ringing from?"

"No, sir. It couldn't have been from here. The only public telephone we have is in the hall. There's a telephone kiosk in Mapleton, that's the nearest village, but I happen to know that it was out of order that night.

My sister lives there and wanted to ring me. There's no box nearer, not that I know of. That call was a proper mystery, sir."

"When you mentioned the matter next day, what did you and Monsieur think Sir Paul might have been doing here? I take it you discussed it."

Henry paused, then he said:

"Monsieur thought Sir Paul might have been keeping an eye on his wife."

"Spying on her?"

"I suppose it was possible, sir."

"By walking along the riverbank?"

"It doesn't seem very likely, not put like that."

"And why should he have wished to spy on his wife?"

"I can't say, I'm sure, sir. I don't think Monsieur was serious. He just said: 'It is none of our business, Henry. Maybe he is keeping an eye on her ladyship.' "

"And that's all you can tell me?"

Henry hesitated. Dalgliesh waited. Then he said:

"Well, there is something else, sir. But it seems daft when I come to think about it. The car park is well lit, sir, but he was walking quickly and in the shadow of the hedge at the far side. But there was something about the way his jacket was clinging, his trousers, too. I think, sir, he'd been in the river, and that's why I say it was daft. He wasn't walking away from the river, sir, he was walking towards it."

He looked from Dalgliesh to Kate, his eyes puzzled as if the full peculiarity of it had only now struck him.

"I'll swear he was wet, sir, soaking wet. But like I said, he was walking towards the river, not away from it."

Dalgliesh and Kate had driven separately to the Black Swan. She was returning directly to the Yard and he driving northeast to Wrentham Green to lunch with the chairman and vice-chairman of Berowne's constituency party. They would meet at the Yard in mid-afternoon to attend the brief formalities of the preliminary inquest before going on to what promised to be a more interesting interview with Paul Berowne's mistress. As Kate unlocked the door of her Metro he said:

"We'd better have a word with the couple who were dining here with Lampart and Lady Berowne on August seventh. They might be able to say when exactly Lampart left the table to fetch the car, how long he was away. Get their names and addresses, will you, Kate? I suggest from the lady, rather than Lampart. And it would be useful to know more about the mysterious Diana Travers. According to the police report on the drowning, she emigrated with her parents to Australia in 1963. They stayed, she came back. Neither of them came over for the inquest or the funeral. Thames Valley had some difficulty in finding someone to identify her. They dug up an aunt, and she made the funeral arrangements. She hadn't seen her niece for over a year, but she had absolutely no doubt about the identification. And while you're at number sixty-two, see if you can get anything more out of Miss Matlock about the girl."

Kate said:

"Mrs. Minns might be able to tell us something, sir. We're seeing her first thing tomorrow." She added:

"There was one thing Higgins said about the Travers drowning which struck me as odd. It doesn't tie up."

So she had noticed the anomaly. Dalgliesh said:

"It seems to have been an evening for river sports. It was almost as odd as Henry's story. Paul Berowne with his wet clothes clinging to him, but walking towards the river, not away from it."

Kate still lingered, her hand on the car door. Dalgliesh gazed out over the high beech hedge which separated the car park from the river. The day was changing. The early-morning air had held a brittle and transitory brightness, but now the storm clouds, forecast for the afternoon, were rolling in from the west. But it was still warm for early autumn, and there came to him as he stood in the almost deserted car park, cleansed of the smell of hot metal and petrol, the scent of river water and sun-warmed grasses. He stood for a moment savouring it like a truant, feeling the pull of the water, wishing that there were time to follow the wraith of that dripping figure through the gateway to the peace of the riverbank. Kate, coming out of her momentary trance, opened the car door and slid in. But she seemed to have shared his mood. She said:

"It all seems so far away from that dingy Paddington vestry." He wondered if she was implying, not daring to say:

"It's Berowne's murder we're supposed to be investigating, not the coincidental drowning of a girl he may hardly have seen."

But now, more than ever, he was convinced that the three deaths were linked, Travers, Nolan, Berowne. And the main purpose of their visit to the Black Swan had been achieved. Lampart's alibi held. Even driving a Porsche, it was hard to see how he could have killed Berowne and still been seated by eight forty.

2

☒

With the electrification of the north-east suburban line, Wrentham Green
had increasingly become a commuter town despite the protestations of
its older inhabitants that it was a county town of character, not a dormitory
suburb of London. The town had woken up sooner than some of its less
vigilant neighbours to the post-war despoliation of England's heritage by
developers and local authorities, and had checked the worst excesses of
that unholy alliance just in time. The broad eighteenth-century high street,
although desecrated by two modern multiple stores, was essentially intact,
and the small close of Georgian houses facing the river was still regularly
photographed for Christmas calendars, even if it required some contortions
on the part of the photographer to exclude the end of the car park and
the municipal lavatories. It was in one of the smaller houses of the close
that the constituency Conservative Party had its headquarters. Passing
through the porticoed door with its gleaming brass plate, Dalgliesh was
met by the chairman, Frank Musgrave, and the vice-chairman, General
Mark Nollinge.

As always he had prepared himself for the visit. He knew more about
both of them than he suspected either would have thought necessary.
Together in amicable harness they had for the last twenty years run the
local party. Frank Musgrave was an estate agent who ran a family business,
still independent of the large conglomerates, which he had originally inherited from his father. From the number of house boards Dalgliesh had
noticed on his drive through the town and the neighbouring villages, the
business was flourishing. The single word MUSGRAVE, bold black lettering

on white, had met him at every turn. Its reiteration had become an irritating, almost premonitory, reminder of his destination.

Musgrave and the general were an incongruous pair. It was Musgrave who at first sight looked like a soldier; indeed his resemblance to the late Field Marshal Montgomery was so marked that Dalgliesh wasn't surprised to hear him speak in a parody of that formidable warrior's staccato bark. The general barely came up to Musgrave's shoulder. He held his slight body so rigidly that it seemed as if his vertebrae were fused, and his tonsured head, the crown ringed with fine white hair, was speckled as a thrush's egg. As Musgrave made the introductions, the general looked up at Dalgliesh with eyes as innocently candid as a child's, but strained and puzzled as if he had looked too long on unattainable horizons. In contrast to Musgrave's formal business suit and black tie, the general was wearing an ancient tweed jacket cut according to some personal whim, with two oblong patches of suede on each elbow. His shirt and regimental tie were immaculate. With his shining face, he had the polished vulnerability of a well-tended child. Even in the first minutes of casual conversation the mutual respect of the two men was immediately apparent. Whenever the general spoke, Musgrave would gaze from him to Dalgliesh with the slightly anxious frown of a parent, worried lest his offspring's brilliance should be underrated.

Musgrave led the way through the wide hall, down a short passage to the room at the back of the house which Berowne had used as his office. He said:

"Kept it locked since Berowne's death. Your people rang, but we'd have locked it anyway. The general and I thought it the right thing to do. Not that there's anything here to shed light. Shouldn't think so, anyway. Welcome to look, of course."

The air smelt stale and dusty, almost sour, as if the room had been locked for months rather than days. Musgrave switched on the light, then strode over to the window and vigorously tugged back the curtains with a rattle of rings. A thin northern light filtered through the plain nylon curtains beyond which Dalgliesh could see a small walled car park. He had seldom, he thought, been in a more depressing room, and yet it was difficult to explain why he should feel this sudden weight of dejection. The room was no worse than any of its kind, functional, uncluttered, impersonal, and yet he felt that the very air he breathed was infected by melancholy.

He said:

"Did he stay in this house when he was in the constituency?"

"No. Just used this room here as an office. He always stayed at the Courtney Arms. Mrs. Powell kept a bed for him. It was cheaper and less trouble than having a flat in the constituency. Talked occasionally about asking me to find one, but it never came to anything. I don't think his wife was keen."

Dalgliesh asked casually:

"Did you see very much of Lady Berowne?"

"Not a lot. Did her bit, of course. Annual fête, appearances at the local elections, that sort of thing. Decorative and gracious all round. Not much interested in politics, would you say, General?"

"Lady Berowne? No, not greatly. The first Lady Berowne was different, of course. But then, the Manstons have been a political family for four generations. I used to wonder sometimes whether Berowne entered politics to please his wife. I don't think he felt the same commitment after she was killed."

Musgrave gave him a sharp glance as if this were a heresy, previously unacknowledged, which even now was better left unspoken. He said quickly:

"Yes, well, water under the bridge. A sad business. He was driving at the time. I expect you've heard."

Dalgliesh said:

"Yes. I had heard."

There was a short, uncomfortable pause during which it seemed to him that the golden image of Barbara Berowne glimmered, unacknowledged and disturbing, in the still air.

He began his examination of the room, aware of the general's anxious, hopeful gaze, of Musgrave's sharp eyes on him as if watching a trainee clerk taking his first inventory. Set in the middle of the floor and facing the window was a solid Victorian desk and a button-backed swivel chair. In front of it were two smaller leather armchairs. There was a modern desk with a heavy old-fashioned typewriter to one side and two more chairs and a low coffee table in front of the fireplace. The only memorable piece of furniture was a bureau-bookcase with brass-bound panes which occupied the recess to the right of the fireplace. Dalgliesh wondered if his companions knew its value. Then he guessed that respect for tradition would forbid its sale. Like the desk, it was part of the room, inviolate, not to be disposed of for a quick profit. Strolling over to it, he saw that it held an oddly assorted collection of reference books, local guides, biographies of notable Tory politicians, *Who's Who*, parliamentary reports, Stationery Office publications, even a few classical novels, apparently gummed together by immutable time.

On the wall behind the desk was a copy of a well-known oil portrait of Winston Churchill with a large colour photograph of Mrs. Thatcher hung to its right. But it was the picture above the fireplace which immediately caught the eye. Moving to it from the bookcase, Dalgliesh saw that it was an eighteenth-century oil painting of the Harrison family by Arthur Devis. The young Harrison, legs elegantly crossed in their satin breeches, stood with proprietorial arrogance beside a garden seat on which sat his thin-faced wife, her arm round a young child. A small girl sat demurely beside her holding a basket of flowers, while to the left her brother's arm was raised to the string of a kite, luminous in the summer sky. Behind the group stretched a gentle English landscape in high summer, smooth lawns, a lake, a distant manor house. Dalgliesh recalled from his interview with Anthony Farrell that Musgrave had been left a Devis. This, presumably, was it. The general said:

"Berowne brought it here from Campden Hill Square. He moved the Churchill portrait and hung it here instead. There was some feeling about it at the time. The Churchill had always hung over the mantelpiece."

Musgrave had moved up beside Dalgliesh. He said:

"I'll miss that picture. Never tired of looking at it. It was painted in Hertfordshire, only six miles from here. You can still see that landscape. The same oak tree, same lake. And the house. It's a school now. My grandfather was agent when it was sold. It couldn't be anywhere else but England. I never knew that painter's work till Berowne brought it here. Rather like a Gainsborough, isn't it? But I'm not sure I don't like it better than that one in the National Gallery—Mr. and Mrs. Robert Andrews. The women are a bit alike, though, aren't they? Thin-faced, arrogant, wouldn't care to be married to either of them. But it's lovely, lovely."

The general said quietly:

"I'll be relieved when the family send for it. It's a responsibility."

So neither of them knew about the legacy, unless they were better actors than he thought likely. Dalgliesh kept a prudent silence, but he would have given much to have seen Musgrave's face when he learned of his good luck. He wondered what spurt of quixotic generosity had prompted the gift. It was surely an exceptionally generous way of rewarding political loyalty. And it was an irritating complication. Common sense and imagination protested at the thought of Musgrave slitting a friend's throat to possess a picture, however obsessively desired, which there was no evidence he even knew had been willed to him. But in the normal course of human life he would have been lucky to have outlived Berowne. He had been at the Campden Hill Square house on the afternoon of Berowne's death. He could have taken the diary. He almost certainly knew that Berowne used a cut-throat razor. Like everyone else who benefited from the death, he would have to be tactfully investigated. It was almost certainly a waste of effort; it would take time; it complicated the main thrust of the enquiry; but it still had to be done.

They were, he knew, waiting for him to talk about the murder. Instead he walked over to the desk and seated himself in Berowne's chair. That, at least, was comfortable, fitting his long limbs as if made for him. There was a thin film of dust on the desk surface. He pulled open the right-hand drawer and found nothing but a box of writing paper and envelopes, and a diary similar to the one found by the body. Opening it, he saw that it contained only engagements and an aide-mémoire for the days he spent in his constituency. Here, too, his life had been ordered, compartmentalized.

Outside, a thin drizzle was beginning to fall, misting the window, so that he saw the brick wall of the car park and the bright curved roofs of the cars as if in a pointillist oil painting. What burden, he wondered, had Berowne brought with him into this sunless and depressing office? Disenchantment with the second job to which he had committed himself? Guilt over his dead wife, his failed marriage? Guilt over the mistress whose bed he had so recently left? Guilt over his neglect of his only child, over the baronetcy which had been rightly his brother's? Guilt because that better-loved elder son was dead and he was still alive? "Most of the things I expected to value have come to me through death." And had there been, perhaps, a more recent guilt, Theresa Nolan, who had killed herself because she had aborted a child? His child? And what was there for him here amid these files and papers, mocking in their meticulous order his disordered life, but the Catch-22 of the well-intentioned? The miserable batten on their victims. If you provide them with what they crave, open your heart and mind to them, listen with sympathy, they come in ever increasing numbers, draining you emotionally and physically until you have nothing left to give. If you repel them, they don't come back and you're left despising yourself for your inhumanity. He said:

"I suppose this room is the place of last resort."

It was Musgrave who understood him the quicker.

"Nine times out of ten that's what it is. They've exhausted the patience of their families, DHSS staff, local authorities, friends. Then it's here. 'I voted for you. Do something.' Some Members like it, of course. Find it the most fascinating part of the job. They're the social workers manqué. I suspect he didn't. What he tried to do, seemed almost obsessed with at times, was explain to people the limits of government power, any government. Remember the last debate on the inner cities? I was in the public gallery. There was a lot of suppressed anger in his irony. 'If I understand the Honourable Member's somewhat confused argument the Government are asked to ensure equality of intelligence, talent, health, energy and wealth while, at the same time, abolishing original sin as from the beginning of the next financial year. What Divine Providence has singularly failed to do, Her Majesty's Government are to achieve by Statutory Order.' The House didn't much like it. Not their kind of humour."

He added:

"It was a lost battle anyway, educating the electorate in the limits of executive power. No one wants to believe it. And anyway, in a democracy there's always an opposition to tell them that anything is possible."

The general said:

"He was a conscientious constituency MP, but it took a lot out of him, more than we realized. I think he was sometimes torn between compassion and irritation."

Musgrave jerked open the drawer of a filing cabinet and pulled out a file at random.

"Take this one, spinster, aged fifty-two. In the middle of the change and feeling like hell. Dad dead. Mum at home and virtually bedridden, demanding, incontinent, getting senile. No hospital bed, and Mum wouldn't go voluntarily even if there were. Or this one. Two kids, both of them nineteen. She gets pregnant, they marry. Neither set of parents like it. Now they're living with the in-laws in a small terraced house. No privacy. Can't make love. Mum will hear through the walls. Baby squalling. Family saying 'I told you so.' No hope of a council house for another three years, maybe longer. And that's typical of what he got every Saturday. Find me a hospital bed, a house, work. Give me money, give me hope, give me love. It's partly what the job is all about, but I think he found it frustrating. I'm not saying he wasn't sympathetic to the genuine cases."

The general said quietly:

"All the cases are genuine. Misery always is."

He gazed out the window to where the drizzle had now strengthened to steady rain, and then said:

"Perhaps we should have found him a more cheerful room."

Musgrave expostulated:

"But the Member has always used this room for his surgery, General, and it's only once a week."

The general said quietly:

"Nevertheless, when we get the new Member he should have something better."

Musgrave capitulated without rancour.

"We could oust George. Or use that front room on the top floor for the surgery. But then the elderly would have to manage the stairs. I don't see how we could re-house the bar."

Dalgliesh half-expected him to call at once for plans and begin the reallocation, his own concerns half-forgotten. He said:

"Did his resignation come as a surprise?"

It was Musgrave who answered:

"Absolutely. A complete shock. A shock and a betrayal. It's no good beating about the bush, General. It's a bad time for a by-election, and he must have known."

The general said:

"Hardly a betrayal. We've never seen ourselves as a marginal seat."

"Anything under fifteen thousand is marginal these days. He should have soldiered on until the election."

Dalgliesh asked:

"Did he explain his reasons? I take it that he did see you both, he didn't merely write."

Again it was Musgrave who answered:

"Oh, he saw us all right. Actually deferred writing to the Chancellor until he'd told us. I was on holiday—my usual short autumn break—and he had the decency to wait until I was back. Came up here late last Friday, Friday the thirteenth, appropriately enough. He said that it wouldn't be right for him to continue as our Member. It was time that his life took a different turn. Naturally I asked what he meant by a different turn. 'You're a Member of Parliament,' I said. 'You're not driving a bloody bus.' He said that he didn't know yet. He hadn't been shown. 'Hadn't been shown by whom?' I asked. He said 'God.' Well, there's not much a man can say to that. Nothing like an answer like that for putting a stopper on rational discussion."

"How did he seem?"

"Oh, perfectly calm, perfectly normal. Too calm. That's what was so odd about it. A bit eerie really, wouldn't you say, General?"

The general said very quietly:

"He looked to me like a man released from pain, physical pain. Pale, drawn, but very peaceful. You can't mistake the look."

"Oh, he was peaceful enough. Obstinate too. You couldn't argue. His decision had nothing to do with politics, though. We did at least establish that. I asked him outright. 'Are you disillusioned with policy, with the party, with the PM, with us?' He said it was nothing like that. He said: 'It's nothing to do with the party. It's myself I have to change.' He seemed surprised by the question, almost amused, as if it were irrelevant. Well, it wasn't irrelevant to me. The general and I have given a lifetime of service to the party. It matters to us. It's not some kind of game, a trivial pursuit that you can pick up and put down when you're bored. We deserved a better explanation and a bloody sight more consideration than we got. He seemed almost to resent having to talk about it. We could have been discussing arrangements for the summer fête."

He began pacing the narrow room, his outrage a palpable force. The general said mildly:

"I'm afraid we were no help to him. None at all."

"He wasn't asking for help, was he? Or for advice. He'd gone to a higher power for that. It's a pity he ever set foot in that church. Why did he, anyway? D'you know?" He shot the question at Dalgliesh like an accusation. Dalgliesh said mildly:

"Out of an interest in Victorian church architecture, apparently."

"Pity he didn't take up fishing or stamp collecting. Oh well, he's dead, poor devil. No point in feeling bitter now."

Dalgliesh said: "You saw that article in the *Paternoster Review*, of course?"

Musgrave had got himself under control. He said:

"I don't read that kind of journal. If I want book reviews I get them from the Sunday papers." His tone suggested that he was occasionally given to such odd indulgences. "But someone read it and cut it out; it was round the constituency pretty sharply. The general's view was that it was actionable."

General Nollinge said:

"I thought that it might be. I advised him to consult his lawyer. He said he'd think about it."

Dalgliesh said:

"He did more than that. He showed it to me."

"Asked you to investigate, did he?" Musgrave's tone was sharp.

"Not really. He wasn't specific."

"Exactly. He wasn't specific about anything in those last few weeks."

He added:

"Of course, when he first told us that he'd written to the PM and was applying for the Chiltern Hundreds, we remembered that *Review* article and braced ourselves for the scandal. Quite wrong, of course. Nothing as human or understandable. There's one odd thing, though, which we thought we'd better mention. Now that he's dead it can't do any harm. It happened on the night that girl was drowned. Diana Something-or-other."

Dalgliesh said:

"Diana Travers."

"That's right. He turned up here that night, well, early morning really. He didn't arrive until well after midnight, but I was still here working on some papers. Something or someone had scratched his face. It was superficial, but deep enough to have bled. The scab had just formed. It could have been a cat, I suppose, or he may have fallen into a rose bush. Equally, the claws could have been a woman's."

"Did he give you any explanation?"

"No. He didn't mention it and neither did I, either then or later. Berowne had a way of making it impossible for you to ask unwelcome questions. It couldn't have had anything to do with the girl, of course. Apparently, he wasn't dining at the Black Swan that night. But afterwards when we read that article, it struck me as an odd coincidence."

It was indeed, thought Dalgliesh. He asked, because the question was necessary, not because he expected any useful information, whether anyone in the constituency could have known that Berowne would be in St. Matthew's Church on the night of his death. Catching Musgrave's sharp, suspicious glance and the general's pained frown, he added:

"We have to consider the possibility that this was a planned murder, that the killer knew he would be there. If Sir Paul told someone in the constituency—telephoned perhaps—there has to be the chance that the conversation was overheard or passed on unwittingly."

Musgrave said:

"You're not suggesting that he was killed by an aggrieved constituent? A bit far-fetched, surely."

"But not impossible."

"Aggrieved constituents write to the local press, cancel their subs and threaten to vote SDP next time. Can't see this as political in any sense. Damn it, man, he'd resigned his seat. He was out, finished, spent, no danger to anyone. After that nonsense in the church, no one was going to take him seriously any more."

The general's soft voice broke in:

"Not even the family knew where he was that night. It would be strange if he told someone here when he hadn't told them."

"How do you know, General?"

"Mrs. Hurrell rang Campden Hill Square shortly after eight thirty and spoke to the housekeeper, Miss Matlock. At least, I understand that it was a young man who answered the telephone, but he handed her over to Miss Matlock. Wilfred Hurrell was the agent here. He died at three o'clock the next morning in St. Mary's Hospital, Paddington. Cancer, poor devil. He was devoted to Berowne, and Mrs. Hurrell rang Campden Hill Square because he was asking for him. Berowne had told her to ring at any time. He'd see that he could always be reached. That's what I find so odd. He knew that Wilfred hadn't long to go, yet he didn't leave a number or an address. That wasn't like him."

Musgrave said:

"Betty Hurrell rang me afterwards to see if he was in the constituency. I wasn't at home. I hadn't got back from London by then, but she spoke to my wife. She couldn't help her, of course. A bad business."

Dalgliesh gave no sign that the call wasn't news to him. He asked:

"Did Miss Matlock say that she'd ask any of the family whether they knew how to contact Sir Paul?"

"She just told Mrs. Hurrell that he wasn't at home and that no one in the house knew where he was. Mrs. Hurrell could hardly press the matter. Apparently he left home shortly after ten thirty and never returned. I called at the house just before lunch, hoping to catch him, but he never came back. I expect they told you I was there."

The general said:

"I tried to reach him later, just before six o'clock, to make an appointment for the next day. I thought it might be helpful if we could have a quiet talk. He wasn't at home then. Lady Ursula answered the telephone. She said she'd look at his diary and ring back."

"Are you sure, General?"

"That I spoke to Lady Ursula? Oh yes. Usually Miss Matlock answers, but sometimes one gets Lady Ursula."

"Are you sure that she said she'd consult the diary?"

"She may have said that she'd see if he were free and ring back. Something like that. Naturally I assumed that meant she would consult his diary. I said not to worry if it was any trouble. She's crippled with arthritis, you know."

"Did she ring back?"

"Yes, about ten minutes later. She said that Wednesday morning seemed all right, but she'd ask Berowne to ring me and confirm next morning."

Next morning. That suggested that she knew that her son wouldn't be back that night. More important, if she had, indeed, gone down to the study and consulted the diary, then it had been there in the study drawer shortly after six on the day of Berowne's death. And at six o'clock, according to Father Barnes, he had arrived at the vicarage. Here at last could be the vital clue linking the murder with Campden Hill Square. This had been a carefully planned killing. The murderer had known where to find the diary, had taken it with him to the church, had partly burnt it in an attempt to add verisimilitude to the suicide theory. And that placed the heart of the murder firmly in Berowne's household. But wasn't that where he had always known that it lay?

He recalled that moment in Lady Ursula's sitting room when he had revealed the diary. The clawed hands shrivelled with age tightening on the plastic. The frail body frozen into immobility. So she had known. Shocked as she was, her mind had still been working. But would any mother shield her son's murderer? Under one circumstance he thought it possible that this mother might. But the truth was probably less complicated and less sinister. She couldn't believe that anyone she personally knew had been capable of this particular crime. She could accept only two possibilities. Either her son had killed himself or, more likely and more acceptable, his murder had been the work of casual unpremeditated violence. If Lady Ursula could bring herself to believe this, then she would see any connection with Campden Hill Square as irrelevant, a potential source of scandal and, worse, a damaging diversion of police energies from their job of finding the real killer. But he would have to question her about that telephone call. He had never in his professional life been afraid of a witness or a suspect. But this was one interview to which he wasn't looking forward. But if the diary had been in the desk at six o'clock, then at least Frank Musgrave was in the clear. He had left Campden Hill Square before two. But his suspicion of Musgrave had immediately struck him as an irrelevance. And then another thought, possibly equally irrelevant, fell into his mind. What was it that Wilfred Hurrell, lying on his deathbed, had been so anxious to say to Paul Berowne? And was it possible that someone had been determined that he shouldn't have the opportunity to say it?

Afterwards the three of them lunched together in the elegant first-floor dining room overlooking the river, now running thick and turbulent under the driving rain. As they were seated, Musgrave said:

"My great-grandfather once dined with Disraeli at this table. They looked out over much the same view."

The words confirmed what Dalgliesh had suspected, that it was Musgrave whose family had always voted Tory and who would find any other allegiance unthinkable, the general who had come to his political philosophy by a process of thought and intellectual commitment.

It was an agreeable meal, stuffed shoulder of lamb, fresh vegetables beautifully cooked, a gooseberry tart with cream. He guessed that both his companions had tacitly agreed not to pester him with enquiries about the progress of the police investigation. They had earlier asked the obvious questions and had met his reticence with tactful silence. He was inclined to put this restraint down to a wish that he should enjoy a meal over which they had obviously taken trouble, rather than to any reluctance to discuss a painful subject, or any fear that they might let slip things best left unspoken. They were served by an elderly black-coated waiter with the face of an anxiously amiable toad, who poured an excellent Niersteiner with shaky hands, but without spilling a drop. The dining room was almost empty—there were only two couples besides themselves and they were at distant tables. Dalgliesh suspected that his hosts had tactfully ensured that he should enjoy his luncheon in peace. But both men found an opportunity to give him their opinion. When, after coffee, the general remembered the need to make a telephone call, Musgrave leaned confidingly across the table:

"The general can't believe it was suicide. It isn't something he'd do himself, so he can't imagine it in his friends. I'd have said the same myself once, about Berowne, I mean. Not so sure now. There's a madness in the air. Nothing's certain any more, least of all people. You think you know them, know how they'd behave. But you don't, you can't. We're all strangers. That girl now, the nurse, the one who killed herself. If it was Berowne's child she aborted, that couldn't have been easy for him to live with. Not trying to interfere, you understand. Your job, of course, not mine. But the case seems pretty straightforward to me."

And it was in the car park when Musgrave had left them to go to his car that the general said:

"I know that Frank thinks that Berowne killed himself, but he's wrong. Not malicious, or disloyal or unkind; just wrong. Berowne wasn't the kind of man to kill himself."

Dalgliesh said:

"I don't know whether he was or wasn't. What I am reasonably sure of is that he didn't."

They watched in silence while Musgrave, with a final wave, negotiated the gate and accelerated out of sight. It seemed to Dalgliesh an additional perversity of fate that he should be driving a black Rover with an A registration.

3

⊠

Half an hour later Frank Musgrave turned into the drive of his house. It was a small but elegant red-bricked country house designed by Lutyens and bought by his father forty years earlier. Musgrave had inherited it with the family business and regarded it with as much obsessional pride as if it had been a two-hundred-year-old family seat. He maintained it with jealous care as he looked after everything that was his, his wife, his son, his business, his car. Usually he drove up to it with no more than customary satisfaction at the old man's good eye for a house, but every six months, as if in obedience to some unstated law, he would halt the car and make a deliberate revaluation of its market price. He did that now.

He had hardly entered the hall when his wife, anxious-faced, came out to meet him. Taking the coat from his shoulders, she said:

"How did it go, dear?"

"All right. He's an odd man. Not altogether friendly, but perfectly civil. Seemed to enjoy his lunch." He paused and added:

"He knows that it was murder."

"Oh Frank, no! What are you going to do?"

"What everyone else concerned with Berowne will do, try to limit the damage. Has Betty Hurrell rung?"

"About twenty minutes ago. I told her that you'd be coming to see her."

"Yes," he said heavily. "I must do that."

He laid his hand momentarily on his wife's shoulder. Her family hadn't wanted her to marry him, hadn't thought him good enough for the only child of a previous lord lieutenant of the county. But he had married her and they had been happy, were still happy. He thought with sudden anger: He's done enough damage. But this is where it stops. I'm not going to risk everything I've worked for, everything I've achieved and my father before me, just because Paul Berowne goes off his head in a church vestry.

4
⊠

Scarsdale Lodge was a large, L-shaped, modern block of flats, brick-built, its front disfigured rather than enhanced by a series of irregular, jutting balconies. A path of stone blocks led between twin lawns to the canopied entrance porch. In the middle of each lawn, a small circular flower bed closely packed with dwarf dahlias ranging in circles through white to yellow and, finally, red glared upwards like a bloodshot eye. To the left a driveway brought them to the rear garage block and to a marked parking lot with a notice warning that it was strictly for the use of visitors to Scarsdale Lodge. It was overlooked by the smaller windows at the back of the building and Dalgliesh, knowing how paranoid flat residents became over unlicensed parking, guessed that a watch would be kept on it for alien cars. Almost certainly Berowne would have judged it safer to leave his car in the public park at Stanmore Station and would have walked the last quarter of a mile uphill, an anonymous commuter with the ubiquitous briefcase, the carrier bag of wine, the offering of flowers probably bought from a stall near Baker Street or Westminster Station. And Stanmore wasn't so very far out of his way. It was, in fact, conveniently on the route to his Hertfordshire constituency. He would be able to snatch the odd hour on a Friday night, that hiatus between his London life and his Saturday-morning constituency surgery.

He and Kate walked in silence to the front door. It was fitted with an intercom—hardly the most effective security, but better than none, and with the advantage that there was no porter to watch comings and goings. Kate's ring and her careful announcement of their names through the grille was answered only by the burr of the released door, and they passed through a hall that was typical of a thousand in similar apartment blocks in suburban London. The floor was of checkered vinyl, polished to mirror brightness. On the left wall was a cork board with notices from the managing agents about the date of lift maintenance and the cleaning contract. To the right a climbing plant in a green plastic pot, inadequately supported, drooped its bifurcated leaves. Ahead of them were the twin lifts. The silence was absolute. Somewhere up there people must be living their cabined lives, but the air, sharp with the tang of floor polish, was as silent as if this were an apartment house of the dead. The tenants would be Londoners, transients most of them, young professionals on their way up, secretaries sharing with each other, retired couples living their self-contained lives. And a visitor could be coming to any one of the forty-odd flats. If Berowne were sensible he would have taken the lift to a different floor each time and walked up. But the risk would be small. Stanmore, for all its high leafiness, was no longer a village. There would be no peeping eyes behind the curtains to watch when he came or went. If Berowne had bought it for his mistress as a convenient, anonymous meeting place, he had chosen well.

Number forty-six was the corner flat on the top floor. They trod silently along a carpeted corridor to the white unnamed door. When Kate rang he wondered whether an eye was regarding them through the peephole, but the door was opened at once as if she had been standing there waiting for them. She stood aside and motioned them in. Then she turned to Dalgliesh and said:

"I've been expecting you. I knew you'd come sooner or later. And at least I'll know now what happened. I can hear someone speak his name, even if it's only a policeman."

She was ready for them. She had done her crying; not all the crying she would do for her lover, but that dreadful howling anguish that tears the body apart was over now, at least for a time. He had had to witness its effects too often to miss the signs: the puffy eyelids, the skin dulled by grief's despoiling power, the lips swollen and unnaturally red, as if the lightest blow would burst them open. It was difficult to know how she normally looked. He thought that she had a pleasant, intelligent face, long-nosed but with high cheekbones and a firm jaw and good skin. Her hair, mid-brown, strong and straight, was drawn back from her face and tied with a tag of crumpled ribbon. A few hairs lay damply across her forehead. Her voice was cracked and strained with recent crying, but she

had it well under control. He felt a respect for her. If grief was the cri-
terion, she was the widow. As they followed her into the sitting room,
he said:

"I'm very sorry to have to trouble you, and so soon. You know why
we're here, of course. Do you feel able to talk about him? I need to know
him better than I do if I'm to get anywhere." She seemed to understand
what he meant, that the victim was central to his death. He died because
of what he was, what he knew, what he did, what he planned to do. He
died because he was uniquely himself. Murder destroyed privacy, laid bare
with brutal thoroughness all the petty contrivances of the dead life. Dalgliesh would rummage through Berowne's past as thoroughly as he rummaged through a victim's cupboards and files. The victim's privacy was
the first to go, but no one intimately concerned with murder was left
unscathed. The victim had at least escaped beyond earthbound considerations of dignity, embarrassment, reputation. But for the living, to be
part of a murder investigation was to be contaminated by a process which
would leave few of their lives unchanged. Murder remained the unique
crime. Peer and pauper stood equal before it. The rich were, of course,
advantaged in this as in everything. They could afford the best lawyer.
But in a free society there was little else they could buy. She asked:

"Would you like some coffee?"

"Very much please, if it's not too much trouble."

Kate asked:

"Can I help?"

"It won't take long."

Kate apparently took the words as an acceptance and followed the
girl into the kitchen, leaving the door ajar. It was typical of her, thought
Dalgliesh, this unsentimental, practical response to people and their immediate concerns. Without hectoring or presumption, she could reduce
the most embarrassing situation to something approaching normality. It
was one of her strengths. Now, above the tinkle of kettle lid and crockery,
he could hear their voices, conversational, almost ordinary. From the few
phrases he could catch, they seemed to be discussing the merits of a make
of electric kettle which both possessed. Suddenly he felt that he shouldn't
be there, that he was redundant as a detective and a man. They would
both get on better without his male, destructive presence. Even the room
seemed inimical to him, and he could almost persuade himself that the
low broken sibilants of female voices were in conspiracy.

There was the grinding roar of a coffee mill. So, she used fresh-ground beans. But of course. She would take trouble over the coffee. It was the drink she and her lover must most often have shared. He looked around the sitting room with its long window giving a distant view of the London skyline. The furniture represented a rather orthodox good taste. The sofa, covered with fawn linen, uncrumpled, still pristine, looked expensive and was probably Scandinavian in the austerity of the design. On each side of the fireplace were matching armchairs, the covers more worn than that on the sofa. The fireplace itself was modern, a simple shelf of white wood above a plain surround. And the fire, he saw, was one of the newest gas models, which gave an illusion of burning coals and a living flame. She would have been able to turn it on as soon as she heard his ring; instant comfort, instant warmth. And if he didn't come, if there was business at the House or at home or in the constituency which kept him from her, there would be no cold ash the next morning to mock her with its easy symbolism.

Above the sofa was a line of watercolours: gentle English landscapes, their quality unmistakable. He thought he recognized a Lear and a Cotman. He wondered if these had been Berowne's gifts, a way perhaps of transferring to her something of value which both could enjoy and which her pride could accept. The wall opposite the fireplace was covered with wooden adjustable units reaching from floor to ceiling. These held a simple stereo system, racks for records, a television set and her books. Walking over to inspect them and flicking them open, he saw she had read history at Reading University. Take away the books and substitute popular prints for the watercolours, and the room could have been a showroom in a newly built block of flats, seducing the prospective buyer with an inoffensive and conventional good taste. He thought: There are rooms designed to be got away from, bleak anterooms where the armour is buckled on to confront the real world outside. There are rooms to come back to, claustrophobic refuges from the arduous business of work and striving. This room was a world in itself, a still centre provisioned with economy and care but containing everything necessary to its owner's life, the flat itself an investment in more than property. All her capital had been tied up here, monetary and emotional. He looked at the row of plants, varied, well tended, glossily healthy, which were ranged on the windowsill. But then, why shouldn't they be healthy? She was always there to tend them.

The two women came back into the room, Miss Washburn carrying a tray with a percolator, three large white cups, a jug of hot milk and sugar crystals. She set it down on the coffee table. Dalgliesh and Kate seated themselves on the sofa. Miss Washburn poured the coffee, including a cup for herself, then carried it over to her seat by the fire. As Dalgliesh had expected, the coffee was excellent, but she didn't drink. She gazed across at them and said:

"The television newsreader said knife wounds. What wounds?"

"Is that how you heard, on the television news?"

She said with great bitterness:

"Of course. How else would I hear?"

Dalgliesh was shaken by a pity so unexpected and so acute that for a moment he dared not speak. And with the pity came a resentment against Berowne which frightened him with its intensity. Surely the man had faced the possibility of sudden death. He was a public figure; he must have known there was always a risk. Hadn't there been someone that he could trust with his secret? Someone who could have broken the news to her, visited her, brought her at least the comfort that he had thought about saving her pain. Couldn't he have found time in his over-busy life to write a letter which could have been privately taken to her if he died unexpectedly? Or had he been arrogant enough to think himself immune from the risks of lesser mortals—a coronary, a car accident, an IRA bomb? The tide of anger ebbed, leaving a slough of self-disgust. It had been directed against himself. He thought: Isn't that how I might have behaved? We're alike even in this. If he had a splinter of ice in the heart, then so have I.

She repeated stubbornly:

"What knife wounds?"

There was no way of telling it gently.

"His throat was cut. His and the tramp's who was with him, Harry Mack." He didn't know why telling her Harry's name should be important as it had been important to speak it to Lady Ursula. It was as if he were determined that none of them should forget Harry.

She asked:

"With Paul's razor?"

"It's probable."

"And the razor was still there, by the body?"

She had said body, not bodies. There was only one which concerned her. He said:

"Yes, by his outstretched hand."

"And the outside door, was it unlocked?"

"Yes."

She said:

"So he let in his murderer just as he let in the tramp. Or did the tramp kill him?"

"No, the tramp didn't kill him. Harry was a victim, not a killer."

"Then it was an outsider. Paul couldn't have killed anyone, and I don't believe he killed himself."

Dalgliesh said:

"We don't believe it either. We're treating it as murder. That's why we need your help. We need you to talk about him. You probably knew him better than any other person."

She said, so low that he could only just catch the whisper:

"I thought I did. I thought I did."

She took up her cup and tried to lift it to her lips, but couldn't control it. Dalgliesh felt Kate stiffen at his side and wondered whether she was controlling an impulse to put her arm round the girl's shoulder and raise the cup to her lips. But she didn't move and, at the second attempt, Miss Washburn managed to get her mouth to the brim. She gulped in the coffee, noisily, like a thirsty child.

Watching her, Dalgliesh knew what he was doing and the more fastidious part of his mind was repelled by it. She was alone, unacknowledged, denied the simple human need to share her grief, to talk about her lover. And it was that need which he was about to exploit. He sometimes thought bitterly that exploitation was at the heart of successful detection, particularly with murder. You exploited the suspect's fear, his vanity, his need to confide, the insecurity that tempted him to say that one vital sentence too many. Exploiting grief and loneliness was only another version of the same technique.

She looked at him and said:

"Can I see where it happened? I mean, without making a fuss about it or being noticed. I should like to sit there alone when they have the funeral. It would be better than sitting at the back of the congregation trying not to make a fool of myself."

He said:

"At the moment the back of the church is being kept locked. But I'm sure it could be arranged once we've finally finished with the place. Father Barnes, he's the parish priest, would let you in. It's a very ordinary room. Just a vestry, dusty, rather cluttered, smelling of hymn books and incense, but a very peaceful place." He added, "I think it happened very quickly. I don't think he felt any pain."

"But he must have felt fear."

"Perhaps not even that."

She said:

"It's such an unlikely thing to have happened, that conversion, divine revelation, whatever it was. That sounds foolish. Of course it's unlikely. I meant that it's an unlikely thing to have happened to Paul. He was, well, worldly. Oh, I don't mean in the sense that he only cared about success, money, prestige. But he was so in the world, of the world. He wasn't a mystic. He wasn't even particularly religious. He usually went to church on Sundays and on the major feast days because he enjoyed the liturgy—he wouldn't attend if they used the new Bible or Prayer Book. And he said he liked an hour when he could think without interruptions, without the telephone ringing. He once said that formal religious observance confirmed identity, reminded one of the limits of behaviour, something like that. Belief wasn't meant to be a burden. Nor was disbelief. Does any of this make sense?"

"Yes."

"He liked food, wine, architecture, women. I don't mean that he was promiscuous. But he loved the beauty of women. I couldn't give him that. But I could give him something no one else could, peace, honesty, total trust."

It was odd, he thought. It was the religious experience not the murder that she needed most to talk about. Her lover was dead and even the enormity of that final, irrevocable loss couldn't blot out the pain of that earlier betrayal. But they would get round to the murder in time. There was no hurry. He wouldn't get what he wanted by rushing her now. He asked:

"Did he explain it to you, that experience in the vestry?"

"He came round the following night. He'd had a meeting in the House and it was late. He couldn't stay long. He told me that he had had an experience of God. That's all. An experience of God. He made it sound perfectly matter-of-fact. But it wasn't, of course. Then he left. I knew then I'd lost him. Not as a friend, perhaps, but then I didn't want him as a friend. I'd lost him as a lover. I'd lost him forever. He didn't need to tell me that."

There were, he knew, women to whom secrecy, risk, treachery, conspiracy, gave a love affair that extra erotic charge. They were women as uncommitted as their men, as fond of personal privacy, who wanted an intense relationship but not at the price of their careers, women to whom sexual passion and domesticity were irreconcilable. But she, he thought, had not been one of them. He recalled word for word his conversation with Higginson of Special Branch. Higginson, in his carefully tailored tweeds, straight-backed, clear-eyed, firm-jawed under the cropped moustache, so like the conventional image of an Army officer that, for Dalgliesh, he walked in an aura of bogus respectability; a conman deferential on suburban doorways, a second-hand-car salesman loitering at Warren Street Station. Even his cynicism seemed as carefully calculated as his accent. Yet the accent was perfectly genuine and so was the cynicism. The worst you could say of Higginson was that he liked his job too well.

"It's the usual thing, my dear Adam. A decorative wife for show, the devoted little woman on the side for use. Only in this case I'm not sure what use precisely. The choice is a little surprising. You'll see. But there's no security problem, never has been. They've both been remarkably discreet. Berowne has always made it plain that he accepted any necessary security precautions, but that he was entitled to take some risks where his private life was concerned. She has never made trouble. I'd be surprised if she makes it now. There'll be no embarrassing little bundle in eight months' time."

Could she, he wondered, really have shut her eyes to the reality, that the affair was documented, every step of its progress noted with almost clinical detachment by those cynical watchers who had decided, no doubt after the normal bureaucratic processes, that she could be classified as a harmless diversion, that Berowne could enjoy his weekly entertainment without official harassment? Surely she couldn't have deceived herself, and neither could he. She was, after all, herself a bureaucrat, a Principal. She must know how the system worked. She was still comparatively junior, but it was her world. One sign that she was a security risk and he would have been warned off. And he would have taken the warning. You didn't become a Minister of State if you hadn't enough ambition, egotism and ruthlessness to know where your priorities had to lie.

He asked:

"How did you meet?"

"How do you expect? At work. I was a Principal in his Private Office."

So it had been as he had expected.

"And then when you became lovers, you asked for a transfer?"

"No, I was due for a transfer. You don't stay long in Private Office."

"Did you ever meet his family?"

"He didn't take me home, if that's what you mean. He didn't introduce me to his wife or Lady Ursula and say, 'Meet Carole Washburn. Meet my mistress.' "

"How often did you see him?"

"As often as he could get away. Sometimes we had a half day. Sometimes a couple of hours. He tried to drop in on his way to his constituency if he was alone. Sometimes we couldn't meet for weeks."

"And he never suggested marriage? Forgive me, this question could be important."

"If you mean that someone could have slit his throat to prevent his asking for a divorce to marry me, you're wasting your time. The answer to your question, Commander, is no, he never suggested marriage. And neither did I."

"Would you describe him as happy?"

She didn't seem surprised by the apparent irrelevance of the question, nor did she need to give it much thought. She had known the answer for a long time. "No, not really. What happened to him—I don't mean the murder—what happened to him in that church, whatever it was, I don't think it would have happened if he'd been satisfied with his life, if our love had been enough for him. It was enough for me; all I wanted, all I needed. It wasn't enough for him. I've always known that. Nothing was enough for Paul, nothing."

"Did he tell you that he'd had a poison pen letter about Theresa Nolan and Diana Travers?"

"Yes, he told me. He didn't take it seriously."

"He took it seriously enough to show it to me."

She said:

"Theresa Nolan's child, the one she aborted, it wasn't his, if that's what you're thinking. It couldn't have been. He would have told me. Look, it was just a poison pen letter. Politicians get them all the time. They're used to them. Why worry about it now?"

"Because anything that happened during the last weeks of his life could be important. You must see that."

"What does it matter, the scandal or the lies. They can't touch him now. They can't hurt him. Nothing can. Not any more."

He asked gently:

"Were there things that hurt him?"

"He was human, wasn't he? Of course there were things that hurt him."

"What things? His wife's infidelity?"

She didn't reply.

He said:

"Miss Washburn, my priority is catching his murderer, not preserving his reputation. They needn't be incompatible. I'll try to see that they aren't. But I'm clear which has to come first. Shouldn't you be?"

She spoke with sudden fierceness:

"No. I've preserved his privacy—not reputation, privacy—for three years. It's cost me a lot. I haven't complained to him. I'm not complaining now. I knew the rules. But I'm going to go on preserving his privacy. It was important to him. If I don't, all those years of discretion, never being seen together, never being able to say, 'This is my man, we're lovers,' always taking second place to his job, his wife, his constituents, his mother, what has been the point of it? You can't bring him back."

That was always the cry when the going got rough: "You can't bring them back." He remembered his second child murderer—the hidden cache of pornographic photographs the police had uncovered in the killer's flat, indecent poses of his victims, pathetic childish bodies violated and exposed. It had been his job as a newly promoted detective inspector to ask a mother to identify her daughter. The woman's eyes had glanced at the photograph once only and then stared ahead, denying knowledge, denying truth. There were some realities which the mind refused to accept even in the cause of retribution, of justice. You can't bring them back. It was the cry of the whole defeated, anguished, grieving world.

But she was speaking.

"There were a lot of things I couldn't give him. But I could give him secrecy, discretion. I've heard about you. There was that business down in the Fens, the forensic scientist who was murdered. Paul told me about it. It was quite a triumph for you, wasn't it? You say, 'What about the victim?' But what about your victims? I expect you'll catch Paul's murderer. You usually do, don't you? Does it ever occur to you to count the cost?"

Dalgliesh felt Kate stiffen at the clear note of dislike and contempt. The girl went on:

"But you'll have to do it without me. You don't really need my help. I'm not going to break Paul's confidences just so that you can notch up another success."

He said:

"There's the matter of the dead tramp, Harry Mack."

"I'm sorry, but I've nothing left over to spare for Harry Mack, not even sympathy. I'm leaving Harry Mack out of my calculations."

"I can't leave him out of mine."

"Of course not, that's your job. Look, I know nothing that can help solve this murder for you. If Paul had enemies, I don't know about them. I've told you about him and me. You knew anyway. But I'm not getting involved any deeper. I'm not ending up in the witness box, photographed on my way into court, pictured on the front page, 'Paul Berowne's Little Bit on the Side.' "

She got to her feet. It was the sign for them to go. When they reached the door, she said:

"I want to get away, just for a couple of weeks. I've plenty of leave in hand. If the papers find out about me, then I don't want to be here when it happens. I couldn't bear that. I want to get out of London, out of England. You can't stop me."

Dalgliesh said:

"No. But we'll still be here when you come back."

"And if I don't come back?" She spoke with the weary acceptance of defeat. How could she live abroad, dependent as she was on her job, her salary? This flat might have lost its meaning for her, but London was still her home and the job would be important to her for more reasons than money. A young woman didn't become a Principal without intelligence, hard work, ambition. But he answered her question as if it had reality.

"Then I should have to come to you."

Outside in the car, buckling on his seat belt, he said:

"I wonder if we would have got more out of her if you'd seen her alone. She might have spoken more freely if I hadn't been there."

Kate said:

"Possibly, sir, but only if I'd promised to keep it confidential, and I don't see how I could have done that."

Massingham, he suspected, would have promised secrecy and then had no compunction in telling. That was one of the differences between them.

"No," he said, "you couldn't have done that."

5
⊠

Back in New Scotland Yard, Kate burst into Massingham's office. She found him alone, surrounded by paper, and had pleasure in interrupting his conscientious but unenthusiastic perusal of the door-to-door enquiry reports with a vehement account of the interview. She had controlled her sense of outrage with difficulty on the drive back to the Yard and was in the mood for a confrontation, preferably with a male.

"The man was a shit!"

"Oh, I don't know. Aren't you being a bit hard?"

"It's the same old story. He basks in his success; she's tucked away in the equivalent of a Victorian love-nest to serve his purpose when he has an odd moment to spare for her. We could be back in the nineteenth century."

"But we aren't. It's her choice. Come off it, Kate! She has a good job, her own flat, a good salary, a career with a pension. She could have chucked him any day she chose. He wasn't coercing her."

"Not physically, perhaps."

"Don't start singing a variation of the old song 'It's the Man What Gets the Pleasure, It's the Girl What Gets the Blame.' Recent history is against you, anyway. There was nothing to stop her having it out with him. She could have given him an ultimatum. 'You've got to choose, it's her or me.' "

"Knowing what his choice would be?"

"Well, that's the risk, isn't it? She might have struck lucky. This isn't the nineteenth century. And he's not Parnell. Divorce wouldn't have harmed his career, not for long, not much."

"It wouldn't have helped it."

"OK. Take your chap, whoever he is. Or any chap you might fancy. If you had to choose between him and your job, would that be so easy? When you're feeling censorious, better ask yourself which you'd choose."

The question disconcerted her. He probably either knew or had guessed about Alan. You didn't keep many secrets in the CID, and her very reticence about her private life would have stimulated curiosity. But she hadn't expected such perception from him or such frankness, and she wasn't sure she liked it. She said:

"Well, it hasn't made me respect him."

"We don't have to respect him. We're not asked to respect him or like him or admire his politics, his ties or his taste in women. Our job is to catch his murderer."

She sat down opposite him, suddenly weary, and let her shoulder bag slip to the floor, then watched him as he began putting his papers together. She liked his office, intrigued by the difference between its sparse masculinity and the murder squad room down the corridor. There the atmosphere was heavily masculine, reminiscent, she thought, of an officers' mess, but as she had once overheard Massingham say to Dalgliesh with the sly malice which his subordinates found offensive and which reminded them of his old nickname of the Honjohn, "Not altogether a first-class regiment, would you say, sir?" The squad were called in to investigate crime at sea and were usually rewarded with a framed photograph of the ship concerned. These were mounted in regular lines along the walls, together with signed portraits of chiefs of police from Commonwealth countries, emblems and badges, signed testimonials, even the occasional photograph of a celebratory dinner. Massingham's walls were decorated only with colour prints of early cricket matches, borrowed, she guessed, from his home. These gentle evocations of long-dead summers—the oddly shaped bats, the top hats of the players, the familiar cathedral spires piercing an English sky, the shadowed grass and the crinolined ladies with their parasols—had at first been a source of mild interest to his colleagues but were now hardly noticed. Kate thought his choice showed a nice compromise between masculine conformity and personal taste. And he could hardly have mounted his school photographs. Eton wasn't exactly unacceptable to the Met, but it wasn't a school to boast about. She asked:

"How is the house-to-house going?"

"As you'd expect. No one saw or heard anything. They were all sitting glued to the box, down at the Dog and Duck, or at bingo. No big fish, but we've netted the usual minnows. Pity we can't throw them back. Still, it'll keep division busy."

"And the cab drivers?"

"No luck. One chap remembered driving a middle-aged gent to within forty yards of the church at the relevant time. We traced the fare. He was visiting his lady friend."

"What? In a love-nest off the Harrow Road?"

"He had somewhat specific requirements. Remember Fatima?"

"Good God, is she still on the job?"

"Very much so. She's also taken to doing a little snouting for Chalkey White. The lady's none too pleased with us at present. And neither is Chalkey."

"And the fare?"

"Well, he's putting in an official complaint. Harassment, interference with personal liberty, the usual. And we've had six confessions to the murder."

"Six. So soon?"

"Three of them we've met before. All certifiable. One did it to protest against Tory policy on immigration, one because Berowne had seduced his granddaughter, and one because the Archangel Gabriel told him to. They've all got the time wrong. They all used a knife, not a razor, and you won't be surprised to hear that none of them can produce it. With a singular lack of originality, they all claim to have chucked it in the canal."

She said:

"Do you ever wonder how much of our job is really cost effective?"

"From time to time. What do you expect us to do about it?"

"Waste less time on the minnows to begin with."

"Come off it, Kate. We can't pick and choose. Only within strict limits, anyway. And it's no different with a doctor. He can't make the whole society healthy, he can't heal the world. He'd go crazy if he tried. He just treats what comes his way. Sometimes he wins, sometimes he loses."

She said:

"But he doesn't spend all his time cauterizing warts while the cancers go untreated."

He said:

"Hell, if bloody murder isn't a cancer, what is? Actually, it's probably a murder investigation, not common crime, which isn't cost effective. Think what it cost to put the Yorkshire Ripper behind bars. Think what this killer will cost the taxpayer before we get him."

"If we get him." And for the first time she was tempted to add: "And if he exists."

Massingham got up from the desk.

"You need a drink. I'll buy you one."

Suddenly she almost liked him.

"OK," she said, "thanks." She picked up her shoulder bag and they went out together to the senior officers' mess.

6

⊠

Mrs. Iris Minns lived in a council flat on the second floor of a block off the Portobello Road. To park anywhere close on a Saturday, the day of the street market, was impossible, so Massingham and Kate left the car at the Notting Hill police station and walked. The Saturday market was, as always, a carnival—a cosmopolitan, peaceable, if noisy, celebration of human gregariousness, curiosity, gullibility and greed. It brought back to Kate memories of her early days in the division. She always walked through the cluttered street with pleasure, although she seldom bought; she had never shared the popular obsession with the trivia of the past. And for all its air of cheerful camaraderie, the market was, she knew, less innocent than it looked. Not all the bundles of notes in various currencies changing hands would find their way into tax returns. Not all the trading was in the harmless artifacts of the past; the usual number of unwary visitors would be relieved of their wallets or purses before they reached the bottom of the road. But few London markets were as gentle, as entertaining or as good-humoured. This morning, as always, she entered the narrow, raucous thoroughfare with a lifting of the spirits.

Iris Minns lived in flat twenty-six of Block Two, a building separated from the main block and from the road by a wide courtway. As they crossed it, watched by several pairs of carefully incurious but wary eyes, Massingham said:

"I'll do the talking." She felt the familiar spurt of resentment but said nothing.

The appointment had been made by telephone for nine thirty, and from the speed with which the front door was opened to their ring, Mrs. Minns must have been among those watching their arrival from behind their curtains. They found themselves facing a small compact figure with a square face, a round determined chin, a long mouth that twitched into a brief smile which seemed less one of welcome than of satisfaction that they were on time, and a pair of dark, almost black, eyes which gave them a quick, appraising glance as if inspecting them for dust. She took the trouble to examine Massingham's warrant card with some care, then stood aside and motioned them in, saying:

"Well, you're on time, I'll say that for you. There's tea or coffee if you fancy it."

Massingham quickly refused it for both of them. Kate's first instinct was to say quickly that she would like coffee, but she resisted the temptation. This could be an important interview; there was no point in jeopardizing its success out of personal pique. And Mrs. Minns wouldn't miss any overt antagonism between them. She couldn't have been mistaken in the flash of intelligence in those dark eyes.

The sitting room into which they were shown was so remarkable that she hoped her surprise didn't show too clearly on her face. Provided by local bureaucracy with an oblong box fifteen feet by ten, a single window and a door opening to a balcony too small for any purpose but giving air to a few pot plants, Mrs. Minns had created a small Victorian sitting room, dark, cluttered, claustrophobic. The wallpaper was a dark olive-green patterned with ivy and lilies, the carpet a faded but serviceable Wilton, while occupying almost the whole of the middle of the room was an oblong table of polished mahogany with curved legs, its surface mirror-bright, and four high-backed carved chairs. A smaller octagonal table was set against one wall holding an aspidistra in a brass pot, while the walls were hung with sentimental prints in maple frames: the *Sailor's Farewell* and the *Sailor's Return*, a child reaching for a flower above a brook, its heedless steps protected by a winged angel wearing an expression of pious imbecility. In front of the window stood a long plant holder of wrought iron painted white, filled with pots of geraniums, and outside on the balcony they could glimpse terra-cotta pots holding ivy and climbing plants whose variegated leaves were entwined with the railings.

The focus of the room was a seventeen-inch television set, but this was less of an anachronism than might first appear, since it was placed against a background of green ferns whose fronds curled against the screen like an ornate but living frame. The window ledge was covered with small tubs of African violets, deep purple and a freckled paler mauve. Kate thought that they were planted in yoghurt tubs, but it was difficult to be sure since each was decorated with a plaited paper doily. A sideboard with an elaborately carved back was covered with china animals, dogs discordant in size and breed, a spotted fawn, and half a dozen china cats in unconvincing feline attitudes, each one on a starched linen mat, presumably to protect the polished mahogany.

The whole room was spotlessly clean, the pungent smell of polish overwhelming. When in winter the heavy red velvet curtains were drawn it would be possible to believe oneself in another setting, another age. And Mrs. Minns could have been part of it. She was wearing a black skirt and a white blouse buttoned to the neck and fastened with a cameo brooch, and with her greying hair dressed high at the front and coiled in a small bun at the nape of the neck, she looked, thought Kate, like an ageing actress dressed for the part of a Victorian housekeeper. The only criticism one could make was that the rouge and eye shadow had been over-lavishly applied. She seated herself in the right-hand armchair and motioned Kate to the other, leaving Massingham to seat himself by turning round one of the dining chairs. In it he looked uncomfortably high and, thought Kate, somewhat at a disadvantage, a male intruder into comfortable female domesticity. In the autumn light, filtered through lace curtains and the green of the balcony plants, his face under the thatch of red hair looked almost sickly, the freckles over the forehead standing out like a splutter of pale blood. He said:

"Can't we have the door closed? I can't hear myself speak."

The door onto the balcony was ajar. Kate got up and went over to close it. To the right she could glimpse the huge blue and white teapot hanging outside the Portobello Pottery and the painted wall panel of the porcelain market. The noise of the street came up to her like the clatter of shingle on a seashore. Then she closed the door and the sound was deadened. Mrs. Minns said:

"It's only on a Saturday. Mr. Smith and I don't much mind it. You get used to it. I always say it's a bit of life." She turned to Kate:

"You live in these parts, don't you? I'm sure I've seen you shopping up at the Gate."

"Very possibly, Mrs. Minns. I'm not far away."

"Oh well, it's a village, isn't it? You see everyone up at the Gate sooner or later."

Massingham said impatiently:

"You mentioned a Mr. Smith."

"He lives here, but you can't see him. Not that he'd be able to tell you anything. But he's off roamin'."

"Roaming? Where?"

"How do I know? On his bicycle. His folk used to live in Hillgate Village in the old days. Proper little slum it was, when his granddad was alive. A hundred and sixty thousand they're asking for the houses now. I reckon he's got gypsy blood, has Mr. Smith. There was a lot of gypsies settled round here after they pulled down the Hippodrome racecourse. He's always roamin'. It's easier for him now that British Rail let his bike go free. Lucky for you he isn't here. He's not too keen on the police. Too many of your chaps pick him up for nothing, only sleeping under a hedge. That's what's wrong with this country, too much pickin' on decent people. And other things I could mention what we're not allowed to say."

Kate could sense Massingham's anxiety to get on with the matter in hand. As if she too had sensed it, Mrs. Minns said:

"It was a proper shock for me, I don't mind telling you. Lady Ursula rang me up just before nine o'clock that night. She told me you'd be sure to be along sooner or later."

"So that was the first you'd heard of Sir Paul's death, when his mother rang to warn you?"

"Warn me? No call to warn me. I didn't slit his throat for him, poor gentleman, nor I don't know who did. You'd have thought Miss Matlock might have taken the trouble to phone earlier. That would have been better for me than hearing it on the six o'clock news. I wondered whether to ring the house, find out if there was anything I could do, but I reckoned they'd be bothered with enough calls without me on the line. Better wait, I thought, until someone rings."

Massingham said:

"And that was Lady Ursula, just before nine?"

"That's right. Nice of her to trouble. But then we've always got on well, me and Lady Ursula. You call her Lady Ursula Berowne because she's the daughter of an earl. Lady Berowne is only the wife of a baronet."

Massingham said impatiently:

"Yes, we know that."

"Oh you do, do you. Millions don't, nor don't care neither. Still, it's as well to get it right, if you're thinking of hanging about Campden Hill Square."

Massingham asked:

"How did she sound when she rang you?"

"Lady Ursula? How do you expect? She wasn't laughing, was she? Wasn't crying neither. That's not her way. She was calm, like she always is. Couldn't tell me much, though. What happened? Suicide was it?"

"We can't be sure, Mrs. Minns, until we know more, get the results of some tests. We have to treat this as a suspicious death. When did you last see Sir Paul?"

"Just before he went out on Tuesday, about half past ten that would be. We was in the library. I'd gone in to polish the desk and there he was, sitting there. So I said I'd come back later, and he said, 'No, come in, Mrs. Minns, I won't be long.' "

"What was he doing?"

"Like I said, he was sitting at the desk. He had his diary open."

Massingham said sharply:

"Are you sure?"

"Of course I'm sure. He had it open in front of him and he was looking through it."

"How can you be certain that it was his diary?"

"Look, it was open in front of him and I could see it was a diary. It had different days on the page, it had dates in it and he'd written in it. Think I don't know a diary when I see one? Afterwards he closed it up and put it in the top right-hand drawer where it's usually kept."

Massingham asked:

"How do you know where it's usually kept?"

"Look, I've worked in that house nine years. I was taken on by her ladyship when Sir Hugo was baronet. You get to know things."

"What else happened between you?"

"Nothing much. I asked him if I could borrow one of his books."

"Borrow one of his books?" Massingham frowned his surprise.

"That's right. I'd seen it on the bottom shelf when I'd been dusting and I fancied reading it. It's there, under the television set, if you're interested. *A Rose by Twilight*, by Millicent Gentle. I haven't seen a book by her for years."

She reached for it and handed it to Massingham. It was a slim book still in its dust cover, a picture of an egregiously handsome dark-haired hero holding a blond girl half-swooning in his arms against a background riot of roses. Massingham flicked through it and said with a note of amused contempt:

"Hardly his kind of reading, I should have thought. Sent to him, I imagine, by one of his constituents. It's signed by the author. I wonder why he bothered to keep it."

Mrs. Minns said sharply:

"Why shouldn't he keep it? She's a good writer is Millicent Gentle. Not that she's been doing much lately. I'm very partial to a good romantic novel. Better than all those horrible murders. I can't be doing with them. So I asked if I could borrow it and he said I could."

Kate took the book and opened it. On the flyleaf was written: "To Paul Berowne, with every good wish from the author." Underneath was the signature, Millicent Gentle, and the date, the seventh of August. It was the date of Diana Travers's drowning, but apparently Massingham hadn't noticed. She closed the book and said:

"We'll take this book back to Campden Hill Square if you've finished with it, Mrs. Minns."

"Please yourself. I wasn't thinking of pinchin' it, if that's what you're thinking."

Massingham asked:

"What else happened after he'd said you could borrow the book?"

"He asked me how long I'd been working at Campden Hill Square. I said nine years. Then he said, 'Have they been good years for you?' I said, as good for me as they have for most."

Massingham smiled. He said:

"I don't think that's what he meant."

"I know what he meant all right. But what did he expect me to say? I do the work, they pay me; four pounds an hour, which is above the going rate, and a taxi home if I'm there after dark. I wouldn't stay if the job didn't suit. But what do they expect for their money? Love? If he'd wanted me to say that I'd spent the best years of my life at Campden Hill Square, then he was disappointed. Mind you, it was different when the first Lady Berowne was alive."

"How do you mean, different?"

"Just different. The house seemed more alive then. I liked the first Lady Berowne. She was a very pleasant lady. Not that she lasted long, poor soul."

Kate asked:

"Why did you continue to work at number sixty-two, Mrs. Minns?"

Mrs. Minns turned on her her bright little eyes and said simply:

"I like polishing furniture."

Kate guessed that Massingham was tempted to ask what she thought of the second Lady Berowne, but he decided to keep to his main line of questioning.

"And what then?" he asked.

"He went out, didn't he?"

"Out of the house?"

"That's right."

"Can you be sure?"

"Look, he had his jacket on, he picked up that hold-all he had, he went through the hall and I heard the front door open and shut. If it wasn't him going out, then who was it?"

"But you didn't actually see him go?"

"I never followed him to the door to kiss him good-bye, if that's what you mean. I have my work to do. But that's the last time I saw him in this world, and I've no expectations of seeing him in the next, that's for sure."

Perhaps prudently Massingham did not pursue this thought. He said:

"And you're certain that he put the diary back in the drawer?"

"He didn't take it with him. Look, what is it about the diary? Are you saying I stole it or something?"

Kate broke in:

"It isn't in the drawer now, Mrs. Minns. Of course, we don't suspect anyone of taking it. It hasn't any value. But it does seem to be missing, and it could be important. You see, if he did make an appointment for the next day, then it wouldn't be very likely that he set out from home meaning to kill himself."

Mrs. Minns, mollified, said:

"Well, he didn't take it with him. I saw him put it back with my own eyes. And if he did come back for it later, it wasn't while I was in the house."

Massingham asked:

"That's possible, of course. When did you leave?"

"Five o'clock. My usual time. I wash up the lunch things and I have my special afternoon job. Some days it might be the silver, some days the linen cupboard. On Tuesday it was dusting the books in the library. I was there from half past two until four, when I went to help Miss Matlock with the tea. He certainly didn't come back then. I'd have heard anyone if they'd come through the hall."

Suddenly Kate asked:

"Would you say it was a happy marriage, Mrs. Minns?"

"Hardly ever saw them together to tell. When I did, they seemed all right. They never shared a bedroom, though."

Massingham said:

"That's not so very unusual."

"Maybe. But there's not sharing and not sharing, if you get my meaning. I make the beds, you see. That may be your idea of a marriage, but it's not mine."

Massingham said:

"Hardly the way to produce the next baronet."

"Well, I did wonder about that a few weeks ago. Off her breakfast she was and that isn't like her. But not much chance, I reckon. Too worried about her figure. Mind you, she's not bad when she's in a good mood. Too gushing though. 'Oh Mrs. Minns, be a darling and fetch my dressing gown.' 'Mrs. Minns, be an angel and run a bath for me.' 'Be a dear and make a cup of tea.' Sweet as sugar, as long as she gets her own way. Well, she more or less has to be. Same with Lady Ursula. She doesn't much care for Miss Matlock helping her to bath and dress. I can see that even if Matlock can't. But there it is. If you get used to having your bath run and your breakfast in bed and your clothes hung up, you have to put up with some inconvenience in return. Different when Lady Ursula was a girl, of course. Servants were seen and not heard then. Pressed back against the wall when the gentry go by in case they have to look at you. Hand the post with a glove so as not to contaminate it. Think yourself lucky to have a good place. My gran was in service; I know."

Massingham said:

"There were no quarrels, then, as far as you know?"

"It would have been better, maybe, if there had been. He was too polite, formal you could say. Now, that's not natural in a marriage. No, there were no quarrels, not till Tuesday morning anyway. And then you could hardly call it a quarrel. Takes two to quarrel. She was screeching fit to reach the whole house, but I didn't hear much from him."

"When was this, Mrs. Minns?"

"When I took up her breakfast tray at half past eight. I do that every morning. Sir Paul used to take up Lady Ursula's. She only has orange juice, two slices of wholemeal bread, toasted, marmalade and coffee, but Lady Berowne has the whole hog. Orange juice, cereal, scrambled egg, toast, the lot. Never puts on an ounce, though."

"Tell me about the quarrel, Mrs. Minns. What did you hear?"

"I got to the bedroom door when I heard her screeching: 'You're going to that whore. You can't, not now. We need you, we both need you. I won't let you go.' Something like that. And then I could hear his voice, very low. I couldn't hear what he was saying. I stood outside the door and wondered what to do. I put the tray down on the table by the door. I usually do that while I knock. But it didn't seem right to go barging in. On the other hand, I couldn't stand there like a daft thing. Then the door opened and he came out. White as paper he was. He saw me and said: 'I'll take the tray, Mrs. Minns.' So I gave it to him. The way he looked, it was a wonder he didn't drop it there and then."

Massingham said:

"But he took it into the bedroom?"

"That's right, and shut the door. And I went back to the kitchen."

Massingham changed the direction of his questions. He asked:

"Did anyone else enter the library that Tuesday as far as you know?"

"That Mr. Musgrave from the constituency did. He waited from about half past twelve to nearly two o'clock, hoping Sir Paul would be back for lunch. Then he gave up and went away. Miss Sarah was there about four o'clock. She'd come to see her grandmother. I told her Lady Ursula wasn't expected back to tea, but she said she'd wait. Then she got fed up too, seemingly. Must have let herself out. I didn't see the going of her."

Massingham went on to ask her about Diana Travers. Kate sensed that he had less faith than had she in AD's belief that the deaths of both girls were somehow connected with Paul Berowne's murder, but he dutifully did what was expected of him. The result proved a great deal more interesting than either of them had thought possible. Mrs. Minns said:

"I was there when Diana arrived. We'd just lost Maria. She was Spanish, her husband worked as a cook in Soho, then she got pregnant with her third and the doctor said to cut down on her outside jobs. She was a good worker, was Maria. Those Spanish girls know how to house clean, I'll say that for them. Anyway, Miss Matlock put a card in the newsagent's window at the end of Ladbroke Grove and Diana turned up. The card couldn't have been there more than an hour. A bit of luck, really, I never thought she'd get any answers. Good cleaning ladies don't have to look in newsagents for jobs these days."

"And was she a good cleaner?"

"Never done it in her life before, you could see that. But she was willing enough. Of course, Miss Matlock never let her touch the best china or polish in the drawing room. She took over the bathrooms, bedrooms, prepared vegetables, did a bit of shopping. She was all right."

"A strange job for her to choose, though, a girl like that."

Mrs. Minns understood what he meant.

"Oh, she was educated all right, you could see that. Well, it wasn't badly paid, four pounds an hour, a good midday meal if you're there for it and no tax unless you're daft enough to pay it. She said she was an actress looking for work and wanted a job she could chuck at once if something turned up. What's so interesting about Diana Travers anyway?"

Massingham ignored the question. He said:

"Did you and she get on well together?"

"No reason why we shouldn't. I told you, she was all right. A bit nosey. Found her one day looking in the drawer of Sir Paul's desk. Didn't hear me till I was on top of her. Bold as brass about it. Just laughed. Asked a lot about the family, too. She didn't get much out of me, nor from Miss Matlock either. No harm in her though, just a bit too keen on chat. I liked her all right. If I hadn't I wouldn't have let her come here."

"You mean she lived here? We weren't told that at Campden Hill Square."

"Well, they didn't know, did they? No reason why they should. She was buying herself a flat in Ridgemount Gardens and there was a hold-up. The owners weren't ready to move into their new place. You know how it is. Anyway, she had to leave her old place and find somewhere for a month. Well, I've got the two bedrooms, so I told her she could move in here. Twenty-five pounds a week including a good breakfast. Not bad. I don't know that Mr. Smith was all that keen, but he was due to be off roamin' anyway."

And there were the two bedrooms, thought Kate. Mrs. Minns's black eyes stared at Massingham, defying him to enquire about the usual sleeping arrangements. And then she said:

"My gran said every woman should marry once, she owes it to herself. But no point in making a habit of it."

Kate said:

"A flat in Ridgemount Gardens? Isn't that a bit up-market for an out-of-work actress?"

"That's what I thought, but she said Daddy was helping. Maybe he was, maybe he wasn't. Maybe it was Daddy, maybe someone else. Anyway, he was in Australia, or so she told me. No business of mine."

Massingham said:

"So she moved in here. When did she leave?"

"Just ten days before she was drowned, poor kid. And you're not telling me there was anything suspicious about that death. I was at the inquest. Natural interest, you might say. Never a mention of where she worked though, was there? You'd have thought they might have sent a wreath to the funeral. Didn't want to know, did they?"

Massingham asked:

"What did she do with herself while she was living here with you?"

"I hardly saw her. No business of mine, was it? Two mornings a week she worked at Campden Hill Square. The rest of the time she said she was off for auditions. She went out a good bit at night, but she never brought anyone here. She was no trouble, neat and tidy always. Well, I wouldn't have had her here if I hadn't known that. Then, the evening after she drowned, before the inquest even, she hadn't been dead twenty-four hours, these two chaps turn up."

"Here?"

"That's right. Just when I got back from Campden Hill Square. Sitting in their car watching out for me, if you ask me. Said they were from her solicitors, come to collect any of her things she might have left here."

"Did they show you any identity, any authority?"

"A letter from the firm. Posh writing paper. And they had a card, so I let them in. I stayed by the door and watched them, mind you. They didn't like it, but I wanted to see what they were up to. 'There's nothing here,' I told them. 'Look for yourselves. She left nearly a fortnight ago.' They properly turned the place over, even turned the mattress up. Found nothing, of course. Funny business, I thought, but nothing came of it, so I let it go. No point in making trouble."

"Who do you think they were?"

Mrs. Minns gave a sudden shout of laughter.

"You tell me! Come off it! They were two of you lot. Fuzz. Think I don't know a policeman when I see one?"

Even in the room's dim arboreal light Kate saw the faint flush of excitement on Massingham's face. But he was too experienced to press further. Instead he asked a few harmless questions about the domestic arrangements at Campden Hill Square and prepared to bring the interview to a close. But Mrs. Minns had her own ideas. Kate sensed that she had something private to communicate. Getting up, she said:

"D'you mind if I use your lavatory, Mrs. Minns?"

She doubted whether Massingham was deceived, but he could hardly follow them. Waiting for her when she came out of the bathroom, Mrs. Minns almost hissed:

"You saw the date in that book?"

"Yes, Mrs. Minns. The day Diana Travers was drowned."

The sharp little eyes gleamed with satisfaction.

"I thought as how you'd noticed. He didn't though, did he?"

"I expect so. He just didn't mention it."

"He never noticed. I know his sort. Too sharp for their own good and then miss what's under their noses."

"When did you first see the book, Mrs. Minns?"

"The next day, August eighth. In the afternoon it was, after he came home from the constituency. Must have brought it with him."

"So she may have given it to him then."

"Maybe. Maybe not. Interesting though, isn't it? I thought as how you'd noticed. Keep it to yourself, that's my advice. He thinks too much of himself, that Massingham fellow."

They had turned out of Portobello Road and were walking down Ladbroke Grove before Massingham spoke, then he laughed.

"My God, that room! I pity the mysterious Mr. Smith, If I had to live there and with her, I'd go roaming."

Kate flared:

"What's wrong with it or with her? At least it's got character, not like the bloody building designed by some bureaucrat with a brief to fit in so many living units with the least possible public expenditure. Just because you've never had to live in one doesn't mean that the people who do like it." She added with fierce defensiveness: "Sir."

He laughed again. She was always punctilious about acknowledging his rank when she was angry.

"All right, all right, I admit the character. They've both got character, she and her room. And what's so wrong with the block? I thought it was rather decent. If the council offered me a flat there, I'd take it quickly enough."

And he would, she thought. He was probably less concerned about the externals of his life, where he ate, where he lived, even what he wore, than she was herself. And it was irritating to discover, once more, how easily in his company she was trapped into insincerity. She had never believed that buildings were all that important. It was people, not architects, who made slums. Even Ellison Fairweather House would have been all right if it had been put up in a different place and filled with different people. He went on:

"And she was useful, wasn't she? If she's right and he did put the diary back in the drawer, and if we can prove that he didn't return . . ."

She broke in:

"That won't be easy, though. It'll mean accounting for every minute of his time. And so far we haven't a clue where he went after he left the estate agent's. He had a key. He could have let himself in and been out again in a minute."

"Yes, but the probability is that he didn't. After all, he went out with his bag, he obviously intended to stay out all day and go straight to the church. And if Lady Ursula did consult the diary before six o'clock when General Nollinge rang, then we know who has to be our chief suspect, don't we? Dominic Swayne."

None of it needed saying. She had seen the importance of the diary as soon as he had. She said:

"Who do you think those men were, the ones who did the search? Special Branch?"

"That's my guess. Either she worked for them and they planted her in Campden Hill Square, or she worked for someone or something a great deal more sinister and they rumbled her. Of course, they could have been who they said they were, men from a solicitor's firm looking for papers, a will."

"Under the mattress? It was a pretty professional search."

If it was Special Branch, she thought, there was going to be trouble. She said:

"They did tell us about Berowne's mistress."

"Knowing that we'd have discovered that for ourselves quickly enough. That's typical of Special Branch. Their idea of cooperation is like a Minister answering a question in the House; keep it short, keep it accurate, make sure you don't tell them anything they don't know already. God, if she was tied up with Special Branch, there's going to be trouble."

She said:

"Between Miles Gilmartin and AD?"

"Between everyone."

They walked in silence for a moment, then he said:

"Why did you bring away that novel?"

She was for a moment tempted to prevaricate. She knew that when the significance of the date had first struck her she had planned to keep quiet about it, to do a little private detection, trace the writer, see if there was anything in it. Then prudence had prevailed. If it proved important,

AD would have to know and she could imagine what his response would be to that particular kind of personal initiative. It was hypocritical to complain about the lack of interdepartmental cooperation while trying to run her own show within the squad. She said:

"The signature is dated seventh August, the day Diana Travers died."

"So what? She signed and posted it on the seventh."

"Mrs. Minns saw it the following afternoon. Since when has the London post arrived that promptly?"

"It's perfectly possible, if she sent it first class."

She persisted:

"It's far more likely that he met Millicent Gentle that day and she gave it to him personally. I thought it would be interesting to know when and why."

He looked at her and said:

"Could be. It's just as likely that she signed it on the seventh, then left it for him at his constituency office." Then he smiled.

"That's what you and Mrs. Minns were having your girlish gossip about."

He gave a slow, secret smile and she knew, with a spurt of irritation, that he had guessed about her temptation to conceal the evidence and was amused by it.

7

⊠

Once back in the Rover and on their way to the Yard she suddenly said:

"I don't understand it, religious experience."

"You mean you don't know how to categorize it."

"You were brought up in it, I suppose. They indoctrinated you from the cradle: nursery prayers, school chapel, that sort of thing."

She had seen the school chapel once on an outing to Windsor. It had impressed her. That, after all, was its purpose. She had felt interest, admiration, even awe, walking under that soaring fan vaulting. But it had still remained a building in which she had felt herself an alien, speaking to her of history, privilege, tradition, an affirmation that the rich, having inherited the earth, could hope to insure similar privileges in heaven. Someone had been playing the organ, and she had sat listening with pleasure to what she thought must have been a Bach cantata, but for her there had been no secret harmonies.

He said, his eyes on the road:

"I'm reasonably familiar with the external forms. Not as much as my father. Compulsory chapel every day for him, or so he claims."

"I don't even feel the need of it, religion, praying."

"That's perfectly natural. A lot of people don't. You're probably in the respectable majority. It's a matter of temperament. What's worrying you?"

"Nothing's worrying me. But it's odd about praying. Most people do pray, apparently. Someone did a survey about it. They pray even if they're not sure who to. What about AD?"

"I don't know what he feels the need of except his poetry, his job and his privacy. And probably in that order."

"But you've worked with him before, I haven't. Don't you think that there's something about this case that's got under his skin?"

He looked at her as if he were sharing the car with a stranger, wondering just how much he could prudently confide. Then he said:

"Yes, yes I do."

Something, Kate felt, had been achieved, a confidence, a trust established. She pressed further.

"What's bugging him then?"

"What happened to Berowne in that church, I suppose. AD likes life to be rational. Odd for a poet, but there it is. This case isn't, not altogether."

"Have you talked to him about it, what happened in that church, I mean?"

"No. I did try once, but all I could get out of him was: 'The real world is difficult enough, John. Let's try to stay in it.' So I shut my mouth, not being a fool."

The light changed. She slipped out the clutch, the Rover moved quickly and smoothly away. They were meticulous in taking turns to drive. He yielded up the seat readily enough but like all good drivers he disliked being a passenger, and it was a matter of pride for her to match his fast competence. She knew that she was tolerated by him, respected even, but they didn't really like each other. He accepted that the team needed a woman, but without being overtly chauvinistic, he would have preferred a man as partner. Her feeling towards him was more positive, compounded of resentment and antipathy. Some of it she knew was class resentment. But at heart there was a dislike more instinctive and fundamental. She found red-haired men physically unattractive. Whatever there was between them, it certainly wasn't the antagonism of an unacknowledged sexuality. Dalgliesh, of course, knew that perfectly well. He made use of it as he made use of so much. For a moment she felt a spurt of active dislike of all men. I'm an oddity, she thought. How much would I care, really care, if Alan chucked me? Suppose I had the choice, promotion or Alan, my flat or Alan? She was given to these awkward self-examinations, imaginary choices, ethical dilemmas, nonetheless intriguing because she knew she would never have to confront them in real life.

She said:

"Do you believe that something really did happen to Berowne in that vestry?"

"It must have, mustn't it? A man doesn't chuck his job and change the direction of his whole life for nothing."

"But was it real? OK, don't ask me what I mean by real. Real in the sense this car is real, you're real, I'm real. Was he deluded, drunk, drugged? Or did he really have, well, some kind of supernatural experience, I suppose?"

"It seems unlikely for a practising member of the good old C of E, which is what he's supposed to have been. That's the sort of thing you expect of characters in a Graham Greene novel."

She said:

"You make it sound as if it were in poor taste, eccentric, a bit presumptuous." She was silent for a moment and then asked:

"If you have a kid, will you have him christened?"

"Yes. Why do you ask?"

"So you believe in it, God, the Church, religion."

"I didn't say so."

"Then why?"

"My family have been christened for four hundred years—longer, I suppose. Yours, too, I imagine. It doesn't seem to have done us any harm. I don't see why I should be the first to break the habit, not without some positive feelings against it, which I don't happen to have."

And wasn't that, she thought, one of the things which Sarah Berowne had resented in her father, the ironic detachment which is too arrogant even to care. She said:

"So it's a matter of class."

He laughed:

"Everything with you is a matter of class. No, it's a matter of tradition, of family piety, if you like."

She said, carefully not looking at him:

"I'm hardly the person to talk to about family piety. I'm illegitimate, if you didn't know."

"No, I didn't know."

"Well, thank you for not telling me it isn't important."

He said:

"It only concerns one person. You. If you think it's important, then OK, it has to be important."

Suddenly she almost liked him. She glanced at the freckled face under a shock of red hair and tried to see him against the background of that college chapel. Then she thought of her own school. Ancroft Comprehensive had certainly had a religion all right, fashionable and, in a school with twenty different nationalities, expedient. It was anti-racism. You soon learned that you could get away with any amount of insubordination, indolence or stupidity if you were sound on this essential doctrine. It struck her that it was like any other religion: it meant what you wanted it to mean; it was easy to learn, a few platitudes, myths and slogans; it was intolerant, it gave you the excuse for occasional selective aggression, and you could make a moral virtue out of despising the people you disliked. Best of all, it cost nothing. She liked to pretend that this early indoctrination had absolutely nothing to do with the cold fury which seized her when she met its opposite, the obscene graffiti, the shouted insults, the terror of Asian families afraid to leave their barricaded homes. If you had to have a school ethos to give the illusion of togetherness, then for her money anti-racism was as good as any. And whatever she might think about its more absurd manifestations, it wasn't likely to lead you to see visions in a dusty church.

8

Dalgliesh had decided to drive alone on the Saturday afternoon to see the Nolans in their Surrey cottage. It was the kind of chore he would normally have entrusted to Massingham and Kate, or even to a detective sergeant and DC, and he could see the surprise in Massingham's eyes when he told him that he had no need of a witness nor of anyone to take notes. The journey itself wasn't unnecessary. If Berowne's murder was linked to Theresa Nolan's suicide, anything he could discover about the girl could be important. She was at present no more than a photograph in a police file, a pale, childish face under a nurse's cap. He needed to animate that shadowy ghost with the living girl. But in intruding on her grandparents' grief he could at least make it as easy as possible for them. One police officer must surely be more tolerable than two.

But there was, he knew, another reason for going himself and alone. He needed an hour or two of solitude and quietness, an excuse to get away from London, from his office, from the insistent telephone, from Massingham and the squad. He needed to escape from the Assistant Commissioner's carefully unspoken criticism that he was making a mystery out of a tragic but unremarkable suicide and murder, that they were all wasting time on a manhunt without a quarry. He needed to escape, however briefly, from the clutter of his desk and the pressure of personalities, to see the case with clearer, unprejudiced eyes.

It was a warm, blustery day. Torn shreds of clouds dragged across a sky of clear azure blue and cast their frail shadows over the shorn autumnal fields. He was travelling via Cobham and Effingham, and once off the A3 he drove the Jaguar XJS into a lay-by and thrust open the car roof. After Cobham, with the wind tearing at his hair, he thought he could smell in its fitful gusts the rich, pine-scented woodsmoke of autumn. The narrow country roads, bleached white between the grass verges, wound through the Surrey woodlands which would suddenly clear to give him a wide view to the South Downs and Sussex. He found himself wishing that the road would straighten before his wheels and run empty, unsignposted, forever, that he could press down the accelerator and lose all his frustrations in the surge of power, that this rush of autumn-scented air screaming in his ears could cleanse his mind as well as his eyes of the colour of blood forever.

He half-dreaded his journey's end, and it came unexpectedly quickly. He passed through Shere and found himself climbing a short hill; and there on the left-hand side of the road, bounded by oaks and silver birch, and separated from the road by a short garden, was an unremarkable Victorian cottage with its name, Weaver's Cottage, painted on the white gate. About twenty yards beyond it the road straightened, and he drove the Jaguar gently onto the sandy verge. When he had turned off the engine the silence was absolute, birdless, and he sat for a moment, motionless and exhausted, as if he had come through some self-imposed ordeal.

He had telephoned, so he knew that they must be expecting him. But all the windows were fastened, there was no woodsmoke from the stack and the cottage had the secretive, oppressive air of a place not deserted but deliberately closed against the world. The front garden was untended, with none of the haphazard exuberance of the normal cottage garden. All the plants were in rows, chrysanthemums, Michaelmas daisies, dahlias, with between them half-denuded rows of vegetables. But the ground was unweeded and the small patch of lawn on each side of the door unmown and shaggy. There was an iron knocker in the form of a horseshoe, but no bell. He let it fall gently, guessing that they must have heard the car, must surely be expecting the knock, but it was a full minute before the door opened.

He said:

"Mrs. Nolan?" and took out his card, feeling, as he always did, like an importunate door-to-door salesman. She barely looked at it, but stood aside to let him in. She must, he thought, be nearer seventy than sixty, a small-boned woman with a sharp, anxious face. The exophthalmic eyes, so like her granddaughter's, gazed into his with a look with which he was only too familiar: a mixture of apprehension, curiosity and then relief that at least he looked human. She was wearing a suit in blue and grey synthetic jersey, ill-fitting at the shoulders and puckered where she had shortened it at the hem. In her lapel was a round brooch of coloured stones in silver. It dragged at the thin jersey. He guessed that this wasn't her usual wear for a Saturday afternoon, that she had dressed up for his visit. Perhaps she was a woman who dressed up to meet all life's ordeals and tragedies: a small gesture of pride and defiance in the face of the unknown.

The square sitting room with its single window looked to him more typical of a London suburb than these deep country woods. It was neat, very clean, but characterless and rather dark. The original fireplace had been replaced by one of mock marble with a wooden overmantel and was furnished with an electric fire, one bar of which was burning. Two walls had been papered in a lurid mixture of roses and violets, and two with a plain paper in blue stripes. The thin, unlined curtains were hung with the patterned side towards the road so that the afternoon sunshine was filtered through a pattern of bulbous pink roses and ivy-clad latticework. There were two modern armchairs, one each side of the fireplace, and a square central table with four chairs. Against the far wall was a large television set, high on a trolley. Except for a copy of both the *Radio Times* and *TV Times*, there were no magazines and no books. The only picture was a garish print of the Sacred Heart over the fireplace.

Mrs. Nolan introduced her husband. He was sitting in the right-hand armchair, facing the window, a huge, gaunt man who responded to Dalgliesh's greeting with a stiff nod but didn't get up. His face was rigid. In the shaft of sunlight between the curtains its planes and angles looked as if they had been carved in oak. His left hand, crossed in his lap, was beating a ceaseless, involuntary tattoo.

Mrs. Nolan said:

"You'd like some tea, I daresay?"

He said:

"Very much, thank you, if it isn't too much trouble," and thought: I seem to have heard that question and spoken those words all my life.

She smiled and nodded as if satisfied, and bustled out. Dalgliesh thought: I say the conventional insincerities and she responds as if I were the one doing the favour. What is it about this job that makes people grateful that I can act like a human being?

The two men waited in silence, but the tea came very quickly. So that, he thought, accounted for the delay in opening the door. She had hurried at his knock to put on the kettle. They sat at the table in stiff formality, waiting while Albert Nolan raised himself stiffly from his chair and edged his way painfully into his seat. The effort set up a new spasm of shaking. Without speaking, his wife poured his tea and set the cup before him. He didn't grasp it, but bent his head and slurped his tea noisily from the side. His wife didn't even look at him. There was a half-cut cake which she said was walnut and marmalade, and she smiled again when Dalgliesh accepted a slice. It was dry and rather tasteless, rolling into a soft dough in his mouth. Small pellets of walnut lodged in his teeth and the occasional sliver of orange peel was sour to the tongue. He washed it down with a mouthful of strong, over-milked tea. Somewhere in the room a fly was making a loud intermittent buzz.

He said:

"I'm sorry that I have to trouble you, and I'm afraid it may be painful for you. As I explained on the telephone, I'm investigating the death of Sir Paul Berowne. A short time before he died he had an anonymous letter. It suggested that he might have had something to do with your grand-daughter's death. That's why I'm here."

Mrs. Nolan's cup rattled in her saucer. She put both hands under the table like a well-behaved child at a party. Then she glanced at her husband. She said:

"Theresa took her own life. I thought you'd know that, sir."

"We did know it. But anything which happened to Sir Paul in the last weeks of his life could be important, and one thing that happened was the arrival of that anonymous letter. We should like to know who sent it. You see, we think it probable that he was murdered."

Mrs. Nolan said:

"Murdered? That letter wasn't sent from this cottage, sir. God help us, we've no call to do such a thing."

"I know that. We never for a moment thought that it was. But I wondered whether your granddaughter ever talked to you about anyone, a close friend perhaps, someone who might have blamed Sir Paul for her death."

Mrs. Nolan shook her head. She said:

"You mean, someone who might have killed him?"

"It's a possibility we have to consider."

"Who could there be? It doesn't make sense. She hadn't anyone else, only us, and we never laid hands on him, though God knows we were bitter enough."

"Bitter against him?"

Suddenly her husband spoke:

"She got pregnant while she was in his house. And he knew where to find her body. How did he know? You tell me that."

His voice was harsh, almost expressionless, but the words came out with such force that his body shook. Dalgliesh said:

"Sir Paul said at the inquest that your granddaughter spoke to him one night about her love of the woods. He thought that if she had decided to end her life, she might choose the only piece of wild woodland in central London."

Mrs. Nolan said:

"We never sent that letter to him, sir. I did see him at the inquest. Dad didn't go, but I thought one of us ought to be there. He just spoke to me, Sir Paul. He was kind really. Said he was sorry. Well, what else can people say?"

Mr. Nolan said:

"Sorry. Aye, I daresay."

She turned to him:

"Dad, there's no proof. And he was a married man. Theresa wouldn't, not with a married man."

"There's no knowing what she might have done. Or him. What does it matter? She killed herself, didn't she? First getting the baby, then the abortion, then suicide. What's one more sin when you've got that on your conscience?"

Dalgliesh said gently:

"Can you tell me something about her? You brought her up, didn't you?"

Mrs. Nolan turned to him almost eagerly.

"That's right. She hadn't anyone else. We only had the one child, her dad. Her mum died ten days after Theresa was born. She had appendicitis and the operation went wrong. A chance in a million, the doctor said."

Dalgliesh thought: I don't want to hear this. I don't want to listen to their pain. That was what the consultant obstetrician had said to him when he had gone to take a last look at his dead wife with her newborn son in the crook of her arm, both of them composed in the secret nothingness of death. A chance in a million. As if there could be comfort, almost pride, in the knowledge that chance had singled out your family to demonstrate the arbitrary statistics of human fallibility. Suddenly the buzzing of the fly was intolerable. He said:

"Excuse me," and seized the copy of the *Radio Times*. He swiped at it violently, but missed. It took another two vehement slaps against the glass before the buzzing finally stopped and the fly dropped out of sight, leaving only a faint smear. He said:

"And your son?"

"Well, he couldn't look after the baby. It wasn't to be expected. He was only twenty-one. And I think he wanted to get away from the house, from us, even from the baby. In a funny way I think he blamed us. You see, we didn't really want the marriage. Shirley, his wife, she wasn't the girl we would have chosen. We told him no good would come of it."

And when no good had come of it, it was them he had blamed, as if their disapproval, their resentment, had hovered over his wife like a curse.

Dalgliesh asked:

"Where is he now?"

"We don't know. We think he went to Canada, but he never writes. He had a good trade, mechanic. He understood cars. And he was always clever with his hands. He said he'd have no trouble finding a job."

"So he doesn't know that his daughter is dead?"

Albert Nolan said:

"He hardly knew she was alive. Why should he care now she's dead?"

His wife bent her head as if to let his bitterness wash over her. Then she said:

"I think she always felt guilty, poor Theresa. She thought she'd killed her mum. It was nonsense, of course. And then her dad leaving her, that didn't help. She grew up like an orphan, and I think she resented it. When bad things happen to a child, she always thinks it's her fault."

Dalgliesh said:

"But she must have been happy here with you. She loved the woodlands, didn't she?"

"Maybe. But I think she was lonely. She had to go to school by bus and couldn't stay for after-school activities. And there weren't other girls of her age anywhere near. She used to love walking in the woods, but we didn't encourage that, not on her own. These days you never know. Nobody's safe any more. We hoped that she'd make friends when she started nursing."

"And did she?"

"She never brought them home. But then there wasn't much here for young people. Not really."

"And you found nothing among her papers, among things she left, to give you any idea who the father of her child could have been?"

"She didn't leave anything, not even her nursing books. She was living in a hostel near Oxford Street after she left Campden Hill Square, and she cleared the whole room, threw everything out. All we had from the police was the letter, her watch, the clothes she was wearing. We threw the letter away. No point in keeping it. You can see her room if you like, sir. It's the one she had since she was a little girl. There's nothing there, just an empty room. We gave everything here, her clothes and her books, to Oxfam. We thought that was what she would have wanted."

It was, he thought, what they had wanted. She led him up the narrow staircase, showed him the room and then left. It was at the back of the cottage, small, narrow, north-facing, with one latticed window. Outside the pine trees and silver birch were so close that the leaves almost trembled against the panes. The room held a green luminosity as if it were under water. A branch of climbing rose with drooping leaves and one tight cankered bud tapped at the window. It was, as she had said, only an empty room. The air was very still and held a faint smell of disinfectant, as if the walls and floor had been scrubbed. It reminded him of a hospital room from which a dead body had been removed, impersonal, functional, a calculated space between four walls, waiting for the next patient to bring his apprehension, his pain, his hope to give it meaning. They had even stripped the bed. A white coverlet was spread over the bare mattress and the single pillow. The shelves of the wall-hung bookcase were empty; surely they were too fragile ever to have held many books. Nothing else remained except for a crucifix over the bed. Having nothing to remember but grief, they had divested the room even of her personality and had closed the door.

Looking down at the stripped and narrow bed, he recalled the words of the girl's suicide note. He had read it only twice when studying the report of the inquest, but he had no difficulty in remembering it word for word.

"Please forgive me. I can't go on in so much pain. I killed my baby and I know that I shall never see her or you again. I suppose I'm damned but I can't believe in hell any more. I can't believe in anything. You were good to me but I was no use to you, ever. I thought when I became a nurse that everything would be different but the world was never friendly. Now I know that I don't have to live in it. I hope that it won't be children who find my body. Forgive me."

It was not, he thought, a spontaneous letter. He had read so many suicide notes since he was a young DC. Sometimes they were written out of a pain and anger which produced its own unselfconscious poetry of despair. But this, despite its pathos and seeming simplicity, was more contrived, the tone of self-regard subdued but unmistakable. She may, he thought, have been one of those dangerously innocent young women, often more dangerous and less innocent than they seem, who are the catalysts of tragedy. She stood on the periphery of his investigation like a pale wraith in her nurse's uniform, unknown and now unknowable, and yet, he was convinced, central to the mystery of Berowne's death.

He had no hope now of learning anything useful at Weaver's Cottage, but his instinct to search made him pull open the drawer of the bedside cabinet, and he saw that something of her remained: her missal. He picked it up and leafed casually through it. A small square of paper torn from a notebook fell out. He picked it up and found himself looking at three columns of figures and letters:

R	D3	S
B	D2	S
P	D1	S
S–N	S2	D

Downstairs the Nolans were still sitting at the table. He showed them the paper. Mrs. Nolan thought that the figures and letters were in Theresa's handwriting, but said she couldn't be sure. Neither of them had any explanation to offer. Neither showed any interest. But they made no difficulty when he said that he would like to take the paper away.

Mrs. Nolan went with him to the front door and, somewhat to his surprise, walked with him down the path to the gate. When they reached it, she looked across at the dark shadows of the wood and said with barely suppressed passion:

"This cottage is tied to Albert's job. We ought to have been out three years ago when he got really bad, but they've been very kind to us. But we'll be leaving as soon as the local authority finds us a flat, and I won't be sorry. I hate these woods, hate them, hate them. Nothing but the wind forever whistling, sodden earth, darkness pressing in on you, small animals screaming in the night."

And then as she closed the gate behind him she looked up into his face.

"Why didn't she tell me about the baby? I'd have understood. I'd have looked after her. I could have made Dad understand. That's what hurts. Why didn't she tell me?"

Dalgliesh said:

"I expect she wanted to save you pain. That's what we all try to do, save those we love from pain."

"Dad's so bitter. He thinks she's damned. But I've forgiven her. God can't be less merciful than I am. I can't believe that."

"No," he said, "I don't think we need believe that."

She stood at the gate watching him. But when he had got into the car and fastened his seat belt he looked back at her and found that, almost mysteriously, she had gone. The cottage had returned to its secret reticence. He thought: There's too much pain in this job. To think I used to congratulate myself, to think it useful, God help me, that people found it easy to confide in me. And what has today's brush with reality brought me? A scrap of paper torn from a notebook with a few jottings, letters and digits which she may not even have written. He felt himself contaminated by the Nolans' bitterness and pain. He thought: And if I tell myself that enough is enough, twenty years of careful non-involvement, if I resign, what then? Whatever Berowne found in that dingy vestry, it isn't open to me even to look for it. As the Jaguar bumped gently back onto the road he felt a spurt of irrational envy and anger against Berowne, who had found so easy a way out.

9
⊠

It was six fifteen on Sunday evening and Carole Washburn stood gripping the rail of the balcony and looking down over the panorama of North London. She had never needed to draw the curtains when Paul had been with her, even late at night. They could gaze out together over the city and know themselves unwatched, inviolate. Then it had been good to step outside, feeling the warmth of his arm through his sleeve, and stand there together, secure, private, gazing down at the busy preoccupations of a world patterned in light. Then she had been a privileged spectator; but now she felt like an outcast, yearning for this distant, unattainable paradise from which she was forever excluded. Each night since his death she had stood watching as the lights had come on, block by block, house by house, squares of light, oblongs of light, light glimmering through curtains of rooms where people were living their shared, or secret, lives.

And now what seemed the longest Sunday she had ever endured was drawing to its close. In the afternoon, desperate to get out of the cage of the flat, she had driven to the nearest open supermarket. There was nothing she needed, but she had taken a trolley and pushed it aimlessly between the shelves, automatically reaching out for tins, packages, rolls of toilet paper, piling the trolley high, oblivious of the glances of her fellow shoppers. But then the tears had started to flow again, splashing over her hands, dropping in an unstoppable stream, splodging the packets of cereal, wrinkling the toilet rolls. She had abandoned her trolley laden with un-wanted, unsuitable goods and had walked out to the car park and driven home again, slowly and carefully, like a novice driver, seeing the world blurred and disorientated, the people jerking like puppets, as if reality were dissolving in perpetual rain.

By evening she had been seized by a desperate need for human companionship. It wasn't the need to begin some sort of life for herself, to plan some sort of future, to cast out her unpractised net into the void she had made around her secret life and begin to draw other people close. Perhaps that would come in time, impossible as it now seemed. It had been a simple uncontrollable longing to be with another human being, to hear a human voice making ordinary, unremarkable human sounds. She had telephoned Emma, who had come into the Civil Service with her from Reading, and who was now a Principal in the Department of Health and Social Security. Before she became Paul's mistress she had spent a fair proportion of her spare time with Emma, quick lunches at a pub or café convenient for both their offices, films, the occasional theatre, even a weekend together in Amsterdam to visit the Rijksmuseum. It had been an undemanding, unconfiding friendship. She had known that Emma would never give up the chance of a date with a man to spend an evening with her; and Emma had been the first victim to her obsessional need for privacy, the reluctance to commit even an hour of time which could be given to Paul. She looked at her watch. It was six forty-two. Unless Emma was spending the weekend out of town she would probably be at home.

She had to look up the number. The familiar digits sprang from the page at her like the key to an earlier, half-forgotten existence. She hadn't spoken to a human being since the police had left, and she wondered if her voice sounded as gruff and false to Emma as it did to her own ears.

"Hello? Emma? You won't believe it. This is Carole, Carole Washburn."

There was the sound of music, joyous, contrapuntal. It could have been Bach or Vivaldi. Emma called:

"Turn it down, darling," and then to Carole:

"Good God! How are you?"

"Fine. It's ages since we met. I wondered if you'd like to see a film or something. Tonight perhaps."

There was a small silence, and then Emma's voice, carefully uncommitted, surprise and perhaps a small note of resentment carefully controlled.

"Sorry, we've got people coming in for dinner."

Emma had always said dinner rather than supper even when they were proposing to eat a take-away Chinese meal at the kitchen table. It had been one of those minor snobberies which Carole had found irritating. She said:

"Next weekend perhaps?"

"Not possible, I'm afraid. Alistair and I are driving down to Wiltshire. Visiting his parents, actually. Another time perhaps. Lovely to hear from you. I must fly, the guests are due at seven thirty. I'll give you a ring sometime."

It was all she could do not to cry out: "Include me, include me! Please, I need to come." The receiver was replaced, voice, music, communication cut off. Alistair. But of course, she had forgotten that Emma was engaged. A Principal at the Treasury. So he had moved into the flat. She could imagine what they were saying now:

"Three years without a word, and she suddenly rings and wants to see a film. And on Sunday evening, for God's sake."

And Emma wouldn't ring back. She had Alistair; a shared life, shared friends. You couldn't cut people out of your life and expect to find them complaisant, readily available, just because you needed to feel human again.

There were two more days of her leave to get through before she was due back in the office. She could go home, of course, except that this flat was home. And it was hardly worth the drive to Clacton, to the square, high-roofed bungalow outside the town where her widowed mother had lived since her father's death twelve years earlier. She hadn't been home for fourteen months. Friday night had been sacrosanct; she could hope for a couple of hours with Paul on his way to his constituency. Sunday she had always kept free for him. Her mother, used to her neglect, seemed no longer to be particularly worried by it. Her mother's sister had the bungalow next door, and the two widows, early acrimonies forgotten, had settled into a cosy routine of mutual support, their brick-boxed lives measured out by small treats: shopping, morning coffee at their favourite café, returning their library books, the evening television programmes, supper on a tray. Carole had almost given up wondering about their lives, why they had chosen to live by the sea when they never went near it, what they talked about. She could telephone now and her mother would be grudgingly acquiescent, resenting the chore of making up the spare bed, the interruption to the weekend programme, the problem of stretching the food. She told herself that she had trained her mother over the past three years to expect neglect, had been grateful that her time with Paul hadn't been threatened by demands from Clacton. It seemed to her ignoble to telephone now, to rush home in search of a comfort for which she couldn't ask and which her mother, even if she had known the truth, wouldn't be able to give.

Six forty-five. If this were a Friday he would have arrived by now, timing his entrance to ensure that there was no one in the hall to see him. There would be the one long ring, the two short peals on the bell which were his signal. And then the bell rang, one long insistent peal. She thought she heard a second and then a third, but that might have been her imagination. For one miraculous second, no more, she thought that he had come, that it had all been an idiotic mistake. She called: "Paul, Paul my darling!" and almost flung herself against the door. And then her mind took hold of reality and she knew the truth. The receiver slid through her moist hands and almost fell and her lips were so dry that she could hear them cracking. She whispered:

"Who is it?"

The answering voice was high, a female voice. It said:

"Could I come up? I'm Barbara Berowne."

She pressed the button almost without thinking and heard the burr of the released lock, the click of the door as it closed. It was too late now to change her mind, but she knew that there had been no choice. In her present desperate loneliness she would have sent no one away. And this encounter had been inevitable. Ever since her affair with Paul had started, she had wanted to see his wife, and now she was going to see her. She opened the door and stood waiting, listening for the whine of the lift, the muted footfalls on the carpet, as she had once waited for his.

She came down the corridor, light-footed, casually elegant, golden, her scent, subtle and elusive, seeming to precede her and then waste itself on the air. She was wearing a coat of cream broadcloth, its wide arms and shoulders pleated, the sleeves fashioned in some finer and differently textured cloth. Her black leather boots looked as soft as her black gloves and she carried a shoulder bag on a slim strap. She was hatless, the corn-coloured hair with its streaks of paler gold twisted at the back into a long roll. It surprised Carole that she could notice the details, could actually wonder about the material of the coat sleeves, speculate where it had been bought, how much it had cost.

As she came in, it seemed to Carole that the blue eyes looked round the room with a frank, faintly contemptuous appraisal. She said in a voice which she knew, without caring, sounded forced and ungracious:

"Please sit down. Would you like something to drink? Coffee, sherry, some wine?"

She, herself, moved over to Paul's chair. It seemed to her impossible that his wife should sit where she had been used to seeing him. They faced each other a few yards apart. Barbara Berowne looked down at the carpet as if satisfying herself that it was clean before placing her bag at her feet. She said:

"No thank you. I can't stay long. I have to get back. We've got some people coming, some of Paul's colleagues. They want to talk about the memorial service. We shan't have it until the police discover who killed him, but these things have to be settled weeks in advance if one wants St. Margaret's. Apparently they don't think he really qualifies for the Abbey, poor darling. You'll come, of course; to the memorial service, I mean. There will be so many people there that you won't be noticed. I mean, you needn't feel embarrassed about me."

"No, I've never felt embarrassed about you."

"I think it's all rather gruesome actually. I don't think Paul would have wanted all that fuss. But the constituency seemed to feel that we ought to have a memorial service. After all, he was a Minister. The cremation will be private. I don't think you ought to go to that anyway, do you? It will be just the family and really intimate friends."

Intimate friends. Suddenly she wanted to laugh aloud. She said:

"Is that why you're here? To tell me about the funeral arrangements?"

"I thought Paul would want you to know. After all, we both loved him in our different ways. We're both concerned to safeguard his reputation."

She said:

"There's nothing you can teach me about safeguarding his reputation. How did you know where to find me?"

"Oh, I've known where to find you for months. A cousin of mine employed a private detective. It wasn't very difficult, just a matter of following Paul's car on a Friday evening. And then he eliminated all the couples in this block, all the old women and all the single men. That left you."

She had drawn off her black gloves and had laid them on her knee. Now she was smoothing them out, finger by finger, with pink-tipped hands. She said without looking up:

"I'm not here to make trouble for you. After all, we're in this together. I'm here to help."

"We aren't in anything together. We never have been. And what do you mean by help? Are you offering me money?"

The eyes looked up, and Carole thought she detected a flicker of anxiety, as if the question needed to be taken seriously.

"Not really. I mean, I didn't think you were actually in need. Did Paul buy this flat for you? It's rather cramped, isn't it? Still, it's quite pleasant if you don't mind living in a suburb. I'm afraid he hasn't mentioned you in his will. That's another thing I thought you ought to know, in case you were wondering."

Carole said, her voice over-loud and harsh even to her own ears:

"This flat is mine. The deposit was paid by me, the mortgage is paid with my money. Not that it's any of your business. But if you have a conscience about me, forget it. There's nothing I want from you or from anyone else connected with Paul. Women who prefer to be kept by men all their lives can never get it into their heads that some of us like to pay our own way."

"Did you have any choice?"

Speechless, she heard the high, childish voice continuing:

"After all, you've always been discreet. I admire you for that. It can't have been easy only seeing him when he hadn't anything better to do."

The amazing thing was that the insult wasn't deliberate. She was capable of being intentionally offensive, of course, but this had been a casual remark born of an egotism so insensitive that she spoke what she thought, not wanting particularly to wound, but incapable of caring whether she wounded or not. Carole thought: Paul, how could you have married her? How could you have been taken in? She's stupid, third-rate, spiteful, insensitive, mean-minded. Is beauty really so important?

She said:

"If that's all you've come to say, perhaps you'll go. You've seen me. You know what I look like. You've seen the flat. This is the chair he used to sit in. That's the table he used for his drink. If you want, I can show you the bed we made love on."

"I know what he came for."

She wanted to cry out, "Oh no you don't. You know nothing about him. I was as happy lying with him on that bed as I've ever been or ever shall be. But that wasn't what he came for." She had believed, still believed, that only with her had he been wholly at peace. He had lived his over-busy life neatly compartmentalized: the Campden Hill Square house, the House of Commons, his ministerial suite at the Department, his constituency headquarters. Only in this high, ordinary, suburban flat did the disparate elements fuse together and could he be a whole person, uniquely himself. When he had come in and sat opposite her, had dropped his briefcase at his feet and smiled at her, she had watched with joy, time and time again, the taut face soften and relax, become already smooth as if they had just made love. There were things about his private life which she knew he had held back from her, not consciously or out of lack of trust, but because, when they were together, they had no longer seemed important. But he had never held back himself.

Barbara Berowne was admiring her engagement ring, holding out her hand and moving it slowly in front of her face; the huge diamond in its setting of sapphires twinkled and flashed. She gave a secretive reminiscent smile, then looked across at Carole and said:

"There's one other thing which you might as well know. I'm having a baby."

Carole cried:

"It isn't true! You're lying! You can't be!"

The blue eyes widened.

"Of course it's true. It isn't something you can lie about, not for long anyway. I mean, the truth will be obvious to the whole world in a couple of months."

"It isn't his child!"

She thought: I'm shouting, screaming at her. I must keep calm. Oh God, help me not to believe.

"Of course it's his child. He always wanted an heir, didn't you know that? Look, you may as well accept it. The only other man I've slept with since my marriage is sterile. He's had a vasectomy. I'm going to have Paul's son."

"He wouldn't have done it. You couldn't have made him do it."

"But he did. There is one thing you can always make a man do. That is, if he likes women at all. Haven't you found that out? You're not pregnant, too, are you?"

Carole buried her face in her hands. She whispered:

"No."

"I thought I ought to be sure." She giggled. "That would have been a complication, wouldn't it?"

Suddenly all control was gone. There was nothing left but naked anger, naked shame. She heard herself bawling like a shrew:

"Get out! Get out of my flat!"

Even in the middle of her anguish and fury, she didn't miss the sudden flicker of fear in the blue eyes. She saw it with a spurt of pleasure and triumph. So she wasn't inviolate after all, she could be frightened. But the knowledge was vaguely unwelcome; it made Barbara Berowne vulnerable, more human. Now she got up almost gracelessly, bent to pick up her shoulder bag by the strap, then scampered to the door, ungainly as a child. Only when Carole had opened it and stood aside to let her out did she turn and speak.

"I'm sorry you've taken it like this. I think you're being rather silly. After all, I was his wife, I'm the injured party."

And then she was hurrying down the corridor. Carole called after her: "The injured party! My God, that's good. The injured party!"

She closed the door and leaned against it. Sickness heaved at her stomach. She rushed to the bathroom, spewed into the basin, grasping the taps for support. And then came anger, cleansing, almost exhilarating. Between fury and grief, she wanted to fling her head back and howl like an animal. She groped her way back into the sitting room and felt for her own chair like a blind woman, then sat gazing at his empty seat, willing herself to calm. When she had herself under control, she fetched her handbag and took out the card with the Scotland Yard extension she had been asked to telephone.

It was Sunday, but someone would be on duty. Even if she couldn't speak to Inspector Miskin now, she could leave a message, ask that she be rung back. It couldn't wait until tomorrow. She had to commit herself irrevocably, and now.

A male voice answered, one she didn't recognize. She gave her name and asked for Inspector Miskin. She said:

"It's urgent. It's about the Berowne murder."

There was a delay of only seconds before the inspector answered. Although she had heard the voice only once before, it came to her with a shock of recognition. She said:

"This is Carole Washburn. I want to see you. There's something I've decided to tell you."

"We'll come round now."

"Not here. I don't want you to come here, not ever again. I'll meet you tomorrow morning. Nine o'clock. The formal garden in Holland Park, the one near the orangery. Do you know it?"

"Yes, I know it. We'll be there."

"I don't want Commander Dalgliesh. I don't want any male officer. Just you. I won't talk to anyone else."

There was a pause, then the voice spoke again, unsurprised, accepting:

"Nine o'clock tomorrow. The garden, Holland Park. I'll be on my own. Can you give me any idea what it's about?"

"It's about the death of Theresa Nolan. Good-bye."

Then she replaced the receiver and leaned her forehead against the cold stickiness of the metal. She felt empty, light-headed, shaken by her heartbeats. She wondered what she would feel, how she could go on living when she was capable of knowing what she had done. She wanted to cry aloud: "My darling, I'm sorry, I'm sorry. I'm sorry." But she had made her decision. There was no going back now. And it seemed to her that there still hung in the room the fugitive scent of Barbara Berowne's perfume, like the taint of betrayal, and that the air of her flat would never be free of it.

BOOK
FIVE

Rhesus
Positive

1

☒

Miles Gilmartin of Special Branch was protected from the importunities of casual visitors and the attention of the ill-intentioned by a series of checks and counterchecks which to Dalgliesh, waiting in thwarted anger and impatience while each was negotiated, seemed more childishly ingenious than necessary or effective. It wasn't a game he was in the mood to play. By the time he was finally ushered into Gilmartin's office by a secretary who irritatingly combined exceptional beauty with an obvious consciousness of her unique privilege in serving the great man, Dalgliesh was beyond considerations of prudence or discretion. Bill Duxbury was with Gilmartin, and they had hardly got beyond the few preliminary courtesies before anger found its relief in words.

"We're supposed to be on the same side, if you people acknowledge any side but your own. Paul Berowne was murdered. If I can't get co-operation from you, where can I expect to get it?"

Gilmartin said:

"I can understand a certain resentment that we didn't tell you earlier that Travers was one of our operatives . . ."

"Operatives. You make it sound as if she were on a production line. And you didn't tell me. I had to discover it for myself. Oh, I can see the fascination of your world. It reminds me of my prep school. We had our little secrets, our code words, initiation ceremonies. But when the hell are you people going to grow up? All right, I know it's necessary, some of it anyway, and for some of the time. But you make it into an obsession. Secrecy for its own sake, the whole vast paper-ridden bureaucracy of spying. No wonder your kind of organization breeds its own traitors. In the meantime, I'm investigating an actual murder and it would help if you stopped playing games and joined the real world."

Gilmartin said mildly:

"I'm not sure that speech wouldn't have been more appropriately made to MI5. There's something in what you say. One ought to guard more against over-enthusiasm, and we're certainly over-bureaucratized. But then what organization isn't? We deal in information, after all, and information is valueless if it isn't properly documented and easily available. Still, pound for pound, I think we give the taxpayers value for money."

Dalgliesh looked at him.

"You really haven't understood a word I've been saying."

"Oh yes I have, Adam. But it's all so unlike you. Such vehemence! You've been reading too many of those espionage novels."

Three years ago, thought Dalgliesh bitterly, Gilmartin might have thought, even if he hadn't dared to speak it: It's all that poetry you write. But he couldn't say that now. Gilmartin went on:

"Are you sure this Berowne murder isn't getting under your skin? You knew him, didn't you?"

"For God's sake, if another person suggests I can't handle the case because I knew the victim, I'll resign." For the first time, a look of concern like a brief spasm of pain passed over Gilmartin's bland, almost colourless face.

"Oh, I shouldn't do that. Not over a small sin of omission on our part. I suppose that Berowne was murdered, by the way. There's a rumour that it could have been suicide. After all, he was hardly normal at the time. This habit he'd developed of sleeping in church vestries. And isn't he supposed to have had some kind of divine revelation? Listening to his voices when he should have been listening to the Prime Minister. And such a very curious church to choose. I can understand an enthusiasm for English Perpendicular, but a Romanesque basilica in Paddington is surely an improbable choice for a good night's sleep, let alone one's personal road to Damascus."

Dalgliesh was tempted to ask him whether he would have found St. Margaret's Westminster a more acceptable choice. Gilmartin, having neatly demonstrated at least a superficial knowledge of church architecture and Scripture to his own evident satisfaction, got up from his desk and began to pace between the windows as if suddenly aware that he was the only one sitting down at a desk and that this lower status might put him at a disadvantage. He could afford a good tailor and dressed with a careful formality which, in a less confident man, might suggest that he was aware of the slightly ambiguous reputation of the security service and was anxious not to reinforce it by any slovenliness in manner or appearance. But Gilmartin dressed to please himself, as he did everything. Today he was elegant in grey. Above the formal suit with its almost invisible darker stripe, the square almost bloodless face and the sleek hair, prematurely white and brushed straight back from the high forehead, reinforced both image and colour scheme: a carefully composed arrangement in grey and silver against which his old school tie, despite its comparative sobriety, hung like a garish flag of defiance.

In contrast Bill Duxbury, stocky, ruddy-faced and loud-voiced, looked like a gentleman farmer whose farming is more successful than his gentility. He stood half looking out of the window like a child ordered to distance himself from the adults and their concerns. Dalgliesh saw that he had recently got rid of his moustache. Without it, his face looked incomplete and naked, as if he had been forceably shaved. He was wearing a tweed checked suit, rather too heavy for the comparatively mild autumn, the jacket cut with a back flap which strained over his large, rather feminine buttocks. When Gilmartin looked at him, which was infrequently, it was with a pained, slightly surprised expression as though deploring both his subordinate's figure and his tailor.

It had early been apparent that Gilmartin was to do the talking. Duxbury would have briefed him, but Duxbury would remain silent unless invited to speak. Dalgliesh was suddenly reminded of a dinner party conversation some years previously. He had found himself sitting with a woman on one of those three-person sofas which can only comfortably hold two. It had been a Georgian drawing room in a North Islington square, but he couldn't now remember the name of his hostess and God knew what he thought he had been doing there. His companion had been slightly drunk, not offensively so but enough to make her flirtatious, merry and then confiding. Memory refused to come up with her name and it didn't matter. They had sat together for half an hour before their hostess, with practised tact, had separated them. He could remember only part of their conversation. She and her husband had a penthouse overlooking a street which was commonly used for student demonstrations, and the police—she was sure they were Special Branch—had asked permission to use their front sitting room to take photographs from the window.

"We said they could, of course, and they were really very sweet about it. But part of me wasn't really happy. I wanted to say: 'They're British subjects. They've got the right to march if they want to. If you want to photograph them, can't you do it openly, in the street?' But I didn't. After all, it was rather fun in a way. The sense of conspiracy, being in the know. And it wasn't up to us to make a stand. They know what they're doing. And it never does to antagonize these people."

It had seemed to him then, and it did now, to sum up the attitude of decent liberals all over the world: "They know what they're doing. It isn't up to us to make a stand. It never does to antagonize these people."

He said bitterly:

"I'm surprised that you and MI5 don't encourage regular secondments to the KGB. You've more in common with them than you have with any outsider. It might be instructive to see how they deal with the paperwork."

Gilmartin lifted an eyelid at Duxbury as if inviting solidarity in the face of unreason. He said mildly:

"As far as paperwork is concerned, Adam, it would help us if your people were a little more conscientious. Massingham, when requesting information about Ivor Garrod, should have put in an IR49."

"In quadruplicate, of course."

"Well, registry need a copy and so, presumably, do you. We're supposed to keep MI5 in the picture. We could look at the procedure again, of course, but I would say that four copies were the minimum."

Dalgliesh said:

"This girl, Diana Travers. Was she the most suitable person you could find to spy on a Minister of State? Even for Special Branch, it seems an odd choice."

"But we weren't spying on a Minister of State, she wasn't assigned to Berowne. As we told you when you enquired about his mistress, Berowne never was a risk. No IR49 submitted there either, incidentally."

"I see. You infiltrated Travers into Garrod's group or cell, whatever he calls it, and conveniently forgot to mention the fact when we enquired about him. You must have known that he was a suspect. He still is."

"It hardly seemed relevant. We all operate, after all, on the 'need to know' principle. And we didn't infiltrate her into Campden Hill Square. Garrod did. Travers's little job for us had nothing to do with Berowne's death."

"But Travers's death might have."

"There was nothing suspicious about her death. You must have studied the autopsy report."

"Which wasn't, I noticed, carried out by the usual Home Office pathologist for Thames Valley."

"We like to use our own people. He's perfectly competent, I assure you. She died from natural causes, more or less. It could have happened to anyone. She had eaten too much, drunk too much, and she plunged into cold water, got tangled in the reeds, gasped and drowned. There were no suspicious marks on the body. She had had, as you no doubt remember from the pm report, a sexual connection just before death." He hesitated a little before the phrase. It was the only time Dalgliesh had seen him even slightly discomposed. It was as if he felt the words "making love" were inappropriate and couldn't bring himself to use a coarser soubriquet.

Dalgliesh was silent. Anger had led him into a protest that now seemed to him humiliatingly childish as well as ineffectual. He had achieved nothing except possibly to exacerbate the simmering professional rivalry between C Division, the Special Branch and MI5, whose uneasy relationship could so easily spill over into high politics. Next time Gilmartin might say: "And for God's sake, put AD in the picture. He's apt to get his knickers in a twist if he doesn't get his share of the lollipops." But what depressed him most and left him with a sour taste of self-disgust was how close he had come to losing his control. He realized how important his reputation for coolness, detachment, uninvolvement, had become to him. Well, he was involved now. Perhaps they were right. You shouldn't take on a case if you knew the victim. But how could he claim to have known Berowne? What time had they spent together, except for a three-hour train journey, a brief ten-minute spell in his office, an interrupted walk in St. James's Park? And yet he knew that he had never felt so great an empathy with any other victim. That impulse to connect his fist with Gilmartin's jaw, to see blood spurting over that immaculate shirtfront, that old school tie; well, fifteen years ago he might have done it and it would have cost him his job. For a moment he almost yearned for the lost uncomplicated spontaneity of youth.

He said:

"I'm surprised that you thought Garrod worth the trouble. He was a left-wing activist at university. It hardly needs an undercover agent to discover that Garrod doesn't vote Tory. He's never made any secret of his beliefs."

"Not of his beliefs, but he has of his activities. His group are rather more than the usual middle-class malcontents looking for an ethically acceptable outlet for aggression and some kind of cause, preferably one that gives them the illusion of commitment. Oh yes, he's worth it."

Gilmartin signalled a glance at Duxbury, who said:

"It's only a small group—cell he calls it. At present four are women. Thirteen of them altogether. He never recruits more nor less. A nice touch of counter-superstition, and, of course, it adds to the mystique of conspiracy. The magic number, the closed circle."

Dalgliesh thought that the number also had a certain operational logic. Garrod could organize three groups of four or two of six for field work and still free himself as coordinator, director, recognized leader. Duxbury went on:

"They're all from the privileged middle class, which makes for cohesion and obviates class tensions. The comrades, after all, aren't noticeable for brotherly love. This lot speak the same language, including, of course, the usual Marxist jargon, and they're all intelligent. Silly, maybe, but intelligent. A potentially dangerous bunch. None is a member of the Labour Party, incidentally. Not that the party would have them. Six of them, including Garrod, are paid-up members of the Workers' Revolutionary Campaign, but they don't hold office. My guess is that the WRC is little more than a front. Garrod prefers to run his own show. A natural fascination with conspiracy, I suppose."

Dalgliesh said:

"He should have joined Special Branch. And Sarah Berowne is a member?"

"For the last two years. A member and Garrod's mistress, which gives her a peculiar prestige in the group. In some ways the comrades are remarkably old-fashioned."

"And what did you get from Travers? All right, let me guess. Garrod introduced her into the Campden Hill Square house. That wouldn't be difficult, given the shortage of reliable domestic help. Sarah Berowne would have tipped them off about the advertisement, if she didn't actually suggest it. Anyone willing to do housework and turning up with good references— and you'd have seen to that—would be pretty sure of a job. That was his cell's function presumably, to discredit selected MPs."

It was Gilmartin who answered:

"One of their functions. They mostly went for the moderate socialists. Dig up the muck, an illicit love affair, preferably homosexual, an ill-advised friendship, a half-forgotten sponsored trip to South Africa, a suggestion of sticky fingers in the party funds. Then when the poor devil goes up for re-selection, spread the manure around judiciously and draw delicate attention to the smell. Discrediting members of the present administration is probably more a matter of occasional duty than enjoyment. I imagine Garrod chose Paul Berowne for personal rather than political reasons. Sarah dislikes more than her papa's party."

So it had been Garrod who had sent the poison pen message to Ackroyd and the gossip writers of the nationals. Well, he had always been Dalgliesh's most likely suspect for that particular mischief. As if hearing his thoughts, Gilmartin said:

"I doubt whether you'll be able to prove he sent that message to the press. They do it very cleverly. A member of the group visits one of those shops where they sell new and second-hand typewriters and let you try out the machines. You know the scene, rows of chained typewriters for the customers to bang away on. The chance of a single prospective customer being recognized is almost nil. We can't keep perpetual watch on all the cell members. They don't warrant that intensity of effort, and I'm not sure, anyway, what particular section or subsection of the criminal law they'd be infringing. The information they use is accurate. It's no use to them if it isn't. How did you get on to Travers, by the way?"

"Through the woman she lodged with before she moved into her flat. Women have a profound contempt for masculine secret societies and a knack of seeing through them."

Gilmartin said:

"The whole sex is one secret society. We wanted Travers to live alone. We should have insisted. But I'm surprised that she talked."

"She didn't. Her landlady didn't altogether believe in an unemployed actress who could yet afford to buy a flat. But it was your men turning up to search her room that confirmed her suspicions. Incidentally, what was your real interest in Garrod, apart from getting some additional names in your activist files?"

Gilmartin pursed his lips.

"There could have been an IRA connection."

"And was there?"

For a moment Dalgliesh thought that he would refuse to answer. Then he glanced at Duxbury and said:

"Not as far as we've been able to discover. Do you think Garrod is your man?"

"He could be."

"Well, good hunting." He seemed suddenly ill at ease, as if uncertain how to bring the interview to an end. Then he said:

"It has been useful talking to you, Adam. We've taken notes of the points you've raised. And you'll watch the procedures, won't you? The IR49. A modest little form, but it has its uses."

As the lift bore him down to his own floor, it seemed to Dalgliesh that he had been closeted with Special Branch for days rather than less than an hour. He felt contaminated by a kind of sick hopelesssness. He knew that he would shake off its symptoms soon enough; he always did. But the infection would still be there in his bloodstream, part of that sickness of the spirit which he was beginning to think he must learn to endure.

But the interview, humiliatingly fractious as it had been, had served its purpose, clearing away a tangle of extraneous brushwood from the main path of his enquiry. He knew now the identity and motive of the poison pen writer. He knew what Diana Travers had been doing at Campden Hill Square, who had put her there and why after the drowning her room had been searched. Two young women were dead, one by her own hand, one by accident. There was no mystery about why and how they had died, and little now about how they had lived. Why then was he still obstinately convinced that these two deaths were not only linked but central to the mystery of Paul Berowne's murder?

2

☒

When he got back from that secretive and self-sufficient world on the eighteenth and nineteenth floors, Dalgliesh found that his own corridor was unusually silent. He put his head in his secretary's office, but Susie's typewriter was shrouded, her desk cleared, and he remembered that she had a dental appointment that morning. Kate was meeting Carole Washburn in Holland Park. Irked by his own bad temper, he had hardly given a thought to the possibilities of that encounter. Massingham was, he knew, visiting the Wayfarers' Refuge in Cosway Street to talk to the warden there about Harry Mack before going on to interview two of the girls who had been in the punt on the Thames when Diana Travers had drowned. According to their evidence at the inquest, neither of them had seen the girl dive into the river. They and the rest of the party had left her with Dominic Swayne on the bank when they pushed out the punt and had seen and heard nothing of her until that awful moment when the punt pole had struck her body. Both had admitted at the inquest that they had been half-drunk at the time. Dalgliesh doubted whether they would have anything more useful to say now that they were sober but, if they had, Massingham was the one best suited to get it out of them.

But Massingham had left a message. As he entered his room, Dalgliesh saw a single sheet of white paper pinned to his blotter with Massingham's paper knife, a long and remarkably sharp dagger which he claimed to have won at a fairground when a child. The dramatic gesture and the few lines of letters and figures in a stark black upright hand said it all. The forensic science laboratory had telephoned the result of the blood analyses. Without pulling out the dagger, Dalgliesh stood silently and looked down at the evidence which, more than any other, was vital to his theory that Berowne had been murdered.

	Berowne	*Mack*	*Smears on carpet and jacket pocket*
Rhesus	Pos	Pos	Pos
ABO	A	A	A
AK	2−1 (7.6%)	1 (92.3%)	2−1
(enzymes)			
PGM	1+ (40%)	2+, 1− (4.8%)	1+
(enzymes)			
Razor blade:			
AK	2−1		
PGM	2+, 1−, 1+		

The PGM system was, he knew, a strong one. There would have been no need to set up a control reaction with the dirty carpet. But the lab must have worked over the weekend despite their heavy load and the fact that, as yet, there was no suspect in custody, and he was grateful. There was blood of two different types on the razor, but that was hardly surprising, the analysis a mere formality. But, more important, the smear on the carpet under Harry's coat wasn't his blood. Dalgliesh had another interview booked for late in the afternoon which promised, in its different way, to be as irritating as the session with Gilmartin. It was helpful that this important piece of scientific evidence had arrived in time.

3

⊠

Holland Park was only a few minutes' walk from Charles Shannon House. Kate had woken early, shortly after six, and by seven had breakfasted and was impatient to get away. After prowling restlessly round an already immaculate flat trying to find jobs to occupy the time, she stuffed a paper bag of crumbs for the birds in her jacket pocket and left three-quarters of an hour early, telling herself that it would be less frustrating to walk in the park than to stay cooped up wondering whether Carole Washburn would actually turn up, whether she might already be regretting her promise.

Dalgliesh had accepted that the agreement with the girl must be kept; she would meet Carole Washburn alone. He had given her no instructions and offered no advice. Other senior officers would have been tempted to remind her of the importance of the meeting, but this wasn't his way. She respected him for it, but it increased her burden of responsibility. Everything might depend on how she handled their encounter.

Just before nine she made her way to the terrace above the formal gardens. When she had last visited the park the beds had been richly patterned with the summer display of geraniums, fuchsias, heliotropes and begonias. But now the time had come for the autumn stripping. Half the beds were already bare—expanses of soft loam littered with broken stems, petals like blobs of blood and a scatter of dying leaves. A council cart, like the dread tumbrel of winter, stood ready for the new strippings. And now, as the minute finger of her watch clicked to the hour the squeals and shouts from the grounds of Holland Park School were suddenly hushed and the park lay in its early-morning calm. An old woman, bent as a witch, with a team of six small discouraged dogs on a lead shuffled along the side path, then paused to pull and sniff at the last flowers of the lavender. A solitary jogger loped down the steps and disappeared through the arches leading to the orangery.

And suddenly Carole Washburn was there. Almost precisely on the hour a solitary female figure appeared at the far end of the garden. She was wearing a short grey jacket over a matching skirt, her head covered by a voluminous blue and white scarf which almost obscured her face. But Kate knew immediately and with a lift of the heart who it was. They stood for a moment regarding each other, then advanced between the denuded flower beds in measured, almost ceremonial, paces. Kate was reminded of spy thrillers, the exchange of defectors at some border crossing, a sense of unseen watchers, ears pricked for the crack of a rifle. When they met, the girl nodded but did not speak. Kate said simply:

"Thank you for coming."

Then she turned and together they passed up the steps out of the garden, across the spongy turf of the wide lawn and into the path through the rose garden. Here the freshness of the morning air was tinged with the remembered scent of summer. Roses, thought Kate, were never finished. There was something irritating about a flower which couldn't recognize that its season was over. Even in December there would be tight and browning buds destined to wither before they opened, a few anaemic heavy heads drooping towards the petal-strewn earth. Pacing slowly between the spiked bushes, aware of Carole's shoulder almost brushing hers, she thought: I must have patience. I must wait for her to speak first. She has to be the one to choose the time and place.

They came up to the statue of Lord Holland, seated on his pedestal, gazing benignly towards his house. Still without speaking, they walked on down the mushy path between the woodlands. Then her companion paused. She looked into the wilderness and said:

"That's where he found her, over there, under that slanting silver birch, the one by the holly bush. We came here together a week later. I think he needed to show me."

Kate waited. It was extraordinary that this wilderness of trees could be close to the centre of a great city. Once over the low palisade, it would be possible to believe oneself deep in the countryside. No wonder that Theresa Nolan, reared among the Surrey woodlands, should have chosen this quiet leafy place in which to die. It must have been like a return to early childhood: the smell of leaf loam, the rough bark of the tree against her back, the scurry of small birds and squirrels in the undergrowth, the softness of the earth making death as natural and friendly as falling asleep. For one extraordinary moment it seemed to her that she entered into that death, was mysteriously one with that lonely dying girl under the far tree. She shivered. The moment of empathy was quickly over, but its power astonished and a little disturbed her. She had seen enough suicides in her first five years of policing to have learnt detachment, and, for her, it had never been a difficult lesson. She had always been able to distance emotion, to think: This is a dead body. Not: This was a living woman. Perhaps, she thought, I can afford a little involvement, a little pity. But it was strange that it should begin now. What was it, she wondered, about the Berowne case which seemed to be changing even her perception of her job? She turned her eyes again to the path and heard Carole Washburn's voice:

"When Paul learned that she was missing, when the nursing home rang to ask if anyone at Campden Hill Square had seen her or knew where she was, he guessed that she might be here. Before he became a Minister and security became a nuisance, he often walked through the park to work. He could cross Kensington Church Street, get into Hyde Park and then into Green Park at Hyde Park Corner, walking nearly all the way to the House on grass and under trees. So it was natural to come and look— I mean, he didn't have to go much out of his way. He wasn't putting himself to any great trouble."

The sudden bitterness in her voice was shocking. Still Kate didn't speak. She dug in her jacket pocket for the small bag of crumbs and held them out on her palm. A sparrow, tame as only London sparrows are, hopped on her fingers with a delicate scrape of claws. His head jerked, and she felt the beak like a pinprick, and then he was gone.

She said:

"He must have known Theresa Nolan very well."

"Perhaps. She used to talk to him in the night hours when Lady Ursula was asleep; tell him about herself, her family. He was easy for women to talk to, some women."

Both of them were for a moment silent. But there was one question which she had to ask. She said:

"The child Theresa Nolan was carrying, could it have been his?"

To her relief the question was taken calmly, almost as if it were expected. The girl said:

"Once I would have said no and been absolutely certain. I'm not certain of anything any more. There were things he didn't tell me, I always knew that. I know it even better now. But I think he would have told me that. It wasn't his child. But he did blame himself for what happened to her. He felt responsible."

"Why?"

"She tried to see him the day before she killed herself. She went to his office, to the Department. It was tactless—the kind of thing only an innocent would do—and she couldn't have chosen a worse time. He was just due to go into an important meeting. He could have made five minutes to see her, but it wouldn't have been convenient and it wouldn't have been prudent. When the young civil servant in his Private Office brought in the news that a Miss Theresa Nolan was in the front hall asking to see him urgently, he said that she was probably one of his constituents and sent down a message asking her to leave her address and he'd get in touch. She went away without saying a word. He never heard from her again. I think he would have got in touch, given time. But he wasn't given time. The next day she was dead."

It was interesting, thought Kate, that this piece of news hadn't come out when Dalgliesh was interviewing Sir Paul's civil servants. Those careful men, by training and instinct, protected their Minister. Were they extending this protection beyond death? They had spoken of Paul Berowne's speed and skill in mastering a complicated submission, but there had been no mention of the inconvenient arrival of an importunate young woman. But perhaps it wasn't surprising. The officer who had taken the message had been comparatively junior. It was another example of the man who had the interesting information not even being questioned. But even if he had been, he might not have thought it important, unless he had read the inquest report and recognized the girl, and perhaps not even then.

Carole Washburn still stood gazing into the woodlands, hands deep in her jacket pockets, her shoulders hunched as if there blew from the tangled wilderness the first chill wind of winter. She said:

"She was slumped against the trunk—that trunk. You can barely see it now, and in high summer it's invisible. She could have been there for days."

Not for long, thought Kate. The smell would soon have alerted the park keepers. Holland Park might be a small paradise in the middle of the city, but it was no different from any other Eden. There were still predators on four legs prowling in the undergrowth and predators on two walking the paths. Death was still death. Bodies still stank when they rotted. She glanced at her companion. Carole Washburn was still staring into the woodland with a painful intensity as if conjuring up that slumped figure at the foot of the silver birch. Then she said:

"Paul told the truth about what happened, but not the whole truth. There were two letters in her jacket pocket, one addressed to her grand-parents asking forgiveness, the one read out at the inquest. But there was another, marked confidential and addressed to Paul. That's what I've come to tell you."

"Did you see it? Did he show it to you?" Kate tried to keep the eagerness out of her voice. Could this, she thought, be physical evidence at last?

"No. He brought it to the flat, but he didn't give it to me to read. He told me what was in it. Apparently while Theresa was nursing at Pem-broke Lodge, she was transferred to night duty. One of the patients had been brought some bottles of champagne by her husband and they'd had a party. It's that kind of place. Anyway, she was a little tipsy. She was gloating over the baby, a son after three girls, and said 'thanks to darling Stephen.' Then she let out that if patients wanted a child of a particular sex, Lampart would do an early amniocentesis and abort an unwanted foetus. Women who hated childbirth and weren't prepared to go through with it just to get a child of the wrong sex knew where to go."

Kate said:

"But he was—he is—taking a terrible risk."

"Not really. Not if there's never anything on paper, never anything specifically said. Paul wondered if some of the pathological reports were falsified to show an abnormality in the foetus. Most of his lab work is done on the premises. Afterwards Theresa tried to get some evidence, but it wasn't easy. When she questioned the patient the next day, she laughed and said that she was joking. But she was obviously terrified. That afternoon she discharged herself."

So this was the explanation of those mysterious jottings which AD had found in Theresa's missal. She had been trying to collect evidence about the sex of the patients' previous children. Kate asked:

"Did Theresa speak to anyone at Pembroke Lodge?"

"She daren't. She knew that someone had libelled Lampart once, and been made bankrupt as a result. He was—he is—notoriously litigious. What could she hope to do, a young nurse, poor, without powerful friends, against a man like that? Who would believe her? And then she found that she was pregnant and had her own problems to think about. How could she speak against what she saw as his sin when she was about to commit mortal sin herself? But when she was preparing to die she felt that she had to do something to put a stop to it. She thought about Paul. He wasn't weak, he had nothing to fear. He was a Minister, a powerful man. He would see that it was stopped."

"And did he?"

"How could he? She hadn't any idea what kind of burden she was putting on him. As I said, she was an innocent. They're always the ones who do the most harm. Lampart is his wife's lover. If he tackled him, it would look like blackmail or, worse, revenge. And his own guilt over her death, the lie about her being a constituent, his failure to help her, that must have seemed morally worse than anything Lampart was doing."

"What did he decide?"

"He tore up the letter while he was with me and flushed it down the lavatory."

"But he was a lawyer. Wasn't his instinct to preserve evidence?"

"Not that evidence. He said: 'If I haven't the courage to use it, then I must get rid of it. There's no compromise. Either I do what Theresa wanted or I destroy the evidence.' I suppose he thought that hoarding it might be degrading, might smack of potential blackmail, carefully preserving evidence against your enemy in case you needed it in future."

"Did he ask your advice?"

"No. Not advice. He needed to think it through, and I was there to listen. That's what he usually needed me for, to listen. I realize that now. And he knew what I would say, what I wanted. I would say: 'Divorce Barbara and use that letter to make sure that she and her lover make no trouble over it. Use it to get your freedom.' I don't know whether I would have said it so brutally, but he knew that's what I wanted him to do. Before he destroyed it he made me promise to say nothing."

"He took absolutely no action, you're sure of that?"

"I think he may have spoken to Lampart. He told me that he would, but we never discussed it again. He was going to tell Lampart what he knew and admit that he had no evidence. And he took his money out of Pembroke Lodge. There was quite a bit, I think, originally invested by his brother."

They began walking slowly down the path. Kate thought: Suppose Paul Berowne had spoken to Lampart. With the evidence destroyed, and pathetically inadequate evidence at that, the doctor would have little to fear. A scandal could hurt Paul Berowne as much as it harmed Lampart.

But after Sir Paul's experience in that vestry, things might be very different. Perhaps the changed Berowne, his own career thrown away, would see it as his moral duty to expose and ruin Lampart, evidence or no evidence. And what of Barbara Berowne, faced on the one hand with a husband who had chucked away both job and prospects, and was even proposing to sell their home, and on the other with a lover who might be facing ruin. Kate decided on a blunt question which in other circumstances she might have felt unwise:

"Do you think Stephen Lampart killed him, with or without her connivance?"

"No. He'd be a fool to involve her in anything like that. And she hasn't the courage or the wit to plan it alone. She's the kind of woman who gets a man to do her dirty work for her and then persuades herself that she knows nothing about it. But I've given you a motive, a motive for both of them. It ought to be enough to make life uncomfortable for her."

"Is that what you want?"

The girl turned round on her and said with sudden passion:

"No, that's not what I want. I want her to be harried and grilled and frightened. I want her disgraced. I want her arrested, imprisoned for life. I want her dead. It won't happen, none of it will happen. And the awful thing is that I've hurt myself more than I can ever hurt her. Once I'd made that call to you, once I'd said I'd be here, then I knew I had to come. But he told me in confidence, he trusted me, he always trusted me. Now there's nothing left, nothing I can remember about our loving that will ever be free of pain and guilt."

Kate looked at her and saw that she was crying. She was making no sound, not even a sob, but from eyes fixed and staring as if in terror the tears ran in a steady stream over the drained face and the half-open quivering mouth. There was something frightening about this steady, silent grief. Kate thought: There isn't a man, any man in the world, who is worth this agony. She felt a mixture of sympathy, helplessness and irritation which she recognized was tinged with slight contempt. But the pity won. There was nothing she could find to say which might comfort, but at least she could make some small practical response, ask Carole back to the flat for coffee before they parted. She was opening her mouth to speak, then checked herself. The girl wasn't a suspect. Even if it were reasonable to think of her in those terms, she had an alibi, a late meeting out of London for the time of death. But suppose Carole were required to give evidence in court, then any suggestion of friendship, of an understanding between them, could be prejudicial to the prosecution. And more than to the prosecution; it could be prejudicial to her own career. It was the kind of sentimental error of judgement which wouldn't exactly displease Massingham if he came to hear of it. And then she heard herself saying:

"My flat is very close, just across the avenue. Come and have coffee before you go."

In the flat Carole Washburn moved over to the window like an automaton and gazed out without speaking. Then she moved over to the sofa and stood regarding the oil painting on the wall above, three triangles, partly superimposed, in a browny-red, clear green and white. She asked, but not as if she greatly cared:

"Do you like modern art?"

"I like experimenting with shapes and different colours laid against each other. I don't like reproductions and I can't afford originals, so I paint my own. I don't suppose they're art, but I enjoy them."

"Where did you learn to paint?"

"I just bought the canvas and oils and taught myself. The small bedroom is a kind of studio. I haven't had time to do much lately."

"It's clever. I like the texture of the background."

"Done by pressing a tissue over the paint just before it dried. Texture's the easy part, it's applying the oil smoothly that I find tricky."

She went into the kitchen to grind the coffee beans. Carole followed and stood listlessly watching from the doorway. She waited until the grinder had been switched off, then suddenly asked:

"What made you choose the police?"

Kate was tempted to reply: For much the same reasons that you chose the Civil Service. I thought I could do the job. I was ambitious. I prefer order and hierarchy to muddle. Then she wondered whether Carole needed to ask, not answer, questions, to reach out, however tentatively, to another's life. She said:

"I didn't want an office job. I wanted a career where I could earn well from the start, hope for promotion. I suppose I like pitting myself against men. And they were rather against the idea at the school I went to. That was an added inducement."

Carole Washburn made no response but watched her for a moment, then drifted back into the sitting room. Kate, hands busy with percolator, mug and saucers, tray and biscuits, found herself recalling that last interview with Miss Shepherd, the careers adviser:

"We had rather hoped that you would set your sights higher, university, for example. You're safe, I'd say, for two As and a B at A-level."

"I want to start earning."

"That's understandable, Kate, but you'll get a full grant, remember. You can manage."

"I don't want to have to manage. I want a job, a place of my own. University would be three wasted years."

"Education is never wasted, Kate."

"I'm not giving up education. I can go on educating myself."

"But a policewoman . . . We had rather hoped that you would choose something more, well, socially significant."

"You mean more useful."

"More concerned, perhaps, with basic human problems."

"I can't think of anything more basic than helping to make sure that people can walk safely in their own city."

"I'm afraid, Kate, that recent research shows that walking in safety has little to do with the level of policing. Why not read that pamphlet in the library, 'Policing the Inner City: A Socialist Solution'? But if this is your choice, naturally we shall do what we can to help. How do you see yourself? In the Juvenile Bureau?"

"No. I see myself as a senior detective." She had been tempted to add mischievously: "And as the first woman Chief Constable." But that, she had known, was as unrealistic as a recruit to the WRAC seeing herself as commanding the Household Cavalry. Ambition, if it were to be savoured, let alone achieved, had to be rooted in possibility. Even her childhood fantasies had been anchored to reality. The lost father would reappear, loving, prosperous, repentant, but she had never expected him to descend from a Rolls-Royce. And in the end he hadn't come, and she had known that she had never really expected him.

There were no sounds from the sitting room, and when she carried in the tray of coffee she saw that Carole was sitting on a chair, stiffly upright, gazing down at her clasped hands. Kate set down the tray, and at once Carole slopped milk into her mug, then clasped both hands round it and gulped avidly, hunched in her chair like an old starved woman.

It was strange, thought Kate, that the girl seemed more distraught, less under control, than at their first meeting, when they had briefly chatted in her own kitchen. What, she wondered, had happened since then to prompt her betrayal of Berowne's confidence, to produce this bitterness and resentment? Had she somehow learned that there was no mention of her in his will? But that, surely, was what she must have expected. But perhaps it mattered more than she had ever thought possible, the public and final confirmation that she had always been on the periphery of his life, officially non-existent after death as she had been in their years together. She thought that she had been indispensable to him, that he had found with her, in that ordinary, seldom-visited flat, a still centre of fulfillment and peace. Maybe he had, at least for a few snatched hours. But she hadn't been indispensable to him; no one had. He had compartmentalized people as he had the rest of his over-organized life, filing them away in the recesses of his mind until he needed what they had to offer. But then, she asked herself, is that so very different from what I do with Alan?

She knew that she wouldn't be able to bring herself to ask what had brought the girl to this meeting, and it wasn't really important to the enquiry. What was important was that Berowne's confidence had been broken and Lampart's motive immensely strengthened. But how far did that really get them? One piece of hard physical evidence was worth a dozen motives. They were back to the old question, could Lampart and Barbara Berowne really have had the time? Someone, Berowne or his killer, had been using the washroom at St. Matthew's at eight o'clock. Three people had seen the gush of water, none of them could be shaken. So either Berowne was alive at eight or the murderer was still on the premises. Either way it was difficult to see how Lampart could have arrived at the Black Swan by eight thirty.

When she had finished her coffee Carole managed a weak smile and said:

"Thank you. I'd better go now. I suppose you want all this on paper."

"We'd like a statement. You could call in at the Harrow Road station, there's an incident room there, or come to the Yard."

"I'll call in at Harrow Road. There won't be any more questions, will there?"

"There could be, but I don't think we'll want you for long."

At the door they stood for a moment facing each other. Suddenly Kate thought that Carole was going to step forward and fall into her arms, and knew that her unpractised arms might even know how to hold and comfort, that she might even be able to find the right words. But the moment passed and she told herself that the thought had been embarrassing and ridiculous. As soon as she was alone she rang Dalgliesh, careful to keep any note of triumph out of her voice:

"She came, sir. There's no new physical evidence, but she has strengthened one of the suspects' motives. I think you'll want to go to Hampstead."

He said:

"Where are you ringing from? Your flat?"

"Yes sir."

"I'll be there in about half an hour."

But it was less than that when the bell of the entry phone rang. He said:

"I'm parked further up Lansdowne Road. Could you come down now?"

He didn't suggest that he should come up, and she hadn't expected it. No senior officer was more scrupulous in respecting the privacy of his subordinates. She told herself that in him it hardly counted for virtue. He was too scrupulously careful to protect his own. Going down in the lift she realized that the more she learned of Berowne, the more alike he seemed to Dalgliesh. She felt a spurt of irritation against both of them. Here waiting for her was a man who might also cause that extremity of grief for a woman unwise enough to love him. She told herself that she was glad that she had that temptation at least well under control.

Stephen Lampart said:

"It isn't true. Theresa Nolan was psychologically disturbed; or, if you prefer bluntness, mad enough to kill herself. Nothing she wrote before that act counts as reliable evidence, even if you have this alleged letter, which I assume you haven't. I mean, if it were actually in your possession you'd be flourishing it in my face, surely. What you're relying on is third-hand information. We both know what that's worth in a court of law, or anywhere else for that matter."

Dalgliesh said:

"Are you telling me that the girl's story is untrue?"

"Let's be charitable and say mistaken. She was lonely, guilt-ridden, particularly about sex, depressed, losing touch with reality. There's a psy-chiatrist's report on her medical file which, stripped of its jargon, says precisely that. Or you can argue that she was deliberately lying, she or Berowne. Neither was a particularly reliable witness. Both, as it happens, are dead. If this is meant to give me a motive, it's absurd. It's also close to slander and I know how to deal with that."

Dalgliesh said:

"As you knew how to deal with libel. A police officer, carrying out a murder investigation, isn't so easily ruined."

"Not financially, perhaps. The courts are so ridiculously indulgent to the police."

The nurse who had received them at Pembroke Lodge had said "Mr.

Lampart has just finished operating, if you would come this way," and they had been shown into a room adjacent to the theatre. Lampart had joined them almost at once, pulling off his green operating cap, peeling off his gloves. The room was small, clinical, seeming full of rushing water and the sound of feet passing in the room next door, of confident voices above the unconscious body of the patient. It was a temporary place, a room for quick clinical exchanges, not for confidences. Dalgliesh wondered if the ploy had been deliberate, a way of demonstrating the subtle power of his professional status, of reminding the police that there was more than one kind of authority. Dalgliesh didn't think that Lampart had dreaded the interview, even if he had thought it prudent to face it on his own territory. He hadn't shown the least sign of apprehension. After all, he had enjoyed power, one kind of power, long enough to have acquired the self-assertive hubris of success. A man who had developed the confidence of a successful obstetrician certainly had the confidence to confront an investigating officer of the Metropolitan Police.

Now he said:

"I didn't kill Berowne. Even if I were capable of a particularly brutal and bloody murder, I certainly wouldn't take Berowne's wife with me and expect her to wait in the car while I slit her husband's throat. As for this other nonsense, even if it were true that I aborted healthy foetuses because they weren't the sex the mother wanted, how do you propose to prove it? The operations were done here. The pathological reports are on the medical records. There's nothing incriminating on any file in this building. And even if there were, you wouldn't have access to it, not without a great deal of trouble. I have strong feelings about the sanctity of medical records. So what can you do? Start interviewing a succession of patients in the hope of tricking or bullying one of them into an indiscretion? And how would you track them down without my cooperation? Your allegation is ridiculous, Commander."

Dalgliesh said:

"But Paul Berowne believed it. He got rid of his shares in Pembroke Lodge after Theresa Nolan's death. I think he spoke to you. I don't know what he said to you, but I can guess. You could trust him to keep silent at that time, but after his experience in that church, his conversion, whatever it was, could you trust his silence then?"

He wondered whether he had been wise to show his hand so soon and so clearly. But the doubt was momentary. Lampart had to be confronted by the new evidence, tenuous as it might be. He had to be given the right to reply. And if it was irrelevant, the sooner it was cleared out of the way, the better.

Lampart said:

"It wasn't like that. We never spoke. And, assuming that he did believe it, he would have been in a somewhat invidious position, rather more invidious than you realize. He wanted a son, but he certainly didn't want another daughter. Nor, incidentally, did Barbara. Barbara might be willing to bear him an heir, if only to consolidate her position. She saw that as part of the bargain. But nine months' discomfort to produce another daughter for him to resent, despise and ignore was asking rather too much of a woman, particularly one who dislikes and fears the thought of childbirth. Assuming the story is true, you could say that Berowne found himself in a curious position, morally anyway. He couldn't stomach the means, but I suspect he wasn't entirely displeased with the ends. That has never been a particularly dignified moral stance, not in my book. Barbara had one miscarriage—a female—eight months after their marriage. Do you suppose he grieved over that? No wonder the poor devil was in a mess psychologically. No wonder he took a razor to his throat. What you've discovered, Commander, if true, is an added reason for suicide, not a motive for murder."

Lampart took down his jacket from a peg, then opened the door for Dalgliesh and Kate with a smiling courtesy that was almost insulting. Then he led the way to his private drawing room, shut the door and motioned them towards the easy chairs before the fire. Sitting opposite, he leaned forward, legs apart, and almost thrust his face at Dalgliesh. Dalgliesh could see the handsome features magnified, the pores of the skin glistening with sweat as if he were still in the heat of the theatre, the taut muscles straining at the neck, the smudge of tiredness under the eyes and the threads of scarlet around the irises, the flecks of dandruff at the roots of the undisciplined forelock. It was still a comparatively young face but the signs of ageing were there, and he could suddenly see how Lampart would look in another thirty years: the skin speckled and bleached, the bones less firmly fleshed, the machismo confidence soured into the cynicism of old age. But now his voice was strong and harsh and the aggression came over to Dalgliesh, powerful as a force.

"I'll be frank with you, Commander, more frank than I would probably think prudent if what you're saying were true. If I had aborted those unwanted foetuses, it wouldn't be giving me a single pang of what you would probably call conscience. Two hundred years ago, anaesthesia in childbirth was regarded as immoral. Less than a hundred years ago birth control was virtually illegal. A woman has a right to choose whether she bears a child. I happen to think she also has a right to choose which sex. An unwanted child is usually a nuisance to itself, to society, to its parents. And a two-month foetus isn't a human being, it's a complicated collection of tissue. You probably don't personally believe that the child has a soul before birth, at birth or after birth. Poet or no poet, you're not the kind of man who sees visions and hears voices in church vestries. I'm not a religious man. I was born with my share of neuroses, but not that one. But what surprises me about those who claim to have faith is that they seem to think that we can find out scientific facts behind God's back. That first myth, the Garden of Eden, is remarkably persistent. We always feel we haven't a right to knowledge or that, when we get it, we haven't the right to use it. In my book we've the right to do anything we can to make human life more agreeable, safer, less full of pain."

His voice grated and there was a gleam in the grey eyes uncomfortably close to fanaticism. He could, thought Dalgliesh, have been a seventeenth-century religious mercenary reciting his credo with drawn sword.

Dalgliesh said mildly:

"Provided, presumably, we don't hurt other people and the act isn't illegal."

"Provided we don't hurt other people. Yes, I'd accept that. Getting rid of an unwanted foetus hurts no one. Either abortion is never justified or it's justified on grounds which the mother happens to think important. The wrong sex is as good a reason as any. I've more repect for those Christians who oppose abortion on any grounds than for those ingenious compromisers who want life on their own terms and a good conscience at the same time. At least the former are consistent."

Dalgliesh said:

"The law is consistent. Indiscriminate abortion is unlawful."

"Oh, but this would have been highly discriminatory. All right, I know what you mean. But the law has no place when it comes to private morality, sexual or otherwise."

Dalgliesh said:

"Where else is it supposed to operate?"

He got up and Lampart saw them out, deferential, smiling, confident. Except for perfunctory courtesies, neither spoke another word.

In the car Kate said:

"It was practically a confession, sir. He didn't even bother to deny it."

"No. But it isn't one he'd ever make on paper or which we could use in court. And it was a confession to medical malpractice, not murder. And he's right, of course. It would be the devil to prove."

"But it gives him a double motive. His affair with Lady Berowne and the fact that Berowne might have felt he had a duty to expose him. Under all that bluff and arrogance, he must know that he's as vulnerable to scandal as any other doctor. Even a rumour wouldn't have done him any good. And coming from someone of Berowne's standing, it would have been taken seriously."

Dalgliesh said:

"Oh, yes, Lampart has got it all—means, motive, opportunity, knowledge, and the arrogance to think he can get away with it. But I accept one thing he told us. He wouldn't have taken Barbara Berowne with him into that vestry, and I can't see her agreeing to be left alone in a car parked in a not particularly salubrious area of Paddington, whatever the excuse. And, always, we get back to the timing. The night porter saw them leaving Pembroke Lodge together. Higgins saw them arriving at the Black Swan. Unless one or both are lying, Lampart has to be in the clear."

And then he thought: Unless we've been misled by that gush of water from the waste pipe. Unless we've got the time of death totally wrong. If Berowne had died at the earliest time Dr. Kynaston had thought possible, say seven o'clock, what happened to Lampart's alibi then? He had claimed to be at Pembroke Lodge with his mistress, but there had to be more ways than one of leaving the Lodge and returning unseen. But someone had been in the church kitchen at eight o'clock; unless, of course, the water had been left deliberately running. But by whom? Someone who had come earlier, at seven o'clock, someone who had arrived in a black Rover? If Berowne had died at seven o'clock, there were suspects other than Stephen Lampart. But what possible purpose would be served by leaving the tap running? There was, of course, always the possibility that it had been left on by accident. But if that were the case, then how and when had it been turned off?

5
⊠

Lady Ursula's friends had expressed their condolences with flowers, and her sitting room was incongruously festive with long-stemmed thornless roses, carnations and imported boughs of white lilac which looked like plastic artefacts sprayed with scent. The flowers had been less arranged than stuck into a variety of vases placed around the room for convenience rather than effect. By her side on the rosewood table was a small cut-glass bowl of freesias. Their scent, sweet and unmistakable, came up to Dalgliesh as he neared her chair. She made no attempt to rise, but held out her hand, and he took it. It felt cold and dry and there was no responsive pressure. She was sitting, as always, bolt upright, wearing an ankle-length black wrapover skirt with above it a high-necked blouse in fine gray wool. Her only jewellery was a double chain in old gold and her rings; the long fingers resting on the arms of her chair were laden with great flashing stones, so that the blue-corded hands with their parchment skin seemed almost too frail to hold the weight of gold.

She motioned Dalgliesh to the opposite chair. When he had seated himself and Massingham had found a place on a small sofa set against the wall, she said:

"Father Barnes called here this morning. Perhaps he thought he had a duty to bring me spiritual comfort. Or was he apologizing for the use made of his vestry? He could hardly suppose I thought it was his fault. If he intended to offer spiritual consolation, I'm afraid he found me a disappointing mourner. He's a curious man. I found him rather unintelligent, commonplace. Was that your opinion?"

Dalgliesh said:

"I wouldn't describe him as commonplace, but it's difficult to see him influencing your son."

"He seemed to me a man who had long ago given up the expectation of influencing anyone. Perhaps he has lost his faith. Isn't that fashionable in the Church today? But why should that distress him? The world is full of people who have lost faith: politicians who have lost faith in politics, social workers who have lost faith in social work, schoolteachers who have lost faith in teaching and, for all I know, policemen who have lost faith in policing and poets who have lost faith in poetry. It's a condition of faith that it gets lost from time to time, or at least mislaid. And why doesn't he get his cassock cleaned? It is a cassock, isn't it? There were what I assumed were egg stains on the right cuff, and the front looked as if he's dribbled on it."

Dalgliesh said:

"It's a garment he practically lives in, Lady Ursula."

"He could buy a spare, surely."

"If he could afford one. And he had made an attempt to sponge off the stain."

"Had he? Not very effectively. Well, that's the sort of thing you're trained to notice, of course."

It did not surprise him that they were discussing ecclesiastical garb while what remained of her son lay headless and dismembered in a mortuary icebox. Unlike herself and Father Barnes, they had been able to communicate from their first meeting. She shifted a little in her chair, then she said:

"But you are not, of course, here to discuss Father Barnes's spiritual problems. What are you here to say, Commander?"

"I'm here to ask you again, Lady Ursula, whether or not you saw your son's diary in the desk drawer when General Nollinge rang this house at six o'clock last Tuesday."

The remarkable eyes looked straight into his.

"You asked that question twice before. I am, of course, always happy to talk to the poet who wrote 'Rhesus Negative,' but your visits are becoming rather frequent and your conversation predictable. I've nothing to add to what I told you before. I find this reiteration rather offensive."

"You do understand the implication of what you're saying?"

"Naturally I understand it. Is there anything else you need to ask?"

"I should like you to confirm that you did, in fact, speak to Halliwell twice on the evening your son died and that, to your knowledge, the Rover was not taken out that night before ten o'clock."

"I've already told you, Commander. I spoke to him at about eight o'clock and then at nine fifteen. That must have been about forty-five minutes before he left for Suffolk. And I think you can safely assume that, if anyone had taken the Rover, Halliwell would have known. Anything else?"

"Yes, I should like to see Miss Matlock again."

"In that case, I would prefer that you see her here and that I remain. Perhaps you will ring the bell."

He tugged at the bell cord. Miss Matlock didn't hurry. But three minutes later she stood in the doorway, wearing again the long grey skirt with its gaping pleat, the same ill-fitting blouse.

Lady Ursula said:

"Sit down, will you, Mattie. The Commander has some questions for you."

The woman took one of the chairs against the wall and brought it over, placing it beside Lady Ursula's chair. She looked stolidly at Dalgliesh. This time she seemed almost without anxiety. He thought: She's beginning to get confidence. She knows how little we're able to do if she sticks to her story. She's beginning to think that it could be easy after all. He went through her account again. She answered his questions about the Tuesday evening in almost the same words she had previously used. At the end he said:

"It wasn't, of course, unusual for Mr. Dominic Swayne to call here for a bath, perhaps a meal?"

"I've told you. He did it from time to time. He's Lady Berowne's brother."

"But Sir Paul wasn't necessarily aware of these visits?"

"Sometimes he was, sometimes not. It wasn't my place to tell him."

"What about the time before last, not the Tuesday, but the time before? What did you do then?"

"He had a bath as usual, then I cooked him supper. He doesn't always have supper here when he comes for his bath, but that night he did. I cooked him a pork chop with mustard sauce, sauté potatoes and green beans."

A more substantial meal, thought Dalgliesh, than the omelette she had cooked on the night of Berowne's death. But on that night he had arrived at shorter notice. Why? Because his sister had telephoned him

after her quarrel with her husband? Because she had told him where
Berowne would be that night? Because his plan of murder was beginning
to take shape?

He asked:

"And after that?"

"He had apple tart and cheese."

"I mean, what did you do after the meal?"

"After that we played Scrabble."

"You and he seem extraordinarily fond of Scrabble."

"I like it. I think he plays to please me. There's no one here to give
me a game."

"And who won that time, Miss Matlock?"

"I think I did. I can't remember by how much, but I think I won."

"You think you won? It was only ten days ago, can't you be sure?"

Two pairs of eyes looked into his, hers and Lady Ursula's. They were
not, he thought, natural allies, but now they sat side by side rigidly upright, motionless as if held in a field of force which both sustained and
linked them. Lady Ursula was, he sensed, almost at the end of her endur-
ance, but he thought he saw in Evelyn Matlock's defiant gaze a glint of
triumph. She said:

"I can remember perfectly. I won."

It was, he knew, the most effective way of fabricating an alibi. You
described events which had, in fact, happened, but on a different occasion.
It was the most difficult of all alibis to break since, apart from the alteration
in time, the parties concerned were speaking the truth. He thought she
was lying, but he couldn't be sure. She was, he knew, a neurotic, and
the fact that she was now beginning to enjoy pitting her wits against his
might be no more than the self-dramatization of a woman whose life had
afforded few such heady excitements. He heard Lady Ursula's voice:

"Miss Matlock has answered all your enquiries, Commander. Should
you propose to continue badgering her, then I think we shall have to arrange
for my solicitor to be present."

He said coldly:

"That, of course, is her right, Lady Ursula. And we're not here to
badger either you or her."

"In that case, Mattie, perhaps you will show the Commander and Chief
Inspector Massingham out."

They were driving down Victoria Street when the telephone rang.
Massingham answered it, listened, then handed the receiver to Dalgliesh.

"It's Kate, sir. I detect a note of girlish enthusiasm. Can't wait until we get back, apparently. But I think she'd like to tell you herself."

Kate's voice, like her enthusiasm, was under control, but Dalgliesh, too, couldn't miss the note of heady optimism. She said:

"Something interesting has turned up, sir. Hearne and Collingwood rang ten minutes ago with Millicent Gentle's address. She's moved since they last published her and hadn't told them where, so it took a little time to trace her. She's at Riverside Cottage, Coldham Lane, near Cookham. I've looked at the ordnance survey. Coldham Lane runs almost opposite the Black Swan. Sir, she must have handed Sir Paul her book on August seventh."

"It seems likely. Have you a telephone number?"

"Yes, sir. The firm wouldn't give me either the address or the number until they'd rung her and checked that she agreed."

"Ring her then, Kate. Ask if she'll see us as early as possible tomorrow morning."

He replaced the receiver. Massingham said:

"The clue of the romantic novelist. I can't wait to meet the author of *A Rose by Twilight*. Do you want me to go to Cookham, sir?"

"No, John. I'll go."

At the Yard entrance he got out of the Rover, leaving Massingham to garage it, then hesitated and strode off vigorously to St. James's Park. The office was too claustrophobic to contain this sudden surge of irrational optimism. He needed to walk free and alone. It had been a hellish day, beginning in Gilmartin's office with peevish ill-temper, ending in Campden Hill Square with unprovable lies. But now the vexations and frustrations fell from his shoulders.

He thought: Tomorrow I shall know exactly what happened at the Black Swan on the night of seventh August. And when I know that, I shall know why Paul Berowne had to die. I may not yet be able to prove it. But I shall know.

6

⊠

Brian Nichols, recently promoted Assistant Commissioner, resented Dalgliesh and found this dislike the more irritating because he wasn't sure that it was justified. After twenty-five years of policing, he regarded even his antipathies with a judicial eye; he liked to be confident that the case against the accused would stand up in court. With Dalgliesh he wasn't sure. Nichols was the senior in rank, but this gave him small satisfaction when he knew that Dalgliesh could have outstripped him had he chosen. This lack of concern about promotion, which Dalgliesh never condescended to justify, he saw as a subtle criticism of his own more ambitious preoccupations. He deplored the poetry, not on principle, but because it had conferred prestige and, therefore, couldn't be regarded as a harmless hobby like fishing, gardening or woodwork. A policeman, in his view, should be satisfied with policing. An added grievance was that Dalgliesh chose most of his friends from outside the force, and those fellow officers he consorted with weren't always of an appropriate rank. In a junior officer that would have been regarded as a dangerous idiosyncrasy, and in a senior it had the taint of disloyalty. And to compound these delinquencies, he dressed too well. He was standing now with easy assurance, looking out of the window, wearing a suit in a subtle brown tweed which Nichols had seen him wearing for the last four years. It bore the unmistakable stamp of an excellent tailor, probably, thought Nichols, the firm his grandfather had patronized. Nichols, who enjoyed buying clothes, sometimes with more enthusiasm than discrimination, felt that it was becoming in a man to own rather more suits and those not so well tailored. Finally, whenever he was with Dalgliesh, he felt inexplicably that he ought perhaps to shave off his moustache and would find his hand moving involuntarily to his upper lip, as if to reassure himself that the moustache was still a respectable appendage. This impulse, irrational, almost neurotic, irritated him profoundly.

Both men knew that Dalgliesh needn't be here in Nichols's tenth-floor office, that the casual suggestion that the AC should be put in the picture was no more than an invitation, not a command. With the new squad officially set up Dalgliesh would, in future, report direct to the Commissioner. But for now Nichols could claim a legitimate interest. It was his Department, after all, which had provided most of the men for Dalgliesh's supporting team. And with the Commissioner temporarily away at a conference, he could argue that he had a right at least to a brief progress report. But, irrationally, part of him wished that Dalgliesh had objected, had given him the excuse for one of those departmental wrangles which he provoked when the job offered less excitement than his restless spirit craved, and which he was adept at winning.

While Nichols looked through the file on the case, Dalgliesh gazed out eastward over the city. He had seen many capitals from a similar height, all different. When he looked down on Manhattan from his hotel bedroom, its spectacular soaring beauty always seemed to him precarious, even doomed. Images would rise from films seen in his boyhood, prehistoric monsters towering above the skyscrapers to claw them down, a vast tidal wave from the Atlantic obliterating the skyline, the light-spangled city darkening into the final holocaust. But London, laid out beneath him under a low ceiling of silver-grey cloud, looked eternal, rooted, domestic. He saw the panorama, of which he never tired, in terms of painting. Sometimes it had the softness and immediacy of watercolour; sometimes, in high summer, when the park burgeoned with greenness, it had the rich texture of oil. This morning it was a steel engraving, hard-edged, grey, one-dimensional.

He turned away from the window with reluctance. Nichols had closed the file but was swivelling his chair and moving his body restlessly as if to emphasize the comparative informality of the proceedings. Dalgliesh moved over and took a seat opposite him. He gave a concise summary of his investigation as far as it had gone, and Nichols listened with a show of disciplined patience, still swivelling, his eyes on the ceiling. Then he said:

"All right, Adam, you've convinced me that Berowne was murdered.

But then I'm not the one who has to be convinced. But what have you got by way of direct evidence? One small smudge of blood under a fold of Harry Mack's coat."

"And a matching stain on the coat pocket. Berowne's blood. He died first. There's no room for doubt. It's identifiable by every known test. We can prove that it's identical with his blood."

"But not how it got there. You know what defending counsel will argue if it ever gets to court. One of your chaps carried it there on his shoes. Or the boy did, the one who found the body. Or that spinster— what's her name—Edith Wharton."

"Emily Wharton. We examined their shoes and I'm confident neither went into the Little Vestry. And, even if they had, it's difficult to see how they could have left a smudge of Berowne's blood under Harry's coat."

"It's a very convenient smudge from your point of view. From the family's too, I suppose. But without it there's nothing to suggest that this isn't exactly what it first appeared—murder followed by suicide. A politi- cian, prominent, successful, has some kind of religious conversion, quasi- mystical experience, call it what you will. He throws over his job, his career, possibly his family. Then, don't ask me how or why, he discovers that it's all a chimera." Nichols repeated the word as if to reassure himself of the pronunciation. Dalgliesh wondered where he had come across it. Then he went on:

"Why did Berowne go back to that church, incidentally? Do you know?"

"Possibly because of a new complication to do with his marriage. I think his wife told him that morning that she was pregnant."

"There you are then. He was already having doubts. He goes back, faces the reality of what he's given up. There's nothing ahead but failure, humiliation, ridicule. He decides to end it then and there. He has the means to hand. While he's making his preparations, burning his diary, Harry comes in and tries to stop him. Result? Two bodies in- stead of one."

"That assumes he didn't know Harry Mack was there. I think he did, he let him in. That's hardly the action of a man contemplating suicide."

"You've no proof that he let him in. None that would satisfy a jury."

"Berowne gave Harry part of his supper, wholemeal bread, Roquefort cheese, an apple. It's on the file. You aren't suggesting that Harry Mack bought his own Roquefort? He couldn't have surprised Berowne. He'd been in the church for some time before Berowne died. He was bedded down in the larger vestry. There's physical evidence, hair, fibres from his coat, apart from the crumbs of food. And he wasn't in the vestry or in the church when Father Barnes locked up after Evensong."

Nichols said:

"He thinks he locked up. Would he swear in the witness box that he turned the key in the south door, that he'd searched every pew? And why should he search? He wasn't expecting a murder. There are plenty of places where Harry, or a murderer for that matter, could have concealed himself. The church was dark presumably, a dim religious light."

The AC had this habit of spattering his conversation with the odd half-quotation. Dalgliesh could never decide whether he knew that he was doing it or whether the words swam into his consciousness from some half-forgotten pool of schoolroom lore. Now he heard him say:

"How well did you know Berowne personally?"

"I saw him a couple of times across a committee room table. We travelled together to the conference on sentencing. He asked to see me once in his office. We walked through St. James's Park to the House together. I liked him, but I'm not obsessed with him. I don't identify with him more than anyone does with any victim. This isn't a personal crusade. But I admit to a perfectly reasonable objection to seeing him branded as the brutal murderer of a man who died after he did."

Nichols said:

"On the evidence of one small smudge of blood?"

"What other evidence do we need?"

"To the fact of murder, none. As I said, you don't have to convince me. But I don't see how you're going to get any further unless you find one irrefutable piece of evidence linking one of your suspects to the scene of the crime." Nichols added: "Sooner rather than later."

"The Commissioner is getting complaints, I suppose."

"The usual thing, two dead bodies, two throats severed, a murderer at large. Why aren't we arresting this dangerous lunatic instead of examining the cars, clothes and houses of respectable citizens? Did you find any traces on the suspects' clothes, by the way?"

It was ironic, thought Dalgliesh, but not surprising: the new division set up to investigate serious crimes with sensitive undertones already accused of crass insensitivity. And he knew where the criticisms would have come from. He said:

"No, but I didn't expect any. This killer was naked or nearly naked. He had the means of washing himself to hand. Three passers-by heard the water gushing away shortly after eight."

"Berowne washing his own hands before supper?"

"If so, he was doing it very thoroughly."

"But his left hand, the unbloodied one, was clean when you found him?"

"Yes."

"There you are then."

Dalgliesh said:

"Berowne's towel was hanging over a chair in the vestry. I think his murderer dried himself with the tea towel in the kitchen. It was still slightly damp, not in places but all over, when I touched it. And he was killed with one of his own razors. Berowne had two, Bellinghams, in a case by the washbasin. A casual intruder, or Harry Mack for that matter, wouldn't have known they were there, probably wouldn't even have recognized the case for what it was."

"And what's a Bellingham, for God's sake? Why couldn't the man use a Gillette or an electric razor like the rest of us? OK, so it was someone who knew he shaved with a cut-throat, knew he'd be at the church that night, had access to the Campden Hill Square house to collect the matches and the diary. You know who best fits that list of requirements? Berowne himself. And all you've got against the suicide theory is one smudge of blood."

Dalgliesh was beginning to think that those four monosyllables would haunt him to the end of the case. He said:

"You're not suggesting, I suppose, that Berowne half-cut his throat, staggered over to Harry to murder him, dripping blood in the act, then staggered back again to the other end of the room to make the third and final cut in his own throat?"

"No, but defence counsel might. And Doc Kynaston hasn't entirely ruled it out. You and I have known more ingenious defences succeed."

Dalgliesh said:

"He wrote something while he was in that vestry. The lab can't identify the words, although they think it possible that he signed his name. The ink on the blotter is the same as the ink in his pen."

"So he wrote a suicide note."

"Possibly, but where is it now?"

The AC said:

"He burnt it with the diary. All right, I know what you're going to say, Adam. Is it likely a suicide would burn a note once written? Well, it's not impossible. He could have been dissatisfied with what he'd said.

Inadequate words, too trite, let it go. After all, the action speaks for itself. Not every suicide goes documented into that good night."

A flicker of pleased surprise passed over his face as if he were gratified at the aptness of the allusion but would rather like to be able to remember where it came from. Dalgliesh said:

"There's one thing he could have written which it's unlikely he would have blotted immediately, and that is something that another person might well wish to destroy."

Nichols was sometimes a little slow in grasping the point, but he was never afraid to take his time. He took it now. Then he said:

"That would need three signatures, of course. It's an interesting theory, and it would certainly strengthen the motive for at least two of your suspects. But, again, there's no proof. We get back to that all the time. It's an ingenious edifice you've built up, Adam, I'm half-convinced by it. But what we need is solid, physical evidence." He added: "You could say it's like the Church, an ingenious edifice erected on an unproved supposition, logical within its terms, but only valid if one can accept the basic premise, the existence of God."

He seemed pleased with the analogy. Dalgliesh doubted if it was his own. He watched while the AC skimmed over the remaining pages of the file almost dismissively. Closing the file, he said:

"Pity that you haven't been able to trace Berowne's movements after he left 62 Campden Hill Square. He seems to have walked into thin air."

"Not altogether. We know that he went to Westertons, the estate agents, in Kensington High Street and saw one of their negotiators, Simon Follett-Briggs. He asked someone from the firm to visit the next day to inspect and value the house. Again, hardly the action of a man contemplating suicide. Follett-Briggs says that he was as unconcerned as if he were giving them instructions to sell a forty-thousand one-bedroom basement flat. He did tactfully express his regrets that the family should be selling a house they'd lived in since it was first built. Berowne replied that they'd had it for a hundred and fifty years; it was time someone else had a turn. He didn't want to discuss it, only to ensure that someone came next morning to carry out the valuation. It was a short interview. He was away by eleven thirty. After that, we haven't been able to trace him. But he could have walked in one of the parks or by the river. His shoes were muddied and subsequently washed and scraped clean."

"Cleaned where?"

"Exactly. It suggests that he could have returned home, but no one admits to having seen him. He might escape notice if he slipped quickly in and out, but hardly if he stopped long enough to clean his shoes. And Father Barnes is certain that he arrived at the church by six. We've seven hours to account for."

"You saw this Follett-Briggs? Extraordinary names these fellows have. He must be feeling pretty sick. That would have been quite a commission. He might get it yet, I suppose, if the widow decides to sell."

Dalgliesh didn't reply.

"Did Follett-Briggs say what he expected it to fetch?"

He could, thought Dalgliesh, have been speaking of a second-hand car.

"He wouldn't commit himself, of course. He hasn't inspected the house and he took the view that Berowne's instructions no longer held. But under a little tactful pressure he did murmur that he would expect to get in excess of a million. That's excluding the contents, of course."

"And it all goes to the widow?"

"It goes to the widow."

"But the widow has an alibi. So has the widow's lover. So, as far as I can see, has every other suspect in the case."

As he picked up his file and moved to the door, the AC's voice pursued him like a plea.

"Just one piece of physical evidence, Adam. That's what we need. And for God's sake, try to get it before we have to call the next press conference."

7

⊠

Sarah Berowne found the postcard on the hall table on Monday morning. It was a card from the British Museum of a bronze cat wearing earrings, with Ivor's message written in his cramped upright hand. "Have tried to ring you but no luck. Hope you're feeling better. Any chance of dinner next Tuesday?"

So he was still using their code. He kept ready a small collection of postcards from the main London museums and galleries. Any mention of telephoning meant a proposal to meet, and this message, deciphered, asked her to be near the postcard gallery of the British Museum on Tuesday next. The time varied with the day. On Tuesdays the assignation was always for three o'clock. Like similar messages, this assumed that she could make it. If not, she was expected to ring back to say that dinner was impossible. But he had always taken it for granted that she would cancel all other engagements when the cards arrived. A message sent in this way was always urgent.

It was, she thought, hardly a code that would defeat the ingenuity of the police, let alone the security forces, if they became interested, but perhaps its very openness and simplicity was a safeguard. There was, after all, no law against friends spending an hour looking round museums together, and the rendezvous was a sensible one. They could pore over the same guidebook, talk in the almost obligatory whispers, move about at will to find the deserted galleries.

In those first heady months after he had recruited her to the Cell of Thirteen, when she was beginning to fall in love with him, she had

looked for these cards as she might for a love letter, lurking in the hall
for the post to fall through the letter box, seizing on the card and poring
over its message as if these cramped letters could say everything that she
needed so desperately to be told but which she knew he would never write,
still less speak. But now, for the first time, she read the summons with
a mixture of depression and irritation. The notice was ridiculously short;
it wouldn't be easy to get to Bloomsbury by three. And why on earth couldn't
he telephone? Tearing up the card, she felt as she never had before, that
the code was a childish and unnecessary device born of his obsessional
need to manipulate and conspire. It made them both ridiculous.

He was, as usual, there on time, selecting cards from the stand. She
waited while he paid and, without speaking, they moved out of the gallery
together. He was fascinated by the Egyptian antiquities and, almost instinctively, they made their way first to the ground-floor galleries and stood
together while he contemplated the huge granite torso of Rameses the
Second. It had seemed to her once that these dead eyes, this finely chiselled
half-smiling mouth above the jutting beard had been a powerfully erotic
symbol of their love. So much had been whispered between them in sly
elliptical phrases while they stood regarding it as if seeing the Pharaoh
for the first time, shoulders touching, and she had fought the need to
stretch out her hand, to feel his fingers in hers. But now all its power
had drained away. It was an interesting artifact, a huge slab of cracked
granite, no more. He said:

"Shelley is supposed to have used these features as a model when
he wrote 'Ozymandias.' "

"I know."

A couple of Japanese tourists, their scrutiny completed, drifted away.
With no change in the level or tone of his voice, he said:

"The police seem more certain now that your father was murdered.
I imagine they've got the pm and forensic reports. They've been to see
me."

A sliver of fear slid down her spine like iced water.

"Why?"

"In hope of breaking our alibi. They didn't, and of course they can't.
Not unless they break you. Have they been back?"

"Once. Not Commander Dalgliesh, the woman detective and a younger
man, a Chief Inspector Massingham. They asked about Theresa Nolan
and Diana Travers."

"What did you tell them?"

"That I'd seen Theresa Nolan twice, once when I'd called to see Grand-mama when she was ill, and once at that dinner party, and that I'd never seen Diana. Wasn't that what you expected me to say?"

He answered:

"Let's go and visit Ginger."

Ginger, named from the colour of the remnants of his hair, was the body of a pre-dynastic man, mummified by the hot desert sands three thousand years before Christ. Ivor had always been intrigued by him, and they never left the museum without this almost ritual visit. Now she gazed down at the emaciated body curled on its left side, the pathetic collection of pots to hold the food and drink which would nourish his spirit on its long journey through the underworld, the spear with which he would defend himself against its ghostly terrors until he reached his Egyptian heaven. Perhaps, she thought, if that spirit could awake now and see the bright lights, the huge room, the moving forms of twentieth-century man, he would think that he had attained it. But she had never been able to share Ivor's pleasure in this memento mori; the body's emaciation, even its attitude, evoked too strongly a modern horror: the pictures and newsreels of the dead at Belsen. She thought: Even when we're here he never asks what I think, what I feel, what I'd like most to see. She said:

"Let's go to the Duveen Gallery. I want to look at the Parthenon screen."

They moved slowly away. As they paced, their eyes on the open guide-book, she said:

"Diana Travers. You told me that she wasn't put into Campden Hill Square to spy on Daddy's private life. You said it was only his job you were interested in, finding out what was in the new Police Tactical Options Manual. I must have been naive. I can't think why I believed you. But that's what you told me."

"I don't need to have a cell member polishing the Berowne family silver to discover what's in the Tactical Options Manual. And she wasn't put there to spy on his private life, not primarily. I put her there to make her think she had a job to do, that she was trusted. It kept her occupied while I decided what to do about her."

"What do you mean, do about her? She was a member of the cell. She replaced Rose when Rose went back to Ireland."

"She thought she was a member, but she wasn't. There's no reason why you shouldn't know. After all, she's dead. Diana Travers was a Special Branch spy."

He had trained her not to look at him when they were talking but to keep her eyes on the exhibits, the guidebook or straight ahead. She gazed straight ahead now. She said:

"Why didn't you tell us?"

"Four of you were told, not the whole cell. I don't tell the cell every-thing."

She had, of course, known that his membership in the Workers' Revo-lutionary Campaign was a cover for the Cell of Thirteen. But even the cell, apparently, had only been a cover for his private inner cabinet. Like a Russian doll, one deceit was unscrewed to find another nestling within it. There were only four people whom he trusted completely, confided in, consulted, and she hadn't been among them. Had he ever trusted her, she wondered, even from the beginning? She said:

"That first time, when you rang me nearly four years ago and asked me to take photographs of Brixton, was that all part of a plan to recruit me, to get the daughter of a Tory MP into the WRC?"

"Partly. I knew where your political sympathies lay. I guessed you wouldn't exactly welcome your father's second marriage. It seemed a pro-pitious time to make an approach. Afterwards, my interest became, well, more personal."

"But was there ever love?"

He frowned. She knew how much he hated any intrusion of the per-sonal, the sentimental. He said:

"There was, there still is, great liking, respect, physical attraction. You can call that love if you want to use the word."

"What do you call it, Ivor?"

"I call it liking, respect, physical attraction."

They had moved into the Duveen Gallery. Above them pranced the horses on the Parthenon frieze, the naked riders with their flying cloaks, the chariots, the musicians, the elders and maidens approaching the seated gods and goddesses. But she looked up at this marvel with unseeing eyes. She thought: I need to know, I need to know everything. I have to face the truth. She said:

"And it was you who sent that poison pen note to Daddy and to the *Paternoster Review*? Doesn't it seem rather petty even to you, the people's revolutionary, the great campaigner against oppression, prophet of the new Jerusalem, reduced to gossip, slander, to childish spite? What did you think you were doing?"

He said:

"Making a little mild mischief."

"Is that what you call it—helping to discredit decent men? And not only my father. Most of them on your own side, men who've given years to the Labour movement, a cause you're supposed to support."

"Decency doesn't come into it. This is a war. Wars may be fought by decent men, but they're not won by them."

A small group of visitors had drifted up. They moved away and walked slowly down the side of the gallery. He said:

"If you're in the job of organizing a revolutionary group, even a small one, and they're going to have to wait for real action, real power, then you must keep them occupied, keen, give them the illusion that they're achieving something. Talk isn't enough. There has to be action. It's partly a matter of training for the future, partly of keeping up morale."

She said:

"From now on you're going to have to do it without me."

"I realize that. I knew that after Dalgliesh had seen you. But I expect you to stay on, at least nominally, until this murder enquiry is over. I don't want to say anything to the others while Dalgliesh is nosing around. Then you can join the Labour Party. You'll be happier there. Or the SDP, of course. Take your choice, there's no difference. By the time you're forty you'll be a Tory anyway."

She said:

"And you still trust me? You've told me all this, knowing that I want to get out?"

"Of course. I know you. You've inherited your father's pride. You wouldn't want people saying that your lover chucked you so you took your revenge by betraying him. You wouldn't want your friends, your grandmother even, to know that you've conspired against your father. You can say I rely on your bourgeois decencies. But there isn't much of a risk. The cell will be dissolved, re-formed, meet elsewhere. That's necessary now anyway."

She thought: That's another aspect of the revolutionary struggle, getting to know people's decencies and using them against them. She said:

"There's something I've learned about Daddy, something I didn't realize until he died. He tried to be good. I suppose those words don't mean anything to you."

"They mean something. I'm not sure what exactly you expect them to mean. I suppose he tried to behave so that he wasn't made uncomfortable by too much guilt. We all do. Given his politics and life-style, that can't have been easy. Perhaps in the end he gave up trying."

She said:

"I wasn't talking about politics. It had nothing to do with politics. I know you think everything has, but there is another view. There is a world elsewhere."

"I hope you'll be happy in it."

They were moving out of the gallery now, and she knew that this was the last time they would be there together. It surprised her how little she cared. She said:

"But Diana Travers, you said you put her into Campden Hill Square until you decided what to do with her. What did you do? Drown her?"

And now for the first time she saw that he was angry.

"Don't be melodramatic."

"But it was convenient for you, wasn't it?"

"Oh yes, and not only for me. There's someone else who had a much stronger motive for getting rid of her. Your father."

Forgetting the need for secrecy, she almost cried:

"Daddy? But he wasn't there! He was expected, but he never arrived."

"Oh, but he was there. I followed him that night. You could call it an exercise in surveillance. I drove behind him all the way to the Black Swan and watched him turn into the drive. And if you should decide to talk to Dalgliesh, who seems for some reason to induce in you the need for sentimental girlish confidences, then that is one piece of information that I shall feel it necessary to pass on."

"But you can't, can you? Not without admitting that you were there, too. If it's a question of motive, Dalgliesh might think there's not a lot to choose between you. And you're alive; he's dead."

"But, unlike your father, I have an alibi. A genuine one this time. I drove straight back to London, to a meeting of senior social workers at the town hall. I'm in the clear. But is he? His memory is unsavoury enough as it is. D'you want another scandal linked to his name? Isn't poor Harry Mack enough for you? Think about that if you're tempted to make an anonymous call to Special Branch."

8
⊠

Tuesday morning couldn't have heralded a better day for a drive out of London. The sunlight was fitful but surprisingly strong, and the sky was a high ethereal blue above the scudding clouds. Dalgliesh drove fast, but almost in silence. Kate had expected that they would drive straight to Riverside Cottage, but the road passed the Black Swan and when they reached it Dalgliesh stopped the car, appeared to think, then turned into the drive. He said:

"We'll have a beer. I'd like to walk along the river, view the cottage from this bank. It's Higgins's property, most of it anyway. We'd better let him know we're here."

They left the Rover in the car park, which was empty except for a Jaguar, a BMW, and a couple of Fords, and made their way to the entrance hall. Henry greeted them with impassive courtesy as if unsure whether he was expected to recognize them and, in reply to Dalgliesh's question, told them that Monsieur was in London. The bar was empty except for a quartet of businessmen conspiratorially bent over their whiskies. The barman, baby-faced above his white starched jacket and bow tie, served them with a notable brew of real ale which the Black Swan took some pride in obtaining, then began industriously washing glasses and re-arranging his bar as if hoping that a show of busyness might inhibit Dalgliesh from asking any questions. Dalgliesh wondered by what extraordinary alchemy Henry had managed to signal their identities. They carried their beer to the chairs each side of the log fire, drank in companionable silence, then returned to the car park and passed through the gate in the hedge to the riverbank.

It was one of those perfect English autumnal days which occur more frequently in memory than in life. The rich colours of grass and earth were intensified by the mellow light of a sun almost warm enough for spring, and the air was a sweet evocation of all Dalgliesh's boyhood autumns: woodsmoke, ripe apples, the last sheaves of harvest and the strong sea-smelling breeze of flowing water. The Thames was running strongly, under a quickening breeze. It flattened the grasses fringing the river edge and eddied the stream into the little gulleys which fretted the bank. Under a surface iridescent in blues and greens, on which the light moved and changed as if on coloured glass, the blade-like weeds streamed and undulated. Beyond the clumps of willows on the far bank, a herd of Friesians were peacefully grazing.

Opposite and about seventy yards downstream he could see a bungalow, little more than a large white shack on stilts, which he guessed must be their destination. And he knew too, as he had known walking under the trees of St. James's Park, that here he would find the clue he sought. But he was in no hurry. Like a child postponing the moment of assured satisfaction, he was glad that they were early, grateful for this small hiatus of calm. And suddenly he experienced a minute of tingling happiness so unexpected and so keen that he almost held his breath as if he could halt time. They came to him so rarely now, these moments of intense physical joy, and he had never before experienced one in the middle of a murder investigation. The moment passed and he heard his own sigh. Breaking the mood with a commonplace, he said:

"I suppose that must be Riverside Cottage."

"I think so, sir. Shall I get the map?"

"No. We shall find out soon enough. We'd better get on."

But he still lingered, feeling the wind lift his hair and grateful for another minute of peace. He was grateful, too, that Kate Miskin could share it with him without the need to speak and without making him feel that her silence was a conscious discipline. He had chosen her because he needed a woman in his team and she was the best available. The choice had been partly rational, partly instinctive, and he was beginning to realize just how well his instinct had served him. It would have been dishonest to say that there was no hint of sexuality between them. In his experience there nearly always was, however repudiated or unacknowledged, between any reasonably attractive heterosexual couple who worked closely together.

He wouldn't have chosen her if he had found her disturbingly attractive, but the attraction was there and he wasn't immune to it. But despite this pinprick of sexuality, perhaps because of it, he found her surprisingly restful to work with. She had an instinctive knowledge of what he wanted; she knew when to be silent; she wasn't over-deferential. He suspected that with part of her mind she saw his vulnerabilities more clearly, understood him better and was more judgemental than were any of his male subordinates. She had none of Massingham's ruthlessness, but she wasn't in the least sentimental. But then in his experience, women police officers seldom were.

He took a final look at the bungalow. If he had walked along the riverbank on that first visit to the Black Swan, as he had been tempted to do, he would have viewed its pathetic pretensions with an incurious and disparaging eye. But now as its fragile walls seemed to shimmer in the slight haze from the river it held for him an infinite and disturbing promise. It was built about thirty yards from the water's edge with a wide veranda, a central stack and to the left, upstream, a small landing stage. He thought he could see a patch of broken earth with clumps of mauve and white, perhaps a patch of Michaelmas daisies. Some attempt had been made at a garden. From a distance the bungalow looked well maintained, the white paintwork gleaming. But even so, it had a summer look; temporary, a little ramshackle. Higgins, he thought, would hardly relish having it in full view of his lawns.

As they looked, the dumpy figure of a woman came out of the side door and made her way to the landing stage, a large dog trotting at her heels. She lowered herself into a dinghy, leaned over to cast off and began rowing purposefully across the river towards the Black Swan, humpbacked over the oars, the dog sitting bolt upright in the prow. As the dinghy crawled closer they could see that he was a cross between a poodle and some kind of terrier, with a woolly body and an anxious, amiable face almost entirely obscured by hair. They watched as the woman bent and rose over the dipping oars, making slow progress against a current that was bearing her downstream away from them. When the dinghy finally bumped the bank, Dalgliesh and Kate walked up to her. Bending down, he caught the bow of the dinghy and held it steady. He saw that her landing place had not been fortuitous. There was a steel stake driven deep into the grass at the water's edge. He slipped the painter over it and held out his hand. She grasped it and almost hopped ashore, one-footed, and he saw that she wore a surgical boot on her left foot. The dog leapt out after her, sniffed at Dalgliesh's trousers, then flopped, discouraged, on the grass as if the physical effort of the journey had all been his. Dalgliesh said:

"I think you must be Miss Millicent Gentle. If so, we're on our way to see you. We telephoned from Scotland Yard this morning. This is Inspector Kate Miskin, and my name is Adam Dalgliesh."

He looked down at a face round and crumpled like an overstored apple. The striped russet cheeks were hard balls under small eyes which, when she smiled up at him, creased into narrow slits, then opened to reveal irises as brightly brown as polished pebbles. She was wearing a shapeless pair of brown slacks and a padded sleeveless jerkin in faded red over a jumper matted with age. Drawn well down over her head was a pixie cap in knitted green and red stripes and with earflaps each ending in a pigtail of plaited wool, decorated with a red bobble. She had an air of slightly battered puckishness like an elderly garden gnome which has weathered too many winters. But when she spoke her voice was deep and resonant, one of the most beautiful female voices he had ever heard.

"I am expecting you, of course, Commander, but not for another half hour. How pleasant to meet you so unexpectedly. I would row you across, but with Makepeace it would mean one at a time and that would be rather slow. I'm afraid it's five miles by road, but perhaps you have a car."

"We have a car."

"Of course, you would have, being police officers. How silly of me. Then I'll be waiting for you. I've just rowed across with my letters. Mr. Higgins lets me put them on the hall table to be posted with his. My postbox is a two-mile walk. It's very kind of him considering that he doesn't really like my cottage. I'm afraid he considers it rather an eyesore. You can't miss the road. Take the first left marked Frolight, then over the humpbacked bridge, then left again at Mr. Roland's farm—there's a sign with a Friesian cow on it—then you'll see a track leading to the river and my cottage. As you can see, you can't really miss it. Oh, and you'll have some coffee, I hope."

"Thank you, we should like that."

"I thought you might. That's partly why I rowed over. Mr. Higgins is kind about selling me an extra pint of milk. It's about Sir Paul Berowne, isn't it?"

"Yes, Miss Gentle, it's about Sir Paul."

"I thought it might be when you telephoned and said you were police. That dear good man. I shall see you both then in about ten minutes."

They watched her for a moment as she limped briskly towards the

Black Swan, the dog lurching at her heels, then turned and made their way slowly back to the car park. They followed her instructions without difficulty, but Dalgliesh drove slowly, knowing them to be still ahead of their appointment and wanting to give Miss Gentle time to row back and be waiting for them. Gentle was, apparently, her real name, not a pseudonym; it had seemed almost too appropriate for a romantic novelist. Driving with irritating slowness, he was aware of Kate's controlled impatience at his side. But ten minutes later they left the side road and turned up the rough track to the cottage.

It ran across an unhedged field and would, thought Dalgliesh, be little more than an impassable quagmire in the worst of winter. The bungalow looked more substantial than it had from a distance. A flower bed, now in its shaggy autumnal decrepitude, bordered the cinder path to the side steps beneath which he could glimpse cans, presumably of paraffin, stacked under a tarpaulin. Behind the bungalow was a vegetable patch: stunted cabbages, and the scarred stems of brussels sprouts, bulbous onions, broken-leaved, and the last of the runner beans, whose dying swatches hung from their poles like rags. The river smell was stronger here, and he could picture the scene in winter, the cold mist rising from the water, the soggy fields, the single mud track to a desolate country road.

But when Miss Gentle opened the door to them and smilingly stepped aside, they walked into cheerfulness and light. From the wide sitting room windows it was possible to imagine oneself on a ship with nothing in view but the white veranda rail and the sheen of the river. Despite an incongruous wrought-iron stove, the room was indeed more typical of a cottage than a riverside shack. One wall, papered with an incongruous design of rosebuds and robins, was almost covered with pictures: dated watercolours of country scenes, twin engravings of Winchester and Wells Cathedrals, four early-Victorian fashion plates mounted in one frame, an embroidered picture in wool and silk of the angel greeting the Apostles at the empty tomb, a couple of rather good miniature portraits in oval frames. The far wall was covered with books, some of them, Dalgliesh noticed, Miss Gentle's own, still pristine in their jackets. On each side of the stove was an easy chair and between them a gate-legged table on which a jug of milk and three flowered cups and saucers had already been placed. Miss Gentle, helped by Kate, drew up a small rocking chair for her second guest. Makepeace, having ambled with his mistress to greet them, slumped down in front of the empty stove and heaved a malodorous sigh.

Miss Gentle brought in the coffee almost immediately. The kettle had been on the boil, she had only to pour the water over the grains. Taking his first sip, Dalgliesh had a moment's compunction. He had forgotten how inconvenient it was for the solitary to be faced with unexpected visitors. That row across to the Black Swan had, he suspected, been more for the milk than to get the letters posted. He said gently:

"You know, of course, that Sir Paul Berowne is dead."

"Yes, I know. He was murdered, and that's why you're here. How did you find me?"

Dalgliesh explained about the finding of her book. He said:

"Anything that happened to him during the last weeks of his life is important to us. That's why we'd like you to tell us exactly what happened on the night of August seventh. You did see him?"

"Oh, yes, I saw him. It was then I gave him the book." She put down her cup and gave a little shiver as if she were suddenly cold. Then she settled down to tell her story as if they were children round the nursery fire.

"I really get on very well with Mr. Higgins. Of course, he would like to buy the cottage and pull it down, but I've said that he can have first refusal from my executors when I'm dead. We have our little joke about it. And the Black Swan is really very respectably run. A nice type of customer, very quiet. But on that night they weren't. I was trying to work and it got very irritating. Young people shouting and screaming. So I went out to the bank and I could just see that there were four of them in a punt. They were rocking very dangerously and two of them were standing up and trying to change places. Apart from the noise, they were behaving very foolishly. I tried to ring Mr. Higgins but my telephone was out of order. So Makepeace and I rowed across. I made for my usual spot—it would have been most imprudent to row up to them and remonstrate, I'm not as strong as I used to be. As I turned the boat to draw up to the bank, I saw the other two men."

"Did you know who they were?"

"Not at the time. It was, of course, dark by then. There was only the reflected light coming over the hedge from the car park. Afterwards I knew one of them, Sir Paul Berowne."

"What were they doing?"

"Fighting." Miss Gentle spoke the words without the least disapproval, almost, Dalgliesh thought, with a note of surprise that he should have needed to ask. Her tone implied that fighting on a riverbank and partly in the dark was an activity to be expected of two gentlemen who had nothing better to do. She said:

"They didn't notice me, of course. Only my head was above the level of the bank. I was afraid Makepeace would bark, but I told him not to and he was really very controlled, although I could see that he wanted to jump out and join in. I rather wondered if I ought to intervene myself, but I decided it would be undignified and really quite ineffective. And it was obviously a private fight. I mean, it didn't look like an unprovoked attack, which I feel one has a duty to try to put a stop to. The second man looked much shorter than Sir Paul, which made it rather unfair in a way. But then he was the younger, so that redressed the balance. They were getting on very well without me or Makepeace."

Dalgliesh couldn't resist a glance at Makepeace, steaming in somnolent calm. It seemed unlikely that he could have raised the energy for a bark, let alone a bite. He asked:

"Who won?"

"Oh, Sir Paul. He landed what I think is called a hook to the jaw. It looked very satisfying. The younger man fell, then Sir Paul picked him up by the collar of his coat and his trousers, very like a puppy, and threw him into the river. He made quite a splash. 'My goodness,' I said to Makepeace, 'what an extraordinary evening we're having!' "

Dalgliesh thought that the scene was beginning to resemble a chapter from one of Miss Gentle's own genre. He said:

"What happened next?"

"Sir Paul waded into the river and fished him out. I expect he didn't actually want him to drown. Perhaps he didn't know whether he could swim. Then he threw him down on the grass, said something which I couldn't hear and walked upstream towards me. As he drew alongside, I popped up my head. I said: 'Good evening. I don't suppose you remember me, but we met last June at the Hertfordshire Conservative fête. I was visiting a niece. I'm Millicent Gentle.' "

"What did he do?"

"He came over, squatted down by the dinghy and shook hands. He was quite unflustered, not in the least disconcerted. He was dripping wet, of course, and his cheek was bleeding. It looked like a scratch. But he was as self-possessed as he had been when we'd met at the Conservative fête. I said: 'I saw the fight. You haven't killed him, have you?' He said: 'No, I haven't killed him. I only wanted to.' Then he apologized and I said there was really no need. He was beginning to shiver—it really wasn't warm enough to be standing around in wet clothes—so I suggested he should come back to the cottage and dry off. He said: 'That's very kind of you, but I think I ought first to move the car.' I knew what he meant, of course. It would be better if he left the Black Swan before anyone saw him or knew that he was there. Politicians have to be so careful. I suggested that he park it somewhere at the side of the road and I'd wait for him a little further upstream until he came back. He could have driven round, of course, but it would have been five miles or more and he really was very cold. He disappeared and I waited. It wasn't long. He was back in less than five minutes."

"And what happened to the other man?"

"I didn't wait to see. I knew he'd be all right. He wasn't alone, you see. He had a girl with him."

"A girl? Are you sure?"

"Oh yes, quite sure. She came out of the bushes and watched when Sir Paul threw him into the river. I couldn't have missed her. She was quite naked."

"Could you recognize her?" Without being asked, Kate opened her shoulder bag and handed over the photograph.

Miss Gentle said:

"Isn't that the girl who drowned? It's possible it was the same one, but I didn't see her face clearly. The light was very poor, as I've said, and they must have been forty yards away."

"What did she do?"

"She laughed. It was most extraordinary. Peal on peal of laughter. When Sir Paul waded in to help him out, she sat on the bank, quite naked, and roared with laughter. One ought not to laugh at another's misfortune, but he really did look very funny. The scene was quite bizarre. Two men stumbling out of the river and a naked girl sitting on the bank and laughing. She had rather an infectious laugh, full-throated, joyous. Ringing across the water, it didn't sound malicious. But I suppose it must have been."

"And what was happening to the party in the punt?"

"They were paddling back upstream towards the Black Swan. Perhaps they were beginning to feel a little frightened. The river is so black at night and so strange, almost sinister. I'm used to it now, I feel at home with it. But I think they wanted to get back to the lights and the warmth."

"So the last you saw of the man and the girl they were together on the bank and you began rowing quietly downstream without being noticed?"

"Yes. The river bends just slightly there and the rushes are taller at the water edge. They were quickly out of sight. I sat quietly and waited until Sir Paul appeared."

"From what direction?"

"Walking upstream, the same direction as I had been rowing. He'd come through the car park, you see."

"Still out of earshot and sight of the boy and girl?"

"Well, out of sight, but I could still hear her laughing as we rowed across. I had to go carefully. With Makepeace and a passenger, we were very low in the water."

The picture of the two of them in that bucket of a dinghy with Makepeace rigid at the prow was ridiculous but endearing. Dalgliesh wanted to laugh. It wasn't an impulse he had expected to feel in the middle of any murder investigation, least of all this one, and he was grateful. He asked:

"The girl, for how long was she laughing?"

"Until we were almost on the opposite bank. And then, suddenly, the laughing stopped."

"Did you hear anything at that moment, a cry, a splash?"

"Nothing. But then, if she had dived cleanly in, there wouldn't have been much of a splash. And I don't think I would have heard it above the noise of the oars."

"What happened then, Miss Gentle?"

"First Sir Paul asked if he could use the telephone to make a local call. He didn't say to where and, naturally, I didn't ask. I left him here and went into the kitchen so that he could feel quite private. Then I suggested that he ought to have a hot bath. I switched on the electric wall heater in the bathroom and lit all my paraffin stoves. It didn't seem a time for economy. And I gave him some disinfectant for his face. I don't think I mentioned that the boy had scratched him quite badly on his cheek. Not a very masculine way to fight, I thought. Then, while he was in the bathroom, I dried his clothes in the spin dryer. I haven't got a washing machine. Well, I don't really need one, just being on my own. I can even manage the sheets, now that we have drip dry. But I don't think I could manage without my spin dryer. Oh, and I handed him my father's old dressing gown to wear while the clothes were drying. It's all wool and beautifully warm. They don't make that quality now. When he came out of the bathroom I thought how handsome he looked in it. We settled down in front of the fire and I made some hot cocoa. Being a gentleman, I thought, he might prefer something stronger, and I offered my elderberry wine. He said he'd rather have the cocoa. Well, he didn't actually say he preferred the cocoa. He would have liked to taste the wine, he was sure it was excellent, but he thought a hot drink might be better. I quite agreed. There's really nothing quite as comforting as good strong cocoa when one is famished with cold. I made it with all milk. I had ordered an extra pint because I planned to have cauliflower cheese for supper. Wasn't that lucky?"

Dalgliesh said:

"Very lucky. Have you spoken of this to any other person?"

"No one. I wouldn't have spoken to you if you hadn't telephoned and he hadn't been dead."

"Did he ask for your silence?"

"Oh, no, he wouldn't have done that. He wasn't that kind of man, and he knew that I wouldn't tell. You know when you can trust a person about something like that, don't you find? If you can, why ask? If you can't, there's no point in asking."

"Please continue to say nothing, Miss Gentle. It could be important."

She nodded but didn't speak. He asked, wondering why it should matter so, why he needed so urgently to know:

"What did you talk about?"

"Not about the fight, at least not very much. I said: 'I expect it was about a woman, wasn't it?' And he said it was."

"The woman who laughed, the naked girl?"

"I don't think so. I'm not sure why, but I don't think so. I've a feeling it was rather more complicated than that. And I don't think he would have fought in front of her, not if he'd known she was there. But then, I don't suppose he did know. She must have concealed herself in the bushes when she saw him coming."

He thought he knew why Berowne had been on the riverbank. He had arrived to join the dinner party, to greet his wife and his wife's lover, to take part in a civilized charade, the complaisant husband, stock figure of farce. And then he had heard the murmur of running water, had smelt, as had Dalgliesh, that strong nostalgic river smell with its promise of a few moments of solitude and peace. So he had hesitated, then walked through the gate in the hedge from the car park to the riverbank. Such a small thing, a simple impulse obeyed, and it had led him to that blood-boltered vestry.

And it must have been then that Swayne, perhaps pulling his shirt over his head, had stepped out of the bushes to confront him like the personification of everything he despised in his own life, in himself. Had he challenged Swayne about Theresa Nolan, or did he already know? Was that one other secret that the girl had confided to him in that final letter, the name of her lover?

Dalgliesh asked again, gently insistent:

"What *did* you talk about, Miss Gentle?"

"Mainly about my work, my books. He was really very interested in how I started writing, where I got my ideas. Of course, I haven't published anything for six years now. My kind of fiction isn't very fashionable. Dear Mr. Hearne, always so kind, so helpful, explained it to me. Romantic fiction is more realistic now. I'm afraid I'm too old-fashioned. But I can't change. People are sometimes a little unkind about romantic novelists, I know, but we're just like other writers. You can only write what you need to write. And I'm very lucky. I have my health, my old age pension, my home and Makepeace for company. And I still keep writing. The next book may be the lucky one."

Dalgliesh asked:

"How long did Sir Paul stay?"

"Oh, for hours, until nearly midnight. But I don't think that he was being polite. I think he was happy here. We sat and talked, and I made scrambled eggs when we got hungry. There was enough milk for that but not, of course, for the cauliflower cheese. At one point he said: 'No one in the world knows where I am at this moment, not a single soul. No one can get at me.' He said it as if I had given him something precious. He sat in that chair, the one you're in now, and he looked so comfortable in Father's old dressing gown and so at home. You're very like him, Commander. I don't mean your features. He was fair and you're so dark. But you are like him: the way you sit, your hands, the way you walk, even your voice a little."

Dalgliesh put down his cup and got up. Kate looked at him, surprised, then rose too and picked up her shoulder bag. Dalgliesh heard himself thanking Miss Gentle for the coffee, emphasizing the need for silence, explaining that they would like a written statement and that a police car would call and take her to New Scotland Yard, if that was convenient. They had reached the door when Kate asked, on impulse:

"And when he left you that night, that was the last time you saw him?"

"Oh, no. I saw him on the afternoon of his death. I thought you knew."

Dalgliesh said gently:

"But Miss Gentle, how could we have known?"

"I thought he would have told someone where he was going. Is it important?"

"Very important, Miss Gentle. We've been trying to trace his movements that afternoon. Tell us what happened."

"There isn't much to tell. He arrived, quite unexpectedly, just before three o'clock. I remember that I was listening to 'Woman's Hour' on Radio Four. He was on foot and he was carrying a bag. He must have walked the four miles from the station, but he seemed surprised when I pointed out how far it was. He said he had felt like a walk along the river. I asked him if he'd had any lunch and he said he had some cheese in his bag and that would do. He must have been famished. Luckily I'd made myself a beef stew for lunch and there was some over, so I made him come in and he ate that and then we had coffee together. He didn't talk very much. I don't think he'd come to talk. Then he left his bag with me and set off for his walk. He came back about four thirty and I made tea. His shoes were very dirty—the river meadows have been so waterlogged this summer— so I gave him my shoe-cleaning box and he sat outside on the steps and cleaned them. Then he took up his bag, said good-bye and was on his way. It was as simple as that."

As simple as that, thought Dalgliesh. The lost hours accounted for, the wedge of mud on his shoe explained. He had gone, not to his mistress, but to a woman whom he had seen only once before in his life, who asked no questions, made no demands, who had given him those remembered moments of peace. He had wanted to spend those few hours where no one in the world knew where to find him. And he must have gone straight from Paddington to St. Matthew's Church. They would have to check the times of the trains, how long the whole journey was likely to have taken. But whether or not Lady Ursula was lying, it seemed highly unlikely that Berowne could have called in at his house, collected his diary, and still arrived at the church at six.

Looking back at the closing door, Kate said:

"I know an old lady who, in her place, would say: 'No one wants my books, I'm poor, I'm lame, and I live in a damp cottage with only a dog for company.' She says: 'I've got my health, my pension, my home, Makepeace for company, and I go on writing.'"

Dalgliesh wondered who it was she had in mind. There was a bitterness in her voice which was new to him. Then he remembered that there was an elderly grandmother somewhere in the picture, and wondered. It was the first time that she had ever hinted at a private life. Before he could answer she went on:

"So that explains why Higgins said that Swayne's clothes were dripping wet. It was a night in August, after all. If he'd been swimming naked and then pulled on his clothes after the drowning, why should they be dripping?" She added:

"It's a new motive, sir, a double motive. Swayne must have hated him. The thrashing, the humiliation, thrown into the river and dragged out like a dog, and in front of the girl."

Dalgliesh said:

"Oh, yes, Swayne must have hated him."

So he had it at last, the motive not only for murder but for this particular murder with its mixture of planning and impulse, its brutality, its over-ingenuity, the cleverness which hadn't quite been clever enough. It was there before him in its pettiness, its arrogance, its essential inadequacy, but in all its terrible strength. He recognized the mind behind it. He had met it before, the mind of a killer who isn't content merely to take a life, who avenges humiliation with humiliation, who cannot bear the searing knowledge that his enemy breathes the same air, who wants his victim not only dead but disgraced, the mind of a man who has felt despised and inferior all his life but who will never feel inferior again. And if his instinct was right and Dominic Swayne was his man, then to get him he would have to break a vulnerable, lonely and obstinate woman. He shivered and turned up the collar of his coat. The sunlight was fading over the meadows, but the wind was freshening and there came from the river a smell, dank and ominous, like the first breath of winter. He heard Kate's voice:

"Do you think we'll be able to break his alibi, sir, by any method we're allowed to use?"

Dalgliesh roused himself and strode to the car.

"We must try, Inspector, we must try."

BOOK SIX

Mortal
Consequences

1
⊠

When Father Barnes had first told Miss Wharton of Susan Kendrick's suggestion that she might like to spend a day or so with them in the Nottingham vicarage until the fuss had died down, she had accepted with gratitude and relief. It was agreed that she would travel to Nottingham immediately after the inquest and that Father Barnes would himself go by tube with her to King's Cross to carry her one case and see her off. The whole plan had seemed like an answer to a prayer. The half-lubricious respect with which she was now treated by the McGraths, who seemed to regard her as a prize exhibit, bolstering their esteem in the road, she found more terrifying than their previous antagonism. It would be a relief to get away from their avid eyes and endless questions.

The inquest had been less of an ordeal than she had feared. Only evidence of identity and of the finding of the bodies had been briefly taken before, at the request of the police, the proceedings were adjourned. The coroner had treated Miss Wharton with grave consideration, and her time in the witness box had been so brief that she was hardly aware of standing there before she was released. Her anxiously searching eyes had failed to see Darren. She had a confused recollection of being introduced to a number of strangers, including a fair-haired young man who said that he was Sir Paul's brother-in-law. No one else from the family was present, although there were a number of sombre-suited men who Father Barnes told her were lawyers. He himself, resplendent in a new cassock and biretta, had been extraordinarily at ease. He had shepherded her with a proprietorial arm past the photographers, had greeted members of the congregation with an assurance she had never before seen in him and had seemed quite at ease with the police. Miss Wharton, for one appalled moment, found herself thinking that the murders seemed to have done him good.

She had known after the first day at St. Crispin's that the visit wasn't going to be a success. Susan Kendrick was heavily pregnant with her first child, but her energy was undiminished and every minute of her day seemed occupied either with parish or domestic concerns or with her part-time physiotherapy clinic at the local hospital. The rambling inner-city vicarage was never empty and, except for Father Kendrick's study, never peaceful. Miss Wharton was constantly introduced to people whose names she couldn't quite catch and whose functions in the parish she never divined. Where the murders were concerned, her hostess was dutifully sympathetic but obviously took the view that it was unreasonable for anyone to be lastingly distressed by dead bodies, however unpleasant their ends, and that dwelling on the experience was at best self-indulgent and at worst morbid. But Miss Wharton had reached the stage when it would have been helpful to talk, and she was missing Darren with a need which was becoming desperate, wondering where he was, what was happening to him, whether he was happy.

She had expressed her pleasure at the coming baby, but nervousness had made her sound coy and her words had sounded gushingly sentimental even to her own ears. Confronted with Susan's robust common sense about her pregnancy, she had been made to feel an absurd old maid. She had offered to help in the parish, but her hostess's inability to find a job suitable to her abilities had drained her confidence further. She had begun to creep about the vicarage like the church mouse they probably thought she resembled. After a couple of days she had nervously suggested that she ought to be thinking of home, and no one had made any attempt to dissuade her.

But on the morning of departure she had brought herself to confide in Susan her worries about Darren, and here her hostess had been helpful. Local bureaucracy held no terrors for her. She had known whom to ring, how to discover the number and had spoken to the unknown voice at the end of the line in the accents of conspiratorial, mutually acknowledged authority. She had made the call from her husband's study, with Miss Wharton seated in the chair conveniently placed for those seeking the vicar's counsel. During the telephone conversation, she had felt like the unworthy recipient of patient professional concern, vaguely conscious that she would have done better had she been an unmarried mother or a delinquent, preferably both, and had been black.

Afterwards Susan Kendrick had given her the verdict. She couldn't see Darren at present; his social worker felt that it wasn't at all desirable. He had been taken before the juvenile court and a supervision order made. They were hoping to arrange a programme of intermediate treatment for him, but until this was satisfactorily under way they didn't think it wise for him to see Miss Wharton. It might only provoke unfortunate memories. He had been very reluctant to talk about the murders, and his social worker felt that when he was ready to do so it should be with someone suitably qualified in social work skills who could work through the trauma with him. He'll hate it all, thought Miss Wharton. He never did like interference.

Lying in bed on her first night at home, wakeful, as she so often was now, she came to a decision. She would go to Scotland Yard and ask the police to help. Surely they would have some authority, or at least some influence, over Darren's social worker. They had always been kind and helpful to her. They would be able to reassure the local authority that she could be trusted with Darren. The decision brought a measure of peace to her troubled mind and she fell asleep.

The next morning found her less confident, but with her resolution unshaken. She would set out after ten o'clock; there was no point in getting caught up in the rush hour. She dressed carefully for the excursion; first impressions were always important. Before setting out, she knelt to pray briefly that the visit might be a success, that she would be met with understanding, that Scotland Yard wouldn't be the terrifying place of her imagination, that Commander Dalgliesh or Inspector Miskin would be willing to talk to the local authority, to explain that she wouldn't even mention the murders to Darren if his social worker thought it unwise. She walked to Paddington underground station and took the Circle Line. At St. James's Park Station she came out of the wrong exit, was for a few minutes lost and had to enquire the way to the Yard. And suddenly, across the road, she saw the revolving sign and the great glass oblong building so familiar from television news pictures.

The entrance hall surprised her. She wasn't sure what she had imagined: a uniformed officer on duty, perhaps a steel grille, even a succession of manacled prisoners being escorted to the cells. Instead she found herself facing an ordinary reception desk with a couple of young women on duty. The hall was very busy with an air of purposeful but relaxed activity. Men and women showed their passes and passed happily gossiping through to the lifts. Except for the flame of remembrance burning on its plinth, it could, she thought, be almost any office. She asked for Inspector Miskin, having decided that this was a matter on which a woman might be more sympathetic than a man and that she could hardly worry Commander Dalgliesh with something so unimportant, except to her. No, she admitted, she hadn't an appointment. She was asked to sit down on one of the chairs set against the left-hand wall, and watched while the girl telephoned. Her confidence grew, and the hands clutching her handbag gradually relaxed. She was able to take an interest in the busy comings and goings, to feel that she had a right to be there.

And suddenly Inspector Miskin was standing beside her. She hadn't expected her to appear. Somehow she had thought that she would be taken by messenger to the inspector's office. She thought: She's saving time. If she thinks it's important, then she'll take me up. And Inspector Miskin obviously didn't think it important. When Miss Wharton had explained her purpose, she sat down beside her and was for a moment silent. Miss Wharton thought: She's disappointed. She hoped I was bringing her some news about the murders, that I'd remembered something new and important. Then the inspector said:

"I'm sorry, but I don't see how we can help. The juvenile court has made a supervision order to the local authority. It's their concern now."

"I know, that's what Mrs. Kendrick told me. But I thought you might be able to use your influence. After all, the police . . ."

"We have no influence, not in this."

The words sounded dreadfully final. Miss Wharton found herself pleading:

"I wouldn't talk to him about the murders, although I sometimes think that boys are tougher than we are in some ways. But I'd be very careful. I'd feel so much better if only I could see him again, even if briefly, just to know that he's all right."

"Why can't you? Did they say?"

"They think he ought not to talk about the murders until he can work through the trauma with someone experienced in social work skills."

"Yes, that sounds like the jargon."

Miss Wharton was surprised by the sudden bitterness in the inspector's voice. She sensed that she had an ally. She opened her mouth to make an appeal and decided against it. If anything could be done, Inspector Miskin would do it. The inspector seemed to be thinking, then she said:

"I can't give you his address: anyway I can't remember it. I'd have to consult the file. I'm not even sure if they've left him at home with his mother, although I suppose they'd have gone for a care order if they'd wanted to remove him. But I can remember the name of his school, Bollington Road Junior. Do you know it?"

Miss Wharton said eagerly:

"Oh yes, I know where Bollington Road is. I can get there."

"They still come out at about three thirty, don't they? You could try passing at the right time. If you met him accidentally, I don't see how they could object to that."

"Thank you, thank you."

Miss Wharton, her perceptions sharpened by anxiety and now relief, guessed that Inspector Miskin was wondering whether to ask her again about the murders; but she said nothing. As they got up and the inspector walked with her to the door, she looked up at her and said:

"You've been very kind. If I remember anything new about the murders, anything I haven't told you, I'll get in touch at once."

Sitting in the tube on her way to St. James's Park Station she had planned that, if all went well, she would treat herself afterwards to coffee in the Army and Navy Stores. But her visit to the Yard seemed to have taken more out of her than she had expected, and even the thought of negotiating the traffic of Victoria Street depressed and discouraged her. Perhaps it would be less exhausting to go without the coffee and make for home. While she was hesitating at the edge of the pavement she felt a shoulder brush against hers. A male voice, young, pleasant, said:

"Excuse me, but aren't you Miss Wharton? I met you at the Berowne inquest. I'm Dominic Swayne, Sir Paul's brother-in-law."

She blinked, confused for a second, and then recognized him. He said:

"We're blocking the pavement," and she felt his hand on her arm, firmly guiding her across the street. Then, without releasing her, he said:

"You must have been to the Yard. So have I. I feel in need of a drink. Please have one with me. I was thinking of the St. Ermin's Hotel."

Miss Wharton said:

"You're very kind, but I'm not sure . . ."

"Please. I need someone to talk to. You'd be doing me a kindness."

It really was impossible to refuse. His voice, smile, the press of his arm were persuasive. He was steering her gently but firmly forward through the station and into Caxton Street. And suddenly here was the hotel, looking so solidly welcoming, its wide courtyard flanked by heraldic beasts. It would be good to have a quiet sit before she started the journey home. He guided her through the left-hand door and into the foyer.

It was, she thought, all very grand: the branching staircase leading to a curved balcony, the glittering chandeliers, the mirrored walls and elegantly carved pillars. Yet she felt strangely at home. There was something reassuring about this Edwardian elegance, this atmosphere of assured, respectable comfort. She followed her companion over the blue and fawn carpet to a couple of high-backed chairs before the fireplace. After they had seated themselves he asked:

"What would you like? There's coffee, but I think you should have something stronger. Sherry?"

"Yes, that would be very nice, thank you."

"Dry?"

"Well, not too dry, perhaps."

Mrs. Kendrick had brought out the sherry decanter before dinner every evening at St. Crispin's vicarage. It had invariably been dry, a pale sour sharpness not really to her taste. But she had missed the evening ritual on her return home. There was no doubt one did get quickly used to these little luxuries. He lifted his finger and the waiter came, swiftly deferential. The sherry arrived, a rich amber, half-sweet, immediately reviving. There was a little bowl of nuts and one of small dry biscuits. How elegant, how soothing it all was. The raucous life of Victoria Street could have been miles away. She sat back, glass at her lips, and looked with tremulous wonder at the ornately carved ceiling, the twin wall lights with their fringed shades, the hugh urns of flowers at the foot of the stair. And suddenly she knew why she felt so at home. Sight, sound, sensation, even the young man's face bent smiling towards her, all fused into a long-forgotten picture. She was in a hotel lounge, surely this same hotel, this very place, sitting with her brother on his first leave after he had gained his sergeant's stripes. And then she remembered. He had been stationed at Bassingbourn in East Anglia. They must have met at a hotel near Liverpool Street, not Victoria. But it had been so very similar. She remembered her pride in the smartness of his uniform, the one winged badge of an air gunner on his breast, the pristine brightness of his three stripes, her sense of importance at being escorted by him, how she had revelled in the unaccustomed luxury, in the assured way in which he had summoned the waiter, ordered sherry for her, beer for himself. And her present companion reminded her a little of John. Like John, he was barely her own height.

"They like us small, we tail-end Charlies," John had said. But he had John's fairness, something of John in the blue eyes and the high curve of the eyebrows, and all of John in his kindness and courtesy. Almost she could imagine that she saw the single-winged emblem of the air gunner on his chest. He said:

"They've been questioning you again about the murders, I suppose. Did they give you a bad time?"

"Oh no, it wasn't at all like that."

She explained the purpose of her visit, finding it easy to talk to him about Darren, their walks along the towpath, their visits to the church, her need to see him. She said:

"Inspector Miskin couldn't do anything about the local authority, but she told me where Darren goes to school. She was really very kind."

"The police are never kind, only when it suits them. They weren't kind to me. You see, they think I know something. They've got a theory. They think my sister might have done it, she and her lover together."

Miss Wharton cried:

"Oh no! But that's a terrible idea. Surely not a woman—and his own wife! A woman couldn't have done it, not this murder. Surely they can't think that."

"Perhaps not. Perhaps they're only pretending to think it. But they're trying to make me say that she confided in me, confessed even. We're very close, you see; we always have been. We only have each other. They know she'd tell me if she were in any trouble."

"But that's awful for you. I can't believe that Commander Dalgliesh really believes that."

"He needs to make an arrest, and the wife or husband is always the obvious suspect. I've had a couple of bad hours."

Miss Wharton had finished her sherry, and, miraculously it seemed, another was in its place. She took a sip and thought: You poor dear. You poor young man. He, too, was drinking, a paler liquid in a tumbler, mixed with water. Perhaps it was whisky. Now he put down the glass and leaned across the table towards her. She could smell the spirit on his breath, masculine, sour, a little disquieting. He said:

"Talk to me about the murders. Tell me what you saw, what it was like."

She could feel his need, strong as a force; and her own need rose to meet it. She, too, needed to talk. She had spent too many sleepless nights fighting off horror, willing herself not to think about it, not to remember. It was better to open that vestry door again and confront reality. So she told him, whispering it across the table. She was back again in that slaughterhouse. She described it all: the wounds like flaccid mouths, Harry Mack with his rigid breastplate of dried blood, the stench, more insistent in imagination than it had been in reality, the pale lifeless hands, drooping like flowers. He leaned over the table towards her, mouth to mouth. Then she said:

"And that's all I can remember. Nothing that happened before, nothing afterwards, only the dead bodies. And afterwards, when I dream about them, they're always naked, quite naked. Isn't that extraordinary?"

She gave a little giggle and lifted her glass carefully to her lips.

She heard him sigh as if the dreadful recital had released something in him. He leaned back in his chair, breathing heavily as if he had been running. Then he said:

"And you didn't go into the room, the vestry where they were found?"

"That's what the Commander kept asking us. He even looked at the soles of our shoes. That wasn't at first, he did that just before we left. And then next day a policeman came and took the shoes away. Wasn't that strange?"

"They were looking for blood."

"Oh yes," she said sadly, "there was so much blood."

Again, he leaned across the table towards her, his face pale and intent. She could see a small bleb of mucus at the corner of the left eye, a dewing of moisture along the upper lip. She took another gulp of the sherry. How warming, how comforting it was. He said:

"Whoever did that, whoever it was, he can't be an ordinary, common intruder. This murder was carefully planned, brilliantly planned too. You're looking for someone with intelligence and nerve. To come back into that room, naked, razor in hand. To confront him, and then to kill. My God, it must have taken courage!" He leaned towards her even closer. "You must see that. You do see it, don't you?"

Courage, she thought. But courage was a virtue. Could a man be as evil as this and yet show courage? She would have to ask Father Barnes, except that it wasn't so easy to talk to Father Barnes nowadays. But it was easy to talk to this young man looking at her with John's eyes.

She said:

"I had a feeling while Darren and I were sitting there in the church waiting to be interviewed that there was something he knew, something he was keeping back, something he was feeling . . . well, perhaps a little guilty about."

"You've told the police about this?"

"Oh no, I haven't told them. It would sound so stupid. There isn't anything he could be keeping back, not really. We were together the whole time."

"But he might have noticed something, something you didn't see."

"But then the police would have seen it too. It's just a feeling I had. You see, I really know Darren quite well. I know when he's feeling . . . well, a little ashamed. But this time I must be wrong. Perhaps I shall know more when I'm able to see him."

"What are you planning to do? Meet him outside the school?"

"I thought so. The inspector said they come out at three thirty."

"But he'll be with other boys. You know what they are, shouting and rushing home. He might not want to leave the gang. He might be embarrassed to see you waiting there."

Miss Wharton thought: Perhaps he'll be ashamed of me. Boys are so odd. It will be terrible if I see him and he won't stop, won't acknowledge me.

Her companion said:

"Why not write him a note and ask him to meet you at the usual place. He'll know that means the towpath. I could take it to him if you like."

"Oh, could you? But you won't know him."

"I'll give it to one of the other kids to deliver. Give him a tip and tell him it's secret. Or I'll ask one of them to point him out. Darren will get it, I promise. Look, let me write it for you. He can read, can't he?"

"Oh yes, I'm sure he can read. He can read the notices in church. He's really an intelligent little boy. His social worker told Mrs. Kendrick that Darren hasn't been going to school. Apparently his mother moved with him to Newcastle, but she didn't find the same opportunities there for her job so they moved back. But she never told the school, and I'm afraid it was all too easy for Darren to truant. It was naughty of him. But I'm sure he can read."

He crooked his finger. The waiter came on silent feet. A few minutes later he was back with a sheet of headed paper and an envelope. Miss Wharton's glass was taken away and a filled one put in place of it.

He said:

"I'll print the message and your name. That'll make it easier for him. And we'd better say to meet you after school. That will be simpler for him than slipping out in the early morning. I may not be able to contact him today but I shall by tomorrow. Suppose we make it Friday at four o'clock on the towpath. Will that be all right for you?"

"Oh yes, yes, perfectly. And I won't let him be too late home."

He wrote quickly, folded the paper then, without showing it to her, put it in the envelope.

"What is his name?" he asked. "His surname."

"Wilkes. He's Darren Wilkes. And the school is Bollington Road Junior, near Lisson Grove."

She watched while he printed it on the envelope and slipped it into his jacket pocket. He smiled across at her.

"Drink up your sherry," he said, "and don't worry. It's going to be all right. He'll be there. You'll see him, I promise."

As they left the hotel and stepped into the wan sunlight, it seemed to Miss Wharton that she was floating in an ecstasy of gratitude and relief. She was hardly aware of giving him her address, of being handed into a taxi, of the five-pound note being slipped into the cabbie's hand. His face, unnaturally large, blocked the cab window.

"Don't worry," he said again. "I've paid the cabbie. There'll be a little change. And don't forget. It's Friday at four o'clock."

Tears of gratitude sprang to her eyes. She held out her hand, seeking for words, but none came. And then the cab moved forward, jerking her back in her seat, and he was gone. For the whole of the journey home she sat bolt upright, hugging her handbag to her chest as if it symbolized this newfound intoxicating happiness. "Friday," she said aloud. Friday at four.

After the taxi was out of sight, Swayne took out and read the message again, his face expressionless. Then he licked the flap and sealed the envelope. The time and place were exactly as he had said. But the date was the following afternoon—Thursday, not Friday. And it was he, not Miss Wharton, who would be waiting on the towpath.

2

⊠

Ten minutes after Kate got back to her office, Massingham came in. He
and Dalgliesh had been interviewing Swayne. She had concealed her disappointment at being excluded from this first important encounter after
the finding of the new evidence, telling herself that her time would come.
Unless they broke Swayne quickly, the interrogations, carefully structured,
conducted within judges' rules and Force regulations, but planned, varied,
persistent, would continue inexorably day after day until that moment when
they would either have to charge him or, for the time being at least, leave
him in peace. From the look on Massingham's face she would get her
chance. He almost threw the file on the desk, then walked over to the
window as if the spectacular view of Westminster's towers and the curve
of the river could help soothe his frustration.

She said:

"How did it go?"

"It didn't. He sits there with his brief at his side smiling, saying less
and less. Or rather, saying the same thing over and over. 'Yes, Berowne
and I did meet on the riverbank. Yes, we did have a scuffle. He accused
me of seducing Theresa Nolan, and I resented him trying to father his
bastard on me. He went for me as if he were crazy. He was crazy. But
he didn't throw me in the river. Berowne had left before I swam out to
the punt. And I didn't kill him. I was with Miss Matlock all that evening.
I was seen arriving at Campden Hill Square. I took Mrs. Hurrell's telephone
call at eight forty. I was there until I left for the pub. I was seen there
from ten forty-five to closing time. If you think otherwise, prove it.' "

"And his brief, who has he got? Someone from Torrington, Farrell and Penge?"

"No. No one from the Berowne connection. I have a feeling Barbara Berowne is distancing herself from her slightly disreputable brother. He's dredged up a bright young pin-stripe from Maurice and Sheldon, perfectly competent and already calculating his fees. There's nothing like a notorious case for getting your name before the public. His strength is that he really believes his client; that must be a rare pleasure for a brief from that firm. You could see how his mind was working. He doesn't think that Swayne has the guts for this particular murder; he can't believe that the motive is strong enough; he can't see how Swayne could have left Campden Hill Square for long enough to commit the murder and returned without Matlock's knowing; and he certainly can't see why she should lie. But mainly, of course, he makes it plain that he doesn't believe that Berowne was murdered, and in that he's getting to be one of the majority. He and the AC should get together."

And so, thought Kate, we try again to break Evelyn Matlock. And she will sit there, chaperoned by Lady Ursula and advised by the family lawyers, half-obstinate, half-triumphant, with that look of dedicated virtue, enjoying her self-imposed martyrdom. In what cause, she wondered. Hatred, revenge, self-glorification, love? For the first time she faced the realization that the case, the first undertaken by the new squad, could end without an arrest in ignominious failure. Massingham turned from the window.

"There still isn't a single piece of physical evidence linking him to the scene. OK, so he had a motive. So did half a dozen others."

"But if he killed out of hate, surely he couldn't conceal it even now?"

"Oh yes he could, well enough, anyway. He's purged it, hasn't he, the worst of his hatred? He's rid himself of its power. He can sit there smiling, the arrogant bastard, because he's free of his enemy forever. He had himself well under control, but he was exulting like a man in love."

She said:

"He killed him and we know he killed him. But we've got to break the alibi. And more than that, we've got to find some physical evidence."

"Oh, Swayne knows that, none better. He's confident that the evidence doesn't exist. It's all circumstantial. If we'd got anything stronger, we'd have produced it by now. And he's actually saying what other people are thinking, that Berowne got Theresa Nolan pregnant, rejected her, and killed himself, partly out of remorse and partly because the dirt in the *Paternoster Review* warned him that the scandal was going to break. My

God, Kate, if the old man's got this wrong, it'll be one hell of a fuck-up."

She glanced at him in surprise. It was rare to hear him use an obscenity. And she guessed that he wasn't thinking only of the success of the new squad, or of those colleagues in C1, and not the most junior, who wouldn't be unhappy to see the maverick Dalgliesh taken down a peg. He had planned his career as carefully as she had hers, and the last thing he wanted was a spectacular failure chalked up against him. But he should worry, she thought bitterly. He was hardly likely to find himself back in division.

She said:

"They'll hardly hold it against you. You'll be off to the Senior Command Course in January anyway, the next step towards the chairmanship of ACPO."

Chairman or not, she thought bitterly, his eventual promotion into that august body, the Association of Chief Police Officers, could be taken for granted.

He spoke almost as if he had forgotten she was there:

"It's not going to be so easy when my father dies."

"He's not ill, is he?"

"Not ill, but he's over seventy, and a lot of life seems to have gone out of him since my mother died last April. I'd like to move out, buy a flat, but it's difficult just now."

It was the first time he had ever spoken of his family. The confidence surprised her. The fact that he had made it must, she supposed, say something about their changing relationship, but she sensed that it would be imprudent to probe.

She said:

"I shouldn't lose any sleep over the title. You can always disclaim it. Anyway, the police'll find it easier to accommodate Chief Constable the Lord Dungannon than they would Chief Constable Kate Miskin."

He grinned.

"Oh well," he said easily, "you could have chosen to join the Wrens, but you'd hardly expect to end up First Sea Lord. It will come in time, the first woman Chief Constable: about a decade after the first female Archbishop of Canterbury, I'd say. Not in my time, thank God."

She didn't respond to the provocation. She was aware of his sudden glance, then he said:

"What's the matter? Something worrying you?"

Is it obvious? she thought, not altogether pleased at his unusual perception. There was little point in never inviting him to the flat if her mind had become so accessible. She said:

"Miss Wharton turned up while you were with Swayne. She wants to see Darren."

"Well, what's to stop her?"

"His social worker, apparently, in the interests of good social work practice. Miss Wharton's fond of the boy. She obviously understands him. They get on well together. He likes her. D'you wonder his social worker is determined to keep them apart?"

He smiled, amused, a little indulgent, a man in whose privileged life the word "welfare" had meant its dictionary definition, nothing more.

"You really hate them, don't you?"

"Anyway, I told her the name of his school. I suggested she could loiter outside and meet him coming out."

"And you're wondering whether the social services will like it?"

"I know damn well they won't like it. I'm wondering if it was wise." She added, as if to reassure herself: "All right, so she'll hang around the school, and with luck get the chance to walk home with him. I can't see what possible harm it can do."

"None, I should think," he said easily. "No possible harm in the world. Come and have a drink."

But before they could reach the door his telephone rang. He went to answer it, then held out the receiver to Kate.

"It's for you."

Kate took it from him, listened in silence for a minute, then said briefly: "All right, I'll come now."

Watching her face as she put down the receiver, Massingham asked: "What's the matter?"

"It's my grandmother. She's been mugged. That was the hospital. They want me to collect her."

He said with easy sympathy:

"That's tough. Is it serious? Is she all right?"

"Of course she's not all right! She's over eighty and the bastards have mugged her. She's not seriously hurt, if that's what you're asking. But she's not fit to be alone. I'll have to take the rest of today off. Probably tomorrow, too, by the sound of it."

"Can't they get someone else to cope?"

"If there was anyone else they wouldn't be ringing me." Then she added more calmly:

"She brought me up. There is no one else."

"Then you'd better go. I'll tell AD. Sorry about the drink." He added, his eyes still on her face: "It's not going to be convenient."

She said fiercely:

"Of course it's not bloody convenient. You don't have to tell me. When would it ever be?"

Walking beside him down the corridor to her room, she suddenly asked:

"What would happen if your father fell ill?"

"I hadn't thought. I suppose my sister would fly home from Rome."

Of course, she thought. Who else? The resentment against him which she had begun to think was fading spurted into angry life. The case was at last beginning to break, and she wouldn't be there. She might be away only for a day and a half, but it couldn't be at a worse time. And it could be longer, much longer. Looking up at Massingham's carefully controlled face as they parted at her door, she thought: He and AD are on their own now. It'll be like the old days. He might be sorry about our missed drink. But that's all he's sorry about.

3
⊠

Thursday was one of the most frustrating days that Dalgliesh could remember. They had decided to give Swayne a rest and there was no further
interrogation, but a press conference called for the early afternoon had
been particularly difficult. The media were getting impatient, not so much
with the lack of progress as with the lack of information. Either Sir Paul
Berowne had been murdered or he had killed himself. If the latter, then
the family and the police should admit the fact; if the former, it was time
for the new squad to be more forthcoming about their progress in bringing
the murderer to book. Both within and outside the Yard there were snide
comments about the squad's being more noted for its sensitivity than for
its effectiveness. As a super in C1 muttered to Massingham in the bar:

"It'll be a nasty one to leave unsolved, the sort that breeds its own
mythology. Lucky that Berowne was on the right, not the left, or someone
would be writing a book by now to prove that MI5 slit his throat for him."

Even the tidying of loose ends, although satisfying, hadn't lifted his
depression. Massingham had reported on a visit to Mrs. Hurrell. He must
have been persuasive; Mrs. Hurrell had admitted that her husband, in
the hours before his death, had confided in her. There had been a small
bill for posters overlooked when the final accounts were prepared after
the last General Election. It would have put the party's expenses over the
statutory limit and invalidated Berowne's victory. Hurrell had himself covered the discrepancy and had decided to say nothing, but it had been on
his conscience and he had wanted to confess to Berowne before he died.
What purpose he thought would be served by the confession was difficult

to envisage. Mrs. Hurrell wasn't a good liar and Massingham reported that she had been rather unconvincingly insistent that her husband hadn't at any time confided in Frank Musgrave. But it wasn't a path they needed to explore. They were investigating murder not malpractice, and Dalgliesh was convinced that he knew his man.

And Stephen Lampart had been cleared of any possible part in Diana Travers's death. His two guests on the night of the drowning, a fashionable plastic surgeon and his young wife, had been seen by Massingham. They apparently knew him slightly, and between pressing drink on him and the gratifying discovery of shared acquaintances, had confirmed that Stephen Lampart hadn't left the table during the meal and had spent less than a couple of minutes fetching the Porsche while they waited chatting with Barbara Berowne at the door of the Black Swan.

But it was useful to clear this detail out of the way, as it was useful to know from Sergeant Robins's enquiries that Gordon Halliwell's wife and daughter had been drowned while on holiday in Cornwall. Dalgliesh had briefly wondered whether Halliwell could have been Theresa Nolan's father. It had never seemed very likely, but the possibility had had to be explored. These were all loose ends neatly tied up, but the main line of the enquiry was still blocked. The words of the AC rang in his brain as insistent and irritating as a television jingle: "Find me the physical evidence."

Strangely, it was a relief rather than an additional irritation to hear that Father Barnes had telephoned while he was in the press conference and would like to see him. The message was somewhat confused, but hardly more so than Father Barnes himself. Apparently the priest wanted to know whether the Little Vestry could now be unsealed and brought into use and when, if at all, the church was likely to get back the carpet. Would the police arrange for it to be cleaned, or was that a matter for him? Would they have to wait until it had been produced at the trial? Was there a chance that the Criminal Injuries Compensation Board might pay for a new carpet? It seemed odd that even someone as unworldly as Father Barnes should seriously expect the statutory powers of the CICB to include supplying carpets, but, for a man beginning seriously to fear that a murder case might never be brought to trial, this innocent preoccupation with trivia was reassuring, almost touching. He decided on impulse that he might as well call on Father Barnes.

There was no answer at the vicarage and all the windows were dark, and then he remembered from his first visit to the church that the noticeboard had shown Evensong at four on Thursdays. Father Barnes would presumably be in church. And so it proved. The great north door was unbolted, and when he turned the heavy iron handle and pushed it open he was met by the expected waft of incense and saw that the lights were on in the Lady Chapel and that Father Barnes, robed only in his surplice and stole, was leading the responses. The congregation was larger than Dalgliesh had expected and the mutter of voices came to him clearly in a gentle, disjointed murmur. He seated himself in the front row just inside the door and sat to listen in patience to Evensong, that most neglected and aesthetically satisfying portion of the Anglican liturgy. For the first time since he had known it, the church was being used for the purpose for which it had been built. But it seemed to him subtly changed. In the branched candleholder where, only last Wednesday, his single light had burned there was now a double row of candles, some newly lit, others flickering with their last tremulous flame. He felt no impulse to add to the glitter. In their light the Pre-Raphaelite face of the Madonna with her flare of crimped and yellow hair under the high crown shone glossily as if newly painted and the distant voices came to him like the ominous premonitory mutterings of success.

The service was short; there was no address and no singing, and within minutes Father Barnes's voice, as if from a far distance but very clear, perhaps because the words were so familiar, was speaking the Third Collect for aid against all perils:

"Lighten our darkness we beseech Thee, O Lord; And by Thy great mercy defend us from all perils and dangers of this night for the love of Thine only Son, our saviour Jesus Christ."

The congregation murmured their amens, got to their feet and began to disperse. Dalgliesh stood up and moved forward. Father Barnes came briskly up to him in a flutter of white linen. He had certainly gained in confidence, almost, Dalgliesh could believe, in physical stature since their first meeting. Now he looked cleaner, more tidily dressed, even plumper, as if a little and a not unwelcome notoriety had put flesh on his bones. He said:

"How kind of you to come, Commander. I'll be with you in a moment. I just have to clear the offertory boxes. My churchwardens like me to keep to schedule. Not that we expect to find much."

He took a key from his trouser pocket and unlocked the box attached to the votive candlestand in front of the statue of the Virgin, and began counting the coins into a small leather draw-string bag. He said:

"Over three pounds in small change and six one-pound coins. We've never done as well as that before. And the ordinary collections are well up, too, since the murders." His face might make an attempt at solemnity but his voice was as happy as a child's.

Dalgliesh moved with him down the nave to the second candlestand in front of the grille. Miss Wharton, who had finished hanging up the kneelers and straightening the chairs in the Lady Chapel, bustled up beside him. As Father Barnes unlocked the box, she said:

"I don't expect there will be more than eighty pence. I used to give Darren a tenpenny piece to light a candle, but really no one else uses this box. He loved stretching his hands out through the grille and striking the match. He could just reach. It's funny, but I'd forgotten about that until now. I suppose it was because he didn't have time to light the candle that dreadful morning. There it is, you see, still unlit."

Father Barnes's hands were busy in the box.

"Only seven coins this time, and a button—rather an unusual one. It looks like silver. I thought at first it was a foreign coin."

Miss Wharton peered closer. She said:

"That must have been Darren. How naughty of him. I remember now, he bent down by the path and I thought he was picking a flower. It really was very wrong of him to steal from the church. Poor child, it must have weighed on his conscience. No wonder I thought he was feeling guilty about something. I'm hoping to see him tomorrow. I'll have a little word about it. But perhaps we should light the candle now, Commander, and say a prayer for the success of your investigation. I think I have tenpence."

She began rummaging in her bag.

Dalgliesh said quietly to Father Barnes:

"May I see the button, Father."

And there at last it was, resting on his palm, the piece of physical evidence they had been seeking. He had seen such a button before, on Dominic Swayne's Italian jacket. A single button. So small a thing, so commonplace, but so vital. And he had two witnesses to its finding. He stood looking at it and there came over him a feeling not of excitement or of triumph, but of immense weariness, of completion.

He said:

"When was this box last cleared, Father?"

"Last Tuesday, it must have been the seventeenth, after morning Mass. As I said, I should have cleared it this Tuesday, but I'm afraid in all the excitement I forgot."

So it had been cleared the morning Berowne was murdered. Dalgliesh said:

"And it wasn't in the box then? Could you have missed it?"

"Oh no, that really wouldn't have been possible. It certainly wasn't there then."

And the whole west end of the church had been closed after the finding of the bodies until today. In theory, of course, someone in the church itself, a member of the congregation or a visitor, could have put the button in the box. But why should they? The obvious box to use, even for a practical joke, was the one in front of the statue of the Virgin. Why walk the length of the nave to the back of the church? And it couldn't have been put in the box by mistake for a coin. No candle had been lit in this stand. But all this was academic. He was countering arguments like a defence counsel. There was surely only one jacket from which this button could have come: it was too great a coincidence to suppose that someone connected with St. Matthew's Church other than Swayne should have dropped it outside the south door.

He said:

"I'm going to place this in one of the envelopes from the Little Vestry and I shall then seal it and ask both of you to sign across the flap. We can unseal the room now, Father."

"You mean, this button is important? It's a clue?"

Miss Wharton said nervously:

"But the owner, do you suppose he'll come looking for it?"

"I don't think for one moment that he's missed it yet. But, even if he has, no one will be in any danger once he knows that the police have it. But I'll send a man round to stay in the church, Father, until we pick him up."

Neither of them asked whose button it was, and he saw no reason to tell them. He went outside to the car and rang Massingham. Massingham said:

"We'd better pick up the boy now."

"Yes, at once. That's the first priority. Then Swayne. And we shall need the jacket. Check the lab report on it, will you, John? There were no buttons missing when we saw Swayne at Campden Hill Square. This is probably the spare. The lab will have noticed if there was a tag on the hem. And see if you can get proof of sale to Swayne. We need the name of the importers and the retailers. But that will probably have to wait now until tomorrow."

"I'll put it in hand, sir."

"But we need a duplicate button now. I'm going to get this one sealed and certified and I haven't a transparent envelope. You recognized the jacket. I suppose it's too much to hope you've got one."

"Much too much. Three hundred–odd quid too much. My cousin has one. I can get hold of a button." He added:

"Do you think there's any danger to Miss Wharton or Father Barnes?"

"Obviously Swayne either hasn't missed the button or has no idea when he lost it. But I'd like someone here in the church until we lay hands on him. But first get hold of Darren and quickly. I'm coming straight back, and then I'd like you to come with me to 62 Campden Hill Square."

"Yes, sir. There's a lot to do. It's a pity we haven't Kate. This tends to happen with women officers, the inconvenient domestic emergency."

Dalgliesh said coldly:

"Not noticeably, John, particularly not with that officer. In twenty minutes then."

4
⊠

It was only the second time since her father's murder that Sarah had called at 62 Campden Hill Square. The first had been on the morning after the news broke. Then there had been a small group of photographers outside the railings, and she had turned instinctively as they had called her name. Next morning she had seen a newspaper picture of herself scurrying fur- tively up the steps like a delinquent housemaid sneaking in at the wrong door under the caption "Miss Sarah Berowne was among the callers today at Campden Hill Square." But now the square was empty of people. The great planes waited in sodden acquiescence for winter, their boughs moving sluggishly in the rain-drenched air. Although the storm was over, the evening was so dark that lights shone palely from first-floor drawing rooms as if it were already night. She supposed that, behind those windows, people lived their secretive, separate, even desperate lives, yet the lights seemed to shine out with the promise of unattainable security.

She had no key. Her father had offered her one when she had walked out, with—or so it had seemed to her at the time—the stiff formality of a Victorian father reluctant to have her under his roof but recognizing that, as an unmarried daughter, she was entitled to his protection and to a room in his house, should she need it. Looking up at the famous facade, at the high elegantly curved windows, she knew that it never had been and that it never could be her home. How much, she wondered, had it really mattered to her father? It had always seemed to her that he lodged in it but had never made it his own any more than it was hers. But had he in boyhood envied his elder brother these dead prestigious stones? Had he lusted after the house as he had lusted after his brother's fiancée? What had he been thinking of when, her mother at his side, he had jammed his foot down on the accelerator at that dangerous corner? What was it out of his past which had finally confronted him in that dingy vestry at St. Matthew's Church?

Waiting for Mattie to answer the door, she wondered how to greet her. It seemed natural to ask "How are you, Mattie?" but the question was meaningless. When had she ever cared how Mattie felt? What possible answer other than an equally meaningless courtesy could she expect? The door opened. Gazing at her with a stranger's eyes, Mattie said her quiet "Good evening." There was something different about her; but then, hadn't they all changed since that awful morning? She had the drained look which Sarah had seen on the face of a friend who had recently given birth, bright-eyed, flushed, but bloated and somehow diminished, as if virtue had gone out of her.

She said:

"How are you, Mattie?"

"I am well, thank you, Miss Sarah. Lady Ursula and Lady Berowne are in the dining room."

The oval dining table was spread with correspondence. Her grand-mother sat stiffly upright, her back to the window. In front of her was a large blotter and to her left boxes of writing paper and envelopes. She was folding a handwritten letter as Sarah came up to her. The girl was intrigued, as always, that her grandmother should be so meticulous over the niceties of social behaviour, having all her life flouted its sexual and religious conventions. Her stepmother apparently either had no letters of condolence to answer or was leaving the chore to someone else. Now she sat at the end of the table preparing to varnish her nails, her hands hes-itating over the ranked bottles. Sarah thought: Surely not blood red? But no, it was to be a soft pink, entirely innocuous, entirely suitable. She ignored Barbara Berowne and said to her grandmother:

"I've come in answer to your letter. The memorial service, it isn't possible. I am sorry, but I shan't be there."

Lady Ursula gave her a long speculative gaze, rather, thought Sarah, as if she were a new lady's maid arriving with somewhat suspect references. Her grandmother said:

"It is not my wish particularly that there should be a memorial service, but his colleagues expect it and his friends seem to want it. I shall be there, and I expect his widow and his daughter to be there with me."

Sarah Berowne said:

"I told you, it's not possible. I'll come to the cremation, of course, but that will be private and for the family only. But I'm not going to display myself suitably clad in black in St. Margaret's Westminster."

Lady Ursula drew a stamp across the dampened pad and stuck it precisely in the right-hand corner of the envelope.

"You remind me of a girl I knew in childhood, the daughter of a bishop. She caused something of a scandal in the diocese when she resolutely refused to be confirmed. What struck me as strange even at thirteen was that she hadn't the wit to see that her scruples had nothing to do with religion. She merely wanted to embarrass her father. That, of course, is perfectly understandable, particularly given the bishop in question. But why not be honest about it?"

Sarah Berowne thought: I shouldn't have come. It was stupid to believe that she would understand or even want to try. She said:

"I suppose, Grandmama, you would have wanted her to conform even if the scruples had been genuine."

"Oh yes, I think so. I would put kindness above what you would call conviction. After all, if the whole ceremony were a charade, which as you know is my opinion, then it could do her no possible harm to let the episcopal hands rest momentarily upon her head."

Sarah said quietly:

"I'm not sure I'd want to live in a world that put kindness before conviction."

"No? But it might be more agreeable than the one we have, and considerably safer."

"Well, this is one charade which I prefer not to have any part in. His politics weren't mine. They still aren't. I should be making a public statement. I shan't be there, and I hope that people will know why."

Her grandmother said drily:

"Those who notice will; but I shouldn't expect too much propaganda value from it. The old will be watching their contemporaries and wondering how long it will be before their turn comes, hoping their bladders will hold out, and the young will be watching the old. But I daresay enough of them will notice your absence to get the message that you hated your father and are pursuing your political vendetta beyond the grave."

The girl almost cried:

"I didn't hate him! Most of my life I loved him, I could have gone on loving him if he had let me. And he wouldn't want me to be there, he wouldn't expect it. He would have hated it himself. Oh, it will all be very tasteful, carefully chosen words and music, the right clothes, the right people, but you won't be celebrating him, not the person, you will be celebrating the class, a political philosophy, a privileged club. You can't get it into your head, you and your kind, that the world you grew up in is dead, it's dead."

Lady Ursula said:

"I know that, my child. I was there in 1914 when it died."

She took the next letter from the top of a pile and, without looking up, went on:

"I've never been a political woman and I can understand the poor and the stupid voting for Marxism or one of its fashionable variants. If you've no hope of being other than a slave, you may as well opt for the most efficient form of slavery. But I must say that I have an objection to your lover, a man who has enjoyed privilege all his life, working to promote a political system which will ensure that no one else gets a chance at what he has so singularly enjoyed. It would be excusable if he were physically ugly; that misfortune tends to breed envy and aggression in a man. But he isn't. I can understand the sexual attraction even if I am fifty years too old to feel it, but you could have gone to bed with him, surely, without taking on all the fashionable baggage."

Sarah Berowne turned wearily away, walked over to the window and looked out over the square. She thought: My life with Ivor and the cell is over, but it was never honest, it never had any reality, I never belonged. But I don't belong here. I'm lonely and I'm afraid. But I have to find my own place. I can't run back to Grandmama, to an old creed, a spurious safety. And she still dislikes and despises me, almost as much as I despise myself. That makes it easier. I'm not going to stand beside her in St. Margaret's like a prodigal daughter.

Then she was aware of her grandmother's voice. Lady Ursula had stopped writing and, leaning both hands on the table, she said:

"Now that you are both here, there is something that I need to ask. Hugo's gun and the bullets are missing from the safe. Does either of you know who has taken them?"

Barbara Berowne's head was buried over her tray of bottles. She glanced up but didn't reply. Sarah, startled, turned quickly round.

"Are you sure, Grandmama?"

Her surprise must have been obvious. Lady Ursula looked at her.

"So you haven't taken it, and presumably you don't know who has?"

"Of course I haven't taken it. When did you find it was missing?"

"Last Wednesday morning, shortly before the police arrived. I thought then that it was possible that Paul had killed himself and that there might be a letter to me with his papers. So I opened the safe. There was nothing new. But the gun had gone."

Sarah asked:

"When was it taken, do you know?"

"I haven't had occasion to look in the safe for some months. That is one reason why I have said nothing to the police. It could have been missing for weeks. It could have had nothing to do with Paul's death, and there was no point in concentrating their attention on this house. Later I had another reason for silence."

Sarah asked:

"What possible other reason could you have had?"

"I thought his murderer might have taken it to use on himself if the police got too close to the truth. That would seem an eminently sensible thing for him to do. I saw no reason to prevent it. Now I think it is time for me to tell Commander Dalgliesh."

"Obviously you must tell him." Sarah frowned, then she said:

"I suppose Halliwell wouldn't have taken it as a sort of memento. You know how devoted he was to Uncle Hugo. He might not like the idea of it getting into someone else's hands."

Lady Ursula said drily:

"Very probably. I share his concern. But whose hands?"

Barbara Berowne looked up and said in her little girl voice:

"Paul threw it away weeks ago. He told me that it wasn't safe to keep it."

Sarah looked at her.

"Nor particularly safe, I should have thought, to throw it away. He could have handed it in to the police, I suppose. But why? He had a licence, and it was perfectly safe where it was."

Barbara Berowne shrugged.

"Well, that is what he said. And it doesn't matter, does it? He wasn't shot."

Before either of the other women could reply, they heard the ring of the front doorbell. Lady Ursula said:

"That may well be the police. If so, they're back rather sooner than I expected. I have a feeling that they may be getting to the end of their enquiries."

Sarah Berowne said roughly:

"You know, don't you? You have always known."

"I don't know, and I have no real evidence. But I am beginning to guess."

They listened in silence for Mattie's footfalls in the marble hall, but she seemed not to have heard the bell. Sarah Berowne said impatiently:

"I'll go. And I hope to God that it is the police. It's time that we faced the truth, all of us."

5

⊠

He went first to the Shepherds Bush flat to collect the gun. He wasn't
sure why he needed it, any more than he was sure why he had stolen
it from the safe. But it couldn't be left at Shepherds Bush; it was time
he found a new hiding place for it. And to have the gun with him reenforced
his sense of power, of being inviolate. The fact that it had once been Paul
Berowne's and was now his made it a talisman as well as a weapon. When
he held it, pointed it, stroked the barrel, something of that first triumph
returned. He needed to feel it again. It was strange how quickly it faded,
so that he was sometimes tempted to tell Barbie what he had done for
her, tell her now, long before it was safe or wise to confide, seeing in
imagination the blue eyes widening with terror, with admiration, with
gratitude and, at last, with love.

Bruno was in his workroom, busy with his latest model. Swayne thought
how disgusting he was with his huge half-naked chest on which a lucky
charm, a silver goat's head on a chain, moved repulsively among the hairs,
his pudgy fingers on which the delicate pieces of cardboard seemed to
stick while he edged them with infinite care into place. Without looking
up, he said:

"I thought you'd moved out for good."

"I have. I'm just collecting the last of my gear."

"I'd like the key, then."

Without speaking, Swayne placed it on the table.

"What shall I say if the police turn up?"

"They won't. They know I've moved out. Anyway, I'm off to Edinburgh
for a week. You can tell them that if they come snooping around."

In the small back room, its walls covered with shelves, which was both Bruno's spare bedroom and a repository for his old models, nothing was ever moved, nothing ever tidied. He stood on the bed to reach the topmost high cluttered shelf, felt under the stage of a model of Dunsinane Castle and drew out the Smith and Wesson and the ammunition. He slipped them into a small canvas bag, together with the last of his socks and a couple of shirts. Then, without a final word to Bruno, he left. It had been a mistake to come in the first place. Bruno had never really wanted him. And the place was a hovel; he wondered how he had stuck it for so long. Paul's bedroom at Campden Hill Square was much more suitable. He ran lightly down the stairs to the front door, rejoicing that he need never enter it again.

He was on the canal path too early, just after three thirty, but it wasn't because he was anxious. He knew that the boy would come. Since the meeting with Miss Wharton, he had had the sensation of being carried along by events, not a mere passenger of fate, but triumphantly borne forward on a crest of luck and euphoria. He had never felt stronger, more confident, more in control. He knew that the boy would come, just as he knew that the meeting would be important in ways that he couldn't at present begin to guess.

Even getting the message to Darren had been easier than he had dared to hope. The school was a two-storey building of grimy Victorian brick set behind railings. He had loitered close but not directly outside, anxious not to attract the attention of the little group of waiting mothers, and hadn't moved up to the gate until he heard the first squeals of the released children. He had chosen a boy as his messenger. A girl, he felt, might be more curious, more noticing, more likely to question Darren about the message. He picked on one of the younger boys and asked:

"Do you know Darren Wilkes?"

"Yeah. He's over there."

"Give him this, will you? It's from his mum. It's important."

He had handed over the envelope with a fifty-pence piece. The boy had taken it with hardly a glance at him, snatching the coin as if afraid that he would change his mind. He had run across the playground to where a boy was kicking a football against the wall. Swayne had watched until he saw the envelope change hands and then had turned and walked quickly away.

He had chosen the meeting place with care: a tangled hawthorn growing close to the canal in whose shelter he could stand and watch the long stretch of path to his right and the forty yards which led to the mouth of the tunnel to his left. Behind him, a few yards to the right, was one of the iron gates to the canal path. His brief exploration had shown that it led to a narrow road bounded by lock-up garages, padlocked yards, the blank faces of anonymous industrial buildings. It wasn't a road to tempt the canal walker on a dark autumn afternoon, and it would give him an escape route from the towpath in case of need. But he wasn't seriously worried. He had been standing here for over twenty minutes and had seen no one.

And the boy, too, was early. Just before ten to four the small figure came into sight, loitering along the canal bank. He looked unnaturally tidy in his obviously new jeans topped with a brown and white zipped jacket. Swayne stepped a little back against the bark of a tree and watched his approach through a shield of leaves. Suddenly he wasn't there, and Swayne felt a wild apprehension until he saw that the boy had climbed down into the ditch and was now reappearing, his hands stretched round the rim of an old cycle wheel. He began bowling it along the towpath. The wheel lurched and bounded. Swayne stepped out of his hiding place and caught it. The boy, no more than twelve yards away, stopped short, looked at him, wary as an animal, seemed about to turn and run. At once Swayne smiled and bowled the wheel back. The boy caught it, still fixing on him his steady unsmiling gaze. Then he swung it round, clumsily twirling, staggered and let it go. It rose out over the water, then fell with a splash which seemed to Swayne so loud that he half expected the canal path to be suddenly alive with people. But there was no one, no calling voices, no running feet.

The ripples widened, then died. He strolled up to the boy and said easily:

"It made a good splash. Do you find many of those in the ditch?"

The boy shifted his glance. Looking out over the canal, he said:

"One or two. Depends."

"You're Darren Wilkes, aren't you? Miss Wharton told me I'd find you here. I was looking for you. I'm an inspector of Special Branch. Do you know what that means?"

He took out his wallet with its credit cards and his old university identity card. How lucky that he'd never given that in after his first and last disastrous semester. It bore his photograph and he flashed it at the boy, not giving him a chance to see more.

"Where is she then, Miss Wharton?"

The question was carefully casual. He didn't want to betray his need, if he had a need. But he had bothered to come. He was here.

Swayne said:

"She can't come. She told me to say that she's sorry, but she isn't feeling very well. Did you bring the note she sent you?"

"What's wrong with 'er then?"

"Only a cold. It's nothing to worry about. Did you bring the note, Darren?"

"Yeah. I've got it."

He thrust a small fist into his jeans pocket and brought it out. Swayne took the crumpled page, glanced at it, then tore it deliberately into small pieces. The boy watched silently as he threw them into the water. They lay on the surface like frail spring petals, then moved sluggishly, darkened, and were lost.

He said:

"Better take no chances. You see, I had to be certain that you really are Darren Wilkes. That's why the note was so important. We have to have a talk."

"What about?"

"The murder."

"I don't know nothin' about the murder. I've talked to the cops."

"The ordinary police, yes, I know. But they're a bit out of their depth. There's more to this than they understand. Much more."

They were moving together slowly upstream towards the entrance to the tunnel. The bushes were thicker here, in one place so thick that even with their summer greenness dropping away, they still provided a safe screen from the path. He drew the boy with him into the semi-darkness and said:

"I'm going to trust you, Darren. That's because I need your help. You see, we in the Special Branch think that this wasn't an ordinary murder. Sir Paul was killed by a gang, a terrorist gang. You know what I mean by the Special Branch, don't you?"

"Yeah. Somethin' to do with spying."

"That's right. It's our job to catch the enemies of the state. It's called special because that's what it is. Special and secret. Can you keep secrets?"

"Yeah. I keep plenty."

The small body seemed to swagger. He looked up at Swayne, the face so like an intelligent monkey, suddenly sharp and knowing.

"Is that why you was there then? Watching 'im?"

The shock was like a physical punch on the chest, painful, disabling. When he could speak Swayne was surprised how calm his voice sounded.

"What makes you think I was there?"

"Them fancy buttons on yer jacket. I found one."

His heart leaped, then for a second seemed to stop, a dead thing in his chest, dragging him down. But then he felt again its regular thudding, pulsing back warmth and life and confidence. He knew now why he was here, why both of them were here. He said:

"Where, Darren? Where did you find it?"

"On the path by the church. I picked it up. Miss Wharton thought I was picking a flower. She never seed me. She give me ten pee for a candle, see, same as always. I always have ten pee for the BVM."

For a moment Swayne's mind seemed to whirl out of control. The boy's words no longer made sense. He saw the peaked face, a sickly green in the gloom of the bush, look up at him with something like contempt.

"The BVM. The statue of the lady in blue. Miss Wharton always give me ten pee for the box. Then I lit a candle, see? For the BVM. Only this time I kept the ten pee and I never 'ad time to light the candle 'cos she called me."

"And what did you do with the button, Darren?"

He had to clench his fists to keep his hands from the boy's neck.

"Put it in the box, didn't I? Only she never knowed. I never tell 'er."

"And you've told no one else?"

"No one arsed me." He looked up again, suddenly sly. "I don't reckon Miss Wharton would like it."

"No. Nor would the police—the ordinary police. They'd call it stealing, taking the money for your own use. You know what they do to boys who steal, don't you? They're trying to get you put away, Darren. They want an excuse to put you in a home. You know that too, don't you? You could be in real trouble. But you keep my secret and I'll keep yours. We'll both swear on my gun."

"You got a gun then?"

For all the childish assumption of nonchalance, he couldn't keep the excitement out of his voice.

"Of course. The Special Branch always go armed."

He drew the Smith and Wesson out of his shoulder bag and held it out in his palm. The boy's eyes fastened on it, fascinated. Swayne said:

"Put your hand on it and swear to tell no one about the button, about me, about this meeting."

The small hand was stretched out eagerly. Swayne watched as it was laid on the barrel. The boy said:

"I swear."

Swayne put his own hand over Darren's and pressed it down. It felt small and very soft and curiously detached from the boy's body, as if it had a separate life like a young animal.

He said solemnly:

"And I swear not to reveal anything that passes between us."

He was aware of the boy's longing. He said:

"Would you like to hold it?"

"Is it loaded?"

"No. I'm carrying the bullets, but it isn't loaded."

The boy took it and began to point it, first at the canal, then with a grin at Swayne, then again over the canal. He held it as he must have seen it held by cops on the television, straight out, grasping it with both hands. Swayne said:

"You've got the right idea. We could do with you in the Branch when you're older."

Suddenly they were aware of the swish of bicycle wheels. Both drew back instinctively into the deeper shelter of the bushes. They had a brief glimpse of a middle-aged man in a cloth cap slowly pedalling against the squelch of the mud, his eyes fixed on the towpath. They stood motionless, hardly breathing, until he had disappeared. But he had reminded Swayne that there wasn't very much time. The canal path could become busier. There could be people taking a shortcut home. He must do what he had to do quickly and silently. He said:

"You want to be careful, playing by the canal. Can you swim?"

The boy shrugged.

"Didn't they teach you how to swim at school?"

"Naw. I ain't been to school that much."

It was almost too easy. He fought back a sudden impulse to laugh aloud. He wanted to lie back there on the mushy earth and gaze upwards through the knotted boughs and shout his triumph. He was invincible, out of their reach, protected by luck and cleverness, and something which had nothing to do with either, but which was now part of him forever. The police couldn't have found the button; if they had they would have confronted him with it, would have taken back the jacket with its tell-tale tag of knotted cotton on the hemline. They must have seen that tag, must have known the spare button was missing when they examined the jacket. But a serious-faced young constable had returned it without comment, and he had worn it almost daily since, feeling superstitiously ill at ease without it. Getting the button wouldn't be difficult. He would first deal with the boy, then go at once to the church. No, not at once. He'd need a chisel to break open the offertory box. He could fetch one from Campden Hill Square, or better, buy one from the nearest Woolworth's. One purchaser among so many wouldn't be noticed. And he wouldn't buy the chisel only. It would be safer to collect a number of small items before queuing at the cash point, that way the cashier would be less likely to remember the chisel. And breaking open the offertory box would look like a simple burglary. It was always happening. He doubted whether anyone would bother to inform the police, and if they did, why should anyone connect it with the murder? And then it struck him that the box might have been emptied. The thought sobered his triumph, but for a moment only. If it had, the button would either have been given to the police or thrown away as useless. And it couldn't have been given to the police, they would have produced it. And even if by ill chance it was still in someone's possession, only the boy knew where it had been found. And the boy would be dead, accidentally drowned, one more child unwisely playing on the canal bank.

He moved out of the shelter of the bushes and the boy followed. On either side the path stretched in empty desolation, the canal sliding thick and brown as sludge between the fretted banks. He shivered. For a second he had been seized with the illusion that no one was coming because there was no one left to come, that he and Darren were the last survivors of a dead, deserted world. Even the silence was eerie, and it struck him that since arriving on the path he hadn't heard the rustle of a single animal, nor the note of a bird.

He was aware that Darren had moved from his side and was squatting beside the water. Pausing beside him, Swayne saw that there was a dead rat caught in the crook of a broken twig; the sleek body, elongated, rippled the surface, its snout pointing like a prow. He squatted beside the boy and they contemplated it in silence. The rat, he thought, looked curiously human in death, with its glazed eye and the small paws raised as if in a last despairing supplication. He said: "Lucky rat," and then it struck him how senseless was that casual statement. The rat, no longer rat, was neither lucky nor unlucky. It didn't exist. No statement about it had any meaning.

He watched while the boy grasped the end of the twig and began moving the body under the water. Then he lifted it. Small eddies broke over its head, and it rose glistening, humpbacked from the suck of the stinking water. He said sharply:

"Don't do that, Darren."

The boy let go the twig and the rat plopped back and began drifting sluggishly downstream.

They walked on. And then suddenly his heart lurched. Darren darted from his side and with a high shout ran leaping into the tunnel mouth. For one appalled second Swayne thought that his victim must have divined his purpose and was dashing to escape. He rushed after him into the semi-darkness; and then he breathed easily again. Darren, whooping and hollering, was running his hands along the tunnel wall, then leaping, arms outflung, in a vain attempt to touch the roof. In his relief Swayne almost leaped with him.

And this, of course, was the place, none better. He would need only a minute, perhaps only seconds. It would have to be swift and sure. Nothing must be left to chance; he would have to do more than merely throw him in. He would need to kneel and hold the head under the water. The boy might struggle, but it would only be brief. He looked too frail to put up much of a struggle. He slipped his arms out of his jacket and folded it over his shoulder; there was no sense in getting an expensive jacket splashed. But the edge of the towpath was concrete here, not earth. He would be able to kneel if necessary without the risk of getting tell-tale mud on his trousers.

He called quietly:

"Darren."

The boy, still leaping at the roof, took no notice. Swayne had drawn breath to call again when suddenly the small figure in front of him swayed, crumpled, fell, silently as a leaf, and lay still. His first thought was that Darren was playing games; but when he came up to him he saw that the boy had fainted. He lay sprawled, so close to the canal that one thin arm was flung out over it, the small half-clenched fist almost touching the water. He was so motionless that he could have been dead; but Swayne knew that he would have recognized death when he saw it. He squatted and gazed intently into the still face. The boy's mouth was moistly open and he thought he could hear the gentle sigh of the breath. In the half-light the freckles stood out against the whiteness of the skin like splashes of gold paint, and he could just see the sparse lashes spiked against the cheek. He thought: There must be something wrong with him. He's sick.

Boys don't faint for no reason. And then he was visited by a sensation which was half pity, half anger. Poor little bastard. They drag him before the juvenile court, put him under supervision, and they can't even look after him. They can't even see he's sick. Sod them. Sod the whole fucking lot of them.

But now that what he had to do was made easier than ever, no more than a gentle nudge away, it had suddenly become difficult. He put his foot under the boy and lifted him gently. The body rose on his shoe, seemingly weightless, so that he could hardly feel it. But Darren didn't stir. One tip, he thought, one small thrust. If he had believed in a god, he would have said to him: "You shouldn't have made it this easy. Nothing should be this easy." It was very quiet in the tunnel. He could hear the slow drip of moisture from the roof, the faint slap of the canal against the pavement edge, the clicking of his digital watch, loud as a time bomb. The smell of the water came up to him, strong and sour. The two half-moons gleaming at the tunnel ends seemed suddenly very far away. He could imagine them receding and shrinking into thin curves of light, and then fading completely, leaving him and the quietly breathing boy sealed up together in black, damp-smelling nothingness.

And then he thought: Do I need to do it? He hasn't done me any harm. Berowne deserved to die, but he doesn't. And he won't talk. The police have lost interest in him, anyway. And once I have the button, it won't matter if he does talk. It will be his word against mine. And without the button, what can they prove? He plucked the jacket from his shoulder and knew as he felt the slip of the lining against his arms that this was the decisive action. The boy would be allowed to live. He savoured for one extraordinary moment a new sensation of power, and it seemed to him sweeter, more exhilarating than even the moment when he had finally turned to gaze down on Berowne's body. This was what it felt like to be a god. He had the power to take life or to bestow it. And this time he had chosen to be merciful. He was giving the boy the greatest gift in his power, and the boy wouldn't even know that it was he who had given it. But he would tell Barbie. Someday, when it was safe, he would tell Barbie, about the life he had taken, the life he had graciously spared. He pulled the body a little further from the water's edge and heard the boy moan. The eyelids flickered. As if afraid to meet the opening gaze, Swayne sprang to his feet, then almost ran to the tunnel end, suddenly desperate to gain that half-moon of light before the darkness closed in on him forever.

6
⊠

It was Sarah Berowne who let them in. Without speaking, she led them across the hall to the library. Lady Ursula was seated at the dining room table on which were stacked letters and documents in three neat piles. Some of the writing paper was edged with black, as if the family had rummaged in their drawers for the mourning paper which must have been fashionable in her youth. As Dalgliesh entered she looked up and gave him a nod, then inserted her silver paper knife in yet one more envelope, and he heard the faint rasp as the paper split open. Sarah Berowne walked over to the window and stood looking out, her shoulders hunched. Beyond the rain-washed panes the heavy swathes of the sycamores drooped dankly in the drenched air, the dead leaves torn by the storm hanging like brown dusters among the green. It was very quiet. Even the hiss of the traffic on the avenue was muted like a spent tide on a far distant shore. But inside the room some of the heaviness of the day seemed still to linger and the diffused frontal headache which had plagued him since the morning intensified and focused behind his right eye, a stabbing needle of pain.

He had never felt in this house an atmosphere of peace or ease, but now the tension quivered on the air. Barbara Berowne alone seemed impervious to it. She, too, was sitting at the table. She was painting her nails; small gleaming bottles and tufts of cotton wool were set out before her on a tray. As he entered, the brush was for a moment poised, its bright tip motionless in the air.

Without looking round, Sarah Berowne said:

"My grandmother is concerned, among other matters, with the arrangements for the memorial service. I suppose you have no views, Commander, on the relative appropriateness of 'Fight the Good Fight' and 'O Lord and Master of Mankind'?"

Dalgliesh walked across to Lady Ursula and held out the button on the palm of his hand. He said:

"Have you seen a button like this, Lady Ursula?"

She beckoned him nearer, then bent her head close to his fingers as if about to smell the button. Then she looked up at him expressionlessly and said:

"Not to my knowledge. It looks as if it came from a man's jacket, probably an expensive one. I can offer no other help."

"And you, Miss Berowne?"

She came over from the window, looked at it briefly and said:

"No, it isn't mine."

"That wasn't my question. I asked if you'd seen it, or one like it."

"If I have, I can't remember. But then, I'm not very interested in clothes or in trivia. Why not ask my stepmother?"

Barbara Berowne was holding up her left hand and blowing gently on her nails. Only the thumbnail remained unpainted. It looked like a dead deformity among the four pink tips. As Dalgliesh came up to her she took up the brush and began to draw careful sweeps of pink along the thumbnail. This done, she glanced at the button, then turned quickly away and said:

"It isn't off anything of mine. I don't think it belonged to Paul either. I haven't seen it before. Is it important?"

She was, he knew, lying, but not, he thought, through fear or any sense of danger. For her, to lie when in doubt was the easiest, even the most natural, response, a way of buying time, fending off unpleasantness, postponing trouble. He turned to Lady Ursula:

"I should like to speak to Miss Matlock, too, please."

It was Sarah Berowne who went across to the fireplace and tugged at the bell.

When Evelyn Matlock came in, all three Berowne women turned as one and gazed at her. She stood for a moment, her eyes fixed on Lady Ursula, then marched across to Dalgliesh stiff as a soldier on a charge. He said:

"Miss Matlock, I'm going to ask you a question. Don't answer it in a hurry. Think carefully before you speak and then tell me the truth."

She glared at him. It was the look of a recalcitrant child, obstinate, malicious. He couldn't remember when he had seen so much hate in a face. Again he took his hand from his pocket and held out on his palm the silver-crested button. He said:

"Have you ever seen this button or one like it?"

He knew that Massingham's eyes as well as his own would be fixed on her face. It was easy to speak a lie, one short syllable. To act a lie was more difficult. She could just about control the tone of her voice, could make herself look up and gaze resolutely into his eyes, but the damage was already done. He hadn't missed that instantaneous flicker of recognition, the small start, the quick flush across the forehead; that, most of all, was beyond her control. As she paused, he said:

"Come closer, look at it carefully. It's a distinctive button, probably from a man's jacket. Not the kind you find on ordinary jackets. When did you last see one like it?"

But now her mind was working. He could almost hear the process of thought.

"I can't remember."

"Are you saying that you can't remember seeing a button like this, or that you can't remember when you saw it last?"

"You're muddling me."

She turned her face to Lady Ursula, who said:

"If you want a lawyer before you answer, you're entitled to one. I can ring Mr. Farrell."

She said:

"I don't want a lawyer. Why should I want a lawyer? And if I did, I wouldn't choose Anthony Farrell. He looks at me as if I'm dirt."

"Then I suggest you answer the Commander's question. It seems a plain enough one to me."

"I've seen something like it. I can't remember where. There must be hundreds of similar buttons."

Dalgliesh said:

"Try to remember. You think you've seen something like it. Where? In this house?"

Massingham, carefully avoiding Dalgliesh's eyes, must have been awaiting his moment. His voice was a careful balance of brutality, contempt and amusement.

"Are you his mistress, Miss Matlock? Is that why you're shielding him? Because you are shielding him, aren't you? Is that how he paid you, a quick half hour on your bed between his bath and his supper? He was getting it cheap, wasn't he, his alibi for murder."

No one did it better than Massingham. Every word was a calculated insult. Dalgliesh thought: My God, why do I always let him do my dirty work for me?

The woman's face flared. Lady Ursula laughed, a tiny cackle of derision. She spoke to Dalgliesh:

"Really, Commander, apart from being offensive, I find that suggestion ridiculous. It's grotesque."

Evelyn Matlock turned on her, hands clenched, her body quivering with resentment:

"Why is it ridiculous, why is it grotesque? You can't bear to believe it, can you? You've had lovers enough in your time, everyone knows that. You're notorious. Well, you're old now, crippled and ugly and no one wants you, man or woman, and you can't bear to think that someone might want me. Well, he did and he does. He loves me. We love each other. He cares. He knows what my life is like in this house. I'm tired, I'm overworked and I hate you all. You didn't know that, did you? You thought I was grateful. Grateful for the job of washing you like a baby, grateful for waiting on a woman too idle to pick up her own underclothes from the floor, grateful for the worst bedroom in the house, grateful for a home, a bed, a roof, the next meal. This place isn't a home. It's a museum. It's dead. It's been dead for years. And you think of no one but yourselves. Do this, Mattie, fetch that, Mattie, run my bath, Mattie. I do have a name. He calls me Evelyn. Evelyn, that's my name. I'm not a cat or a dog, I'm not a household pet." She turned on Barbara Berowne: "And what about you? There are things I could tell the police about that cousin of yours. You planned to get Sir Paul even before your fiancé was buried, before his own wife was dead. You didn't sleep with him. Oh no, you were too cunning for that. And what about you, his daughter? How much did you care about him? Or that lover of yours? You only used him to hurt your father. Not one of you knows what caring is, what love is." She turned again on Lady Ursula: "And then there's Daddy. I'm supposed to be grateful for what your son did. But what did he do? He couldn't even keep Daddy out of prison. And prison was torture for him. He was claustrophobic. He couldn't take it. He was tortured to death. And how much do you care, any of you? Sir Paul thought that giving me a job, a home, what you call a home, was enough. He thought he was paying for his mistake. He never did pay. I did all the paying."

Lady Ursula said:

"I didn't know that you felt like this. I should have known. I blame myself."

"Oh no you don't! Those are just words. You never have blamed yourself. Not ever. Not for anything. Not all your life. Yes, I did sleep with him. And I shall again. You can't stop me. It's no affair of yours. You don't own me body and soul, you only think you do. He loves me and I love him."

Lady Ursula said:

"Don't be ridiculous. He was using you. He used you to get a free meal, a hot bath, his clothes washed and ironed. And in the end he used you to get an alibi for murder."

Barbara Berowne had finished her manicure. Now she surveyed her finished nails with the pleased complacency of a child. Then she looked up.

"I know that Dicco made love to her, he told me. Of course he didn't murder Paul, that's silly. That's what he was doing when Paul died. He was making love to her on Paul's bed."

Evelyn Matlock swung round on her. She cried:

"It's a lie. He couldn't have told you. He wouldn't have told you."

"Well, he did. He thought it would amuse me. He thought it was funny."

She looked at Lady Ursula, a conspiratorial glance of mingled amusement and contempt, as if inviting her to share a private joke. Barbara Berowne's high, childish voice went on:

"I asked him how he could bear to touch her, but he said he could make love to any woman if he shut his eyes and imagined it was someone else. He said he kept his mind on the hot bathwater and a free meal. Actually, he didn't mind the love-making. He said she hasn't a bad figure and he could quite enjoy it as long as he kept the light off. It was all the sloppy talk, all that messing over him afterwards that he couldn't bear."

Evelyn Matlock had sunk down on one of the chairs against the wall. She put her face in her hands, then looked up into Dalgliesh's face and said in a voice so low that he had to bend his head to hear:

"He did go out that night, but he told me he wanted to talk to Sir Paul. He wanted to find out what was going to happen to Lady Berowne.

He told me they were dead when he arrived. The door was open and they were dead. They were both dead. He loved me. He trusted me. Oh God, I wish he'd killed me too."

Suddenly she began crying, great retching sobs which seemed to tear her chest apart and rose to a whopping crescendo of agony. Sarah Berowne moved swiftly over to her and awkwardly cradled her head. Lady Ursula said:

"This noise is appalling. Take her to her room."

As if the half-heard words were a threat, Evelyn Matlock made some attempt to control herself. Sarah Berowne looked across to Dalgliesh and said:

"But surely he couldn't have done it. There wouldn't have been time to commit the murders, clean up afterwards. Not unless he went by car or by bicycle. He'd never have risked a cab. And if he took the cycle, Halliwell must have seen or heard him."

Lady Ursula said: "Halliwell wasn't there to hear him."

She lifted the receiver and dialled a number. They heard her say: "Could you please come over, Halliwell."

No one spoke. The only sound in the room was Miss Matlock's muted sobbing. Lady Ursula looked at her with a calmly speculative gaze, without pity, almost, it seemed to Dalgliesh, without interest.

And then they heard footsteps on the marble floor of the hall and Halliwell's stocky figure stood in the doorway. He was wearing jeans and a short-sleeved, open-necked shirt, and stood there completely at ease. The dark eyes flicked briefly from the police to the three Berownes, then to the sobbing, huddled figure in Sarah Berowne's arms. Then he closed the door and looked calmly at Lady Ursula, undeferential, relaxed, wary, shorter than the other two men, but seeming in his calm self-confidence momentarily to dominate the room.

Lady Ursula said:

"Halliwell drove me to St. Matthew's Church on the night my son died. Describe to the Commander what happened, Halliwell."

"Everything, my lady?"

"Of course."

He spoke directly to Dalgliesh:

"Lady Ursula rang me at ten to six and asked me to have the car ready. She said that she would come out to the garage and we were to leave as quietly as possible by the back door. When she was seated in the car she said that I was to drive to St. Matthew's Church, Paddington. It was necessary for me to consult the road map and I did so."

So they had left, thought Dalgliesh, nearly an hour before Dominic Swayne had arrived. The flat over the garage would have been empty. Swayne would have assumed that Halliwell had already left for his next day's leave. The chauffeur went on:

"We arrived at the church and Lady Ursula asked me to park outside the south door at the back. Her ladyship rang the bell and Sir Paul answered it. She went inside. About half an hour later she returned and asked me to join them. That must have been about seven o'clock. Sir Paul was there with another man, a tramp. There was a sheet of paper on the table covered with about eight lines of handwriting. Sir Paul said he was about to sign his name and wanted me to witness his signature. Then he signed and I wrote my name underneath. The tramp did the same."

Lady Ursula said:

"It was fortunate that Harry could write. But then he was an old man. He was at a state school when the young were taught these skills."

Dalgliesh asked:

"Was he sober?"

It was Halliwell who answered.

"His breath smelt, but he was steady enough on his feet, and he could write his name. He wasn't so drunk that he didn't know what he was doing."

"Did you read what was written on the paper?"

"No sir. It wasn't my business to read it and I didn't."

"How was it written?"

"Apparently with Sir Paul's fountain pen. He used the pen to sign his name and then handed it to me and to the tramp. When we had signed, he blotted the paper. Then the tramp went out through the door to the right of the fireplace and Lady Ursula and I left. Sir Paul stayed in the vestry. He didn't see us to the door. Lady Ursula then said that she would like to be taken for a drive before returning home. We drove to Parliament Hill Fields and then to Hampstead Heath. She sat in the car on the edge of the heath for about twenty minutes. Then I drove her home and we arrived back about half past nine. Lady Ursula asked me to drop her at the front door so that she could enter the house unobserved. She told me to park the car in Campden Hill Square and I did so."

So they had been able to leave and return unobserved. And she had asked for her supper to be brought up on a tray, the thermos of soup, the smoked salmon. No one would disturb her until Miss Matlock came to put her to bed.

He said to Halliwell:

"After you had signed that paper, did Sir Paul say anything?"

Halliwell looked at Lady Ursula but, this time, he got no help. Dalgliesh asked again:

"Did he say anything, to you, to Harry Mack, to his mother?"

"Harry wasn't there. Like I said, he signed and stumbled off. Not much of a man, I'd say, for company or conversation. Sir Paul did speak, to her ladyship. Only the three words. He said: 'Look after him.' "

Dalgliesh looked across at Lady Ursula. She was sitting very still, her hands in her lap, looking out across the room beyond the green tapestry of the trees to some imagined future, and he thought he saw the trace of a smile on her lips. He turned again to Halliwell:

"So you now admit that you lied when I asked if a car or the bicycle could have been taken out that night? You lied about being in your flat the whole of that evening?"

Halliwell said calmly:

"Yes sir, I lied."

Lady Ursula broke in:

"I asked him to lie. What had happened between me and my son in that vestry wasn't relevant to his death, whether or not he killed himself. It seemed to me important that you should spend your time and effort finding his killer, not meddling in the private affairs of the family. My son was alive when I left him. I asked Halliwell to say nothing about our visit. He is a man accustomed to obeying orders."

Halliwell said:

"Some orders, my lady."

He looked across at her and gave her a grim fleeting smile. She answered his glance with a small, self-satisfied nod. It seemed to Dalgliesh that they were for a moment oblivious to anyone else in the room, united in their private conspiratorial world which had its own compulsions. They stood together now as they had from the first. And he had no doubt what it was that bound them. Hugo Berowne had been his commanding officer; she was Sir Hugo's mother. He would have done a great deal more than lie for her.

They had almost forgotten Barbara Berowne. But now she sprang up from the table and almost threw herself at Dalgliesh. The pink fingers scrabbled at his jacket. The spurious sophistication dropped away and he was being clutched by a frightened child. She cried:

"It isn't true, he didn't do it! Dicco didn't leave the house. Can't you see? Mattie is jealous because he never really cared for her. How could he? Look at her. And the family have always hated him, him and me." She turned to Lady Ursula. "You never wanted him to marry me. You never thought I was good enough for your precious sons, either of them. Well, this house is mine now, and I think it would be better if you left."

Lady Ursula said quietly:

"I'm afraid it isn't."

With difficulty she turned and lifted the strap of her handbag from the back of her chair. They watched as the distorted fingers fumbled at the clip. Then she took out a folded sheet of paper. She said:

"What my son signed was his will. You are adequately, but not extravagantly, provided for. This house and the rest of his property is left to me in trust for his unborn child. If that child does not survive, then it comes to me."

Barbara Berowne had tears brimming her eyes, a frustrated child. She cried:

"Why did he do it? How did you make him?"

But it was to Dalgliesh that Lady Ursula turned as if it were he who was owed the answer. She said:

"I had gone there to remonstrate with him, to make sure that he knew about the child, knew whether it was his, to ask what he intended. It was the presence of the tramp that gave me the idea. You see, I had the necessary two witnesses. I told him: 'If she's carrying your child, I want to ensure that he's born safely. I want to safeguard his future. If you should die tonight, she'll inherit everything and your child will have Lampart as a stepfather. Is that what you want?' He didn't reply. He sat down at the table. I took a sheet of paper from the top drawer of the desk and placed it in front of him. Without speaking, he wrote out the will, just the eight lines. A reasonable annual income for his wife and everything else in trust for the child. He may have wanted to get rid of me; I think he did. He may have been beyond caring; that is possible. He may have taken it for granted that he would be alive to make more formal arrangements next day. Most of us make that assumption. Or he may, somehow, have known that he wouldn't survive the night. But that, of course, is ridiculous."

Dalgliesh said:

"You lied about speaking to Halliwell later that evening. Once the bodies were discovered you knew that he could be at risk. He would lie at your request. You felt you owed him at least an alibi. And you lied about your son's diary. You know that it was in this house at six o'clock that evening. You went down to the study and took it from the desk drawer when the general telephoned."

She said:

"At my age the memory is bound to be a little defective." She added, with what sounded like grim satisfaction: "I don't think I've ever lied to the police before. My class seldom has the need to. But if we do, then I can assure you that we're quite as ready to and just as good at it, probably better, than other people. But then I don't think you've ever doubted that."

Dalgliesh said:

"You were waiting, of course, to see how much we had discovered, to be sure that your grandchild's mother wasn't a murderess or the accomplice of a murderer. You knew that you were concealing vital information, information which could have helped your son's butcher go free. But that wouldn't have mattered, would it? Not if the family line continued, not if your daughter-in-law produced an heir."

She corrected him gently:

"A legitimate heir. It may not seem very important to you, Commander, but I am over eighty and we have different priorities. She isn't an intelligent woman, not even an admirable one, but she'll be an adequate mother, I'll see to that. He'll do all right. He'll survive. But to grow up knowing that your mother was her lover's accomplice in the brutal murder of your father, that's not a heritage any child could cope with. I didn't intend that my grandson should have to cope with it. Paul asked me to look after his son. That is what I have been doing. There is a peculiar authority about the last wishes of the recently dead. In this case they coincided with my own."

"That is all you care about?"

She said:

"I am eighty-two, Commander. The men I have loved are all dead. What on earth else is left for me to care about?"

Dalgliesh said:

"We shall want new statements, of course, from all of you."

"Naturally, you people always want statements. Aren't you sometimes in danger of believing that everything important in life can be put down in words, signed and admitted in evidence? I suppose that's the attraction of the job. All the messy, incomprehensible muddle reduced to words on a sheet of paper, exhibits with tags and numbers. But you're a poet—or were once. You can't possibly believe that what you deal in is the truth."

Dalgliesh said:

"Dominic Swayne is living here now, isn't he? Do any of you know where he is?" There was no reply. "Then we shall leave a police officer here until he returns."

It was then that the telephone began ringing. Barbara Berowne gave a gasp and glanced from the instrument to Dalgliesh with something very like fear. Lady Ursula and Sarah Berowne ignored it as if neither the room nor anything in it was any longer their concern. Massingham moved over to it and lifted the receiver. He gave his name, listened in silence for a couple of minutes during which no one moved, then spoke so quietly that the words were unintelligible and replaced the receiver. Dalgliesh moved over to him. Massingham said very quietly:

"Darren has arrived home, sir. He won't say where he's been and Robins says it's obvious he's hiding something. His mother isn't back yet and no one knows where she is. They're trying her usual pubs and clubs. Two officers are staying with Darren until we pick up Swayne, and they've rung the social services to try to contact his supervisor. No luck there. It's after office hours."

"And Swayne?"

"No trace yet. That designer he shared a flat with says that he looked in at Shepherds Bush earlier to collect his gear. Said he was off to Edinburgh."

"Edinburgh?"

"He has friends there, apparently, people he met when he was doing a fringe show at this year's festival. Robins is in touch with Edinburgh. They may be able to pull him off the train."

"If he took it."

He walked over to Evelyn Matlock. She lifted to him a face devastated by grief, and he saw in her eyes something so like trust that it turned his heart over. He said:

"He used your affection for him to make you lie for him; that was a betrayal. But what he felt for you and what you felt for him is your business and his, no one else's, and no one but you can know the truth about it."

She said, looking up at him, willing him to understand:

"He did need me. He never had anyone else. It was love. It was love."

Dalgliesh didn't reply.

Then she said in a voice so low that he could hardly catch the words:

"He did take a box of matches with him when he left. I wouldn't have known, only the electric kettle in the kitchen was broken. Halliwell was mending it for me. I had to light the gas with a match and I needed a new box. The one by the stove was missing."

She began to cry again, but now almost soundlessly, a stream of silent tears washing down her face as if she wept out of a weariness and hopelessness that had gone beyond pain.

But there were still questions that he needed to ask and to ask now, while she had passed beyond the extremity of misery and loss into an acceptance of defeat. He said:

"When Mr. Swayne arrived, did he go alone into any part of the house other than your sitting room and the kitchen?"

"Only to take his toilet bag to the bathroom."

So he would have had the chance to enter the study. He asked:

"And when he came back, was he carrying anything?"

"Only his evening paper. He had it with him when he arrived."

But why not leave it in the back of the house? Why carry a newspaper with him to the bathroom unless he proposed to use it to conceal something, a book, a file, private letters? Suicides commonly destroyed their papers; he would find something in the house to take with him and burn. It had probably been fortuitous that he had opened the drawer and found the diary ready to hand.

He turned to Sarah Berowne and said:

"Miss Matlock is obviously distressed. I think she would like a cup of tea. Perhaps one of you could go to the trouble of making it for her."

She said:

"You despise us, don't you? Every one of us."

He said:

"Miss Berowne, I am in this house as an investigating officer. I have no other right here and no other function."

He and Massingham had reached the door before Lady Ursula spoke, her voice high, unwavering.

"Before you leave, Commander, I think you should know that a gun is missing from the study safe. It belonged to my elder son, a Smith and Wesson .08. My daughter-in-law tells me that Paul got rid of it, but I think it would be safer to assume that she is—" She paused and then added with delicate irony, "That she is mistaken."

Dalgliesh turned to Barbara Berowne.

"Could your brother have got hold of it? Did he know the combination of the safe?"

"Of course he didn't. Why should Dicco want it? Paul got rid of it. He told me. He thought it was dangerous. He threw it away. He threw it in the river."

Lady Ursula spoke as if her daughter-in-law were not present.

"I think you can assume that Dominic Swayne knows the combination of the safe. My son changed it three days before he died. He had the habit of noting the new combination in pencil on the last page of his diary until he was sure that he and I had memorized it. His practice was to circle the digits on next year's calendar. That was the page which I think you showed me, Commander, had been torn out."

7
⊠

It was nearly five o'clock by the time he had bought the chisel, the strongest
the shop had on display. There hadn't in the end been time to get to a
Woolworth's, but he had told himself that it didn't matter and bought the
chisel in a hardware shop off the Harrow Road. The assistant might remember him, but then, who was going to ask? The theft would be seen
as an unimportant break-in. And afterwards he would throw the chisel
in the canal. Without the chisel to match with the marks on the edge
of the box, how could they possibly link him with the crime? It was too
long for his jacket pocket, so he placed it with the gun in the canvas bag.
It amused him to carry over his shoulder that innocuous commonplace
bag, to feel the weight of the gun and the chisel bumping against his
side. He had no fear of being stopped. Who would want to stop him, a
respectably dressed young man walking quietly home at the end of the
day? But the assurance was more deeply rooted. He walked the drab streets
head high, invincible, and could have laughed aloud at the grey, stupid
faces, staring ahead as they passed him, or bent to the ground as if instinctively searching the pavement in the hope of finding a dropped coin.
They were corralled in their hopeless lives, endlessly trudging the same
bare perimeters, slaves of routine and convention. He alone had had the
courage to break free. He was a king among men, a free spirit. And in
a few hours he would be on his way to Spain to the sun. No one could
stop him. The police had nothing to justify holding him, and now the
only physical evidence linking him with the scene of crime was within
his reach. He had enough money to last for the next two months and

then he would write to Barbie. The time wasn't ripe to tell her yet, but one day he would tell her and it had to be soon. The need to tell someone was becoming an obsession. He had nearly confided in that pathetic spinster over drinks at the St. Ermin's Hotel. Afterwards he had been almost frightened by that urge to confess, to have someone marvel at his brilliance, his courage. He would tell Barbie. It was Barbie who had a right to know. He would tell her that she owed her money, her freedom, her future to him. She would know how to be grateful.

The afternoon was so dark now that it could have been night, the sky thick and furred as a blanket, the air heavy to breathe and with the sharp metallic taste of the coming storm. Just as he turned the corner of the road and saw the church, it broke. The air and sky glittered with the first flash of lightning, then almost at once there came the crack of thunder. Two large drops stained the pavement in front of him and the rain sheeted down. He ran into the shelter of the church porch, laughing aloud. Even the weather was on his side; the main approach road to the church had been empty, and now he looked out from the porch into a wash of rain. Already the terraced houses seemed to shiver behind a curtain of water. From the glistening road spurts rose like fountains and the gutters ran and gurgled in torrents.

Gently he turned the great iron handle of the door. It was unlocked, slightly ajar. But he had expected to find it open. With part of his mind he believed that churches, buildings of sanctuary and superstition, were always left open for their worshippers. But nothing could surprise him, nothing could go wrong. The door squeaked as he closed it behind him and stepped into the sweet-smelling quietness.

The church was larger than he had imagined, so cold that he shuddered and so still that he thought for a second that he heard an animal panting before he realized that it was his own breath. There was no artificial light except for a single chandelier and a lamp in a small side chapel where a crimson glow stained the air. Two rows of candles burning before the statue of the Madonna gusted in the draught from the closing door. There was a locked box attached to the branching candleholder, but he knew that it wasn't this that he sought. He had questioned the boy carefully. The box containing the button was at the west end of the church in front of the iron ornamental grille. But he didn't hurry. He moved into the middle of the nave facing the altar and spread his arms wide as if to take possession of the vast emptiness, the holiness, the sweet-smelling air. In front of him the mosaics of the apse gleamed richly gold, and turning to look up at the clerestory, he could see in the half-light the ranks of painted figures, one-dimensional, harmlessly sentimental as cut-outs from a child's picture book. The rainwater ran down his hair to wash over his face, and he laughed as he tasted its sweetness on his tongue. A small pool gathered at his feet. Then slowly, almost ceremoniously, he paced down the nave to the candleholder in front of the grille.

There was a padlock on the box, but it was only small, and the box itself more fragile than he had expected. He inserted the chisel under the lid and heaved. At first it resisted, and then he could hear the gentle splinter of the wood and the gap widened. He gave one more heave and suddenly the padlock sprang apart with a crack so loud that it echoed through the church like a pistol shot. Almost at once it was answered by a crack of thunder. The gods, he thought, are applauding me.

And then he was aware of a dark shadow moving up to him and heard a voice, quietly untroubled, gently authoritative.

"If you're looking for the button, my son, you've come too late. The police have found it."

8

⊠

Last night Father Barnes had dreamed again the same dream which had visited him on the night of the murder. It had been terrible—terrible on first waking and no less terrible when he thought about it later—and like all nightmares, it had left him feeling that it had been no aberration but was firmly lodged in his subconscious, powered with its own terrible reality, crouched ready to return. The dream had been a Technicolor horror. He had been watching a procession, not part of it but standing on the edge of the pavement, alone, disregarded. At its head was Father Donovan in his richest chasuble, prancing in front of the processional cross while the congregation streamed out of his church behind him: laughing faces, bodies leaping and steaming, the clash of the steel drums. David, he thought, leaping before the Ark of the Lord. And then came the sacrament borne high under a canopy. But when he drew close, he saw that it wasn't a proper canopy but the faded, grubby carpet from the Little Vestry of St. Matthew's, its fringe swaying as the poles lurched, and what they were carrying wasn't the sacrament but Berowne's body, pink and naked like a stuck pig with its gaping throat.

He had woken up calling out, fumbling for the bedside lamp. Night after night the nightmare had returned and then, last Sunday, mysteriously, he had been free of it and for three blessed nights his sleep had been deep and undisturbed. As he turned to lock the dark and empty church after Dalgliesh and Miss Wharton had left he found himself praying that it wouldn't revisit him tonight.

He glanced at his wristwatch. It was only quarter past five, but the evening was as dark as midnight. And when he reached the edge of the porch the rain began falling. First came a flash of thunder, so loud that it seemed to shake the church. He thought how unmistakable and how eerie it was, that unearthly sound, something between a growl and an explosion. No wonder, he thought, men have always feared it, like the anger of God. And then, immediately, came the rain spilling from the porch roof in a solid wall of water. It would be ridiculous to set out for the vicarage through such a storm. He would be soaking wet in seconds. If he hadn't insisted on staying on for a few minutes after Dalgliesh had left to enter the candle money in his petty-cash register, he could probably have had a lift home. The Commander was dropping Miss Wharton at her flat on his way to the Yard. But now there was nothing for it but to wait.

And then he remembered Bert Poulson's umbrella. Bert, who sang tenor in the choir, had left it in the bell room after Sunday's Mass. He could borrow it. He went back into the church, leaving the north door ajar, unlocked the door in the grille and made his way into the bell room. The umbrella was still there. Then it occurred to him that he ought, perhaps, to leave a note on the peg. Bert might turn up early on Sunday and begin agitating when he found it was missing; he was that sort of man. Father Barnes went into the Little Vestry and, taking a sheet of paper from the desk drawer, wrote: "Mr. Poulson's umbrella is at the vicarage."

He had hardly finished writing and was putting his pen back in his pocket when he heard the sound. It was a loud crack and it was very close. Instinctively he moved out of the Little Vestry and into the passage. Behind the grille was a young man, fair-haired, chisel in hand. And the collection box gaped open.

And then Father Barnes knew. He knew both who it was and why he was here. He remembered Dalgliesh's words: "No one will be at risk once he knows that we've found the button." But for one second, no more, he felt fear, an overwhelming, incapacitating terror which rendered him speechless. And then it passed, leaving him cold and faint but perfectly clear-headed. What he felt now was an immense calm, a sense that there was nothing he could do and nothing he need fear. Everything was taken care of. He walked forward as firmly as if he were greeting a new member of his congregation and knew that his face showed the same conscious, sentimental concern. His voice was perfectly steady. He said:

"If you're looking for the button, my son, you've come too late. The police have found it."

The blue eyes blazed into his. Water was flowing like tears over the young face. It looked suddenly like the face of a desolate and terrified child, the mouth, half-open, gaped at him, speechless. And then he heard a groan and saw with disbelieving eyes the two hands stretched towards him, shaking; and in the hands was a gun. He heard himself say: "No, oh no, please!" and knew that he wasn't pleading for pity because there was none. It was a last impotent cry against the inescapable. And even as he made it he felt a thud and his body leaped. It was only seconds later as he hit the ground that he heard the gunshot.

Someone was bleeding over the tiles of the nave. He wondered where it was coming from, this steadily spreading stain. Extra cleaning, he thought. Difficult to get off. Miss Wharton and her ladies wouldn't be pleased. The red stream crept, viscous as oil, between the tiles. Like that TV advert, liquid engineering. Somewhere someone was groaning. It was a horrible noise, very loud. They really ought to stop. And then he thought: This is my blood, this is me bleeding. I'm going to die. There was no fear, but only a moment of dreadful weakness, followed by a nausea more terrible than any physical sensation he had ever experienced. But then that, too, passed. He thought: If this is dying, it is not so very difficult. He knew there were words he ought to say, but he wasn't sure he could remember them and it didn't matter. He thought: I must let go, just let go. After that thought there was no other.

He was unconscious when at last the blood stopped flowing. He was beyond hearing when almost an hour later the door was pushed slowly open and the heavy footsteps of a police officer moved down the nave towards him.

9

⊠

From the moment she walked into the casualty department and saw her grandmother, Kate had known that there was no longer any choice. The old lady had been sitting on a chair against the wall, a red hospital blanket around her shoulders, and had a pad of gauze taped to her forehead. She had looked very small and frightened, her face greyer and more wizened than ever before, her anxious eyes fixed on the entrance door. Kate was reminded of a stray dog brought into the Notting Hill nick and awaiting transfer to the Battersea Dogs' Home which had sat tied by a string to a bench and had gazed quivering at the door with just such an intensity of longing. As she walked up to her, it seemed that she was seeing her grandmother with shocked eyes as if they had been parted for months. The tell-tale signs of deterioration, of the draining away of strength and self-respect, that she had either ignored or pretended not to see were suddenly all too plain: the hair, which her grandmother had always tried to dye back to its original red, now hanging in vertical stripes of white, grey and a curious orange each side of the sunken cheeks; the blotched hands thin as talons; the ridged nails on which the remnants of polish, months old, clung like dried blood; the eyes still sharp, but glittering now with the first glint of paranoia; the sour smell of unwashed clothes, unwashed flesh.

Without touching her, Kate sat beside her on the vacant chair. She thought: I mustn't make her ask, not now, not when it has become so important. At least I can spare her that humiliation. Where did I get my own pride if not from her? She said:

"It's all right, Gran. You're coming home with me." There had been no hesitation and no choice. She couldn't look into those eyes and see for the first time real fear, real despair and still say no. She had left her side only for a few minutes to speak to the staff nurse and confirm that it was all right for her to leave. Then she had led her, docile as a child, to the car, driven her to the flat and put her to bed. After all the scheming and agonizing, the self-justification, the determination that she and her grandmother would never again live under the same roof, it had been as simple and inevitable as that.

The next day had been hectic for both of them. By the time Kate had seen the local CID, driven her grandmother back to her flat and packed a case with Mrs. Miskin's clothes and the odd collection of possessions from which she couldn't bear to be parted, left notes for the neighbours to explain what had happened and spoken to the social service department and the housing office, it was mid-afternoon. Then on their arrival back at Charles Shannon House there had been tea to make, drawers and a cupboard to clear for her grandmother's things, her own painting gear to be stowed away in the corner. God knows, she thought, when I'll be able to use that again.

It was after six before she was free to set off to the Notting Hill Gate supermarket to shop for enough food to leave ready for the next few days. She only hoped that she would be able to get back to work the next morning, that her grandmother would be well enough to be left. She had insisted on accompanying Kate and had stood up well to the day's exertions. But now she was looking tired, and Kate was filled with a desperate worry that she might refuse to be left next morning. She had struck her head and bruised her right arm when the youths had jumped on her. But they had been content to grab her purse without kicking in her teeth, and the physical damage was superficial. Her head and arm had been X-rayed; the hospital were satisfied that she was fit to be at home if there was someone to keep an eye on her. Well, there was someone to keep an eye on her, the only person in the world she had left.

Pushing her trolley along the aisles at the supermarket, Kate marvelled at the amount of additional food which one other person made necessary. She needed no list. These were the familiar items demanded by her grandmother which she had shopped for every week. As she placed them in the basket she could still hear the echo of that old confident, disgruntled voice in her ears. Ginger biscuits ("not those soft ones, I like them hard for dipping"), tinned salmon ("red, mind you, I can't be doing with that pink muck"), tinned pears ("at least you can get your teeth into them"), custard powder, packets of cut ham ("keeps fresher that way and you can see what you're getting"), the strongest-tasting teabags ("I wouldn't bath a newt in that stuff you bought last week"). But this afternoon had been different. Since coming to the flat she had sat without complaint, a pitiable, tired, docile old woman. Even her expected criticism of Kate's latest paint-ing—"I don't know why you want to stick that thing on the wall, looks like a kid's drawing"—had sounded more like a ritual objection, an attempt to revive her old bravado, than genuine outrage. She had let Kate set off for the shops with nothing but a sudden deepening of fear in the faded eyes and an anxious:

"You'll not be long then?"

"Not long, Gran. Just off to the supermarket at Notting Hill Gate."

Then, as Kate reached the door, she called her back and raised her small gallant pennant of pride:

"I'm not asking to be kept. I've got me pension."

"I know, Gran. There's no problem."

Manoeuvring her trolley down the aisles stacked with tinned fruit, she thought: I don't seem to need a supernatural religion. Whatever hap-pened to Paul Berowne in that church vestry, it's as closed to me as painting is to the blind. Nothing is more important to me than my job. But I can't make the law the basis of my personal morality. There has to be something more if I'm to live at ease with myself.

And it seemed to her that she had made a discovery about herself and about her job which was of immense importance, and she smiled that it should have happened while she was hesitating between two brands of tinned pears in a Notting Hill Gate supermarket. Odd, too, that it should have happened during this particular case. If she was still with the squad at the end of the enquiry she would like to say to AD: "Thank you for having me on the case, for choosing me. I've learnt something about the job and myself." But immediately she realized that it wouldn't be possible. The words would be too revealing, too confiding, the sort of girlish en-thusiasm she wouldn't be able to recall afterwards without a flush of shame. And then she thought: For God's sake, why not? He's not going to demote me, and it's the truth. I shouldn't be saying it to embarrass him or impress him or for any other reason except that it's true and I need to say it. She knew that she was over-defensive, probably she always would be. Those early years couldn't be wiped out and they couldn't be forgotten. But surely she could let down one small drawbridge without yielding the whole fortress. And would it matter so much if it was yielded?

She was too clear-sighted to expect this mood of exaltation to last long, but it depressed her how quickly it drained away. A wind was blustering around Notting Hill Gate, shaking out the sodden litter from the raised flower beds and swirling it damply against her ankles. On the parapet an old man corded in rags and surrounded by bulging plastic bags lifted his querulous voice and ranted feebly against the world. She hadn't brought the car. It was hopeless to try to park near Notting Hill. But the two bags were heavier than she had expected and their weight began to drag on her spirits as well as her shoulder muscles. It was all very well to indulge in self-congratulation, to muse on the imperatives of duty, but now the reality of the situation struck her like a physical blow, filling her with a misery close to despair. She and her grandmother would be locked together now until the old lady died. She was getting too old to cope with independence and soon she would compensate for its loss by persuading herself that she didn't really want it. And who now would give her priority for a single-person flat or a place in an old people's home, even if she would accept it, with so many more urgent cases on the waiting list? And when she was too old to be left during the day, what then? How could she, Kate, carry on her job and at the same time nurse a geriatric patient? She knew what officialdom would say. "Can't you ask for three months' compassionate leave, or find a part-time job?" And the three months would become a year, the year might be two or three, her career would be finished. No hope now of a place on the Bramshill course, of planning for a senior command. What hope even of staying on in the special squad with its long unpredictable hours, its demand for total commitment?

The storm was over now, but the great plane trees in Holland Park Avenue still shook down heavy drops of rain which seeped, disagreeably cold, under the collar of her coat. The evening rush hour was in full spate, and her ears were battered by the grind and roar of traffic, a noise which normally she hardly noticed. As she waited to cross Ladbroke Grove, a van hissing too fast through the running gutters splashed her ankles with dirt. She shouted her protest, unheard above the thunder of the road. The storm had brought down the first autumn fall of leaves. They drifted sluggishly against the barks of the plane trees and lay, delicately veined skeletons, on the tacky pavement. As she trudged past Campden Hill Square she gazed up towards the Berowne house. It was hidden by the trees of the square garden, but she could picture its secret life and had to resist the temptation to cross the road and walk up to it to see if the police Rover was parked outside. She seemed to have been away from the squad for weeks rather than a single day.

She was glad to turn from the roar of the avenue into the comparative quiet of her own road. Her grandmother didn't speak when she rang the bell and called her own name into the entry phone. But there was a burr and the door was released with surprising speed. The old lady must have been near the door. She humped her carrier bags into the lift and was borne upwards past floor after floor of empty and silent corridors.

She let herself into the flat and, as she always did, turned her key in the security lock. Then she hauled the bags of groceries onto the kitchen table and turned to walk the three yards across the hall to the sitting room door. The flat was silent, unnaturally so. Surely her grandmother would have turned on the television? Small facts unregarded in her self-obsessed mood of resentment and misery suddenly came together: the sitting room door tight closed when she had left it open, the swift but voiceless response to her ring at the street door, the unnatural silence. Even as her hand touched the knob and she pushed open the sitting room door, she knew with absolute certainty that something was wrong. But by then it was too late.

He had gagged her grandmother and tied her to one of the dining chairs with strips of white cloth—probably, she thought, a ripped sheet. He himself stood behind her, eyes blazing above the smiling mouth like a bizarre tableau of triumphant youth and age. He was holding the gun with both hands, steadying the barrel, his arms stretched rigid. She wondered if he was used to firearms or whether this was how he had seen a gun held in TV crime series. Her mind was curiously detached. She had often wondered how she would feel if faced with this kind of emergency, and it interested her that her reactions were so predictable. Disbelief, shock, fear. And then the surge of adrenaline, the gears of the mind taking hold.

As their eyes met he slowly lowered his arms, then placed the muzzle of the gun against her grandmother's head. The old lady's eyes above the mouth gag were immense, great black pools of terror. It was extraordinary that those restless eyes could be filled with such an intensity of pleading. Kate was seized with such pity and such anger that, for a moment, she dared not speak. Then she said:

"Take off that gag. Her mouth's bleeding. She's had one shock already. D'you want to kill her with pain and fright?"

"Oh, she won't die. They don't, these old bitches. They live forever."

"She isn't strong, and a dead hostage isn't much use to you."

"Ah, but I'll still have you. A policewoman, rather more valuable."

"Will you? D'you think I care a damn except for her? Look, if you want any cooperation from me, take off that gag."

"And have her hollering like a stuck pig? Not that I know what a stuck pig sounds like, but I know the kind of noise she'd make. I'm in a particularly sensitive mood, and I never could stand noise."

"If she does, then you can gag her again, can't you? But she won't. I'll see to that."

"All right. Come and take it off yourself. But be careful. Remember, I've got this gun against her head."

She moved across, knelt and put her hand against her grandmother's cheek.

"I'm going to take off the gag. Now, you mustn't make a noise. Not a sound. If you do, he'll put it on again. Promise?" There was no response, nothing but terror in the glazed eyes. But then her head jerked twice.

Kate said:

"Don't worry, Gran. I'm here. It's going to be all right."

The stiff hands with their parched swollen knuckles clasped the chair ends as if fastened to the wood. She put her own hands over them. They felt like dry crêpe, cold and lifeless. She pressed down her warm palms and felt the physical transfer of life, of hope. Gently she put her right hand against her grandmother's cheek and wondered how she could ever have found this crumpled flesh repulsive. She thought: We haven't touched each other for fifteen years. And now I am touching her, and with love.

When the gag dropped off, he waved her back and said:

"Stand over there against the wall. Now." She did as she was ordered. His eyes followed her.

Bound in her chair, her grandmother was rhythmically opening and shutting her mouth like a fish gasping for air. A thin dribble of bloodstained mucus dripped over her chin. Kate waited until she could control her voice. Then she said coolly:

"Why this panic? We've got no real evidence. You must know that."

"Ah, but now you have."

Without moving the gun, he turned up the corner of his jacket with his left hand.

"My spare button. Your people at the lab won't have missed this broken twist of thread. Pity the buttons are so distinctive. This comes of having expensive taste in clothes. Papa always said it would be my undoing."

His voice was high, brittle, the eyes large and bright as if he were on drugs. She thought: He's not really as calm as he wants to sound. And he's been drinking. Probably got at my whisky while he was waiting. But that made him more dangerous, not less. She said:

"That's not enough, a single button. Look, don't be a fool. Stop play-acting. Hand over the gun. Go home and call your lawyer."

"Ah, but I don't think I can do that, not now. You see, there's this damned officious priest. Or rather, there was this damned officious priest. He had a taste for martyrdom, poor sod. I hope he's enjoying it."

"You've killed him? Father Barnes?"

"Shot him. So you see I haven't anything to lose. If I'm aiming for Broadmoor rather than a high security jail, you could say the more the merrier."

There was, she remembered, a mass murderer who had said just that. Who was it? Haigh?

She said:

"How did you find me?"

"The telephone directory, how else? Rather a coy and uncommunicative entry, but I guessed it was you. No difficulty in getting the old woman to open the door, incidentally. I just said I was Chief Inspector Massingham."

"All right, so what's the plan?"

"I'm getting out. Spain. There's a boat at Chichester harbour which I can handle. The *Mayflower*. I've sailed on her. She belongs to my sister's lover, in case you're interested. You're going to drive me there."

"Not now I'm not. Not till the roads are clear. Look, I'm as anxious to live as you are. I'm not Father Barnes, I'm no martyr. The police pay me well, but not that well. I'll get you to Chichester, but we have to wait until the A3 is clear if we're going to get through. For God's sake, it's the rush hour. You know what the traffic's like getting out of London. I don't fancy getting stuck in a traffic jam with a gun at my back and every other motorist peering in the car."

"Why should they? The police will be looking for a single man, not a man, wife and his dear old grandma."

She said:

"They won't be looking for anyone yet, button or no button. Not unless they've found the priest or know that you've got the gun. As far as the police know, there's no hurry. They don't even know that you've found out about the button. If we're to get well away fast and unnoticed, we have to have a clear drive to Chichester. And there's no point in carting along my grandmother. She'll only be a hindrance."

"Possibly, but she's coming. I need her."

Of course he needed her. His plan was plain enough. She would be expected to drive, he would sit at the back, the gun against the old lady's head. And when they reached the harbour she would be expected to help with the boat, at least until they got out to sea. And what then? Two gunshots, two bodies bundled over the side. He seemed to be considering, then he said:

"All right, we'll wait. Just for an hour. How much food is there?"

"Are you hungry?"

"I shall be, and we'll need provisions. Everything portable that you've got."

This she knew could be important. Hunger, shared need, shared food, a natural human want satisfied. It was one way of establishing that empathy on which their survival might depend. She remembered what she had been taught about sieges. The prisoners identified with their captors. It was those sinister watching eyes outside, those unseen intelligences, their guns, their listening devices leeched to the walls, their false insinuating voices which became the enemy. She wouldn't identify with him or with his kind if they were together until they starved, but there were things she could do. Use "we" not "you." Try not to provoke him. Try to ease tension and, if necessary, cook for him. She said:

"I could go and see what we've got. I don't keep much fresh food, but there'll be eggs, tins, pasta, and I could cook what I had planned for tonight: spaghetti bolognese."

He said:

"No knives."

"You can't do much cooking without a knife of some sort. I'll need to chop onions and the liver. My recipe uses chopped liver."

"Then do without them."

Spaghetti bolognese. Strong tasting. Was there anything that she could put into the sauce which would incapacitate him? Her thoughts ranged over the contents of her medicine chest. But she rejected the idea as nonsensical. There would be no opportunity. He wasn't a fool. He'd see to that. And he wouldn't eat anything which she didn't share. Her grandmother began muttering. Kate said:

"I've got to speak to her."

"All right. But keep your hands behind your back and be careful."

She had to get hold of the gun, but now wasn't the time. It was pressed hard against her grandmother's skull. One suspicious move on her part and he would press the trigger. She went up again to the chair and bent her head. Her grandmother whispered. Kate said:

"She wants to go to the lavatory."

"That's too bad. She's staying where she is."

Kate said angrily:

"Look, d'you want a stink in the room for the next hour? And in the car, come to that. I'm fastidious, if you're not. Let me take her. What possible danger can she be?"

Again there was a moment's silence while he thought.

"All right. Untie her. But leave the door open. And remember I'll be watching you."

It took her a full minute to undo the clumsy knots, but at last the linen dropped away and her grandmother fell forward into her arms. She drew her up, marvelling at the lightness of her body, brittle as a bird's. Holding her gently and murmuring encouragement as she might to a child, Kate half-carried her into the lavatory. Supporting her with one arm, she pulled down her knickers and lowered her onto the seat, aware of him standing braced against the passage wall less than two yards away, the gun pointed at her head. Her grandmother whispered:

"He's going to kill us."

"Nonsense, Gran. Of course he won't kill us."

The old lady directed a look of venomous hatred across Kate's shoulder. She hissed:

"He's been at your whisky. Bloody cheek."

"I know, Gran. It doesn't matter. Better not talk, not now."

"He's going to shoot us. I know." Then she said, "Your dad was a copper."

A policeman! Kate could have laughed aloud. It was extraordinary to learn that now, in this place, at this moment, astonishing to learn it at all. Still shielding her grandmother's body with her own, she said:

"Why didn't you tell me?"

"You never asked. No point in telling, anyway. He was killed before you were born, in a car smash, chasing a villain. And he had a wife and two kids. Little enough for them on a police pension without letting on about you."

"So he never knew?"

"That's right. And no point in telling his wife either. Nothing she could do about it. More grief, more trouble."

"So you were landed with me. Poor Gran. I haven't been much use."

"You've been all right. No worse than any other kid. I never felt right about you. I always felt guilty."

"Guilty! You! Why on earth?"

"When she died, your ma, I wished it had been you."

So that had been at the root of all the estrangement. She felt a spring of joy. Here crouching by a lavatory seat, a gun at her head, with death perhaps seconds away, she could have laughed. She put her arm round the old lady, helping her to her feet, then let her rest against her while she drew up her knickers. She said:

"But of course you did. It was natural. It was right. She was your daughter. You loved her. Of course you wished it had been me who died if one of us had to go." But she couldn't make herself say, It would have been better if it had been me. Her grandmother muttered:

"I've felt bad about it all these years."

"Well, stop feeling bad about it. We've got a lot of years ahead."

And then she heard his step as he moved into the doorway, felt his breath on the back of her neck. He said:

"Get her out of here and start cooking that meal."

But there was something she needed to ask. For over twenty years she hadn't asked, hadn't even cared. But now, amazingly, it had become important. Ignoring him, she said to her grandmother:

"Was she glad about me? My mother?"

"Seemingly. Before she died she said 'my sweet Kate.' So that's what I called you."

So it had been as simple as that, as wonderful as that.

His voice rasped with impatience:

"I said, get her out of here. Take her into the kitchen. Tie her to one of the chairs, against the wall, by the door. I want my gun against her head while you're cooking."

She did as she was told, fetching the strips of sheeting from the sitting room, drawing her grandmother's wrists gently behind her back, tying them as loosely as she dared, careful not to hurt her. Keeping her eyes on the knots, she said:

"Look, there's something I must do. I've got to ring my boyfriend. He's coming to supper at eight."

"It doesn't matter. Let him come. We'll be gone by then."

"It does matter. If he finds the flat empty he'll know something is wrong. He'll check the car. Then he'll ring the Yard. We've got to put him off."

"How do I know he's expected?"

"You'll find his initials on that wall diary behind you on the clipboard." She was grateful now that, absorbed with the business of settling in her grandmother, she had telephoned Alan to cancel their date but hadn't rubbed out those faint pencilled initials and the time. She said:

"Look, we've got to get to Chichester before anyone knows we've gone. He won't be altogether surprised to be chucked. We had one hell of a row last time he was here."

He was silent; considering. Then he said:

"All right. What's his name and the number?"

"Alan Scully, and he works at the Hoskyns Theological Library. He won't have left yet. He stays late on Thursday."

He said:

"I'll ring from the sitting room. You stand back against the wall. Don't come to the telephone till I tell you. What's the number?"

She followed him into the sitting room. He motioned her back against the wall to the left of the door, then moved over to where the telephone stood on the shelf of the wall unit, the answering machine beside it, the directories neatly stacked beneath. She wondered if he would remember the risk of leaving his palm print. As if the thought had communicated itself to him, he took a handkerchief from his pocket and draped it over the receiver. He said:

"Who will answer, this man Scully or a secretary?"

"At this hour, he will. He'll be alone in his office."

"Let's hope he is. And don't try anything. If you do, I'll shoot you first and then the old witch. And maybe she won't die quickly. You will, but not her. I might have a little fun with her first, switch on the electric stove, clamp down her hand on the hot plate. Think about that if you're tempted to be clever."

She couldn't believe that, even now, he'd bring himself to do it. He was a killer but not a torturer. But the words, the horror of the picture they evoked, made her shudder. And the threat of death was real enough. He had already killed three men. What had he to lose? He would prefer a live hostage, prefer to let her do the driving, to have an extra pair of hands on the boat. But if he needed to kill, he would, trusting that he could get well on his way before their bodies were found.

He said:

"Right, what's the number?"

She gave it and watched, heart pounding, while he dialled. The call must have been quickly answered. He didn't speak but after less than four seconds he held out the receiver and she moved across and took it from his hand. She began speaking loudly and very fast, desperate to drown any questions, any response.

"Alan? It's Kate. Tonight's off. Look, I'm tired, I've had one hell of a day, and I'm fed up with cooking for you every bloody time we meet. And don't ring back. Just come tomorrow if you feel like it. Maybe you'll take me out for a change. And Alan, remember to bring me that book you promised. The Shakespeare *Love's Labour's Lost*, for Christ's sake. See you tomorrow. And remember the Shakespeare." She banged down the receiver. She found that she was holding her breath, and let it out gently and silently, afraid that he would notice the release of tension. Had her words sounded even remotely credible? The message seemed to her so obviously false. Could he possibly have been deceived? But after all, he didn't know Alan, he didn't know her. That might be typical of the way they spoke to each other. She said:

"That's OK. He'll keep away."

"He'd better."

He motioned her back to the kitchen and took up his stance beside her grandmother, the gun again to her head.

He said:

"You've got wine, I suppose?"

"You should know. You've been at the drinks cupboard."

"So I have. We'll have the Beaujolais. And we'll take the whisky and a half-dozen bottles of the claret with us. I've a feeling I'm going to need alcohol before I get across the Channel."

How experienced a sailor was he? she wondered. And what kind of boat was the *Mayflower*? Stephen Lampart had described it, but she couldn't now remember. And how could he be sure that the craft would be fuelled and ready for sea, that the tides would be right? Or had he passed beyond the borders of reason, of precarious sanity, into a fantasy in which even the tides would run to his bidding?

He asked:

"Well, aren't you going to get on with it? We haven't much time."

She knew that every action must be slow, deliberate, unfrightening, that any sudden movement might be fatal. She said:

"I'm going to reach up and take a frying pan from that top cupboard. Then I'll need the minced beef and the liver from the refrigerator and a tube of tomato paste and the herbs from this cupboard on my right. OK?"

"I don't need a cookery lesson. And remember, no knives."

As she started her preparations she thought of Alan. What was he doing? What was he thinking? Would he stand still for a moment, consider, come to the conclusion that she was drunk, hysterical or mad, then go back to his books? But he couldn't! He must know that she was none of these things, that if she did go mad, it wouldn't be in that way. But it was impossible to picture him actually taking action, ringing the Yard, asking for Commander Dalgliesh. It seemed to her that she was expecting him to act a part as out of character as it would be for her to take over his job, catalogue his library. But surely that reference to *Love's Labour's Lost* had been unmistakable. He must know that she was trying to convey an urgent message, that she was under duress. He couldn't have forgotten their talk about Shakespeare's Berowne, the attendant lord. She thought: He reads the newspapers, he must know that these things happen. He can't not know what sort of world we live in. And she would never normally speak to him in those terms, in that tone of voice. He knew her well enough to be sure of that. Or did he? They had been happily making love for over two years. There wasn't anything about her body that wasn't familiar to him, as his was to her. Since when did that mean that two people knew each other?

Standing back against the wall, the gun still pressed to her grand-mother's head, Swayne kept his eyes fixed on her while she took the package of minced steak and the one of liver out of the refrigerator for the frying pan. He said:

"Ever been to California?"

"No."

"It's the only place to live. Sun. Ocean. Brightness. People who aren't grey and frightened and half-dead. You wouldn't like it. Not your kind of place."

She asked:

"Why don't you go back?"

"I can't afford to."

"The air fare or the expense of living there?"

"Neither. My stepfather pays me to stay away. I'll lose my allowance if I go back."

"Couldn't you get a job?"

"Ah, but then I might lose something else. There is a little matter of step-papa's Seurat."

"That's a painting, isn't it? What did you do to it?"

"Clever. How did you know that? The history of art isn't in the police curriculum, is it?"

"What did you do to it?"

"Stuck a knife through it several times. I wanted to spoil something he cared about. Actually he didn't much care about it. But he cared about what it cost. Well, it wouldn't have been much good sticking a knife in Mama, would it?"

"What about your mother?"

"Oh, she keeps in with my stepfather. She more or less has to. He's the one with the money. Anyway, she's never much cared for children, not her own, anyway. Barbara's too beautiful for her. She doesn't really like her. That's because she's afraid my step-papa does, too much."

"And you?"

"They don't want to know about me, either of them. They never have. Not this stepfather, nor the one before. But they will. They will."

She tipped the minced steak from the paper into the frying pan and began moving it around with a spatula. Keeping her voice calm as if this were an ordinary dinner and he an ordinary guest, she said above the hiss of singeing meat:

"This really ought to have onions in it."

"Forget about the onions. What about your mother?"

"My mother's dead, and I never knew my father. I'm a bastard." She thought: I might as well tell him. It could evoke some emotion, curiosity, pity, contempt. No, not pity. But even contempt would be something. Contempt was a human response. If they were to survive, she had to get some relationship established that was other than fear, hatred, conflict. But when he spoke his voice held nothing but an amused tolerance.

"One of those, are you? They've all got chips on their shoulders, bastards. I should know. I'll tell you something about my father. When I was eleven he made me have a blood test. A doctor came and stuck a needle in my arm. I could see my own blood flowing out into the syringe. I was terrified. He did it to try and prove that I wasn't his son."

She said, and meant it:

"That was a terrible thing to do to a child."

"He was a terrible man. But I got my own back. Is that why you're a policewoman, getting your own back on the rest of us?"

"No, just earning a living."

"There are other ways. You could have been a decent whore. There aren't enough of those around."

"Are those the women you fancy, whores?"

"No, what I fancy isn't so easily come by. Innocence."

"Like Theresa Nolan?"

"So you know about that? I didn't kill her. She killed herself."

"Because you made her abort your child?"

"Well, she could hardly expect to have it, could she? And how are you so sure that it was mine? You never can be sure, any of you. If Berowne didn't sleep with her, he wanted to. By God, he wanted to. Why else should he have thrown me into that river? I could have done a lot for him, helped him, if he'd let me. He couldn't be bothered even to talk to me. Who did he think he was? He was going to leave my sister, my sister, for his dreary whore or for his God. Who the hell cares which? He was going to sell his house, make us poor and despised. He humiliated me in front of Diana. Well, he chose the wrong man."

His voice was still low but it seemed to her that it rang out filling the room, charged with anger and triumph.

She thought: I might as well ask him about it. He'll want to talk. They always do. She spoke almost casually, squeezing the tomato paste into the pan, reaching up for the jar of mixed herbs.

"You knew that he'd be in that vestry. He wouldn't have left home without saying where he could be found, not when there was a risk that a dying man would send for him. You told Miss Matlock to lie to us, but she knew where he was and she told you."

"He gave her a telephone number. I guessed it was the number of the church, but I rang directory enquiries. The number they gave me for St. Matthew's was the one he'd given Evelyn."

"How did you get from Campden Hill Square to the church? Cab? Car?"

"By bicycle, his bicycle. I took the key to the garage from Evelyn's cupboard. Halliwell had left by then, whatever he told the police. His lights were out and the Rover had gone. I didn't take Barbie's Golf. Too conspicuous. A bicycle was just as quick, and I could wait in the shadows until the road was clear and pedal quickly away. And I didn't leave it outside the church where it might have been seen. I asked Paul if I could bring it in, leave it in the passage. It was a fine night, so I didn't have to worry about muddy tyre marks on the floor. I thought of everything, you see."

"Not everything. You took away the matches."

"But I put them back. The matches prove nothing."

She said:

"And he let you in, you and the bicycle. That's what I find odd. That he actually let you in."

"It's odder than you think. Much odder. I didn't realize at the time, but I do now. He knew I was coming. He was expecting me."

She felt a frisson of almost superstitious horror. She wanted to cry out: But he couldn't have known! It isn't possible!

She said:

"And Harry Mack. Did you really have to kill Harry?"

"Of course. It was his bad luck that he came blundering in. But he was better dead, poor sod. Don't worry about Harry. I did him a favour."

Turning to face him, Kate asked:

"And Diana Travers. Did you kill her too?"

He gave a sly smile and seemed to gaze straight through her as if re-living a secret pleasure.

"I didn't need to. The weeds did it for me. I trod water and watched as she dived in. There was a flash of whiteness cleaving the surface. And then it settled and there was nothing, only that liquid darkness. So I waited, counting the seconds. And then quite close to me, a hand rose out of the water. Just a hand, pale, disembodied. It was uncanny. Like this. See, like this."

He shot up his left hand, the fingers tautly splayed. She could see the stretched sinews under the milk-white flesh. She didn't speak. Gently he relaxed his fingers and let his arm fall. He said:

"And then that, too, disappeared. And I waited, still counting the seconds. But there was nothing, not even a ripple."

"And you swam on, leaving her to drown?"

His eyes focussed on her as if with an effort, and she heard again in his voice the charge of hatred and triumph.

"She laughed at me. No one does that. No one will, ever again."

"What did you feel like afterwards, knowing what you'd done in that vestry, the butchery, the blood?"

"You need a woman and I had one handy. Not the one I would have chosen, but you have to take what you can get. It was clever too. I knew she'd never break after that."

"Miss Matlock. You used her in more ways than one."

"No more than the Berownes did. They think she's devoted to them. Do you know why? Because they never bother to ask themselves what she really thinks. So efficient, so devoted. Almost one of the family, except, of course, that she isn't, is she? She never was. She hates them. She doesn't know it, not really, not yet, but she hates them, and one day she'll wake up to it. Like me. That dreadful old bitch, Lady Ursula. I've seen her trying not to cringe when Evelyn touches her."

"Evelyn?"

"Mattie. She does have a name of her own, you know. They found a pet name for her as they might for a cat or a dog."

"If they've been overworking her for years, why didn't she leave?"

"Too scared. She went off her head. Once you've had one spell in the funny farm and your dad's a murderer, people get wary. They're not sure you're safe looking after their precious kids or let loose in the kitchen. Oh, the Berownes had her where they wanted her, all right. Why should they think she got a kick out it, fussing over that selfish old woman, washing under her droopy old tits? Christ, I hope I never get old."

She said:

"You will. Where you're going, they take good care of you. Healthy diet, daily exercise, locked up safely at night. You'll grow old, all right."

He laughed.

"But they won't kill me, will they? They can't. And I'll be out again. Cured. You'll be surprised how quickly they'll cure me."

"Not if you kill a police officer."

"Let's hope I don't have to, then. When is that stuff going to be ready? I want to get on."

She said:

"Soon. It won't be long now."

Already the kitchen was beginning to fill with the savoury smell of the sauce. She reached up for her pasta jar and tipped out a handful of spaghetti, breaking it. The thin cracks sounded unnaturally loud. She thought: If Alan has telephoned the police, they could be outside already, boring through the wall, looking, watching, listening. How would they play it? she wondered. Telephone, and begin the long process of negotiation? Crash in? Probably neither. As long as he was ignorant of their presence, they would watch and listen, knowing that sooner or later he would leave the flat with his hostages. That would give them their best chance to disable him. If they were there. If Alan had acted.

Suddenly he said:

"My God, this place is bloody pathetic. You can't see it, can you? You think it's all right. No, you think it's better than all right. You think it's really something. You're proud of it, aren't you? Dull, orthodox, ghastly, conventional good taste. Six bloody awful mugs hanging on their little hooks. You don't need any more, do you? Six people are quite enough. No one else can drop in because there isn't a mug for him. And the same in the cupboard. I've had a look. I know. Six of everything. Nothing broken. Nothing chipped. Everything neatly arranged. Six dinner plates, side plates, soup bowls. Christ, I've only got to open this cupboard behind me to know what you're like. Don't you ever want to stop counting the crockery and start living?"

"If by living you mean mess and violence, no, I don't. I had enough of that when I was a kid."

Without moving the gun he reached up his left hand and slipped the catch on the cupboard. Then he took out the dinner plates one by one and placed them on the table. He said:

"They don't look real, do they? They don't look as if they'd break." He took one of the plates and smashed it down against the side of the table. It cracked neatly in two. Then he took the next. She went quietly on with her cooking and heard as plate after plate was carefully smashed, the two pieces neatly arranged on the table. The pyramid grew. Each crack was like the small report of a gun. She thought: If the police are actually here, if they've got their listening devices on, they'll pick that up, try to identify it. The thought must have occurred to him. He said:

"Lucky for you the fuzz aren't outside. They'd wonder what I'm doing. It would be a shame for the old bitch if they broke in. Plates don't make a mess, but blood and brains, you can't stack those up neatly on the table."

He was able to keep the gun steadily pointed at her grandmother's head and still, one-handed, manage the cupboard door and crack the plates. So he was ambidextrous or as near as made no odds. It was important to remember that, if it came to a fight.

She said:

"How did you do it? How did you manage to surprise him? I mean, you must have burst in on him half-naked, razor in hand." She had asked the question to propitiate him, flatter him. What she hadn't expected was his reply. It almost burst out of him, as if they were lovers and he had been longing to confide. He said:

"But you don't understand! He wanted to die, God rot him, he wanted it! He practically asked for it. He could have tried to stop me, pleaded, argued, put up a fight. He could have begged for mercy. 'No, please don't do it. Please!' That's all I wanted from him. 'Please.' Just that one word. The priest could say it, but not Paul Berowne. He looked at me with such contempt. And then he turned his back. I tell you he turned his back on me! When I came in half-naked, his razor in my hand, we stood and looked at each other. He knew then. Of course he knew. And I wouldn't have done it, not if he'd spoken to me as if I were even half-human. I spared the boy. I can be merciful. And that boy is sick. If you get out of here alive, do something about it, for Christ's sake. Or don't you bloody care?"

The blue eyes were suddenly luminous. She thought: He's crying. He's actually crying. And he was crying soundlessly, without a twitch of the face. And now her blood ran cold because she knew that anything was possible. She felt no pity, only a detached curiosity. She hardly dared breathe, terrified that his hand would shake, that the gun pressed again against her grandmother's head would go off. She could see the old lady's eyes wide and glazed as if she were already dead, her figure rigid with terror, not daring even to wince at the hurt of the metal hard against the defenceless skull. He took control of himself. With a sound between a sob and a laugh, he said:

"Christ, I must have looked daft. Naked, or practically. Just my pants. And the razor. He must have seen the razor. I mean, I wasn't hiding it or anything. So why didn't he stop me? He didn't even look surprised. He was supposed to be terrified. He was supposed to prevent it happening. But he knew what I'd come for. He just looked at me as if he were saying 'So it's you. How strange that it has to be you.' As if I had no choice. Just an instrument. Mindless. But I did have a choice. And so did he. Christ, he could have stopped me. Why didn't he stop me?"

She said:

"I don't know. I don't know why he didn't stop you." And then she asked: "You said you spared the boy. What boy? Have you spoken to Darren?"

He didn't reply. He stood staring at her, but as if he weren't seeing her, suddenly remote as if he'd entered a private world. Then he said in a voice so cold, so full of menace, that she could hardly recognize it:

"That message about the Shakespeare: *Love's Labour's Lost*. That was a code, wasn't it?"

He smiled a grim, self-satisfied smile, and she thought: Oh God, he knows and he's glad that he knows. Now he's got the excuse he wants, the excuse to kill us. Her heart began thumping, a leaping animal hurling itself against her chest. But she managed to keep her voice steady.

"Of course not. How could it be? What on earth gave you that idea?"

"Your bookcase. I had a look at it while I was exploring the flat before you came back. Quite a little self-improver, aren't you? All that usual boring stuff people think they ought to have when they are trying to make an impression. Or is the boyfriend trying to educate you? Some job. Anyway, you've got a Shakespeare."

She said solidly through lips that seemed to have grown dry and huge: "It wasn't a code. What possible code could it be?"

"I hope for your sake that it wasn't. I'm not going to get myself banged up in this hole with the police outside waiting for an excuse to burst in and kill me. That would be tidy. No awkward questions. I know how they operate. No death penalty any more, so they set up their own execution squads. Well, it isn't going to work with me. So you'd better pray that we get away from here safely before they arrive. Look, you can leave that stuff. We're going now."

Oh God, she thought, he means it. It would have been better to have done nothing, not to have telephoned Alan, to have got away from the flat as soon as possible, to trust to the hope of crashing the car. And then her heart seemed for a moment literally to stop and she was seized with a dreadful coldness. There was a difference in the room, in the flat. Something had changed. And then she knew what it was. The ceaseless background roar of the traffic along the avenue, faint but continuous, had stopped, and nothing was moving down Ladbroke Road. The police were diverting the traffic. Both roads were closed. They weren't risking a shootout. The siege had begun. And any minute he, too, would realize it.

She thought: I can't bear it. He'll never be able to stand a siege. Neither of us will. He meant what he said. As soon as he realizes the police are outside, as soon as they ring, then he'll shoot us. I've got to get that gun. I've got to get it now.

She said:

"Look, this is ready now. I've cooked it. We may as well eat it. It'll only take a few minutes, and it's not as if we can stop on the road."

There was a silence, and then he spoke again in a voice like ice.

"I want to see that Shakespeare. Go and fetch it."

She forked a strand of spaghetti from the saucepan and tested it with trembling fingers. Without looking round, she said:

"It's about ready. Look, I'm busy. Can't you fetch it? You know where it is."

"Go and fetch it, unless you want to rid yourself of this old bag."

"All right."

It had to be now.

She willed her hands into stillness. With her left fingers she slipped undone the two buttons at the top of her shirt as if the kitchen had suddenly become too hot. The slab of liver lay on the draining board in front of her, bleeding into its wrapping. She plunged her hands into it, tearing at it, squeezing it, smearing her hands until they were thick with blood. It was the work of seconds, no more. Then with an instantaneous gesture she drew her bloody hand fiercely across her throat and swung round, wide-eyed, head thrown back, and thrust out at him the blood-clotted hands. Without even waiting for the terror in his eyes, his gasp like a sob, she flung herself at him and they crashed down together. She heard the clatter of the gun as it spun out of his hand and then a thud as it ricochetted against the door.

He had been trained. He was as good at combat as she was and as desperate. And he was strong, far stronger than she had expected. With a sudden convulsive jerk, he was on top of her, mouth to mouth, fierce as a rapist, his harsh breath rasping down her throat. She ground her knee into his groin, heard his yelp of pain, prised his hands from her throat and slid her bloody hands over the floor, feeling for the gun. Then she almost screamed with agony as he jammed his thumbs into her eyes. With their bodies locked, both were reaching desperately for the gun. But she couldn't see. Her eyes were dancing stars of coloured pain, and it was his right hand which found the weapon.

The shot shattered the air like an explosion. Then there was a second explosion and the door of the flat burst open. She had a bizarre sensation of male bodies leaping through the air, then standing, arms stretched, guns rigid, their bodies towering over her like dark colossi. Someone was pulling her up. There were shouts, commands, a cry of pain. And then she saw Dalgliesh in the doorway and he was moving towards her, deliberately, gently, like a film in slow motion, speaking her name and, as it seemed, willing her to fix her eyes only on him. But she turned and looked at her grandmother. The sunken eyes were still fixed in that glazed extremity of fear. The hair still hung in its multicoloured strands. The pad of gauze was still taped to the forehead. But nothing else was there. Nothing. The bottom of her face had been shot away. And strapped to her execution chair by the linen bands which Kate herself had fixed, she couldn't even fall. In that second in which she could bear to look, it seemed to Kate that the rigid figure fixed on her a glance of sad, reproachful astonishment. Then she was sobbing wildly, burying her head against Dalgliesh's jacket, smearing it with her bloody hands. She could hear him whispering:

"It's all right, Kate. It's all right. It's all right." But it wasn't. It never had been. It never would be.

He stood there, holding her in his strong clasp among the loud masculine voices, the commands, the sounds of scuffling. And then she pulled away from him, fighting for control, and saw over his shoulder Swayne's blue eyes blazing, triumphant. He was handcuffed. An officer she didn't know was dragging him out. But he looked back at her as if she were the only person in the room. Then he jerked his head at her grandmother's body and said:

"Well, you're free of her now. Aren't you going to thank me?"

BOOK SEVEN

Aftermath

1
⊠

Massingham had never been able to understand why it was traditional for police officers to attend the funeral of a murder victim. When a crime was still unsolved there might be some justification for it, although he had never himself believed in the theory that a killer was likely to expose himself to the public gaze merely for the satisfaction of watching his victim's corpse go underground or into the fire. He had, too, an unreasonable aversion to cremation—his family had for generations preferred to know where the bones of their forebears lay—and disliked canned religious music, a liturgy denuded of grace and meaning and the hypocrisy of attempting to dignify a simple act of hygienic disposal with a spurious significance.

Mrs. Miskin's funeral enabled him to indulge all these prejudices. He was further disgusted when it came to the ritual of examining the wreaths, a pathetically small line of floral contrivances set out along the crematorium wall, to find that a particularly florid example was from the squad. He wondered who had been given the job of buying it and whether the somewhat fulsome message of sympathy was directed at Mrs. Miskin, who wouldn't see it, or Kate, who wouldn't want it. But at least the affair had been brief and, by luck, had coincided with the extravagant vulgarity of a pop star's funeral in the neighbouring chapel, so that public and press interest in their more subdued entertainment had been mercifully small.

They were to go back to the Lansdowne Road flat. Waiting for Dalgliesh in the car, he only hoped that Kate had provided an adequate amount of refreshment; he badly needed a drink. The experience, too, seemed to have soured his chief's temper. On the drive south into London he was more than usually uncommunicative. Massingham said:

"Did you read that article by Father Barnes in one of the Sunday heavies, sir? Apparently he's claiming that some kind of miracle happened at St. Matthew's, that Paul Berowne had stigmata on his wrists after his first night in that vestry."

Dalgliesh's eyes were fixed on the road ahead.

"I read it."

"Do you think it's true?"

"Enough people will want it to be to fill the church for the foreseeable future. They should be able to afford a new carpet for the Little Vestry."

Massingham said:

"I wonder why he did it? Father Barnes, I mean. It won't exactly please Lady Ursula. And Berowne would have hated it, I imagine."

Dalgliesh said:

"Yes, he'd have hated it. Or perhaps it would have amused him. How can I possibly know? As for why he did it, even a priest apparently isn't immune to the temptations of becoming a hero."

They were driving down the Finchley Road before Massingham spoke again.

"About Darren, sir. Apparently his mum has finally taken off. The council are applying to the juvenile court to convert the supervision order into a care order. Poor little sod, he's fallen into the clutches of the welfare state with a vengeance."

Dalgliesh said, his eyes still on the road:

"Yes I heard, the social service director found time to ring me. And it's just as well. They think he has leukaemia."

"That's tough."

"There's an excellent chance of a cure. They've got it early. They admitted him to Great Ormond Street yesterday."

Massingham smiled. Dalgliesh glanced at him.

"What's amusing you, John?"

"Nothing, sir. I was thinking about Kate. She'll probably ask me if I seriously suppose that God would kill off Berowne and Harry to get young Darren cured of his leukaemia. It was Swayne, after all, who first pointed out that the kid was sick."

It had been a mistake. His chief's voice was cold:

"It would argue a certain extravagant use of human resources, wouldn't you say? Watch your speed, John, you're over the limit."

"Sorry, sir."

He eased his foot from the accelerator and drove on in silence.

2

⊠

An hour later, balancing a plate of cucumber sandwiches on his knee, Dalgliesh thought that all the funeral teas he had attended had been curiously alike in their mixture of relief, embarrassment and unreality. But this one evoked a stronger and more personal memory. He had been thirteen at the time and had returned with his parents to a Norfolk farmhouse after his father had conducted the funeral service of a local tenant farmer. Then, watching the young widow in new black clothes which she couldn't afford passing round the home-made sausage rolls and sandwiches, pressing on him the fruit cake which she knew was his favourite, he had felt for the first time an adult and almost overwhelming sense of the sadness at the heart of life and had marvelled at the grace with which the poor and the humble could meet it. He had never thought of humility in connection with Kate Miskin, and she had nothing in common with that country widow and her desolate and uncertain future. But when he saw the food brought in, the sandwiches made before she left for the crematorium, then covered with foil to keep them fresh, the fruit cake, he saw that it was almost exactly the same food, and it evoked the same surge of pity. It had, he guessed, been difficult for her to decide what should suitably be offered, alcohol or tea. She had decided on tea and she was right; as far as he was concerned, it was tea they needed.

It was a small and curiously assorted party. A Pakistani who had been her grandmother's neighbour and his very beautiful wife, both of them more at ease at this funeral than he guessed they might have been at a festivity, sat together in gentle dignity. Alan Scully helped hand round the teacups with a vague self-effacement. Dalgliesh wondered whether he was anxious not to give the impression that he had a right to treat the flat as his own, then decided that this interpretation was over-subtle. Here, surely, was a man supremely unworried about what other people might think. Watching Scully handing round plates with the air of a man unsure what exactly he was holding, or what he was expected to do with it, Dalgliesh recalled that surprising telephone conversation, the persistence with which Scully had ensured that he spoke only to Dalgliesh himself, the clarity of the message, the extraordinary calmness of his voice and, not least, those perceptive last words.

"And there's another thing. There was a pause after I lifted the receiver before she spoke, and then she spoke very fast. I think someone else actually dialled the number and then handed over the receiver. I've given it some thought, and there's only one interpretation which fits all the facts. She's under some kind of duress."

Watching Scully's gangling six-foot-two body, the mild eyes behind the horn-rimmed spectacles, the lean, rather handsome face, the long strands of fair untidy hair, he thought how unlikely a lover for Kate he seemed, if lover he was. And then he caught Scully's glance at Kate as she was talking to Massingham, speculative, intense, for a moment vulnerable in its open longing, and thought: He's in love with her. And he wondered whether Kate knew, and if she did, how much she cared.

It was Alan Scully who was the first to leave, fading gently away rather than making a definite exit. When the two Khans had also said their good-byes, Kate carried the tea things into her kitchen. There was a sense of anticlimax, the usual uncomfortable hiatus at the end of a vaguely social occasion. Both men wondered if they should offer to help wash up, or whether Kate wanted them out of the way. And then, suddenly, she said that she would like to go back to the Yard with them and, indeed, there seemed no good reason why she should stay at home.

But Dalgliesh was a little surprised when she followed him into his office and stood in front of the desk as rigid as if she had been summoned for a reprimand. He looked up and saw her face flushed and almost bloated with embarrassment; then she said gruffly:

"Thank you for choosing me for the squad. I've learnt a lot." The words came out with a harsh ungraciousness which made him realize what it had cost her to say them. He said gently:

"One always does. That's what so often makes it painful."

She nodded as if it were she dismissing him, then turned and walked stiffly to the door. Suddenly she swung round and cried:

"I shall never know whether I wanted it to happen like that. Her death. Whether I caused it. Whether I meant it. I shall never know. You heard what Swayne called out to me. 'Aren't you going to thank me?' He knew. You heard him. How shall I ever be sure?"

He said what it was possible to say:

"Of course you didn't want it to happen. When you think about it calmly and sensibly you know that. You're bound to feel partly responsible. We all do when we lose someone we love. It's a natural guilt, but it isn't rational. You did what you thought was right at the time. We can't any of us do more. You didn't kill your grandmother. Swayne did, his final victim."

But with murder there never was a final victim. No one touched by Berowne's death would remain unchanged: himself, Massingham, Father Barnes, Darren, even that pathetic spinster, Miss Wharton. Kate knew that perfectly well. Why should she suppose that she was different? The well-worn reassuring phrases sounded false and glib even as he spoke them. And some things were beyond his reassurance. Berowne's foot, hard on the accelerator at that dangerous corner; her bloodstained hands thrust out to the killer. There was action and there was consequence. But she was tough, she would cope. Unlike Berowne, she would learn to accept and carry her personal load of guilt, as he himself had learnt to carry his.

3

⊠

Miss Wharton's only experience of a children's hospital was fifty years
ago when she had been admitted to her local cottage hospital to have her
tonsils out. Great Ormond Street could hardly have been more different
from her traumatic memories of that ordeal. It was like walking into a
children's party; the ward so full of light, of toys, of mothers and happy
activity that it was difficult to believe that this was a hospital until she
saw the pale faces and the thin limbs of the children. Then she told herself: But they're ill, they're all ill, and some of them will die. Nothing can
prevent it.

Darren was one of those in bed but sitting up, lively and occupied
with a jigsaw on a tray. He said with happy self-importance:

"You can die with what I've got. One of the kids told me."

Miss Wharton almost cried out her protest.

"Oh, Darren, no, no! You aren't going to die!"

"I reckon I won't. But I could. I've gone to foster parents now. Did
they tell you?"

"Yes Darren; that's lovely. I'm so glad for you. Are you happy with
them?"

"They're all right. Uncle's going to take me fishing when I get out
of here. They're coming in later on. And I got a bicycle—a Chopper."

Already his eyes were on the door. He had hardly looked at her since
she had arrived, and when she had walked up to the bed she had glimpsed
in his face a curiously adult embarrassment and had suddenly seen herself
as he saw her, as all the children must see her, a pathetic and ridiculous

old woman carrying her gift of an African violet in a small pot. She said:

"I miss you at St. Matthew's, Darren."

"Yeah. Well, I reckon I won't have time for that now."

"Of course not. You'll be with your foster family. I quite understand."

She wanted to add: But we did have happy times together, didn't we? then stopped herself. It was too like a humiliating plea for something she knew he couldn't give.

She had brought him the violet because it had seemed more manageable than a bunch of flowers. But he had seemed hardly to look at it and now, gazing round the toy-filled ward, she wondered how she could possibly have imagined that it was a suitable gift. He didn't need it, and he didn't need her. She thought: He's ashamed of me. He wants to get rid of me before his new uncle arrives. He hardly seemed to notice when she said good-bye and slipped away, handing the violet to one of the nurses on her way out.

She took the bus to the Harrow Road and walked to the church. There was plenty for her to do. Father Barnes, refusing a period of convalescence, had been back only two days, but the number of services, and the size of the congregations, had increased since that article in the paper about a miracle, and there would be a long line of penitents waiting for confession after this afternoon's Evensong. St. Matthew's would never be the same again. She wondered how long there would be a place in it for her.

This was the first time she had gone alone to the church since the murder, but in her misery and loneliness she was hardly aware of apprehension until she tried to fit her key in the lock and found, as she had on that dreadful morning, that she couldn't get it in. The door, as then, was unlocked. She pushed it open, her heart pounding, and called:

"Father, are you there? Father?"

A young woman came out of the Little Vestry. She was an ordinary, respectable, unfrightening girl, wearing a jacket and a blue headscarf. Seeing Miss Wharton's white face, she said:

"I'm sorry. Did I startle you?"

Miss Wharton managed a faint smile.

"It's all right. It's just that I wasn't expecting anyone. Was there anything you wanted? Father Barnes won't be here for another half hour."

The girl said:

"No, there's nothing. I was a friend of Paul Berowne. It's just that I wanted to visit the Little Vestry, to be alone here. I wanted to see where it happened, where he died. I'm going now. Father Barnes said to return the key to the vicarage, but perhaps I could leave it with you, as you're here."

She held it out and Miss Wharton took it. Then she watched as the girl went to the door. When she reached it, she turned and said:

"He was right, Commander Dalgliesh. It's just a room, a perfectly ordinary room. There was nothing there, nothing to see."

And then she was gone. Miss Wharton, still trembling, locked the outside door, went along the passage to the grille and gazed up through the church to the red glow of the sanctuary lamp. She thought: And that, too, is only an ordinary lamp made of polished brass with a red glass. You can take it apart, clean it, fill it with ordinary oil. And the consecrated wafers behind the drawn curtain, what are they? Only thin transparent discs of flour and water which come neatly packed in little boxes, ready for Father Barnes to take them in his hands and say the words over them which will change them into God. But they weren't really changed. God wasn't there in that small recess behind the brass lamp. He wasn't any longer in the church. Like Darren, he had gone away. Then she remembered what Father Collins had once said in a sermon when she first came to St. Matthew's: "If you find that you no longer believe, act as if you still do. If you feel that you can't pray, go on saying the words." She knelt down on the hard floor, supporting herself with her hands grasping the iron grille, and said the words with which she always began her private prayers: "Lord, I am not worthy that thou shouldest come under my roof, but speak but the word and my soul shall be healed."

A Note on the Type

This book was set in a digitized version of a face called Primer, designed by Rudolph Ruzicka (1883–1978). Mr. Ruzicka was also responsible for the design of Fairfield and Fairfield Medium, Linotype faces whose virtues have for some time been accorded wide recognition.

The complete range of sizes of Primer was first made available in 1954, although the pilot size of 12-point was ready as early as 1951. The design of the face makes general reference to Linotype Century—long a serviceable type, totally lacking in manner or frills of any kind—but brilliantly corrects its characterless quality.

Composed by
Maryland Linotype Composition Company,
Baltimore, Maryland

Printed and bound by Fairfield Graphics,
Fairfield, Pennsylvania
Typography and binding design by
Tasha Hall